THE WOMAN WHO STOLE EVERYTHING

AND OTHER STORIES

THE WOMAN WHO STOLE EVERYTHING

AND OTHER STORIES

ARNOLD BENNETT

WILDSIDE PRESS

Originally published in 1927,

Published by Wildside Press LLC.
wildsidepress.com

CONTENTS

THE WOMAN WHO STOLE EVERYTHING

CHAPTER I

IN THE HOTEL

MR. HENRY KEARNS sat after lunch in the lounge of the hotel, where he had eaten alone. He was a man of fifty, with hair dark brown and silver grey, carefully brushed.

Although middle-aged by the clock of time, he felt himself quite honestly to be a decade younger than his years; and he proclaimed this feeling—common nowadays to all men of fifty—by the exhibition of certain dandyisms, such as the harmony of colour between his necktie, his handkerchief, and his socks, to show that in his own opinion he was not yet laid by on the shelf. Besides, the hotel was the most select in London. Better than any other, its servitors maintained the social traditions of the grand eighteenth century, which traditions divided mankind into flunkeys who exulted in humility, and nobles—from Chicago and elsewhere—who haughtily deigned to give orders to the flunkeys. The knee-breeches of the gigantic attendants in the lounge were a sufficient proof that no hint of the French revolution had ever slipped in through the revolving doors of the splendid portico.

A small group, wafted forward by the powerful bowings of a *maître d'hôtel* and several waiters, emerged from the music-haunted restaurant. It consisted of a young man and two elderly ladies. The young man was slim and elegant. Henry Kearns envied him his slimness and his youth. "Never," thought the full-bodied Henry, "shall I be like that again!"

The elderly ladies, obviously sisters, were elaborately and fashionably clad. They moved with distinction in their short skirts, and the expression of their rouged and powdered faces—the dark eyes hard-glittering—showed the habit of unquestioned authority. They would have been a credit to any select hotel; and their fixed determination to be taken for ten years younger than they were, about fifty instead of about sixty, amounted to a certificate of force of character. For thirty years they had been steadily inspired by this ideal. They patronised their young man, but at the same time admitted the magic of his looks and his years. They marshalled their femininity to allure him. They willed themselves to believe that they could still allure a young man by the decayed vestiges of a beauty which had once been renowned. To Harry Kearns they were a spectacle—pitiable, tragic, disgusting.

"Why in God's name can't they be old with decency?" thought he, clinging to his own vestiges of masculine attractiveness. Yet at the same time he felt that every woman has sexual charm and that somehow they had it. And he yearned to be under the influence of sexual charm, realising all that he had missed in this respect, and rather glad that there was now a prospect, known to none but himself, of tasting at last sensations which hitherto had never been his. Nothing in life, he decided, really counted except women. He was mysteriously excited.

The young man stared at Henry Kearns in passing down the lounge; but the elderly ladies would not share his attention with any other phenomenon. He noticed their subtle protests against the roving of his young eye, and at once made amends and escorted them with exaggerated intentness to the lift. They took leave of him with condescension—masking wistfulness; he took leave of them with a non-committal deference; his back indicated a sure conviction that he held all the cards. They soared out of sight.

Then the young man moved towards the gentlemen's cloak-room, hesitated, and returned to the lounge.

"Excuse me," said he, somewhat nervously addressing the man of fifty. "Are you Mr. Henry Kearns?"

Mr. Kearns perceived instantly that the youth was not quite the man of the world always at ease in every situation.

"I am," answered Mr. Kearns rather stiffly.

"I thought I couldn't be mistaken—you're so like your photograph. I'm your niece's husband." He smiled suddenly and delightfully.

"Not Nick!" Mr. Kearns exclaimed, and he, too, smiled suddenly and delightfully, and jumped up and seized the young man's somewhat limp, hot hand.

"Sit down, do! This is most satisfactory. I'm so glad you spoke to me. How's Cora?"

"Very well, thanks, so far as I know."

They sat side by side. Mr. Kearns felt not a bit older than his nephew-in-law. He wondered whether his elegant nephew-in-law, who apparently achieved sartorial style without taking thought, would approve his necktie and handkerchief. They were both shy, constrained again: no smooth flow of chat. They talked, not glibly, in a few exchanges, of matters entirely devoid of interest, each privately estimating the other.

"And who were your guests?" Henry Kearns demanded, plunging rashly into the avuncular rôle.

"Those hags?" said Nick Ussher, with disdainful negligence. "They weren't my guests; I was theirs. Just a couple of clients, very well off. For some reason they invited me to lunch. They're staying here." A pause. Nick continued: "I suppose you're going down to Cander?"

"I'm going down there this afternoon."

"Oh! This afternoon!" Nick had come to the conclusion that this uncle-in-law was a sympathetic human being. He went on, in a new, confidential tone: "I should have liked to have a chat, but I can't stop now—sorry!"

"Urgent?"

"Well—" The young man was slightly blushing.

"See here!" Henry Kearns burst out, benevolently. "Come and dine with me somewhere to-night. I'll go down to Cander to-morrow morning."

Nick Ussher thought:

"This is the fellow that Cora takes after. Always changing his plans." He said aloud, generously appreciative: "It's awfully decent of you. But really I couldn't—No!"

"Oh, stuff, my boy!" Henry Kearns familiarly insisted. "It simply doesn't matter a damn whether I go to Cander to-day or to-morrow or next year. I'll expect you about eight. Here. It's as good as anywhere, I expect. And bring Cora. I know I ought to have let her know I was in town. But you know how you let things slide. Tell her she must come and forgive me."

"Afraid Cora can't come. The fact is, I believe she's engaged to-night."

Why did the boy say "the fact is"—a phrase which always means equivocation? A solicitor ought to know better than that. Then the phrase about Cora's health, "So far as I know." Why didn't he know completely about his wife's health?

"Something wrong," thought Henry Kearns, apprehensive, as he replied lightly: "Well, come alone then."

Nick Ussher accepted.

"I suppose you couldn't make it eight-thirty?" Nick suggested. "I'm frightfully busy."

"Of course I could. Eight-thirty be it." Kearns thought: "I've let myself in for something."

CHAPTER II

AFTER DINNER

"Now," said Henry Kearns, sympathetically but quite cheerfully. "We're beginning to know each other. Let's talk straight, shall we—Nick?" It was the first time he had used the Christian name to young Ussher.

The waiters had withdrawn. And Henry, after telling about himself, had led the conversation to Nick and his business, and then his wife: and the husband had cautiously but not unwillingly admitted domestic friction.

Nick gave a very faint cough, pulled at the front of his collar, straightened his black tie, with the latest butterfly ends, and shifted his long legs.

"I'd like to," said he, with a warm, candid smile.

Kearns answered the smile with another, equally warm and candid. Intimacy was born all of a sudden.

"Your marriage isn't quite a success?"

"That's right—uncle," Nick laughed—a laugh curt and self-conscious. Henry Kearns liked to be addressed as "uncle."

They had dined in Henry's private room, and were sitting in easy-chairs on either side of a dead fireplace, with the round dinner-table and its orange-shaded lamp behind them. No other light in the over-upholstered room. A delicate night-breeze, and the distant sounds of traffic, came through the heavy silken curtains of the large window. Uncle Henry was impressed by the situation so swiftly and clearly revealed. And he was pleased with himself for having surmised it earlier in the day. He felt that he had stepped into a new, romantic and formidable world—the world of sexual complications, the world of women.

For many years he had travelled, in Britain and abroad, as agent for a very large firm of contractors. A sort of commercial traveller; but not one of the ordinary sort. He had travelled "in" such things as bridges and similar public works. A single order might come to a million pounds, on which his modest commission might come to thousands—not counting the considerable item of expenses; Henry had been accustomed to move from place to place in the most luxurious style, for display was part of his successful method, and the firm willingly paid for it all.

He had made money and saved money, and had put a lot of it into shares of the firm when the firm was launched as a large limited company. The shares had risen high. He was rich, rich enough at any rate to offer himself the best of everything, from cigars to suites in hotels. He had triumphed by virtue of his gift of tongues and of persuasive diplomacy.

A year earlier, after living half his life without cost to his private purse, he had bought the house at Cander. The notion of retiring and settling had been in his mind, and now the notion was being realised. He had begun to tire of the life of business. It was a life in only two dimensions; he vaguely and instinctively wanted the third dimension—women. Never had he been worried by aught but the most transitory sentimental complications. He was free; he was bound to consult the wishes of nobody but himself; and nobody but himself had the right to criticise him. Now he desired not to be free; or, more accurately, to be both free and tied.

He looked at Nick Ussher with the concealed superiority of his gift of tongues, of his wide familiarity with countries and men, of his expertise in diplomacy, of his perfect freedom. But also he envied young Nick, though the envy seemed to him to be morbid. Nick was in a mess; yet he envied him, because the youth was more fully alive, was living in three dimensions instead of in two.

He liked Nick, except for his moist, flabby hand—he had shaken hands with him again on his arrival for dinner, his exactly punctual arrival. In addition to being handsome and elegant, Nick was evidently a very serious and dependable person. He had a good chin, a firm voice, and a manner which, if a little shy and awkward, was well poised. Harry Kearns had shown a discreet, cordial curiosity about him, and all Nick's responses had been frank and satisfactory. Partner in an important legal firm. Very industrious. Genuinely keen on his work. Sound, broad political ideas. Sound ideas on finance—national and domestic. Anxious to learn. Quick to pick up. A substratum of rocky hardness, as indeed was proper. And the young man was fit, too. He sometimes rode a hack in the mornings; played squash rackets of a Sunday; had his preferences among Swedish exercises. He insisted on his physical fitness. But there was a tired look in his eyes, round about which the skin was drawn into a perhaps unnatural smoothness: as if by force of will he rose from his bed untimely. Yes, he had the mien of a man who is the slave of a daily implacable programme. Withal, human, appealing—possibly rendered so by his servitude to the programme.

"Cora hasn't left you, by any chance?" Uncle Henry asked, with a gentle, disarming smile.

"No—" Nick hesitated. It seemed to him that the interview was sliding quicker and quicker down a slope into the last depths of utterly unreserved self-revelation. And this to a man whom he had met for the first time that day!

Henry Kearns silently passed a cigar-box to his guest.

"Take a fresh cigar. Don't relight that one. Now! Let's hear the trouble."

"Yes. That's all very well," said Nick, with the cigar in his mouth and a match at the end of the cigar. "That's all very well, but Cora's your niece, and I've always understood you're rather fond of her. You mightn't like—"

"So I am rather fond of her. But what then? That won't prevent me from being impartial. Be as blunt as you please. You needn't have the least fear of putting my back up. I'm not that sort. You go right on."

Nick puffed violently, and then examined the ignition.

"Oh! It's so difficult to describe. It's so darned silly. There are a million things—you know."

"Quite!" observed Henry Kearns, sagely comprehending—the wise elder!

Nick thought:

"There's no 'quite' about it. You're a decent, kindly old cove, but you know nothing about women and they don't interest you. You haven't a care. You do yourself thundering well, and you're only interested in yourself."

This reflection, however, was tinged with bravado; it lacked perfect sincerity; Nick was admiring his uncle-in-law, and also he was passionately envying the old cove's freedom from cares of a certain kind. In that moment Nick regarded singleness as the highest form of earthly bliss.

"Yes," said Henry Kearns. "I know there are a million things—there always are. Just tell me one. Tell me the last one."

"I will!" The young husband's tone was decided. "I'll tell you the very last one. She won't let me get enough sleep. I took her out to the Legation Club last week. It's infernally expensive, but she wanted to go, so I took her. Well, we dance and so on. She likes my dancing, and I'm very fond of dancing. At twelve o'clock I say to her, 'Look here, my girl, we must be hooking it. I've got a day's work in front of me to-morrow, and even as it is I shan't be asleep before one o'clock.' I say to her I can't work if I don't sleep, and if I don't work I can't find the money to take her about to places like the Legation Club. Plain enough, eh? Stands to reason, doesn't it? Mind you, *she* sleeps till ten or eleven after an evening out, but I have to be up at seven as usual. What about it?"

"Quite, quite!" Henry Kearns eagerly encouraged the husband. "She jibbed, eh?"

"Well, of course they're very clever, all of 'em. She said we might just stay a little longer—she was quite nice about it. Of course you asked me to tell you, and I'm telling you. It may *sound* nothing, it *is* nothing, but—. Well, at twelve-thirty or so, I said to her, 'Now what about going home?' Then she said a late night now and then would do me all the good in the world. I needed it. Mustn't get in a rut. Mustn't get middle-aged. Quite a new tack, you see. She was enjoying her evening, no mistake. Funny how they can enjoy it when they know somebody else isn't! But they can, somehow. At one o'clock I told her straight I was going home. Gloves were off then. She said *she* shouldn't go, anyway, and there were several friends there who'd be glad of her company even if I wasn't. She danced with one or two of them. I said, by all means stay. We stopped at a table and she began to talk. I said, 'Well, I'm off, Cora.' She said to the people at the table, 'Here's my tyrant insists on taking me home. We're both middle-aged.' She came with me. It always takes her about ten hours to undress. She came into my room at three-fifteen—three-fifteen, if you please—and asked me if I was asleep. Fat lot of difference it would have made if I had been! We had a regular old scene. Lasted till after four. I had to get up in less than three hours. Of course I had no sleep. When I got up at seven I thought it would do her good to wake her. She was sound asleep. She wanted some waking. But I woke her all right. Never more surprised in her life! I said I thought she might like to know how it felt to be kept awake when you wanted to sleep. She simply couldn't think of anything to say. I left her. She didn't follow me. You see, we're very busy in our office, and I'm the youngest partner, and I like to be there by nine o'clock, or soon after. And, by God, I am!" Nick laughed courageously. "Well, that's one thing."

Flushed, he leaned back in his chair.

As for Henry Kearns, he took the man's part without any reservation. He knew Cora as a very charming girl, an enchanting girl; and how Tommy, his deceased elder brother, a dull, honest fellow, had contrived to be the father of such a girl, he never could understand! Cora and Henry were great friends; he gave her fine presents. But he was absolutely convinced of the truth and justice of Nick's narration, and quite ready to revise his rosy estimate of Cora. After all, he was not attached to Cora, and he could judge her as objectively as anyone. Further, by her conduct thus revealed, she had put him, as her uncle, in a position of humiliation, and he resented that, and blamed her for it.

"She was very naughty," he said kindly, but not too seriously; for he had an instinct against disparaging his own kin. Sort of disloyalty in so doing!

"But you see how *cruel* it was, don't you?" cried Nick passionately, sitting up straight again in sudden excitement. "You don't defend her, do you? If you can offer any defence of her I should very much like to hear it. Because I can't think of any. I've tried to. Now do be frank with me!"

Nick gave such a display of emotion that Uncle Henry was startled, positively frightened by it. He could feel perspiration on his forehead—but it was a warm night.

"No, I don't see any defence," he agreed, quiet and compassionate.

"It's so *cruel*!" Nick repeated fiercely, just as if Uncle Henry had disagreed instead of agreeing. "It's so *cruel*! That's what I say. What can you do? What can a man do? What *is* there to do? How *can* you handle a woman when she behaves like that? Just think of me all that day! And the next night! And the day after! Just *think* of me!"

The young man seemed to have lost all shame, all reserve. Uncle Henry wished the scene could end. He had an acute sense of awkwardness. A young solicitor, in large practice, prim like most lawyers, immersed in his profession—breaking out like this! It was terrible; it was shocking.

Uncle Henry tried to reassure himself by thinking:

"It's nothing to do with me, anyhow. I shan't let it disturb me."

The self-centred, confirmed bachelor, without a care! He was aghast at the unexpected glimpse of the horrors of marriage. Aghast! How wise he had been to remain single! What a life! But had he not always known, in his heart, that women were like that?

Nick leaned forward still more.

"And that's only one thing!" he exclaimed, waving a hand towards Henry. He kept the pose, arm outstretched, lips tight, gaze fixed on Henry. Almost a menace! The glowing end of Nick's cigar fascinated Henry. Certainly the young man had entirely forgotten any diffidence he might have had in criticising the niece to the uncle.

"See, how long have you been married?"

"Well, you ought to know. You sent her an A1 ring. She's lost it."

"The deuce she has!" said Uncle Henry, aggrieved. The ring had cost him a hundred and fifty pounds.

"She loses everything. Three years—we've been married, nearly. Yes, that's it. Three years, nearly."

"I suppose there's nothing I can do?" Henry's conscience compelled him to suggest.

"It's awfully good of you. But I doubt if there's anything to be done." (Henry was much relieved; his mind lightened.) "Ah! Well! Things may settle down. Let's hope so. I don't know why I should come here bothering you like this. It was just seeing you—happening to see you—I thought— You must excuse me."

The young man's tone was now changed to the resigned, the calm, and the matter-of-fact. He had returned to his senses, in a sweat. He was ashamed of his outspokenness about a private and most intimate affair. He felt as though he had just wakened up to find himself parading a fashionable thoroughfare in pants and undershirt.

"I suppose she doesn't happen to have taken a fancy to anybody else?" Henry Kearns timidly suggested. A daring suggestion!

"God knows! I don't! . . . No, honestly I don't think it's that. It's— Well, what's the use? . . . You've been very nice about it."

"You ought to have a child."

"Cora! A child! You should hear her on that point."

The interview ended thus.

CHAPTER III

CANDER

Kearns left the train the next afternoon at Cander. It was a train crowded with passengers for a large seaside resort which lay at the river's mouth twelve miles farther on. Kearns had spent an hour and three-quarters with two middle-aged men and a young one, and two gaudy, respectable, young-ish women, one of whom was continually sighing about the heat and gazing anxiously at her face in a tiny mirror and powdering her nose or rouging her lips; while the other passed the time in half-heartedly trying to keep a pink cotton skirt below her knees.

Bags of golf-clubs, suit-cases, and hat-boxes littered the racks. The talk was of golf, tennis, hotels, food, revues, royalty, parties, and the dangerous folly of French politicians and of idle, grasping, misled British working-men; seasoned with dry giggles about suspected fornications.

Kearns had said nothing, but he was interested, even diverted. In the back of his mind dwelt Cora and Nick, but especially Cora; the compart-ment seemed to him to be an extension of the world which, according to Nick, was Cora's favourite world.

He stepped down on to the sunlit platform, despatch-case in hand, and the next moment the train pulled out, having casually remembered and dis-dainfully forgotten Cander within the space of a few seconds. . . . The huge train was a spot on the distance; it vanished into the black orifice of a tunnel under the downs; it was silenced.

Two people gave up tickets to a red-cravated porter at the wicket. Ke-arns stood alone on the long, empty, glaring platform, and saw his two trunks lying on the springy asphalt of the platform forty yards off; the trunks were as solitary as himself. By magic the world of the compartment had given place to another world—of placid, sunstruck solitude. He looked up and saw the lace curtains of the station-master's bedroom, which it was the life-work of the station-master's wife to maintain in whiteness against the attacks of flying engine-soot. He saw the old station-master, who after thirty years of incessant attention to business had arrived at five pounds a week and a gold-braided authoritative cap. The station-master, connecting Kearns with the two trunks, waited uncertainly hovering, and in due course received a request from Kearns that the luggage should be sent by the car-rier to "Pomegranates" in the village. The station-master, at the name of the house, recognised Kearns, whom his blinking eyes had seen only once before.

Kearns left the station and strode down the approach-road to the bridge which carried the railway over the highway. The village was a mile off; the station stood where it did, at the crossing of the main line and the highway to the sea, because it would have been accessible nowhere else; the villagers and visitors had to accept the mile with good grace. Kearns could just see the antique walls of Cander Castle beyond a mound of the landscape. In front of him was the old bridge which carried the highway over the tidal stream—whose name certainly ought to have been Meander, for it flowed for thirty miles to reach what the crow would reach in a dozen. The tide was slowly bearing rushes and seaweed northwards, and in a few hours it would be slowly bearing them southwards again, through the immense hayfield flats which once had been a sea-floor. A sign over a wooden shed said "Tea and boats"; but the shed seemed to be deserted, and the boats were moored cushionless in a row under the grassy bank. Two young persons lounged on the old bridge. The public-house, calling itself a hotel, lay under the burning sun as enchanted as the whole countryside. And not a vehicle on the road, while every avenue out of London was blocked with tens of thousands of motors! Henry Kearns set off to cover the rolling mile.

To the south, protecting the road from all the sea-winds except the prevailing south-west, rose the great green rampart of the downs, on whose lower slopes the wheat was turning. Kearns walked and walked, up one hill and down another, and walked and walked, wishing that he had had the trustfulness to confide his despatch-case also to the carrier. No shade anywhere. An enormous char-à-banc, roofed in summer hats, glided past him with the smoothness of a train; it was closely followed by six others. Then a small car rushed to meet him. Then solitude once more, and silence.

Then he descried the running white figures of cricketers. He stopped at the recreation ground (not styled the village green) to watch cricket over the hedge. On benches round the field sat the villagers, including mothers of families. In one corner were swings on which families were swinging. In another corner was a tennis-court; but at Cander cricket was still the premier game, and during a cricket match tennis might not be played. On the other hand, as Kearns had heard, tennis was lawful on Sundays, whereas the spectacle of cricket on Sundays would have raised a riot of outraged villagers. A middle stump flew out of the ground! Clapping! The bowler wore black trousers.

" 'E's been bowling for Cander for thirty years," said a man in the way of gossip to Kearns, over the hedge, proudly. " 'E's one of the old uns."

Kearns smiled and nodded.

"What a world!" thought Kearns. "Nothing changes in it."

He was forgetting the tennis-court, absorbed as he was in the drama of the contrast between this world and the world which he had left in London and in the train.

Unwillingly he moved on towards the village.

Cander was one of the show villages of Sussex. Rapturous sightseers said that every cottage in it had a genuine old thatched roof: a statement about half true; half the cottages were thatched, with far-projecting eaves, and quite a dozen dated back five centuries; they had survived intact revolutions and civil wars and subtler national changes. The general aspect of the place was incredibly picturesque, and, in the way of picturesqueness, beautiful. Externally, it well exemplified the conventional dreams of an American tourist concerning rural England. But Henry Kearns had once inspected the interiors of two of the cottages, and been positively shocked by their twilit gloom, due to the overhanging eaves and the smallness of the dormers and the casemented windows, by the lowness of the bent ceilings and the narrowness of the stairs, by the stuffiness, and by the absence of water.

The few shops specialised in picture-postcards, candles, lamp-oil and rat poison. Rats, indeed, were the chief and dominant inhabitants of the village. They bred as fast as unlimited bane could kill them. The night was theirs; in the night they scuttered across floors and beds and cots; they dragged clothing to and fro; they disported themselves under the hedges in the road; they made meals of poison; morning saw their dead bodies in hundreds; and the next night they were as rampant and voracious as ever. Kearns had heard that only two houses in the village were rat-free, the huge vicarage and his own. A great ruling race!

Unrecognised and scarcely saluted, Kearns passed slowly up the street under a blazing afternoon sun, amid playing, shrieking children, with flowery gardens and creeper-covered, ancient, half-timbered walls on either side. Insecure aerials were multiplying over the roofs; the villagers had growing contact with the world they had never seen and never would see, and when they chose could plainly hear Savoy Bands, excerpts from *Die Walküre* or *Don Giovanni*, or lectures upon the North Pole, or the manufacture of costly perfumes at Grasse. None could say that civilisation was not marching on.

He came to his own house, "The Pomegranates." It was the largest in the village. Built by an American family in discreet, tasteful imitation of the picturesque-antique, it had a lovely tiled roof, many dormers and casements, a wrought-iron lantern above the front-door, copied precisely from a lantern in a Florentine palazzo, and a wonderful shoe-scraper to match. It stood back a dozen feet from the road, and the intervening space was populated with lilies in bloom. It had an artesian well, an electric-light plant, telephone-wires, a garage, a dovecot with real doves; but no aerial. Its windows were exquisitely curtained, and through the withdrawn curtains could be seen glimpses of artistic lamp-shades, "period" furniture, and old china.

Henry had bought the house complete with everything in it at a very low price, because the Americans were tired of it and a couple of thousand pounds more or less was naught to them. The Americans, it was said, had a palazzo in Rome, where they always wintered, continually improving and refining their taste in the arts and in the literatures of several nations. For years they had arrived in Gander punctually on the first of July, with a train of Italian servants, who leaned on gates and chatted among themselves in the evenings. And punctually on the thirtieth of September they departed again, having conscientiously spent the summer in ruralising, reading, motoring, and offering perfect meals to friends and acquaintances nearly as cultured as themselves. They had tried in all seriousness, and with a noble lack of humour, to improve and refine the taste of Cander, and—to put it briefly and crudely—they had failed. And so they had abandoned Cander and gone elsewhere to continue their summer lives of ardent self-perfecting and doing themselves extremely well. And Cander had forgotten them as casually and totally as Rome herself would one day forget them.

Kearns had a spasm of horrible misgiving as he walked under the archway which connected his house with his garage. For the first time he was ashamed of his ownership, and perceived the bad taste of it: a change of heart somehow brought about by the interview with his nephew-in-law. But why? How?

Nobody to be seen. True, he had only telegraphed that he would probably arrive some time that afternoon. Through the half-open doors of the garage he saw gleams of the eight-cylinder Packard. Then he was on the first lawn, admirably shaven, with a playing fountain in the middle and flowers all round. Three marble steps down to the second lawn, with an oblong marble-sided pool in the middle! Three marble steps down to the third lawn, netted for tennis. And then, below, the immense view, cunningly framed in foliage, of several miles of the Flats, under hay.

The view was unique; the meandering river, the thin strip of railway, dykes, rush-lined straight ditches intersecting the vast plain, cattle, mowing-machines and hay-wains and horses and men, diminished by the distance into midgets! On the horizon, blue hills of Surrey. It might be Saturday afternoon, but hay was being got, because it had to be got, diligently. A whole flock of children, just like doves, flew across the field eagerly to announce to their fathers the haymakers that they had had their tea and wanted to help in agriculture. The sun shone warmly and implacably on every square foot of the shimmering scene.

"Four bathrooms and central heating!" thought Henry Kearns disconnectedly. Strange man!

He thought he heard far off behind him the hoot of a motor; he took no notice—he was dreaming. Then his ear caught the sound of feet on the hard marble steps. He turned; a young woman in a flowing fawn dust-coat was standing on the steps. She hesitated, appeared to wish to retreat, but with a devil-may-care gesture approached him. A dark, handsome man was following her. As she came nearer he noticed that she was rather agitated and trying, without success, to be easy and natural.

"Uncle!" she cried, in an uncertain, semi-hysterical voice. "I'd no idea—!"

Yes, she was excessively perturbed. The man had stopped.

"Come along!" she called sharply to the man. "This is Uncle Henry Kearns." And she pecked at Uncle Henry, and Uncle Henry sniffed her strong perfume. This was Cora; in the first moments of her onrush he had hardly recognised her, so altered and matured was she.

CHAPTER IV
THE MARTYR

"WELL, uncle, how do you think I'm looking?"

These were Cora's first words as she dropped into an easy-chair in a small sitting-room on the first-floor with a view over the lawns and the Flats. Henry Kearns took a chair opposite to her. In the garden she had murmured meaningly to him: "I'm dying to have a chat, uncle. Do take me inside." And when Kearns indicated her companion, who had been very summarily introduced, she had said with a certain nonchalance: "Oh, *he*'ll be all right here," and louder: "Shan't you, Sweeney?"

"How do I think you're looking?" Henry repeated her words.

"Yes. Aren't I looking rather nice?"

She seemed to be craving for admiration. She gave him a beseeching smile. She was now twenty-seven; she had been married for nearly three years and Henry Kearns had not seen her for four years.

With her hat, she had thrown off the dust-coat, and the pale attire thus revealed was of the slightest and flimsiest. One knee was crossed over the other and both were showing. Sturdy, graceful calves, comely ankles, a glimpse of powerful thighs; small feet, most fashionably sheathed; bare arms which matched the calves; hands long, but too narrow, with pointed, dyed nails and a few rings on the thin fingers. Brown hair mechanically waved.

What Henry chiefly noticed about the arrangement of the face was the touch of added red in the nostrils, which, like the small mouth, had the appearance of a wound half-healed. Every visible part of her epidermis, except perhaps on the nape of the neck, had been cosmetically treated, changed, transformed, in the intention to beautify. The result was a highly finished product. Her physique was magnificent, and she had made the best of it, after years of minute study of every inch and every attribute of her body. She had left nothing to itself. Even her attitude, as she threw her arms wide on the arms of her chair and slanted her head, was thought out, willed in detail. Her face could scarcely be called beautiful, and assuredly it was not pretty—the features were too large and accentuated, the expression too masterful, for that—but she was good-looking. The glance of the fine, hazel eyes was brazen, defiant, challenging; but apparently she could soften it at will, just as at moments she could put on an ingenuous simper which turned her into the pretty, frankly foolish, feminine creature who pleads for guidance and firm support from wise, strong males—turned her even into the virgin again. Whatever else she might be, she was something very definite and unmistakable, a remarkably representative specimen of a type.

Henry Kearns was amazed, and he was saddened, by the spectacle of her maturity. He had last seen her a wild girl with the lights of innocence in her eyes. He now saw her as the woman who had eaten to repletion of the tree of knowledge; hardened, coarsened; omniscient in physical sensations; meditating always upon her learning therein, savouring it, delving into it with her tireless thoughts. But she was wonderful, and she was his niece, and he had known her since babyhood, and he felt an affection for her.

The question he nervously asked himself was:

"Is she good-natured at bottom, or is her egotism ruthless?"

It seemed very odd to him, and quite disconcerting, that, such as she was, she was his niece. Women of her type were rarely relatives; one did not expect them to be relatives. Other men's nieces—by all means! But one's own!

He saw Nick's difficulties in a new light. His sympathies floated forth towards distant Nick, but they enveloped also the too sophisticated head of Cora. She was she. And could she help it?

"Yes. I do think you look rather nice," said Kearns, in an indulgent tone. He could see no advantage in frankness.

"But you aren't quite satisfied. You're disappointed." Cora went on her way with determination. She seemed to imply that he had been living in the hope of seeing her in the most splendid bloom and that this hope had been his main interest in existence.

"Not at all!" he answered. "I think you look fine."

"Of course two hours in an open car don't exactly help a woman. I feel all blown away. I—"

"I think you look fine," he said again.

"I'm so glad," she smiled confidingly, weakly. Then she hardened. "Do I look older?"

"Well, you've been married since I saw you last."

"I'm changed?" she exclaimed, suddenly apprehensive. "I do look older? Do I look my age?"

"Let's see; how old are you?"

"Twenty-six. Some of my friends say I don't look a day older than twenty-three."

"I thought you were twenty-seven."

"Yes, so I am," she calmly admitted. "That's right. But it was only the other day. You needn't be so particular, uncle darling. So I look twenty-seven, do I? Well, everyone doesn't think so."

Henry understood then that it was a matter of terrific importance to her to look younger than her years, and that the suspicion of having changed ever so little with the passage of time was repugnant to her, intolerable. Her anxiety was sincere to the point of being tragic. It really touched Henry, so that he spoke reassuringly, as to an invalid about an invalid's health, when he said, falsely and heartily:

"I never accused you of looking twenty-seven. If I didn't know, I should give you twenty-three or four."

"You are a dear. But you always were," she responded, appeased and grateful. "I do admire your taste in villages, uncle. And in houses, too. Oh! What wouldn't I give to bury myself in the country—for years and years, away from everything!" She gave a long sigh, as it were yearning after the realisation of an impossible and heavenly dream. "A cottage like one of those down the road. I shouldn't mind how simple."

"But a bathroom—hot and cold."

"Oh, of course, if there *could* be a bathroom."

"All the cottages here are full of rats," said Henry. "You adore rats, I suppose."

"How horrid you are, uncle!" She frowned. "As if rats couldn't be put right quite easily. But you do like to tease me. You always did. It's growing on you." She smiled softly. "I'm frightfully thirsty It's the dust. You can't *imagine* how dusty it was. It's nonsense about tar preventing dust." Her tone incriminated all road authorities. "Would you like to offer me just a tiny drink?"

"Certainly. I'll ask for tea." He jumped up and rang the bell.

"I suppose I daren't ask for a dry Martini," she suggested.

"You dare," said Henry. "But what about your friend in the garden?"

"Oh, he can wait. Surely he can wait just a minute or two!" said Cora carelessly.

Henry rang the bell, and said to the maid, who entered somewhat scared—for the staff had only just heard, and indirectly, of the master's arrival:

"Good afternoon, Annie. Mrs. Ussher will have a dry Martini cocktail, if there's one to be had. And you can bring me some tea."

"Yes, sir. If you please, sir, the housekeeper told me to ask when it would be convenient for you to see her. She only knew a minute since that you'd come, sir."

"Any time. Any time. Tell her."

"Uncle," said Cora, when the maid had gone away "I do wish you hadn't said the cocktail was for me. I thought you'd order two cocktails. That would have been all right. They're always so funny about women having anything but tea in the afternoon."

"Who are funny?"

"Servants." Cora pouted.

"Don't let that trouble you," said Henry soothingly. "They won't think anything here. But I'm sorry I didn't think of it, all the same."

"It doesn't *matter*," Cora negligently pardoned him. "But—" She left the "but" in the air, feeling by instinct that it would be more effective so.

The tea and the Martini cocktail were brought in with surprising speediness—and by the housekeeper herself, a plumpish woman of forty, clearly very intelligent and capable, but with little regard for the conventionalities of professional costume. She was wearing a mauve skirt and a crimson blouse; she belonged to the village, and had probably never seen a fashionably correct housekeeper in her life.

"Good afternoon, Mrs. Hickett," Kearns greeted her; and as soon as she had set down the tray, he half rose and shook hands with her.

"Good afternoon, sir." Mrs. Hickett had a pleasant smile for him, and a pleasant, energetic, self-respecting manner. She seemed to be not in the least overset by the honour of having her hand shaken by the master of the house.

"You all right, Mrs. Hickett?"

"Yes, thank you, sir. And I hope you are."

"Oh yes. . . . This is my niece, Mrs. Ussher."

Cora's recognition of Mrs. Hickett might perhaps have been detected by some instrument of scientific sensitiveness and precision.

"Good afternoon, madam," said Mrs. Hickett, in a firm, impartial voice, looking straight at Cora, who thereupon ornamented her first recognition with a ghastly insincere smile.

"Can't the little fool see that it always pays to be a bit more than civil to head servants?" Kearns reflected. "She might be coming down here to stay, one day. . . . To put it no higher!" he added to himself. He knew that Mrs. Hickett was forming her estimate of Cora, and that the estimate had certain reserves. He was ashamed of Cora, or rather, he definitely did not care for Mrs. Hickett to know he had for niece such a woman as Cora appeared to the eye to be. He saw Cora with Mrs. Hickett's eye. He felt as though he ought to explain Cora to Mrs. Hickett, but he knew that any attempt to do so, even were it possible, must fail. Cora could never be established in the good opinion and sympathies of Mrs. Hickett. The two women became at once inimical, on terms of equality. There are very frequently occasions on which women lose the sense of relative rank. This was one of them.

The maid arrived with a cake-stand, which Mrs. Hickett took from her and put in exactly the most convenient position for a cake-stand. When the maid had gone, and when Mrs. Hickett had reached the door, Mrs. Hickett turned round.

"I'm sorry I wasn't downstairs to meet you when you arrived, sir."

"Not at all. I went straight into the garden. Nobody even saw me."

"No, sir. You see, sir, I got the two telegrams together, yours and Mrs. Ussher's, and seeing I didn't expect either of them just now, there was a good bit to do. I thought you might be driving down, sir. Oh! And your luggage has just come, sir. Your room is quite ready, sir. And the two spare rooms will be ready in a few minutes, sir. I sent to ask if Mr. Ussher would take anything, but he said not yet, sir. Thank you, sir."

Exit Mrs. Hickett, with nothing but a somewhat bewildered nod of approbation from her employer.

Cora leaned forward and, seizing cake, stuffed a large piece of it into her mouth.

"You *did* say I should be welcome to come and stay here whenever I liked," said Cora, through the cake thickly. "You said you preferred the house to be occupied, and the servants to have something to do."

Kearns recalled that some time before he had casually so written to his niece.

"Yes," he agreed. A pause. "I did." A pause "And here you are." He was collecting himself from an incredible blow.

"You also said you'd warn your housekeeper."

"I did say so, and I did warn her."

"So I thought I'd run down for a week-end."

"Quite! But this 'Mr. Ussher' in the garden?"

"Of course it's just my luck. I never do have any luck," Cora complainingly protested. "I'd no idea you'd be here. I didn't even know you were in England. I had the notion of coming down this morning—and you know how impulsive I am. I admit I'm all in the wrong, and naturally you'll blame me. But it was so tempting. It sounded such a lovely idea. And Sweeney's so hard up, poor thing. We couldn't have afforded an hotel—at least not our sort of hotel. I must be comfortable. If I can't be comfortable, I'd as soon be dead. Yes, I mean it, though you don't believe me. Besides, hotels—"

"Whose car did you come down in?"

"Oh, I hired a car, and I shall pay for it. Why shouldn't I? Can't a woman offer a man a seat in a car? I should like to know why not indeed. All these old-fashioned ideas are all gone now, you know—but perhaps you don't know. Anyhow, I'm entitled to hire a car and ask who I like to sit in it, and I'm entitled to pay for it. And considering Sweeney drives himself and saves a chauffeur—"

"You mean Nick's entitled to pay for it," Kearns interrupted her flow. "Unless, of course, you've come into money and never told me."

"Now, uncle, please, please—"

Her voice broke. At first, after the incursion of Mrs. Hickett, she had been most painfully, if not ludicrously, constrained. The constraint, however, had yielded to the magic of her arguments in her own favour, had melted visibly in the warmth of them, like snow in the sun. But now, at the mention of Nick, it had all returned, more painful or ludicrous than before. She wept, bowed her head, extended her hand nervously towards Henry Kearns; her fingers moved as if groping for something they could not find. Suddenly she sprang up and hysterically snatched Kearns's handkerchief from his pocket and dropped back into her seat with the plunder.

"Excuse me; excuse me," she begged, dabbing her eyes. "I must have left my bag somewhere; it's always losing itself. Physical objects have a grudge against poor me. I've often no—no—noticed it." She was sobbing.

Kearns was amazed, he was nearly stupefied, by the enormity of her indiscretion. It was inconceivable that she should have realised, in imagination, all the consequences, or half the consequences, of her utterly crazy bad taste. He said to himself that a woman who would do what she had done would stick at absolutely nothing for the satisfaction of a caprice. And the man—Sweeney, as she called him! The man! In order to restore his own calm he very carefully poured himself out a cup of tea. The cocktail had vanished down that elegant throat. Crumbs of cake littered the pale, fragile lap. He waited for her, and had not to wait long.

"My life's been hell," she murmured and muttered, gazing curiously at the pattern of Henry's handkerchief. "What a sporting hanky! I'm not one to complain. I never complain. I might have written and told you some things. But I didn't. Nobody ever went into marriage with higher ideals than I did. I wanted marriage to be *everything*. I must have affection, tenderness. Yes, tenderness. If I don't have it, I'm like a flower without water. And romance! Did I tell you Sweeney's the finest driver in London? Why shouldn't life be romantic? But I've had nothing. Business, business, health, fitness, economy, all day, every day! I've had *nothing*. I couldn't stand it any more. Of course I might have killed myself. That might have been the best for every-one—certainly for me it would have been. But we're so weak. I suppose we oughtn't to be. . . . I thought surely there must be *some* romance in the

world, waiting for me. And then poor darling Sweeney came into my life."
(She's quoting from some novel she's read, reflected Henry.) "And why
shouldn't we be happy, Sweeney and me? Isn't everybody entitled to happiness if they can find it? That's my religion anyway. Sweeney adores me.
The way he looks at me sometimes—it makes me feel giddy, yes it does."
She smiled plaintively. "You can't say I'm not being frank with you. . . .
Well, I know I oughtn't to have done it. I oughtn't to have come here like
this, with Sweeney, and not told you. I say it again quite plainly, I blame
myself. I've nothing to answer. I'm defenceless. But if you knew—if you
knew—if you could realise! You can't, though." She seemed to imply that
since she had thus candidly and unreservedly judged and condemned herself, no one else ought to judge and condemn her. Indeed she had raised
herself to be the chief saint and martyr of the whole situation.

Henry Kearns said not a word; he felt that no speech would be adequate, but his real reason for silence was fear of the impossibility of defeat-
ing her by argument. She was now half-lying in the easy-chair, her dress in
extreme disarray, the skirt rucked up, one short sleeve slipping down her
shoulder. This frock was less a covering than an exposition.

And she had a general air of dampness which strangely became her,
and enhanced her attractiveness, giving her the charm of a soft victim. She
was aware of this, and, further, she exulted in the ruin of the costly frock,
which was part of her martyrdom. A superb and unhappy animal twisting
and curving and cowering in its lair! She was exciting, never more sensu-
ous than in her woe.

She fascinated Henry Kearns. Without looking at him she knew that
his gaze was upon her. She stirred afresh into a new posture, lifted her
head, smiled at him with a new smile, languorous, exhausted with emotion,
supplicating, ravishing, darting at him delicious danger; and yet humble,
niece-like, pure. This was the child he had known. See her! The mature,
highly finished, unscrupulous, irresistible feminine!

"But it's all right now you're here," she astoundingly said. "You've
saved me by being here. Sweeney can go away. He must, in fact, poor
darling! Shall have to find a reason for him going. Your Mrs. Hickett need
never know he isn't my husband. Of course it means that Nick won't ever
be able to come to see you; but I expect you won't mind that. I'm sure *he*
won't."

"Yes, but supposing I hadn't happened to be here. Think of the—"

"How like a man to say that! What's the good of supposing? You *are*
here. And oh, uncle! I can say this for myself at any rate. I'm not merce-
nary, am I? All I ask for is affection. I'm willing to give up everything for
that. Everything. Poor Sweeney hasn't a cent. He's only himself. I'll just
go and speak to him."

Henry was nonplussed—so colossal was her assumptions, her omissions, her suppressions. She rendered him speechless. He thought of Nick. Nick had had the management of this young woman! He had lived alone with her in a flat for three years, trying to cope with her. It was terrible. And how was Henry himself to contend with her?

CHAPTER V

IN THE GARDEN

MR. SIMEON TODD had found a shady and screened corner in the garden, and was reclining fairly comfortably on a crescent-shaped marble bench with a curved back to it and ends carved into the shape of heraldic lions.

Known throughout the West End of London as "Sweeney," he was a muscular man of thirty-nine or forty at least, with hairy hands, arms and chest, well-shaved expanses of slaty-blue on his chin and upper lip, very white and very regular teeth, and black eyes. The hair on his head was black, and it shone. He had been a Territorial major, an actor, and a club secretary. He had sold motor-cars, champagne, and cigars on commission, and was ever ready and anxious to take up agencies for something or anything. The Turf Club would generally "find" him. No other address could be relied on. He frequented the racecourses near London, and his deep, vibrating voice made a familiar sound in all the finest West End restaurants. He was always spending money, yet never had money. He carried a cheque-book, but seldom had the courage to use it. Women, one heard, had died for him. Sweeney, however, though once he had been bankrupt, still lived.

Cora searched for him in the empty garden, flitting from lawn to lawn.

"Oh! There you are!" she exclaimed. "I've been looking for you for ages. I thought you'd run off with the car and deserted me."

She stood smiling at him, ecstatic, and then sat down closely by his side. Sweeney's policy was one of benevolent inaction.

"Oh! You've found my bag. I knew you would." She seized and opened the bag. "Don't look at me while I do my face. I'm a fright. Now don't dare to look at me. You needn't be jealous of this hanky—it's uncle's; he lent it me." She worked away at her features, a mirror in one hand and apparatus in the other. "Uncle's a queer old thing—did you notice him? Not you! He thinks he understands everything, but really he understands nothing. I'll tell you what he is—he's neuter." She laughed. "He likes me simply awfully and I like him—we're the greatest friends—but there's not much to him. Now he *can* sell things on commission; all this place here comes from commission—think of it! *He* comes out on the right side every time. No bankruptcies for *him*! Are you thirsty, darling?"

"I am," said Sweeney, with true feeling.

"I was afraid you must be. Uncle offered me a dry Martini—or what they suppose is a dry Martini in this house. Why don't you look at me? Why do you keep on staring at the grass? I know why it is. I'm hideous. Uncle thinks I look my full age. He didn't say so, but I'm sure he thought it. I'm too old. I'm too old for you, and you don't hide it. You hate me. I can't thrill you any more."

"You asked me not to look at you, Corry."

"Yes, you needn't tell me that." Her voice rasped. "You know I didn't mean it. You're so literal. I've yet to meet the man that isn't. . . . Great silly!"

She suddenly turned and faced him and laughed victoriously as she caught the expression in his black eyes. She kissed him. He held her by the shoulders, and his clutch hurt her. She was happy, oblivious of everything but her happiness.

"Darling!"

Her voice was silken again, fainting, dying. She leaned on him. He continued to gaze at her with a serious air. He knew exactly what his eyes could do. Nevertheless, being still passionately fond of her and always uneasy when away from her, his gaze and mien were quite sincere.

She remembered that she had not re-packed and closed her handbag (some of whose contents she lost daily, not to say the bag itself). When she had set the important matter right, and given herself a little murmurous praise for doing so, she melted into him again, and her shoulders seemed to be aching for the clutch of his strong hands, which slowly he gave them. Perfect bliss shone from her features. Few human beings could have experienced an intenser felicity than was hers then. At worst she knew what she wanted, and how to procure it; and when procured it fulfilled all her hopes. She was not of those who strive, and strive in vain, living for a future which never comes. Her wisdom was practical; it achieved an entirely satisfactory result by the simplest means. Thus her absolute belief in herself was justified; she had nothing whatever to learn from philosophy and might legitimately boast to the rest of mankind: "What you go down to the grave without winning—for all your efforts, I attain daily." She was unanswerable.

She put her lips on his. He shifted.

"If anybody happens to come round these bushes suddenly—" he began.

She frowned, and her neck flushed in an instant.

"There!" she cried, tragically resentful. "If you were really in love with me you couldn't say a thing like that. You just couldn't say it. I know I'm hideous. I know I'm old, *passée*. And it's all through you. Here, I've just done my face," she blubbered feebly, "and you make me cry again!" But she managed to restrain her tears.

Sweeney pinched her pale forearm, pinched it to excruciate. Cora winced, and was brave. She liked to suffer at his hands, liked every manifestation of his physical strength.

"That'll be black to-morrow," she breathed contentedly. "But I shan't powder it. I shall keep it to look at." Her bliss was restored as quickly as it had been marred. She leaned her hair on the back of the seat and closed her eyes, and ejaculated low:

"Sweeney! Darling!"

The powerful darling's hand was still on her arm, but if he had withdrawn it no Paul Pry could have accused Cora of anything graver than dozing in the heat of the summer afternoon and neglecting her handsome companion.

She said dreamily, her eyes still closed:

"You don't seem to realise, you sleepy old thing, you being here with me has got me into a most terrible mess. I was never in such a hole. It's simply frightful." She sighed.

This was her first reference to the predicament in which she found herself, and though the words she used were grievous, the tone belied them; it was almost serene. Nor did she criticise her conduct—only the result of it. Not the conduct, but the result, was an enormity.

"Yes," Sweeney agreed with her estimate of the result. He said no more at the moment. His tactic was to wait; and he could have waited for hours. "Let 'em begin. If you begin yourself you're sure to be wrong," was his thought, guiding his invariable practice with women in a delicate dilemma.

"You've got me into it, and it's up to you to get me out of it, darling. I'm surprised I have to remind you of that."

"I didn't want to come here, my child. I said so several times. I most distinctly objected."

"You didn't object enough," said Cora, sitting up "You ought to have refused absolutely. You're so weak."

"Only where you're concerned, my dearest."

Cora smiled, flattered.

"I acted for the best, as I always do," she went on. "You've no money. Nor me either. I saw a way of saving twenty pounds. How could I have guessed that uncle would be here? It was my luck again. The usual thing. Well, something has to be done. And please I can't do *all* the thinking and planning and scheming."

"Seems to me we'd better hook it right away." He knew by experience that she had already formed a plan, and that she would stick to it; and he hoped that his suggestion would not be at variance with her plan. But if it was, he would not mind very much. Any plan would suit him. He had nothing to lose—neither reputation nor money. She would not deprive him of her society, and he was indifferent as to the precise spot on the earth's surface which she would appoint to him for the enjoyment of her society.

"Darling!" she gravely and forbearingly expostulated. "How can you possibly suggest that we should both go? Can't you see I have to put things right with uncle? Somehow I must get him on our side. It'll take hours and hours. He's fearfully obstinate and old-fashioned and bourgeois. Of course I can *do* it, but it'll take time. And I couldn't begin to do it if you stayed on here."

"I'm not going to leave you, girlie. You mustn't ask me too much."

"Darling!" She was enraptured. "Now I've got to deal with him"—she stroked "his" sleeve—"as well as with uncle. Darling, you must be reasonable. You must go away at once—now! I think the luggage is still in the car. Be sure you don't run off with mine, by the way, and don't just throw it out of the car as you generally do with luggage. Put it down gently. You'd better go to that hotel at Pulborough where we had a drink. And don't worry about the bill. We'll see to that later. Now, darling, do be reasonable! Your girlie implores you."

"I won't do it," said he, chiefly as a matter of form.

She kissed him tenderly.

"Be good!" she mumbled, her lips on his. "Shall I have to go down on my knees to you?"

"All right!" he yielded gloomily. He was honestly surprised that she should advocate a separation for the night. And, as happens occasionally to all men who think that they have nothing to learn about women, he was visited by a doubt whether women were not after all utterly incalculable—even to the greatest masters of them.

As for Cora, she was both pleased and displeased, and perhaps rather more displeased than pleased. He had yielded too easily. He ought to have been obstinate to the point of a scene. He ought to have insisted on a *quid pro quo* for his acquiescence. Was he letting her slip from him without a pang?

"Can you bear to lose me till to-morrow—on our week-end?" she demanded.

He shook his head, several times: a reply which she expected, for with her it was a fundamental article of faith that every wish ought to be gratified and that the frustration of a desire was matter for a real grievance against destiny. She could not admit the value of self-control, which seemed to her monstrously unnatural.

"You shall not, dearest. I've thought of a scheme. You'll take the car out again at about eleven o'clock to-night and meet me at the corner of the road at the end of the village here, say eleven-thirty. I'll be there—waiting for you."

He nodded. He well knew that he would have to wait for her and not she for him, since there was no record of her ever having been punctual for an appointment; but he merely nodded as if he believed her; he would probably not have to wait more than three-quarters of an hour.

"I can see you think I shan't be able to get away," she proceeded softly. "But I shall. I know Uncle Henry. He's one of those who are always wanting to go to bed, always wanting to get up. He's bound to send me off to bed at eleven. Besides, I shall say I'm tired." She smiled; for just as she was never punctual, so she was never tired. "Then I'll slip out to you. I'll run—run down the road, and you'll be waiting for me, and we'll drive off into the night, very fast—very fast. You'll drive faster than you've ever driven, through the night, and I shall be terribly afraid. But you won't care, you cave-man." She was whispering now. "You'll drive up on to the downs, and over the top of the downs—you know we saw it all as we came along this afternoon; even then I was thinking how lovely it would be to do that. And we'll go on till we come to one of those 'Rings'—you know, trees in a ring, Druid or something, I forget—sacred, frightfully old—Celtic, was it?—and we'll get out there and rest. And there won't be anyone within miles and miles of us. We shall be all alone under the trees, and I do hope the moon will be shining through the leaves. But that doesn't matter though—the darker the better. I'm so glad it's so lovely and hot."

Her dream was smouldering and burning in her eyes. She thrilled passionately to the stimulus of the dream, as to a magic annunciation. Her whispering voice trembled to it. She was uplifted, transfigured. She was drenched in the very fluid of poetry. Sweeney thought she was wondrous, miraculous, unique. He had never known any woman comparable to her, and he had known quite a few women of her type. He also thought that there were no roads on the downs; but that was a possible difficulty which could be met when the time came, and which to mention to her in her present mood of exaltation would be tactless.

"Go! Go!" she urged him, living in the dream. "Get away before uncle or anyone else comes into the garden. I want you to be clear away when he asks. We mustn't have any hitches. Where have I put that handkerchief of his? Oh, in the bag. Do you think I ought to give it him back?"

CHAPTER VI
HENRY'S HEART

HENRY KEARNS had a heart of his own, which, after causing him no trouble for some fifty years, was at last beginning to claim a certain amount of attention. Cora had not long left the small upstairs drawing-room to deal with Sweeney in the garden, when a maid came in with a telegram. Henry read the telegram—smiled a rather sardonic smile all to himself, and then drew a letter from his side-pocket and studied it afresh for the fourth or fifth time. It was the only letter on his person; as a man of order, proud of his orderliness, he did not usually carry letters in his pockets; having promptly answered them, he either filed them away or destroyed them. This letter was written on thick, quarto paper in a large, decided, feminine hand. It ran thus:

"Dear Henry Kearns. (I don't like 'Mr.' to a friend, or 'Miss' from a friend.) I wonder whether you would care to dine with me on Friday next—8.30—at my flat. If so I would ask just one or two people to meet you; not more than six of us altogether and perhaps only four. I should much like to have you here. I feel we have quite a lot to say to each other, and I think also you would find my friends interesting. And perhaps we could then hit on an evening for that theatre which you suggested. I am going away for the week-end— I seldom spend Sunday in town—but I shall be back on Tuesday. If I get your answer here then, that will give me time to arrange things—assuming of course you say yes, which I hope you will. I've been thinking over your arguments about the Allied Debts.
"Very sincerely yours,
"CYNTHIA SMYTHE."

He had met Cynthia Smythe at a dinner at The Hague, in a Foreign Office—Peace Palace circle, and not thought more than twice of her. Then again, on a flying visit to London, at a miscellaneous party with a basis of international trading relations, held at the house of the second partner in his late firm; in which house he had been invited to spend the night. At the end of the second evening, during which he had talked to her a great deal, and she quite as much to him, he had said to himself: "There's more in that girl than I thought there was."

Not that she was precisely a girl. But she was a spinster. She looked— well—thirty-four. Therefore Henry, to be on the safe side, had given her forty years. She was slim, if firm of body, and very well-dressed—in her own style. It was apparent that she had means and plenty of friends, and was accustomed to formulate her ideas clearly, and to have them listened to seriously. She was acquainted with things in general and with languages. She said she had only once been in a night-club, and she regarded night-clubs as the resort of individuals of both sexes who had never grown up and who had no intellectual resources. What attracted him to her was her candour, her girlish laugh, a charming trick of raising her left shoulder, and her low voice and exquisite articulation. When his mind dwelt on her it was the shoulder-raising and the quiet, frank laugh that he thought of—saw and heard.

The telegram said:

"Address till Tuesday, The Fowl Hatch House, Stoke Mandev-ille. Cynthia Smythe."

He wondered, and wondered sardonically, why she had telegraphed her address, since she had told him that Tuesday would be soon enough for his reply. . . . She desired to have a letter from him with the minimum of delay. He had indeed mentioned a theatre—the Chekhov play—but very vaguely—not a definite proposition.

The telegram somehow struck him as dramatic. It seemed to have given a new turn to his existence. It revealed to him that his mind had been dwelling on her very considerably. He dropped the letter on to his knee, whence it floated to the floor, and carefully examined the telegram, which had been despatched from the Great Central Station at 2.52. She must have been on the way to her week-end in the country when the idea of sending it had occurred to her. She had chanced his address: Kearns, Cander, Sussex. He had mentioned Cander once, and quite casually: she had remembered the name; the name had sunk into her consciousness. He had told her that he was leaving London for an indefinite period. Had she forgotten the fact—she who remembered a name heard once—or was she assuming that he would come specially to London for her dinner? No doubt the latter. A piece of cheek, eh? But he was flattered and excited. Yes, he was flattered by the notion that he had made an impression. His sedate heart was stirring. He said to himself: "I am a simpleton." But he did not really believe that he was a simpleton.

Cora ran most informally and startlingly into the room; but of course with an uncle she was entitled to be girlish. She saw the telegram in Henry's hand, and the large, bold page on the carpet.

"Oh! What a masculine sort of a woman!" she cried impulsively, almost with malicious glee. It was uncanny, unnerving. The insight of women, the agility of their wits, was utterly disconcerting; but Henry kept his presence of mind, picked up the letter, put it in his pocket, looked grave.

"Aren't we awful?" Cora went on, as if genuinely concerned.

"Who—awful?"

"Women. I can't understand why men ever have anything to do with us!" She seemed to be quite sincere in her condemnation of women.

Her words destroyed the original drama of the letter, and created a new one in Henry's mind. Henry was suddenly terrified. He recoiled panic-stricken from the prospect of further relations with Cynthia Smythe. He feared the name Cynthia; he feared the name Smythe. He feared her hand-writing, her notepaper. He thought: "She's forty and she's a virgin, and so damned self-confident, and she must be so set in her habits—finicky habits of course, like mine." His liberty, his priceless, beloved liberty: which he was just beginning to enjoy to the full! Was he to let it go? He could not. He was free, free; was he to purchase chains and eternally bind himself? He pictured the sharing of a bathroom with Cynthia Smythe! God knows why at that moment he should picture such a disturbing fragment of daili-ness; but he did. And he was affrighted. But through his alarms, as through a gauze, he could see Cynthia lifting enchantingly her left shoulder, and hear her quiet laugh.

"Well," said Cora cheerfully. "Sweeney's gone. I've packed him off. You'll never see him again. So that's all right."

Evidently, he thought, she meant to stay on. She had been caught in the attempt to use his home as a house of assignation; but she could perceive therein no reason against her staying on.

CHAPTER VII

LATE

DINNER was for eight o'clock.

"Sharp," said Henry, with a reluctant smile to Cora, whom he had avoided until seven o'clock, on the plea of having to occupy himself with household affairs.

"Yes, uncle. I know how particular you bachelors are about meal-times."

Her tone and mien were quite submissive. She went upstairs to her room at once. Kearns walked in the garden, regarding neither the lawns, the flowers, nor the scenery. He was debating in his mind whether or not to telephone to Nick Ussher and ask him to come down to Cander at once—that night. For a while he could not decide between the pros and the cons of the scheme. He was afraid of the possible consequences of telephoning for Nick; but what in the end persuaded him to do so was the very fact that he had been afraid. He returned into the house guiltily full of the project.

The telephone was in the hall; there was no privacy about the telephone. He glanced up the stairs, lest Cora might perchance be leaning over the banisters of the landing, or one of the servants wandering about. The Exchange gave the opinion that on a Saturday night it ought to be easy to get London. He clearly articulated the number, having consulted the book; he articulated it twice. Whereupon he felt that he had cast the die, burned his boats, crossed the Rubicon; and immediately regretted his action as a foolish action that could lead to nothing but trouble—chiefly for himself. He got London in ten minutes, which seemed like ten hours to his fuming and pacing in the tiled hall. Mr. Nicholas Ussher was not at home, but he was at his club, or one of his clubs. Henry demanded the Club. More fuming and pacing. He distantly heard bells ringing at intervals, and now and then the scampering above of some maid who had gone upstairs by the back-staircase. In another ten minutes he got London again, and the Club, and finally—it seemed both miraculous and terrible—he recognised Nick's voice in the receiver. Henry's heart was noticeably beating. For a few seconds he could not think what the devil to say to the poor fellow. Then he saw that he must be brief and blunt:

"Cora's here at Cander. Can you come down? Yes, to-night. Now. Drive down. You'll be here in two hours or a bit more. Finish your dinner and come."

Nick had too much sense to ask for reasons and explanations. He relied on his uncle-in-law's common sense and good judgment, and said he would come, and cut off the communication.

Henry blew out breath; he was perspiring.

"My God!" he thought. "What have I let myself in for?"

Then he said to himself superiorly, and with false calm, that of course he had done the right thing, the only thing, and that he and Nick between them would be a match for any woman. At least matters would be brought to a head. The hall clock struck the hour, in silver, and the hour was eight. He had already observed that the clock was five minutes fast. He ran upstairs. Having enjoined punctuality on the disorderly Cora, he could not afford to be late; yet he would inevitably be late. His clothes had not been laid out in the master's stately bedroom. Why not? It was twelve minutes past eight (Greenwich) when he descended, somewhat flustered and quite resigned to being apologetic.

Nobody in the ground-floor drawing-room, with its orange-shaded glowing lamps! Nobody in the dining-room, with its white-shaded glowing lamps and its dazzling table-array! (He would show the slut that a bachelor could have as good a notion of comfort and luxury as any woman.) Not a sound! He paced the drawing-room as he had paced the garden, smoked a cigarette, smoked another cigarette, drew the blinds—though he had given orders that they should not be drawn.

"Damn it all!" he muttered in exasperation. "I shall begin."

He rang the bell. He heard the bell ring. No reply. He rang again. After an interval he heard a scuttering on the main stairs, and a girl, the house-maid, dashed rather rustically into the drawing-room. He instantly assumed the calm of a god.

"What is your name?"

"Amy, sir."

"Well, Amy, where is the parlourmaid?"

"She's upstairs with Mrs. Ussher, sir. We've both been up there."

"Well, will you kindly go back to Mrs. Ussher and give her my compliments, and say that dinner is waiting. Thank you."

He knew that dinner was not waiting, because the parlourmaid could not be simultaneously serving the dinner and attending upon Cora.

"I'm not *very* late, am I, dear uncle?" Cora said, strolling into the drawing-room at twenty-five minutes to nine. She smiled innocently. She wore a white embroidered frock, cut passably low in front and extremely low behind: it was an old frock, good enough for a country week-end.

"Not at all!" Henry replied lightly. "It's the soup that's early."

What was the use of showing any trace of annoyance? She was a fact which existed, and doubtless no more responsible for her mind than a hunchback for his hunch. You could not be annoyed with a hunchback. But what a life—with her! He had said "sharp" and she was thirty-five minutes late, and thought absolutely nothing of it! Not a syllable of excuse! The parlourmaid did not immediately announce dinner. How could she? Six more minutes passed.

"I *am* glad I'm not late," said Cora, with significance.

A cat! She probably assumed that dinner ought to have been waiting, and magically keeping hot, all ready to be swept from the kitchen into the dining-room the very moment her ladyship deigned to appear.

They went in to dinner. During the meal Cora chatted for the improvement and the impressing of the parlourmaid. As for Henry, he was continuously self-conscious, with an entirely illogical feeling of guilt—because he had secretly sent for her husband. In less than three hours the man would arrive. Then what? He dreaded the scene, which, however, he was bringing on himself. He could not face the hours before Nick's arrival. At least he could not face them in inaction.

"Shall we take a walk?" he suggested, when she lit a cigarette at the end of dinner. "It's easy to get up on to the downs from here."

She paused, then said:

"Oh, uncle, what a heavenly idea! Do let's." And she rose at once. "I needn't put anything on, need I?"

"Yes, you need, my child. You can't go down our village street in only that frock."

"But it's dark."

"It's not dark enough," he insisted firmly.

"It's so hot," she said, repining, and added, brightly acquiescent: "But just as you wish, uncle."

Butter, apparently, wouldn't melt in her little mouth.

CHAPTER VIII

CONFESSION

"THIS is a tumulus," Henry Kearns remarked, stopping by a grassy mound which rose irregularly out of the vast expanse of turf rolling around them in tremendous contours. "At least, so I'm told," he added.

They had climbed very slowly to the second hilltop of the Downs above the village, and were five or six hundred feet above sea-level. In front of and below them, to the north, lay the measureless Flats, with long tongues of white mist lying across the land in places, and the twinkling of domestic lamps in the windows of County Council cottages, and a gleam of water here and there from the river.

"What is a tumulus?"

Henry exclaimed that a tumulus was a prehistoric sepulchre.

"How perfectly thrilling and horrid!" said Cora. "But I suppose they're nothing but bones now. Why don't people open them and see?"

"They do, sometimes. But there's such a thing as a sense of decency. I vote we sit."

Henry was hot after the exercise. They sat, side by side. No sooner had they left the confines of the village than Cora had taken off the Spanish shawl which covered her bare shoulders and carried it in her hand, waving it to and fro. She now threw it on the grass, but did not sit on it. There it was spread, its big red flowers and veridian leaves darkly showing. Henry leaned back in physical relief against the mound, found his cigarette case and passed a cigarette to Cora, who sat up straight enough. The brief flare of a match; the red ends of two cigarettes.

An enormous orange-tinted moon swam swollen and as if bursting with the potentialities of light over the summit of an eastern hill. The sky first, and then the earth, began to be illuminated as the colour of the moon changed from orange to pale yellow. The stars faded. Shadows appeared vaguely, and then sharply, defined. The turf brightened. Every blade of grass under the eyes of the pair could be distinguished from its neighbour. The daisies had wilted away, as the wheat on the lower slopes turned, ripening. No wind! No sound! No sound, as it seemed, in the whole world! But in the great, benignant heat of the night, black figures could be described afar off, moving solemnly in twos and threes, or solitary, on the surface of the downs. The heat had drawn the adventurous up to the heights; and awe was subduing every one of them.

"Uncle," Cora breathed, in a melting, sad, sweet voice. "I must tell you. I think you've taken this business simply magnificently. Far better than I deserve. I know I'm wicked. I wish you could realise how awful I feel about it all."

Her tones seemed to be sanctified by the secret yearnings for righteousness with which they were laden. She was sincerity itself, aspiration itself. And in her white, thin frock, which enveloped her only as a vapour might have done, she was vaporous too; so ethereal that a rough sigh from Henry might have blown her away.

Henry agreed privately that he had indeed behaved rather marvellously in the affair. While offering no reply to her intense assertions, he saw a chance of mastery and took it.

"Have you broken with Nick?" he asked bluntly and curtly, putting at the same time a shade of good-humoured, tolerant benevolence into his question.

"Oh, no! I don't think so. Oh, no! I wouldn't say I'd broken with him."

"Does he know about this—who-is-it?"

"No."

"Does he suspect? I'm not being inquisitive. I should like to help you—both."

"I doubt if he even suspects. Men never do. They can't believe that you could prefer anybody else to them. Too proud."

True perhaps (thought Henry), if feline.

He demanded, more firmly:

"What's the trouble between you and Nick? Now you can either talk quite freely to me, as if you were talking to yourself, or not at all. I don't mind which, but it must be one or the other."

"It's all very vague," she said submissively. "It's a something, a *je ne sais quoi*—"

"*Je ne sais quoi* be hanged," Henry exclaimed with calculated brutality. He felt that he was subjugating her, and that she needed, even perversely desired, the whip. "Tell me about the last great row you and he had." He was curious to hear her version of the dance-club affray.

"Last great row! Oh, uncle."

"Well there must have been one—you being a Kearns."

"It was about money," said Cora dismally.

"The usual thing!"

"No. Nick isn't mean. I know he thinks I'm extravagant, but he never says so. Only he makes me feel it, and that's worse than saying so. I'm not blaming him. He said I'd had I forget how much money last month. I said I hadn't. I couldn't believe it. You know I can't keep accounts, and I've given up trying to. So he brought down his private account-book that he keeps locked up, and he showed it me. I'd never seen it before. Of course he could point out all the items—it was all so neat, it made me angry—well, it didn't make me angry, because I was angry before, and I said I didn't take his damned account-book. I said he might make mistakes like other people. He went cold and formal, like he does sometimes; he didn't say any more. But next day, when it was all smoothed over and I asked him for some money he said 'Certainly,' quite nicely, and fetched his account-book and entered it up; and then he said, 'Now you'll initial this, please. We won't have any more disputes of this sort any more.' Naturally I was furious. I said it was an insult for a husband to ask a wife to sign for money. As if he couldn't trust me, indeed! But no, he wouldn't see it. And he wouldn't give me the money until I had signed. And I wouldn't sign. But as I had to have some money I did sign in the end. But I never forgave him for that—I meant for using what you'd call his economic power. . . . I suppose I was right to sign. Was I?"

"My good girl," said Henry, with an air of disgust. "What a fool you were! If all your rows have been like that—! Here you disputed his accounts to start with—that is to say, you didn't trust him—at least you pretended to yourself you didn't trust him—because naturally you knew in your heart all the time that his accounts were correct—and then you refuse to do a perfectly ordinary thing—that everybody does as a matter of course. Do you call it an insult to be asked for a receipt? There's no question of trust or distrust. Surely you can see that."

"Yes," said Cora softly. "I can see it now you explain it. But I'm not a man, and it's no use pretending I am. I only wish Nick would explain things to me like that. But he doesn't. He just goes white and taps his foot, and there we are—a scene! It isn't that I don't like Nick. I do. I was mad about him at one time—he's such a fine dancer. I mean really fine."

"Do you ever go out dancing together?" Henry asked, feigning simplicity.

"Oh, yes!"

"Even after your rows?"

"Oh, yes!"

"And I expect you want him to stay up too late, and he hates it, eh?"

"How funny you should say that! It's quite true. That was the beginning of our *very* last row. But you see he's always so hard about it. Time, time, time! Business, business, business! He simply can't see there's another side of life at all! That's what I say."

"Quite. But you do ask him for money, and he does have to earn it; and how can he earn it if you keep him up half the night? What's your defence?"

"Oh!" she yielded. "I haven't any defence. I'm quite capable of seeing *that*. But it's only now and then. It isn't every night. After all—. Well, what's the use? I was wrong. There! When I'm wrong I always admit it. Nick never admits he's wrong. Never! And even if he never is wrong, he might pretend he's wrong sometimes, just to please me. Nobody likes living day and night with a perfect paragon."

"There's not much sense in that," said Henry Kearns. "You can't expect Nick to say he's wrong when you both know he's right."

A couple of wanderers approached them on the wide grassy path. The girl was leaning rather heavily on the tall young man's arm, and looking up at him. He looked downwards, with bent head. The girl was talking, the man listening. She was dressed in white; all the girls were dressed in white. Her voice came into hearing. A soft, sad, wistful voice, like Cora's, seemingly charged with mysterious significances, as if saying lovely and solemn things about the deeps of existence. The immense concave of the sky might have subdued this couple also, as it had subdued Cora. Their tread was soundless on the resilient turf.

"I said, 'If that's how you look at it, my dear,' I said," the girl was saying.

Henry caught just those words and no more. The voice diminished to a murmuring again. The clinging girl glanced round at Henry in his dinner-jacket and straw hat, and at Cora in her evening frock, and at the Spanish shawl; she stared with hard impudence at Cora during a few steps, and then, sharply turning her head towards her young man, she ignored Cora as something negligible or contemptible. A common Cockney voice; thick ankles; no distinction of carriage! But still the passing was impressive, implicit with obscure portents. The couple were far down the slope now. Cora had apparently not noticed them.

"Yes," she said meekly, after a long pause. "Yes."

Henry Kearns had once more the apprehension of imminent drama. He envisaged Nick Ussher driving swiftly towards Cander. Should he tell Cora that Nick was on the way? Was she sufficiently vanquished to receive the news in the spirit in which it ought to be received? He nearly told her, and then recoiled from the step in alarm. Cora leaned back against the slant of the tumulus.

"Oh, how heavenly it is, the feel of the grass against your spine!" she softly exclaimed, wriggling and pressing her spine into the grass. "And this grave has never been opened for thousands of years!"

She shuddered with emotion. With what ardour she was capable of living, at moments! Henry Kearns almost envied her her extraordinary capacity for emotion! He was a mere learned fish compared to her. But how dangerous was her terrible latent store of emotion! He saw Nick getting nearer and nearer, and wished to God that to-morrow had dawned.

"If you aren't breaking with Nick," he said, judicially. "I suppose you'll break with this what's-his-name?"

"I suppose so," she admitted. She gave a sob, then controlled herself. "Yes," she said, apparently courageous. "I must—of course. But what have I to live for? That's what I ask myself."

"Well, now," said Henry Kearns persuasively. "You're coming down to bed-rock now. What *do* you live for as it is? Tell me about yourself, my dear. Tell me just what your life is. Tell me your ordinary day. I'm very interested."

CHAPTER IX

HER LIFE

"I GET up," said Cora. "That's the beginning, I suppose."

"What time?"

"Oh! It depends. I never allow anybody to call me. You see it's most important for me to have all the sleep I can. Nothing ages you like loss of sleep. The doctor says so. He says I ought to have nine hours if possible. But of course it isn't often I do have nine hours. Houses are so noisy in the mornings. Servants simply will not be quiet. They don't understand. Servants have a mentality of their own, and they're all the same. I've tried dozens of servants."

"When do the servants get up?"

"They're *supposed* to be down by seven o'clock; but do you think they are?"

"And you get up—when?"

"Well, I have my breakfast in bed—on a tray. It saves so much trouble. And, of course, though they never consider you, you have to consider them. Besides, I always feel rather queer when I wake up."

"Ten or eleven o'clock, I expect?"

"Yes."

"And the rest of the morning?"

"Well, I have to dress. I've no maid. The housemaid is supposed to maid me, but her notion of maiding—" Cora laughed derisively. "The parlourmaid looks after Nick much better than the housemaid looks after me. I suppose that's right. Nick's the most important—the breadwinner, as they say, and he must have all the care."

"By the time you're dressed I suppose it's time for lunch?"

"Not at all. I'm never later than twelve-thirty, Then there's shopping, and a million things that a woman has to do."

"Housekeeping?"

"Oh! I never bother about housekeeping. I was never taught that, or brought up to it. I see the cook, unless I'm in a very great hurry. She's a sort of cook-housekeeper. We only have the three servants, you see."

"And you lunch?"

"I'm not very keen on lunch, unless I'm invited out. Nick *never* accepts an invitation to lunch. So I have to go alone. Some hostesses don't care so frightfully for that. In the ordinary way either I have an egg at home, or I go to the Club—I mean my own Club—not the Legation."

"And then?"

"Well, you mustn't forget there's such a thing as clothes, darling uncle. Clothes take a long time, especially for a poor woman like me, who has to make things last, and with no maid to help her. I know women who have a maid who can alter dresses, and it saves them the maid's wages over and over again. Only husbands can't see that. Oh no! Husbands simply say that they can't afford to pay for a maid. It's very short-sighted."

"And later in the afternoons?"

"Well, I have a few friends who stick to me in spite of all my faults. We may play Bridge, or we go to art-galleries, or the pictures. I think the film has a very great future, and it's our duty to watch it and encourage it. Some people don't see it in that light; but I do. Or we go to a matinée, but I don't care so much for the matinées, because the audience is nearly all women and they will giggle."

"I expect by the time you get back home, Nick's back, too."

"That's just where you're wrong, darling uncle. Nick is always late. Office, naturally! Everything has to give way to the office. I'm always home first, and I try to be all ready for him and looking as nice as I can. I only dress to please him, and because I want him not to be ashamed of me. What a bad thing it would be for him in his business if he had a shabby wife!"

"Then you see Nick for the first time in the day when he comes home?"

"No! Not always. If I happen to be awake I call to him while he's dressing, and he comes in to say good morning. That's the time I should love a good long gossip with him, but he's generally in such a frightful hurry. Yes, he can't spare me any time in the morning, and at night he always says he must get to sleep. So what *am* I to do? The fact is, I never see him."

"But you spend the evenings together?"

"Sometimes he has to work in the evenings. Then I play the piano a bit, or read a book, and I slip off to bed quietly so as not to disturb him at his work. But of course we dine out, or have people to dinner, now and then. Not that you can entertain, really, with only three servants. We go to first-nights. I adore first-nights. I'd go to all of them if I could, but Nick's so easily bored at the theatre. And we dance sometimes at the Legation—but you know about that. . . . And that's about all, I think. Of course there's Sundays. We have been known to go away for a week-end—but the fuss on Monday mornings about Nick being late for the office!"

"And holidays?"

"This year we went to Cannes in January. But only for a fortnight. I should love to spend months in Cannes, months, like other people do. And last summer we were at Le Touquet for a month, nearly. I danced every night. I never went to bed till two o'clock. It was simply heavenly. But at Le Touquet people really do understand how to enjoy themselves. This summer's a bit muddled. God knows what will happen these next few weeks! Nick hasn't *mentioned* a holiday, and I wasn't going to be the first to mention it."

Henry Kearns made no comment. They both smoked again, and not a word said. A faint murmur rose to them over the Downs from the far distance of the Flats; it was like the hum of an insect's wings. Then it increased into the noise of the last train from London. It was a resounding roar. There could be seen a red glow from the funnel of the engine, dragging furiously after it a long procession of pale lights. A momentarily still louder roar as the train crossed the iron bridge over the river! The racket of the train seemed to awaken the whole firmament and to fill it.

"Oh, uncle!" cried Cora, suddenly. "How cruel of you, with your questions, making me tell my life like that! Do you think I didn't notice the sarcasm in your questions: the way you put them?"

"Not at all," Henry protested, soothingly. "I only wanted to get at the facts. There wasn't any sarcasm."

"Oh yes, there was!" she insisted. "Yes, there was! And you were quite right. I should be sarcastic myself if I were in your place."

The sound of the train diminished; it was the hum of an insect's wings; it was nothing. Silence.

"Let's go back to the house," Cora went on, in a fatigued, repining voice. "I can't *stand* being here."

And with the emphasis on the word "stand," she threw away her cigarette, which curved in the air and lay abandoned, but burning, on the grass a dozen feet off. "It's too big up here, and I can't stand it; and men and women's bones underneath me and everything!" She did not rise to go, but pulled a tiny handkerchief from her bag and began to fan herself feebly. "I've told you my life is terrible, and so it is! I know that as well as anybody. But is it my fault? What am I to do? I was brought up like that, and I can only be myself. Do you think I haven't thought of all this before? Do you think I don't want to be different? I suppose you imagine I'm happy! I *do* want to be different, but I can't. Every day it's the same. You won't believe me if I say I'd like my bones to be inside this tumulus; but it's true!"

Her tone, tragic, sincere, and distressed, was really heart-rending; it was as if a great tortured soul struggled to escape through her little rouged mouth.

"I won't sit on a grave. In a thousand years my bones will be somewhere, too, and some girl will be sitting on them. But what does it matter?" She moved across to the Spanish shawl, and lay down on it, her left hip rising out of the rest of the body like a hill.

Henry was afflicted. He desired intensely to be of help to his niece; for he had made the astounding discovery that a human being was not utterly evil; that Cora had a troubled conscience, aspirations towards righteousness, and a secret, withdrawn, piteous life, throbbing painfully beneath the dailiness of her worldly existence. And, he thought, perhaps too complacently:

"*I* have brought this to the surface, and nobody else has."

And he pictured Nick still coming nearer and nearer, and he had hopes, for her and for Nick, of a marvellous re-birth, all due to himself, which hopes made him feel creative like a god.

"I'll tell you how it strikes me," he said very quietly, leaving the tumulus and sitting close by her on the shawl. He did not look at her, nor touch her, but gazed vaguely over the Flats. "What you need, my dear girl, is to see yourself, and you aren't doing it. Your arguments about yourself are all upside down. And what's more, there's a part of your mind that knows they're upside down. Now, for instance, you don't really believe that you dress in order to please Nick and help him in his business. All that's only an excuse. You spend money on dress because you like to look your best, and no other reason. If you didn't you'd excuse your dowdiness by saying that you didn't spend money on dress because you wanted to save his money for him. The fact is, you're jealous of his business and you'd like him to make money without earning it. You haven't understood that money has to be paid for, somehow, like everything else. You say you lie in bed in the morning because you must have sleep, and not enough sleep ages you. Rot, my dear! Cocktails will age you, but you go on drinking 'em. If you need sleep, why in the name of sense don't you go early to bed? Well, you don't go early to bed because you enjoy staying up late and drinking cocktails and dancing, and all these things are more important to you than your health and your looks and Nick's health and Nick's breakfast. That's the size of it—trust me!"

"You *are* preaching, darling uncle!" Cora interjected feebly.

"I know I am. But, dash it—you're asking for preaching, the way you go on. And what else can I do? Look at your attitude to servants. It's all wrong. You have the infernal impudence to say they're 'supposed' to get up at seven—and you get up at eleven, and have your breakfast brought to you. Do you know the difference between you and your servants? Your servants earn money and you only spend it. They work and you're idle. They've learnt a job and they can do it, and you can't do any job on earth. You're 'supposed' to be the mistress of a house, and you couldn't run it to save your life. You can't even keep accounts, though anyone could learn to keep your sort of accounts in a fortnight. I expect you'll be telling me next you've forgotten the blooming multiplication table! Your servants could teach you lots of things, but you couldn't teach them anything—yes, you could, you could teach them how to powder their noses. And you look down on them! And that's not the worst. The worst is that they think you've got the right to look down on them. That's what's up with society to-day. And you think yourself ill-used because there are two of you and you've only got three of these immortal souls that you call servants who pass their whole lives in waiting on you and Nick hand and foot. Yes, by God! I *am* preaching. What have you ever done to be proud of? You're simply an incapable, who wants everything for nothing. When you married Nick he took the responsibility of keeping you, and before you married you took jolly good care to be sure that he *could* keep you. And what do you give him in return—except your bare body? Nothing. Not a thing! You steal everything—that's what it amounts to. And yet you have the nerve to have grievances! Supposing Nick happened to be ruined—you couldn't even cook for him; you wouldn't know how to nurse him if he was ill; I'm dashed if you could do his mending. Are you humble about it all? Not you! You're proud of it. Hasn't it ever struck you that you're only something nice to look at—and you won't be even that for very long if you continue at your present rate. What do you think you'll be like in another twenty years? You'll be nothing but a damned nuisance to anybody you have to live with."

Cora stirred, and her uneasy movement warned Henry Kearns to rise off the shawl. He walked away—just a few yards—restless and nervous. The mass with the mound in the middle, which was Cora, heaved itself up, and Cora stood. She seemed to shiver, stooped for the shawl, and draped it with conscious craft round her shoulders. Then she gazed at Henry, the light of the moon full on her. She looked at him plaintively, not protesting, not defiant; but rather as if she were saying: "Is that all? Have you finished with me? Or have I still more to endure? I know I'm at your mercy."

Henry was ashamed of his preaching—he with the damnable superiority of the untempted man! Yet what could he do but preach? She had to be told, and she had to be told emphatically, even violently, if any result was to be obtained. Thus he sought to justify himself and extinguish his shame—and failed to do so. How facile his arguments and how unanswerable!

Yet there was falsity in his reasoning, and especially in his comparison of her, to her disadvantage, with cooks, parlourmaids, and housemaids. She had what they had not and could never have. In her sloth, and her absorption in herself, and her determination to get all that it was possible to get out of the world of men and women, she had achieved an ideal far beyond their reach. She was desirable; she was marvellous to look upon; to watch her gave pleasure to Henry Kearns. And neither the fact that her mere face was not strictly beautiful, nor his sharply aroused sense of her vices and faults, could lessen his pleasure and his admiration. She was desirable, marvellous and magnificent. She had a sovereign power, and she knew it. She had a prestige. The moon and the wide sky and the vastness of the Downs could not reduce her to triviality or the contemptible. She challenged them and matched them. She was one of the finished products of a civilisation. Arguments were futile against her and could not scathe her. There she was! Was he to criticise God?

She said sadly:

"Why didn't you talk to mamma and papa twenty years ago? I was brought up like that. It's not my fault. However can I help being myself?"

Henry was about to reply that everybody was responsible for himself, and that it was the business of children to correct in themselves the errors of their parents. But he refrained: the matter was too complex: he saw with the easy, clear insight of one who had observed many societies and instinctively avoided all blinding emotions, that not Cora's father and mother were to blame for her defects and her misfortune, but the mighty stream of evolution itself.

"Let's go back home," he suggested compassionately.

Time was passing and he did not want to be late for Nick. He was just as apprehensive as ever of the clash and upshot of the encounter which he had secretly and too rashly planned.

CHAPTER X

THE SOVEREIGN QUEEN

WHEN Nicholas Ussher drove in the brilliant moonlight along the Pulborough road in the direction of Cander, his chauffeur, who was quite unacquainted with the district, stopped to ask the way of the occupant of another car which was standing at the corner of a cross lane. The lane, he was told, led northwards to Cander at a distance of a few hundred yards. Ussher, tired and impatient, caught sight of the giver of information, and jumped out of his car.

"Hullo! Todd!" he exclaimed. "Is that you?"

Sweeney started, almost violently, and then recovered himself.

"Yes," he said, very calmly.

There was a pause, and Sweeney also stepped down into the road.

By a common impulse of caution, and without a word, they moved a few paces southwards up the cross lane towards the Downs, so as to be out of hearing of Nick's chauffeur.

Nick despised Todd, and despised him all the more because of his great reputation as a conquering Lovelace: of which reputation he had a certain morbid but instinctive envy. Nick's thoughts pieced themselves together very rapidly into a seemingly coherent whole.

Cora had danced with Todd at the Legation Club on the night when she had deprived Nick of his full ration of sleep. He now suspected that she had insisted on staying late chiefly in order to dance with Todd. He recalled, or imagined that he recalled, disturbing glances and gestures between them. Cora had not told him where she was going for the week-end, nor when she would return. But he had not questioned her: nor even seen her; she had left a note for him announcing her departure: such a thing had never happened before. Why Henry Kearns should have telephoned to him to come instantly to Cander to meet Cora he did not comprehend. But Cora was assuredly at Cander, and Todd was waiting alone in a car at a late hour at the corner of the lane leading to Cander! Henry Kearns could not possibly be aware of that fact. Or was he aware of it? Lastly, Todd had a constrained, confused air of agitation. A good-looking rascal—with just the shifty, appealing, half-savage, unreliable face to attract women, who were all as silly when confronted by such a face as by a military uniform worn dashingly.

Thus Nicholas Ussher to himself as regards the circumstances precedent to the situation. As to the situation itself, he reflected:

"I am a man who has experience of the world. I must keep quite calm and I must be dignified. I can handle this contemptible middle-aged scoundrel all right."

He did not consciously recognise that his dignity was more important to him than anything else just then; but it was so; and his dignity was in jeopardy He knew not what he should say to Todd. He gathered, however, that Todd was waiting for him to begin.

"Have you seen my wife to-day?" he asked, not choosing his words, nor his tone, which was hard, tight, and challenging, whereas, if he had considered it at all, he had meant it to be lofty, easy and perhaps light—the tone of a man who could control and was controlling the entire affair by moral and mental superiority.

He hated to mention his wife; his wife was his, and to share even her name or appellation with this fellow hurt him. He hated still more the implied admission that this fellow with the grotesque nickname of "Sweeney" might be better acquainted than himself with Cora's doings and movements.

"Yes," Sweeney answered with tranquillity, sticking his hands into his pockets as it were preparatory to an elaborate discussion. "As a matter of fact I drove her down here this afternoon. Didn't you know?"

If Sweeney had not uttered the last three words the scene might have developed differently. But those last three words exasperated Nick because they had the effect of twitting him with his ignorance of Cora's plans. He became intensely jealous. Jealousy flamed in him scorchingly, monopolising his mind. He had a desire to kill the fellow on the spot, or at least to knock him senseless; he was no longer a self-possessed man with experience of the world, but a savage animated by the most primitive instincts. He vaguely acknowledged to himself that he could not charge the fellow with a breach of decorum for driving Cora down to her Uncle's house; but of course it never occurred to him that Cora had not expected to find her uncle at home. Still, the admission made no difference to the trend of his accusing ideas. The fellow was somehow guilty: his mere demeanour was proof enough of that. The fellow simply could not be natural. (And this was not surprising, seeing that Sweeney was every moment apprehending the appearance of Cora in the lane on her way to him from the village!) Damn the insolent fellow with his "Didn't you know!"

"That's my business, whether I knew or not," snapped Nick. Not quite the remark of a superman handling a situation! But now Nick did not care what happened.

"Yes," Todd agreed nonchalantly.

"What were you waiting there for, may I ask?"

"Well," said Todd, and there was deliberate offensiveness in his voice: "That's my business what I was waiting there for. Unless, of course, you own the bally road."

Although still quite close to the highway, they were out of sight of the two automobiles and of the chauffeur. The hedge, at this point of the mounting, curving lane rose high over the heads of the rivals for Cora, and cut them off from direct moonlight. But they could see each other's faces plainly enough. Their faces were together, for Nick had made a half-turn towards his foe.

"Well?" muttered Sweeney, with defiance.

"Well?" repeated Nick.

Not another word was said. All disguise had been abandoned. Nick's attitude denounced Sweeney as Cora's paramour. Sweeney's attitude desperately acknowledged the relationship. Sweeney now did not care how soon Cora showed herself in the lane; he glanced quickly across the highway to see if by chance she was coming. Nick had absolutely no fear of Sweeney. He knew that the fellow had some renown as an amateur boxer, but he regarded him as a middle-aged decadent weakling. He seized Sweeney by the shoulder, and Sweeney freed himself instantaneously and jumped back, watching warily for an opening to lay Nick flat.

But Nick, too, had done some boxing. They were animals with scarcely a thought above the physical plane. They breathed loudly. Nick snorted. He was in a sort of ecstasy of fury, and delighted in it. He flinched from no consequences and from no publicity. The whole world might have made a ring round them and Nick would not have cared.

Then they both heard on the rough stones footsteps coming, not from the direction of the village, but from the Downs, and they saw Cora in the Spanish shawl and Kearns, and by immense overruling efforts they became human again.

None of the four completely understood the situation. Cora was amazed to see her husband. Henry Kearns was startled to see Sweeney—especially with Nick. Sweeney could not understand why, having regard to Cora's passionate secret appointment with himself, she should be approaching his car in company with her uncle. And Nick knew nought of the situation except a fragment of it heard on the telephone, and the fact of Sweeney's presence.

But all realised very acutely that something terrible had been about to happen, and that something terrible might still happen. All hearts were beating excitedly in fear. Henry Kearns, saying to himself that he was the oldest and the most important person there, called urgently on his brain for the best method of assuming the lead. But it was Cora herself who took the initiative. Cora knew beyond any questioning that not Henry Kearns but herself was by far the most important person there, and that alone her mysterious power over men had created the situation, and that only she could resolve it.

She ran forward, thinking thrice as quickly as any of the men. She stood between the antagonists, and very close to both of them. Strange influences invisibly radiated from her. The antagonists looked at her soft, dominating brilliance, and were nonplussed. They could do nothing, and were reduced, like Henry Kearns, to waiting for her.

"Whatever do you two imagine you're doing?" she demanded, in the tone of a benevolent but sovereign queen admonishing unruly subjects.

She felt pleasure in the sight of two men desperately quarrelling over her; it gave her confidence; she had no remorse at having by sheer negligence bungled her own arrangement with Sweeney. Nor did she trouble about the circumstances which had brought Nick dramatically on the scene.

The chauffeur peeped round the corner of the lane, and then prudently drew back, feeling that it would be safer for him to see nothing and to hear nothing.

"Why is this fellow here?" growled Nick peremptorily, indicating Sweeney. He was a lawyer, and after all he had legal rights over his woman; he owned her more effectively than anybody else could own her. "He tells me he drove you down here? Is it true?"

"My dear Nick, of course it's true. And why shouldn't he drive me down to uncle's?" Cora replied lightly, with a gentle, soothing laugh.

"Is he sleeping at your place?" Nick asked Henry Kearns.

"No, he isn't," said Kearns, and he said no more.

"I asked you a question, Cora," Nick resumed fiercely. "What is this fellow doing here?"

"Why on earth are you so melodramatic, my poor boy?" Cora calmly retorted. "I haven't the slightest idea what he's doing here. I've been for a walk with uncle on the Downs. Sweeney, what *are* you doing here?"

She was sublime in her impudence. But Sweeney did not regard it as impudence. He regarded her move as one which, according to the code to which he was accustomed, she was quite entitled to make. He had been "there" before, and more than once. The responsibility in these cases was the man's, and on such occasions as the present Sweeney had a certain practical conception of chivalry. Also he was capable of bringing much ingenuity to bear on a difficulty.

"It's all very simple," said he, coldly and resentfully. "I should have told Ussher straight off, if his manner had been different. I was meaning to sleep at Pulborough, but I thought I'd be more comfortable at Brighton, and I was just driving to Brighton. On the slope about a quarter of a mile back I saw two people coming down the hill, and I thought I recognised Mrs. Ussher's Spanish shawl, and so I was just waiting here to see if I was right, and say a couple of words if I *was* right. That's all."

"What a simply frightful liar he is!" thought Cora, almost frightened at the man's miraculous duplicity. As for Kearns, he felt that Sweeney was lying, and that grave and sinister things were hidden from himself. But he kept silence.

"Well," said Nick, ominously and rudely to Sweeney. "My advice to you is to get on to Brighton."

Nick believed the story, partly because he wanted to believe it, because the easiest course was to believe it. Moreover, it was convincingly plausible.

"Nick!" Cora protested plaintively. "Nick! Surely there's no need to talk like that."

"Don't let that trouble you, Cora," Sweeney sniggered. "It doesn't trouble me a bit."

And he walked off, and Nick Ussher somewhat absurdly followed after him for a few steps, as if showing a suspicious character off the premises and satisfying himself that the suspicious character really did leave the said premises. The male portion of this group made a poor spectacle.

Cora, on the contrary, continued to dominate. While Nick was menacing the rear of Sweeney (who took care not to turn his head) she murmured to Henry Kearns:

"Don't breathe a word to Nick about me not knowing you were at Cander until I got here. He might kill me."

Her demeanour as she said this, whether histrionic or not, was magnificent. She seemed to be warning her uncle against the temptation to commit a blunder, an act of baseness, a fatal crime. It was she who was the innocent, and Kearns the potential miscreant. Kearns wondered if she in fact did fear death at the hands of a raging husband. He could not credit that she did: yet her superb manner nearly convinced him against reason of her utter sincerity. He muttered to her an "Of course I shan't."

"Nick!" she cried. "Nick!" A heavenly, irresistible appeal was in her voice.

Nick swung round. She advanced and threw herself upon him, clasping his neck so tightly that he could hardly breathe. Innumerable times she kissed his face—not merely his mouth and eyes, but every part of his face. She buried him in her kisses as in rose-petals, and he rose up out of them at intervals struggling for air. Her fiery breath consumed and burnt out his anger and even his doubts of her. He could feel himself softening, melting; and defeat was delicious to him, though he was rather ashamed that any third person should see the display. Cora did not mind a witness at all, and especially a sympathetic uncle; for he was witness of her triumph. She was still a sovereign queen, and Kearns knew it and Nick knew it.

"Nick!" she cried again, with abandonment and supplication. "How did you find me? It must have been one of those instincts that nobody understands." Nick was not in a position to contradict her. "Is that your car down there? Take me away in it." Her voice grew richer and softer. "Take me away—now. I know I've not been being nice to you lately; but I can't help it sometimes. I've only you in the world. I'll do anything you ask. You must be hard on me. I want more than anything else to be your slave. Oh, Nick! If only you knew how to treat me. Take me away. This minute. . . . Home!" She laid her head on his shoulder, and Nick felt victorious and yet silly.

Kearns said discreetly:

"Come to my place, and go home to-morrow if you want to. You can't drive back to London at this time of night. Besides—in that frock! You'd have to change. And the chauffeur'll be tired."

Cora reproached him with a long look.

"Chauffeur!" she repeated. "Frock! What ever does it matter? What's a chauffeur for? Tell him to drive fast—fast."

She was ruthless. She was imploring to be allowed to be Nick's slave, his thing. But she was ruthless.

"Take me home now, Nick! I need it." She sobbed. "I must have you to myself."

She raised her head from his shoulder and gazed at him, still sobbing at intervals—short, childlike sobs. The Spanish shawl was slipping and revealing her shoulders.

"All right! Come on!" Nick yielded, with masculine gruffness. He was now excited.

Henry Kearns could think of nothing to say—nothing.

Cora mounted into the car as into a war-chariot, the chieftainess returning from some Amazonian campaign. The resplendent shawl was across the full width of the car. The chauffeur, with the resigned fatalism of chauffeurs at late hours, started the car.

"Stop!" Cora enjoined him, and leaned out. "Darling uncle. You've been simply frightfully kind. I must kiss you."

She kissed him.

"So that's her kiss!" he thought, curiously.

The car turned round. It was gone. Cora had dropped her head again on Nick's shoulder.

"Hold me! Hold me tight!" she was whispering, so that the chauffeur should not hear.

"My God!" Henry Kearns exclaimed in Cora's bedroom, into which he had gone for a moment to see what sort of a mess she had left there. He could almost have wiped his brow in the tumult of his sensations. "Women!"

Whom did Cora love, if she loved anyone? He could not answer the query. Perhaps not Cora herself could have answered it—if it had troubled her. But it did not trouble her. She was living tremendously in the moment.

Kearns felt very sorry for Nick. He thought of the young man's moist, limp hand.

"But," he reflected, "so long as she's got that power over him, he must be prepared to pay the price of it. Anyway she's marvellous. My God! Women!" And he kept ejaculating in his peaceful solitude: "Women! Women! My God!"

In his promenade through the silent house he encountered the letter from Cynthia Smythe, which he had laid aside. It seemed to be lying in wait for him. He picked it up, read it again; it fascinated him; it teased him. He saw Cynthia raising her left shoulder.

"Oh, hang it!" he muttered, and sat and wrote the answer: "My dear Cynthia Smythe. I am delighted to accept your charming invitation for Friday."

A PLACE IN VENICE

I

A GLOWING noon in late August on the Lido. The unclouded sun, whose in-candescent brightness no eye might safely meet, dominated the vast beach with its downpour of dazzling fire. A few figures bobbing in the shallow blue water, or sculling in comic boats, or sitting on the edge of rafts. Many more figures walking on the beach, male and female, clad in costly, gaudy bathing-costumes, or in costly, gaudy pyjamas, or in mere loin-cloths, with tanned skins—and vermilion lips most of them. A bewilderment of gay, clashing colours, thin legs and arms, thick legs and arms, slim bodies, Fal-staffs of both sexes, beauty, repulsive ugliness, smiles, scowls, innocence, vice—the wealth of half a dozen nations collected together.

Behind, up the beach, an endless row of bathing-tents, rented at a hun-dred lire a day, with tinted awnings and beds under them on which sprawled the idle and the exhausted; and beyond the tents the high white façade of the huge hotel, whose rooms were let at four hundred lire a night, with its terraces, bars, divans, lounges, and restaurants, from which emanated thinly the sounds of a jazz band.

I lay prone on the hot sand, in flannels, with a panama hat lodged on the back of my neck. I had come over from Venice, not to bathe but to see. I saw; and what I saw was a strange sight—somehow semi-oriental; but the life of Venice and the lagoons has in summer always had a flavour of the East.

A fruit-seller, with a little boy who ran errands to the tents, came along and offered me bruised peaches out of a basket at a price which would have been dear in London. I suggested half of what he asked. He smiled scornfully and passed on, knowing by experience that the Anglo-Saxon who would not pay any price demanded was exceptional and might profit-ably be ignored.

And then approached a man of about thirty-five in the least possible black bathing-costume. He had a melancholy, brown-bearded face; which was odd in that scene; but more odd was his fair skin amid all the wander-ing men extravagantly bronzed by much bathing and exposure to sunshine. I wondered that he had the courage to show his white body in a place where obviously to be well tanned was a state of grace and matter for self-satisfaction. Undoubtedly the poor fellow was sunning himself for the first time. A wet towel protected his head from the torrent of heat.

He circled hesitant around, and dropped on the sand at a distance of perhaps ten feet from me. I could not say that he was going to join me, but he had laid himself open to the suspicion thereof. "Presently," I said to myself, "this chap is going to speak to me," and at once I began to fancy evil traits in his face. I was English; he, too, seemed to be English, and I regretted his approaching lapse from the English code of public manners. True, the Lido is an island; but it is not a desert island, and if it had been a desert island the sacred code might still have held firm.

He did speak to me; his voice was peculiar, disturbing.

"Hottest day we've had this summer," said he.

Then the fellow had been in Venice all the summer, and yet was now sunning himself for the first time! Suspicious! But he was English, right enough, and educated.

"Yes," I responded, reluctant, non-committal, repellent.

My tone ought to have beaten him off, but I was not sure of its efficacy.

I said to myself, "This chap is going to ask me for something." I hated the man. He was bathing on the Lido under false pretences; he was an adventurer; but I ought not to have been surprised; necessarily in a place like the Lido, full of mugs, adventurers male and female must be rife.

"If by any chance you should want a guide—" he began.

"No, thanks." I stopped him sourly. To a travelled tourist the word "guide" is the most antagonising in the language.

Then he said:

"I only mention it because I'm down and out."

"And you aren't the only one on this beach, I bet," I replied indifferently, aware that rooms at four hundred lire a night are not infrequently occupied by bluffers and down-and-outs, sharpers, swindlers, the equivalent in the fashionable world of three-card-trick operators at a country race-meeting.

No sooner had I said this than a memory stirred within me, awakened by the peculiarity of his voice.

"Excuse me," I said, in a new and somewhat apologetic tone of interest. "Were you at Oundle?"

"I was," he answered grimly.

"We were there together. You were in the Sixth while I was in the Lower Fifth. Then your name must be—must be—wait a sec—Byatt."

"It is," he answered grimly.

"My dear chap," said I, eager to atone. "I'm really awfully sorry I didn't recognise you at once."

"Who are *you*?"

I named myself.

"No recollection of you at all—not the slightest."

It was a rebuff, but then he had had a rebuff from me. I felt sorry for him. Also, the freemasonry of the public school began to influence my mood.

"If I can help you in any reasonable way, Byatt," I said, and I raised my body on my right elbow and adjusted my hat anew against the sun, and examined his sad face.

"Reasonable way be damned!" said he, with cold fire. "You turned me down without the smallest enquiry when you did not know who I was. But as soon as you find I was at a public school—yours—ours—your class instincts get busy and you think you ought to help. Yes, well, I don't happen to see things like that—that's all. Let's pretend I wasn't begging." He was sitting up.

"All right," I agreed cheerfully. "And come and have lunch with me, will you? Pity old Sanderson died, wasn't it? He was a great Head. Let's lunch here, eh?" I pointed in the direction whence came the sounds of jazz.

"He was a great Head. But we can't lunch there. *You* can't lunch there because only bathing-costumes are admitted. And *I* don't care to go into the big restaurant upstairs."

"Well, somewhere else, then."

"No!" said Byatt, shortly. "I'm hanged if I'll take any free meals. You needn't think I'm starving. I'm not."

"I'm sorry you refuse."

"You can prove how sorry you are by coming and having lunch with me, then," said Byatt.

I hesitated a moment, and replied:

"I'll come with pleasure. Where?"

"Oh! My place in Venice."

I nodded, reflecting upon the queerness of a down-and-out and a would-be professional guide having a "place in Venice."

"I'll be back in a minute or two," he said, springing up.

And in a few minutes he was back, clad in a worn suit of grey flannels. His face was sensitive, refined, set, implacable; with twitching nostrils.

"We'll take the penny steamer," he said, as we crossed the huge lounge of the hotel, full of the salt of the earth. And he pulled at his short, outspreading beard.

"I've got a gondola here with two gondoliers." I protested. "It'll have to return and we may as well go in it."

I was afraid he might decline again, but he said:

"Oh! If it's like that—"

We boarded the black gondola at the landing-stage of the hotel, and Byatt spoke to the gondoliers in Italian, giving them an address.

A stately way of crossing the lagoon! Beneath a white-fringed awning we reclined side by side on cushions, our legs on cushions, while the two bright-scarved gondoliers, towering above us, forward and aft, swept the shallow, narrow craft swiftly through the glittering water with slow, powerful strokes. If there had been a breath of wind they would not have ventured forth; but there was no breath of wind. The incomparable panorama of the campaniles, domes, and shipping of Venice spread itself in front of us. Richness and beauty and warmth everywhere. And Byatt was down-and-out. A large English steam-yacht—it could not have been less than a thousand tons—passed us as we got near the mouth of the Grand Canal, turned ahead of us, and stopped; an anchor fell out of her with a quiet plop, and two sailors in a smart dinghy tied her up by the stern to a mooring buoy. A tremendous spectacle of wealth, this yacht, flying the burgee of a well-known yacht club. And Byatt, down-and-out, regarded her grimly. He spoke not a word during the short voyage; neither did I.

Presently, some distance up the Grand Canal, the gondola turned away to leave the wide thoroughfare of palaces, and, neatly avoiding a motor-launch and a plying passenger-steamer, came to a halt in the Rio Carducci before a crazy building of extreme picturesqueness.

"Here we are," said Byatt, quite nicely. "What time do you want your gondola to come back for you?"

Then he translated my reply. He had assumed, correctly if humiliatingly, that my command of Italian was imperfect.

II

A large and lofty hot room, with a broken ceiling through whose holes could be seen the rafters of the sloping roof of the building. Dark, though so high up, because lit by only one small window that had no prospect save the view of another and loftier house at a distance of about seven feet! The sole furniture consisted of a small deal table in a corner near the window, an enormous wardrobe (of Italianate-Empire style) whose open doors disclosed emptiness, one chair, and an enormous ancient oak-bedstead, the mosquito curtains of which, hung from a point in the ceiling, were torn here and there and hence quite useless; the bed itself in a dirty disorder. Grime, decay, and slatternliness everywhere. Such was the "place" of the old Oundelian. Outside one imagined all the marvellous antique beauty of Venice.

"Got a match?" asked Byatt, after feeling in his pockets.

I gave him a box, and he lighted a foul lamp on the small table in the corner, and began to warm up a mess that resembled vermicelli. As he totally ignored me, I walked about in the room, and finally looked out of the window, and far below saw hundreds of pieces of linen hung to dry, and a very narrow canal with refuse floating upon it, and a strong odour of the past arising from it. I brought my nose within the room again. Church-bells clanged loudly at intervals; one of them was so deafening that it might have been on the roof.

"Take your coat off," said Byatt, and set me the example. "It's more comfortable."

As there was no dining-table, my host put the plates on the broad window-sill; he fixed the one chair for me, and stood up himself. And thus we ate—first some slices of the fag-end of an unholy Italian sausage, and secondly the vermicelli. The drink was the remainder of the contents of a bottle of Fiuggi water.

"I hope you've enjoyed your meal," said Byatt, bitterly, at the close. "Sorry there's no coffee. Anyhow the coffee on the Lido would have been filthy. Can you give me a cigarette?" he added, after feeling in the pockets of his jacket lying on the floor.

"The lunch was excellent," I said.

"Glad you liked it," said he, still bitterly. "It will now be in order if you invite me to dinner to-night, or to lunch to-morrow."

"I'll be delighted."

We both walked about the room, smoking. For myself, I was in great mental discomfort.

"Well," he began again. "What about it all? The facts of the case are before you, except that you don't yet know that what you see here are my entire worldly possessions, and I haven't a centime—Yes, I have." He pulled out two or three Italian coins, worth in all about sixpence, and planked them savagely on the window-sill. "There! My total fortune. . . . Go on. Speak freely."

He stared at me, his chin pushed forward defiantly, as if to say to me: "Are you clever enough to solve the problem, you prosperous devil?"

"If I'm to be frank," I replied, "and there's no object in not being— what I don't understand is why, if you were so hard up, so near the end of your resources, you should have been chucking money about on the Lido this morning. You don't bathe on the Lido for a penny three farthings."

"Oh!" said he, haughtily. "You certainly don't. It's ten lire for the smallest cubicle, beside the tip and the hire of a costume. And there's the steamer fare, and the tram along the Lido afterwards. And that wasn't all. I had a drink at Florian's before I started, and I went into the hotel divan and had a most costly cocktail—a side-car, if you want to know—and two sandwiches that came to twenty lire.

"But I'll tell you how it happened. I saw a fifty-lire note floating on the canal this morning and I fished it out and dried it in the sun. You see, I'm just round the corner from the Accademia, where the big Titians are, and some American woman must have dropped the thing overboard from a gondola and nobody saw it. Fifty lire's no use to me, so I thought I'd have a fling—hastening the end sort of business, you know—rashness of despair sort of thing. Quite usual, I believe, in these cases. That's the whole explanation. Of course if I'd used the fifty wisely I shouldn't have been without a centime now, but I should have been without a centime in another three days or so—and where's the difference between then and now?"

"Quite!" I answered.

"Moreover, I've had the Lido, and I've met my old fellow-Oundelian."

I resented the man's misfortune. I wished I'd never met him. I'd no responsibility towards him, and he'd no right to expect anything from me. I was entitled to walk out. But could I? No! I was confined in the squalid room by the mere power of his unhappiness over my sense of pity, and by the august traditions of Oundle School. Nevertheless I did harshly resent the man's misfortune. He walked to and fro, nervous, superior, shabby, and I thought I could read in his face the history of his fall from Oundle to perdition. I scorned him at one moment; at the next I was most painfully sorry for him.

"Well," he said. "Don't think I don't realise I'm putting you in a damned awkward position. Good-bye! I won't accept any return hospitality. Like that, I shall be one up on you." He held out his hand stiffly.

At this juncture the rickety door opened, and a youngish, good-looking, charming woman came in. She was expensively and very fashionably dressed, and wore valuable jewellery, and had brown hair and brown eyes and a troubled, frightened expression. I thought of her in those fragile and lovely clothes climbing the long, dark, frowsy, slippery stairs that led up from the splendid picturesqueness of the canal to Byatt's miserable "place."

She said nothing. Byatt said nothing. They gazed at one another. Byatt's frame shook. The woman's white hand on the door was trembling.

I turned towards the window, embarrassed. Also I absurdly did not like being caught in my shirtsleeves by the modish creature. Not a word from either of them. I waited, interminably. Then:

"Here!" I heard Byatt's angry, rising voice. "You get out of this. Do you hear me? Get out of this. And quick!" His tone was terrible.

A silence. Movement. When I turned round again the woman was gone, and Byatt was seated in the sole chair, his face hidden in his hands, crying.

"I've let myself in for something," I thought, rancorous, yet pleasurably expectant. Life seemed to be a frightful, dramatic and absorbing affair—for some people.

What struck me was the contrast between Byatt's present demeanour and the awful ferocity with which he had forced the visitor to depart the moment she arrived. He was now pitiful to me in his weakness, and I was touched, though I had contempt for a man who permitted himself to cry in front of another man. And I had doubts about the justifiableness of his treatment of the woman, whose face had pleased me by its kind, rather wistful expression; she had showed, indeed, absolutely none of the arrogance of the very well dressed!

Byatt looked up, not a trace of shame on his delicate bearded features.

"You saw that lady?" he said loudly, having mastered his sobs. He repeated, imperiously: "You saw that lady?"

"Yes."

"She was the cause of my ruin, and I haven't set eyes on her since she did me in. You can imagine how I feel about meeting her again. You married?"

I shook my head.

"Well, I was. Hunting woman. Oh no, not *her*. My wife, I mean. I'd no profession and no money. I got myself made secretary of a Hunt in the Dukeries. Five hundred a year and a house. Fancy *me* secretary of a Hunt! Still, there it was. My father had died leaving nothing, though he'd been living at the rate of a good ten thousand a year. Usual thing. I had to keep myself somehow. I didn't make a bad Hunt-secretary, I think. My wife helped me. The mischief with my wife was that she'd do anything for me. Stick at nothing. She *did* stick at nothing. She died for me."

"What do you mean—she died for you?" I put the question in a tone as sympathetic as I could manage.

Byatt jumped up and walked about, and kicked his coat lying on the dirty floor. A child, still a child! But I began to be anxious, to be afraid, about the probably distressing quality of the child's story. Children can suffer. A solemn mood was coming over me.

"This lady you've just seen—I forget her surname; she's married; her Christian name's Ethel. It's no good beating about the bush. Ethel fell in love with me—violently. She didn't hide it; didn't trouble to hide it. Well, damn it, she was very attractive. Still is; you could see that for yourself. I say you could see that for yourself."

"Of course."

"Well, when an attractive young woman makes straight *at* you—when she shows you she's your slave—what's a fellow going to do about it? She *was* attractive. No man—anyhow awfully few men—could resist such an attack, and I didn't. I won't deny it. We saw a lot of one another. If I'd lifted my finger she'd have run away with me. It don't sound nice for a man to say such things, but there it was, and why should I beat about the bush? Yes, yes, I was in love with her. My wife fell ill. Pleurisy. Pneumonia. Had to go into a nursing-home. She was very ill. I saw as much as I could of her. And I did not see Ethel at all. Ethel wrote to me; but I didn't answer her letters either. Sense of decency towards my wife, I suppose. Jolly few women have that sort of a sense of decency.

"Well, I had to run up to London for a night on urgent Hunt business. What happens? While I'm away, Ethel forces her way into the nursing-home and sees my wife. *Forces* her way! I have the evidence of the nurse on that point, anyhow. Can you imagine it? I don't know directly what Ethel said to my wife. But I know what my wife said to the nurse afterwards—perhaps her mind was wandering, but she said it all the same. I mean perhaps she didn't intend to say it, because you don't make such confidences to a nurse. However, she said it. She said that Ethel was in love with me, and I was in love with Ethel, and so she felt—my wife felt—she was only in the way, because she wanted my happiness more than anything, and if my happiness meant Ethel's happiness, she wanted Ethel to be happy too. And the next day my wife went and died. I say she just went and died. And that was that. Can you conceive it?"

"I hardly can."

"Well, you'd better set about conceiving it, then. That's what women are—some of them. Ethel must have been mad—completely carried away by her feelings for me. But there's some varieties of madness that oughtn't to be forgiven, and can't be. I never saw her again, until to-day. She didn't write, and you may be sure I didn't. She cleared out, and a good thing, too! I heard afterwards she'd married some plutocrat."

At this point poor Byatt dropped into abuse which, though there was not a word in it that couldn't be printed, was so appalling that I don't care to reproduce it. Moreover I couldn't possibly reproduce the tone—icy, icy, and so deliberate.

I didn't speak, because I couldn't think of anything adequate to say. I couldn't even look at the unhappy man. Somehow I was ashamed before him, as though I'd done something wrong to him. I expect I was ashamed of not being as unhappy as he was. For the whole tragedy, apparently years old, was quite fresh in his mind. The coward in me that is in all of us would have given almost anything to be a hundred miles away.

He proceeded:

"And look at me. I'm the result. Of course there was a vast deal of talk. For scandalmongering give me a hunting county! I threw up my job—and if I hadn't thrown it up of my own accord I should have been asked to. Sold the furniture—the furniture was practically all I had on earth. Lower and lower, naturally! At last touting for jobs as a guide in Venice! See this beard? Do you think I wore a preposterous beard in those days? Not much! I let my beard grow because one day I dropped my safety razor out of the window here—cleaning it, and hadn't the money to buy another. Besides, why should I shave? Men in my state get careless and idle."

A clock struck noisily on some tower.

"Your gondola's here," said Byatt, and moved towards the door.

"But I can't leave you like this," I burst out.

"Yes, you can. I've no claim on you whatever, and you can't help me."

"Listen," I said, resuming my coat. "I can't talk now. I—I'm too sorry for you to be able to talk about it. But you owe me your company at dinner, and I'll expect you to-night."

"Shan't come."

"Then I'll call for you—eight o'clock. Yes, I will."

He was shaking his head as I hurriedly left, but he was not shaking it with any real conviction.

IV

"Ethel" was standing nearly at the bottom of the frowsy flights of marble stairs. She made a charming, appealing, pathetic picture in a dark corner, as she half-sprang at me.

"Excuse me, are you his friend?" she timidly asked in an exquisite voice.

For an instant I understood that she could indeed be irresistible when she chose; she was choosing. I explained my relations with Byatt, and added:

"Are you thinking of going up to him again? I doubt if that would be very wise."

"Do you know his story?" she asked.

"I know *his* story," I replied frankly. "He's just told me." The situation seemed to have rendered us intimate without any preliminaries.

She said, with quick submission:

"I'll do whatever you consider best. But could we have a talk—I mean you and I?"

"My gondola is waiting. Will you come with me?"

"I have my launch here," she said. "If you wouldn't mind. It's more private than a gondola. I've just arrived on my yacht."

"That big yacht?"

"Yes. You must have seen us. I saw the gondola. At first I didn't quite recognise Mr. Byatt because of his beard"—she gave a little shudder—"but afterwards I could be sure by his way of moving his hands."

I had noticed nothing remarkable in the movement of his hands; women, however, notice and remember the tiniest trifles in the deportment of the men they have loved.

"I'll come with you with pleasure," I said. "To the yacht?"

She was evidently, despite her modest demeanour, a personage of consequence, the number of people who have control of a very big yacht is exceedingly few.

She nodded. "I'm alone on board, but I'm expecting friends at the end of the week. I suppose he told you my husband was dead."

"He didn't know," I answered, and said further, perhaps callously: "He didn't even know your married name."

I dismissed my gondola. Ethel's launch, with its crew of three, was a craft as smart as only the launch of a big yacht can be smart. It had a glazed cabin, closed forward, with a door aft. Once in the cabin we were shut off completely from the crew. The launch, almost silent, got away with an entirely un-Venetian speed; it passed everything on the ruffled bosom of the Grand Canal. Owing to its enclosed "Kitchin" propeller, it could pull up with suddenness of a motor-car; gondoliers and the engineers of other launches were at first terrorised, then relieved, then angry; Ethel's British crew magnificently ignored all Venetian manifestations of feeling.

"I followed you as soon as the launch could be lowered," said Ethel, "but the moment I got inside the house and enquired for Mr. Byatt I hesitated to go upstairs. . . . And is that his home?"

I nodded. She shuddered again.

We were approaching the great white side of the yacht.

"No!" she cried. "Not on board! Not on board! Let us go to Torcello. We can talk in the cathedral there. I went there last year in the launch. There's not a place quite like it."

I assented, though I had always regarded Torcello as a day's excursion. Ethel gave an order, peeping forth from the cabin. A man touched his cap. The launch swerved. The engineer opened out and the pace was doubled.

We had covered the six sunlit miles to Torcello and were shooting up the village canal making huge plutocratic waves on either side by the time I had recounted to Ethel the narrative just heard from Byatt. I had no scruples about being perfectly candid with her; neither regard for her sensibilities nor a sense of loyalty to Byatt could prevent me from making a complete disclosure.

She wept a little, but very discreetly. A strange scene! Though our acquaintance extended over a space of but half an hour, we might have been lifelong intimates. To be with this dissolving, wonderful creature in the privacy of the cabin aroused in me emotions both delicious and sad. "Does she still love him?" I asked myself. She was the mistress of a big yacht, and doubtless also of big houses; and Byatt had grown a beard because he had no money to buy a razor, and they were bound together by a dead woman . . .

We were in the cold, bare, deserted, lovely Cathedral of Santa Maria. The dark and beautiful Venetian girl who was our cicerone sat down on a stone step by the door to await placidly the pleasure of the tourists; and the childishly naïve twelfth-century mosaics of the Last Day, the Crucifixion, and Hell were spread in front of us.

"This is the most touching church in the world," Ethel murmured.

I thought so, too.

"I didn't force my way into the nursing-home," she said quietly, after a pause, and sat down on the balustrade that guarded the chancel and sighed. "At least I *did*. But Mrs. Byatt had sent a note. The page-boy at the Home brought it, and I don't think anybody else in the Home knew anything about it. The note was just this: 'I'm very, very ill. Please come and see me here. It's urgent.' Scrawled in pencil. I was ashamed to go. But of course I felt I must go. I knew I couldn't look her in the face. I knew I'd done her wrong, a wrong. I admit all that. I had great difficulty in getting in to her. Well, I *did* force my way in. But after her note, wasn't I bound to see her? She smiled at me very kindly. I burst into tears at once—the moment the nurse was out of the room—she asked the nurse to leave. She didn't cry, Mrs. Byatt didn't. And she was terribly ill. She said she wanted me to tell her honestly if I was in love with her husband—with Edgar. How could I tell her a lie? Then she said she knew Edgar was in love with me. I couldn't speak. I only nodded. She beckoned me to come close to her, and she took my hand and kissed it. Yes! And she was frightfully ill and her breathing was awful, but she seemed perfectly calm in herself. I'm afraid I must have made a dreadful noise sobbing. The nurse came back, and the doctor was with her. I had to go. They pushed me out. Afterwards, the next day, I heard she was dead. I went away to London. I never heard from Edgar, and why should he write to me? And I couldn't bring myself to write to him. I married—perhaps you know how you marry at the first chance when you're—when you're like I was, with nothing on earth to live for. In two years my husband died. That's the story."

After a long interval of silence she began to talk about the mosaics, and the carvings on the balustrade of the chancel. The beautiful girl at the door sat waiting for us with everlasting patience.

At last Ethel said:

"It's the feel of this church that has helped me to tell you. I knew it would. . . . And I never saw him again until to-day. He's very poor and unhappy, isn't he? Why did you say I mustn't go upstairs to him again?"

V

I fetched Byatt out of his lair, and he dined with me at one of the open-air restaurants which are a feature of Venetian summer life. It happened to be a week when low-tide occurred in the evenings, and the aroma of the canals which on three sides bounded the restaurant was added to the odours of the dishes. At the end of the meal cigar smoke mitigated the battle of the smells.

"How could I have guessed that my wife had sent for her?" he said gloomily, after I had told him, with my customary frankness and fullness, all that Ethel had told me.

"You'd have known all about it if you'd taken steps to see her," I answered.

"But how could I see her when I thought she'd practically killed my wife?" he objected.

"But she didn't know you thought that of her," I said. "She didn't even suspect it."

"Then it's nobody's fault. The nurse was quite sincere. It was just one of those things that are nobody's fault. . . . My luck! Her luck, if you like."

"Do you want to hear my view?"

"As you wish."

"My view is that you were too proud—and she was too proud. You've suffered for your pride."

He retorted in a bitter, rather loud voice:

"I suppose in my place you'd have acted quite differently."

I looked at the table-cloth:

"I dare say I should have acted just as you did. But I should have been wrong all the same. However, it's no use discussing that. The point now is that you can put yourself right."

"How?"

"By going to see her. She's paid you a visit, and you can return it. She gave way first, anyhow—that's something."

"Go and see her on her yacht, eh?"

"It's where she lives."

"Never!" he cried fiercely, hitting the table. "Never! I'll die first. She's rolling in wealth—rolling in it, and me—look at me! No! Never! I'd a thousand times sooner be unhappy for ever and ever."

"And would you far sooner she should be unhappy for ever and ever, too?"

He hesitated.

"Yes!" he exploded savagely. "A ruined man and a pauper making up to a rich widow! Not on your life!"

"If *you* were rolling in wealth, would you go and see her?" I demanded.

"I might."

"And you won't because you're a pauper—as you say?"

"I won't."

"Then besides being a pauper," I said resentfully, "you're a fool, and a proud fool, and a cruel fool."

He pushed back his chair violently and seized his hat.

"Thanks for your charming hospitality," he said acidly, and strode away.

He could not leave by water, as he had no money for a gondola, but in Venice there are hidden footpaths from everywhere to everywhere. I paid the bill and hurried in my gondola to his abode, and there lay in wait. Presently I saw him, through the central passage, enter the house from some alley at the back. He began to climb the stairs, wearily, a broken man, a pitiable, a heart-rending spectacle. I cautiously and silently followed him up the dim steps. Then I stopped, petrified.

Under a feeble glim, in the very corner of a landing where I had met her earlier in the day, she had been waiting for him again. Her hand was on his shoulder. She was timorously smiling at him. Invincible, yielding woman!

I crept downstairs swiftly, like a would-be thief in imminent fear of detection. I had seen, beneath the flickering flame in its dirty glass, on the frowsy landing, the most beautiful and reassuring sight I had ever seen. And I can still shut my eyes and see it afresh.

The next morning at my hotel I received a note:

"Please lend me fifty pounds if you can. She can get me a job, but I must have money in my pocket. I admit I was a cruel fool. But she was not. Don't come down. And thank you.—E. B."

He must have brought the note himself. I put good English banknotes into an envelope, and addressed the envelope and gave it to the waiting boy. And I did not go down.

THE TOREADOR

I

CLIFFE was standing, a suit-case in either strong hand, on one of the plat-forms of the Maritime station at Calais, when he glimpsed Lucy through the window of one of the luxury-trains that waited here and there, casu-ally—as it seemed, to be assaulted, stormed, and taken possession of by imperious throngs of well-dressed travellers who knew what they wanted, were determined to get it, were evidently accustomed to get it, and were in fact getting it. Cliffe had recently paid a tailor's bill, and he knew that there was scarcely an overcoat in that throng worth less than fifteen pounds; as for the women's plain but perfect apparel, he could not face the estimate of its value; but he knew the cost of their apparently simple handbags, for on the previous afternoon he had been pricing handbags, for his mother, in Bond Street. He was positively shaken at the thought of the amount of loose money in the world and of the number of persons in the world who were so placed as to be able to devote themselves to expensive pleasures involving large movements over the world's surface.

And he was the more shaken because he had just escaped from a north-ern town, appropriately called Workington, where he worked upon research in the laboratories of a vast chemical manufactory, the property of a limited company with a capital of seven million pounds. At Workington his sur-roundings were ugly, squalid, smoky, even filthy; ninety-nine out of every hundred of the inhabitants toiled laboriously amid the smoke for weekly sums which these occupiers of luxury-trains would spend without a second thought on trifles like an umbrella, a scarf, or a bottle of scent; probably none of them had ever travelled farther than the Isle of Man, and all of them had to take their brief, crowded holidays in August.

The astonishing contrasts of life, however, did not seriously disturb Cliffe's peace of mind. He was twenty-three, tall and muscular; he had the boundless, careless, cheerful confidence which comes to a small extent from a good education and training at an ancient university, and to a large extent from perfect health. He had a fortnight's leave, a passport, and a couple of hundred pounds—the product partly of earnings and partly of bonuses; and he was going to join one or two fellows in Paris for Easter.

It was by no means his intention to scatter all the two hundred pounds, but you never knew what might happen to you.

On the previous evening he had made the acquaintance of Lucy at a dance in London, and since the encounter he had passed many hours in thinking about her and in wondering how and when he might plan to meet her again. Then he had seen her on the Dover-Calais steamer, and had been prevented by the crush and her strange, flitting elusiveness from getting at her; and now he saw her for the third time with only a pane of glass between them. She had not noticed him.

He perceived from a metal disc dangling from the side of the coach the words, "*4ème voiture.*" At the door at the end of the carriage was a uniformed attendant.

"Is this the fourth carriage?" he demanded of the attendant, with that calm, jolly assurance which is the outcome of spacious homes, public schools, and Universities.

"Yes, sair."

"Right. You just take these, will you?"

And the attendant eagerly hauled up the two suit-cases. Cliffe followed the suit-cases. The compartments and saloon of the coach were full of a disorder of travellers finding their places and generally settling themselves.

"Hul*lo*, Lucy!" he exclaimed, lightly smiling at the princess of his thoughts.

"Hul*lo*, Cliffe!"

(They had acquired in a night the easy intimacy of post-war manners.)

"Where are you going to?" she inquired, shaking hands.

"If it comes to that, where are *you* going to?"

"Seville, for Easter."

"So am I," said Cliffe.

"How ripping!" she exclaimed, simply.

There can be no doubt that the princess was pleased to be pleased.

"All alone?" he questioned.

"Yes, except for auntie's maid. I'm joining uncle and auntie in Seville."

"I must just get my place," said he, and left her. He vanished, not only from her sight, but also from the sight of the coach-conductor. It was not until after the train had well started that he approached Lucy again, with an admirable simulation of a long face.

"I say," said he. "I'm in the dickens and all of a mess. It seems you have to book your places in advance in these trains, and I didn't book a place. Did you?"

"Of course!" said Lucy, astounded and superior. "Weeks since! Do you mean to say you didn't know?"

"How should I?" he retorted. "I've never had time to go to the Continent since I was a boy and carted about like a parcel. The head mandarin here is fearfully cross, and he can only speak thirteen and a half words of English, and I can't speak any French. Do be a sport and tell him I didn't know. I expect you talk French like one o'clock."

Lucy laughed freely, very freely. The sequel proved that she did talk French like one o'clock. Trouble there assuredly was, and much of it. But, after a somewhat heavy financial transaction of a secret nature, the tangle with the train authorities was smoothed out, and Cliffe was accommodated with the berth of the head mandarin himself. True that during the daytime, if he wanted to sit, he had to sit on a tip-up seat in the corridor, but he did not much mind that. Lucy benevolently passed many moments in the corridor. It was during one of these moments—the train was dawdling round the outskirts of Paris—that she said to him:

"You know, I can't get over you not knowing that in these big expresses all the places are booked in advance."

And he said to her:

"But of course I knew. Only when I saw you in the train I decided all of a sudden to go wherever you were going. So I jumped in and chanced it."

Lucy blushed; Lucy frowned; Lucy left the corridor; Lucy did not appear in the restaurant-car for dinner. Cliffe thought how strange girls were. You always knew where you were with any man, but never with any woman. Still, he admired her reserve, though he feared her incalculableness. So much so that he slept little in the tiny berth of the head mandarin.

When, the next morning, at the Spanish frontier, they changed trains, Cliffe had to be diplomatic and generous towards another head mandarin without Lucy's aid. But she did speak to him later on, as the train was switchbacking over the interminable mountains of Spain.

II

Lucy was a tall, dark girl, indeed nearly as tall as Cliffe, who reached five foot ten quite. Her father, now retired from the Army, had done service in every British war from 1895 to 1918. In no matter what part of the earth the integrity of the British Empire had been menaced, Colonel (once for a space Brigadier-General) Brest had been there to defend it. In the pursuit of duty he had suffered from frost-bite and from sunstroke, he had often been wounded, and he had lost the best part of an arm. Consequently he was very poor; it was easier to die than to live on his retired pay.

Consequently Lucy was poor. Nevertheless, Lucy, being familiar with a large number of well-to-do people, contrived to have a wonderful life of pleasure: suppers, dinners, lunches, automobile excursions, theatres, dances, and yet again dances. She got everything for nothing. Her very cigarettes were given to her; even books were given to her. Thus she was thoroughly accustomed to the fruits of money, while having none; and she had the fastidiousness, the yearning for the absolute best, of a millionaire. How she managed to be always smartly dressed I cannot explain; she herself could not have explained; it was just a girl's miracle. But many such girls accomplish many such miracles.

Her uncle and aunt, Mr. and Mrs. John Brest, did a lot for her, because she amused them and often saved them from their customary tedium. John Brest, having manufactured military uniforms instead of wearing them, was, of course, very rich. Still, not a bad fellow—and generous.

Since their first encounter, at the dance, Lucy had passed hours in thinking about Cliffe Forrest, and in wondering whether he would have the sense to take any measures to see her again. He did not belong to "her crowd," of which most of the young male members somewhat bored her. She could not quite make him out, add him up, nor take him down. Hence, though breezy with him, she had been careful. Any ordinary youth, who had bored her less than usual, she would have casually asked where, if ever, they were to meet once more.

Cliffe attracted her because he did and knew few of the things that her crowd did and knew, and because he was obviously very keen on certain strange and horrible toil in which he laboured in a strange and horrible town of which she had never previously heard. His descriptions were amusingly phrased. And he had sang-froid. The calmness with which he recounted to her how something (she understood not what) had exploded under a pressure of two hundred atmospheres (what were two hundred atmospheres?) and left naught but a few tiny fragments of two workmen both frightened and enchanted her. Yet I doubt whether Cliffe would have seriously attracted her if he had not danced rather masterfully, had not had a fair complexion with fair hair, had worn a moustache, had not had sparkling eyes and a funnily deep voice.

When she glimpsed him on the steamer she had ingeniously avoided him and could not explain to herself why. When she saw him through the carriage window she had dropped her gaze. When he accosted her in the carriage and told her he was going to Seville she had begun to believe in fate. When he sought her aid to get him out of a most absurd and inconceivable mess she was really delighted. Could such ignorance as his exist? She felt like a protective aunt to him, and enjoyed the feeling.

But when he brightly and impudently informed her that the mess was of his own deliberate making and that he had audaciously changed his destination to Seville for the sole reason that Seville was her destination too—then she became stiff, queerly resentful. And she was afraid. Further, she suddenly ceased to feel like a protective aunt to him, and constituted herself a protective aunt to Mrs. Brest's maid, who was sampling the continent for the first time and mournfully considered that for all practical purposes it was inferior to England.

On the second morning of the long journey when she entered the breakfast-car, with that false vivacity and vigour which come of two consecutive imperfect nights in two different trains, Cliffe was already there and eating a Spanish breakfast—consisting, strangely enough, of fried eggs and something called ham. Although there were plenty of empty places in the car, she was bound by one of those conventions which hold the structure of society together to seat herself at his table. It was a very bright morning, and Cliffe was very bright, and they were in Andalusia, the land of sunshine and love, oranges and lemons, cactus and Judas-trees. They talked of all these matters (except love), and of the nearness of Seville and the marvels of Seville. And then the conversation sagged, and to lift it Cliffe began on the subject of his old father, who was gradually, in an amateurish and obstinate way, losing his fortune in the enterprise of raising farm stock. And the conversation sagged again, and Lucy in her turn lifted it by a discourse on her fragile, hypochondriacal aunt, whose new maid she was taking out.

Then she asked whether Cliffe had got a room in Seville, well knowing that he had not. She told him with cynicism that there would assuredly not be a room to be obtained anywhere at any price in Seville for Easter—there never was! He laughed and replied that in a city of a quarter of a million inhabitants a room, and many rooms, would beyond doubt be discoverable.

She said:

"Very well, you'll see," yawning.

And to herself she said:

"This youth is beginning to bore me, like all the others."

The arrival in the romantic and burning city of Seville was extremely trying. The train seemed to throw out all the tourists in the world. Rows of hotel omnibuses and rows of hackney carriages blistered in the sun, and scores of uniformed men were shouting the names of hotels. The porter of the Hôtel de Madrid assumed charge of Lucy and many other travellers. Cliffe vanished into a mass of humanity. Presently he came with his two suit cases to the crowded omnibus of the Hôtel de Madrid.

"Have you any rooms?" he blandly asked the porter, who was busy with hand-luggage.

Lucy waited with a superior smile for the answer.

"I could perhaps find a room for you outside," said the porter in good English.

And Lucy ceased to smile superiorly and pretended that she was smiling benevolently.

"How much?"

"Seventy pesetas, sir."

"Not a night?"

"Yes, sir."

"Rot!" exclaimed Cliffe, impatiently.

The porter shrugged his shoulders.

As the omnibus drove away, Lucy saw Cliffe hail a one-horse victoria and put his bags into it.

"He is an idiot," she reflected. "What does he hope for in Seville at Easter? And he does bore me—terribly."

But her diagnosis of her mental condition was wrong. She was merely very, very exhausted after forty-eight hours' continuous travelling.

III

The circumstances which led to his taking her to the great Easter Sunday bull-fight—perhaps the greatest annual event of the kind in Spain—were as follows. It was Saturday night. The large Moorish restaurant of the Hôtel de Madrid was just a little less crowded and tinkling and noisy than it had been half an hour earlier. Lucy was dining at a small table in the company of an old gentleman, who presently rose to his feet.

"I must go and see how your auntie is getting on," said he.

"I'll just finish my cigarette, uncle," said she.

"Aren't you coming now?" he asked, suggesting by his tone that she certainly ought to come now.

"I shan't be long," said the obstinate creature, with a deliberately seductive smile.

The old gentleman glanced at his watch, sighed, and departed with much dignity. Anybody would have guessed him to be a general rather than an Army clothier.

Lucy, resplendent in a newly-given gorgeous Spanish shawl, was determined to await events alone. She had seen Cliffe Forrest eating by himself at the distant other end of the restaurant. She knew "intuitively" (that is, she guessed or hoped or feared) that he had noticed her presence, but he had shown no sign of having noticed it. Three days and two nights had passed since he had left her in order to hail the victoria, and she had had no least glimpse of him. Odd! Exceeding odd! Especially having regard to the fact that his declaration about coming to Seville because she was coming to Seville had presented itself to the singular Lucy almost as a declaration of love! He knew where she was staying. Why pursue a girl over a thousand miles of mountain and plain if you practise a policy of neglect at the end of the journey? But men were always thus illogical! Anyhow, the enigmatic youth could not get out of the restaurant without skirting her table. She lit a cigarette and draped her flashing shawl afresh and waited.

At length Cliffe folded the newspaper which he had been reading, paid his bill, and stood up.

"She's alone now," thought Cliffe. "I'll have a shot at her. A couple of days to herself won't have done her any harm. She may be rather glad to see me."

"Hul*lo*, Cliffe!" she exclaimed, looking up as he stopped, hesitatingly and innocently, at her table. "You staying here after all?"

He rose high over her, very fair and ingenuous in appearance, and she thought: "What fun to bring him down!" She pulled the shawl more tightly about her, held the cigarette loose between her lips, and imagined herself as a sort of super-Carmen.

"Rather not," he answered. "Seventy pesetas a night! I got a room without any trouble in a house in the Calle Gomez—six pesetas a night."

"But what kind of a room?" She spoke with an ironic inflection, though she was impressed by his skill in falling on his feet.

"Well, it's clean," he said, shortly. She looked lovely to him, and dangerous, and he thought: "She mustn't be allowed to get above herself. And why doesn't she ask me to take a chair?"

"And what have you been doing with yourself?" she demanded negligently.

"Oh, everything! Seeing life. Gallery. Gardens. Cathedral. Midnight service. Torchlight processions. And so on."

"I saw Thursday night's procession from the front of the Town Hall," said she, grandly.

"So did I," said he.

"I suppose you're going to the bull-fight to-morrow afternoon?" she ventured.

"I certainly am. I hear it's not at all a nice spectacle, but I think it ought to be seen—once."

"So do I," said she. "And I wish I was going to see it." She then told him that her hypochondriacal aunt, the most charming of middle-aged ladies, considered herself to be ill, and that her uncle would not dream of leaving her, his wife being his passion, and that therefore the bull-fight was impossible for her, Lucy.

"But surely you wouldn't *care* to see it?"

"Oh, wouldn't I? And why not, indeed? It's just like a man, that is, especially a young man! Uncle would have taken me. If a male can see it, why can't a female?"

"Oh, no reason at all!" he admitted, with an enrapturing smile. "I only thought—"

"Not a bit!" she stopped him. "You merely didn't think. Sit down. Here! Have a cigarette."

He sat down and accepted a cigarette from her tiny jewelled case.

"If only you were holding a rose in your mouth you'd look just like Carmen," he said.

"Oh, should I? A work-girl and a bad lot! Thanks!"

"Still, you *would*. I say, I wish I could take you to the bull-fight."

"But you can't!"

"No, they wouldn't let you go."

"That's not why," she retorted, quickly. "Do you think I'm a baby in arms? Of course they'd let me go. To begin with, I shouldn't ask them. I should just go."

"Well, do, then—if you mean it. But you'd have to ask them and I don't think they *would* let you go. They don't know me."

"No, they don't. If they *did* know you they naturally wouldn't consent." She laughed. He laughed.

"Come, then."

"No!"

"Listen," said he. "It begins at five; I'll call for you at four."

"Have you got seats?"

"No. But I'll get them."

She was about to say that seats were unobtainable, but, profiting by her experience of him, she refrained.

"No, thanks, I won't come."

"They wouldn't let you."

"You can't catch me like that," she said, easily. "But I won't come, thanks. If I really wanted to go—"

"You just said you did want to go."

"I was only joking. If I wanted to go, there are at least a dozen people in this hotel who'd take me quick enough. Half London's here."

"Well," said he, "I'll call for you at four with a carriage."

"But I've told you I won't go."

"I know," he said. "But you might change your mind. There's a hundred to one chance of you changing your mind. And I'll call for you on that chance."

"Oh, will you?" she murmured. "Well, I shan't change my mind."

"I don't care," he said, smoothly. "I'll call for you all the same and risk it."

"She's the goods," he reflected afterwards, in the dark, mysterious Southern street full of tramcars and mantillas and vendors of lottery tickets.

"There's something steady at the back of that youngster's silly eyes," she reflected, in bed. "I'm sure he's deliciously dangerous."

IV

The bull-ring. Two minutes to five in the afternoon. An enormous amphitheatre, with a tawny sanded ring in the middle large enough for the final of the English Football Cup. Fifteen thousand people, mostly men, on the boundless rising tiers of the amphitheatre. The tower of the Giralda jutting up into the blue sky beyond the mountain of spectators to the east; and a hot wind shaking the lofty awnings that topped the mountain of spectators to the west. The sun ruthlessly blazing down upon the whole of the ring and upon more than half of the spectators. A brassy orchestra making a great deal of noise. The flutter of a thousand fans. The raucous calls of men in white selling water, pea-nuts, and strange sweets. The air vibrating with heat and excitation.

Two of the fifteen thousand were Cliffe and Lucy. She had come. She had nearly not come; but Cliffe's coachman was specially dressed in toreador fashion, and that splendid detail had decided her. She had entrusted herself to Cliffe.

In the matter of seats, he had not succeeded quite as well as she had expected. The fashionable seats were on high, and Cliffe's seats, though happily in the shade, were rather low down, among the populace. Lucy was the only woman within fifteen yards. Still she did not really mind. He would protect her from the primitiveness of the populace. The dark faces near to her were too clear, the faces a little farther off were clear; and gradually the faces dwindled off into the distances, so that on the upper rows across the ring they were mere pinhead blobs of white punctuating the mass of clothes. Lucy felt herself to be in the midst of a frightening, heaving ocean of humanity. Cliffe alone was her lifebelt. And even he— What could she make of a young man who had followed her from the Channel to Seville and then carefully avoided her for two full days? He was, he must be, in some secret and undiscovered way, formidable. She put on a courageous and defiant air, but she had her private and exquisite alarms.

"You'd better take that shawl off, I think," said Cliffe. "Too conspicuous down here."

She took it off. Above and behind them, in the select *palcas*, similar bright shawls hung over the balconies.

A bugle. From the east there entered the procession—espadas, banderilleros, picadors on horseback, and all the train of performers; gorgeously attired, the espadas in gold. The procession advanced with slow dignity across the ring to the west, bowed deeply to the Presidential box, and broke up into units, each to his proper station. The glittering units were like dolls on the sand.

Suddenly a magnificent black bull rushed into the arena and stood still, lonely, friendless, and terrible. Lucy's heart throbbed and she thought: "I am at a bull-fight. It has begun." And Cliffe's heart throbbed and he thought: "Well, here goes, anyway."

The bull was thinking:

"Where am I? This isn't a field. I've never been here before. What's all this about? It's so bright I can scarcely see."

Then in the shimmer of sunshine he saw something offensively pink and dashed for it, head down.

Cliffe watched the proceedings with extreme intensity. Lucy divided her gaze between the proceedings and Cliffe, whom she glanced at every now and then sideways. He was oblivious of her. The toreadors teased the bull, tempting him with their rich pink cloaks and springing away at his onset. He was bewildered, could not select his prey, ran first at one and then at another, aimed his horns at cloaks instead of at bodies, and soon had a sensation of fatigue and boredom. Another bugle. The bull, near the side of the arena, saw a horse with a man on its back. "This at any rate shall not escape me," thought the bull. And he was right. The horse made no attempt to escape. He just stood broadside on. The next instant the bull lifted horse and rider into the air. The rider fell on to the bull's back and rolled into safety and scrambled up. Part of the horse walked quietly away. Lucy drew her breath in sharply and lowered her head.

"Steady on!" whispered Cliffe, without looking at her. "The nag's doped."

Then the moving part of the horse dropped down, agitated its legs violently, and died, and was covered with a cloth. And the bull saw other horses. Lucy glanced behind her, up the mountain of spectators, as if looking for a way of escape.

"No, you don't," breathed Cliffe. "You wanted to come, and you've got to stick it."

When the tangled remains of three horses had been covered with three cloths, yet another bugle sounded, and the banderilleros came forward and stuck long coloured darts, two at a time, into the bull's back as, missing his aim, he lunged past them. The bull mistook the darts for stinging flies, but he was now too tired to occupy himself with such trifles, and indeed he had a more important matter to attend to. For presently the golden espada, or matador himself, with a long sword and a cloak more exasperatingly red than any of the other offensive cloaks, was facing him.

"Well, surely they don't call this bull-fighting?" murmured Lucy, when the espada, having taken careful aim, hit the bull in the wrong place, so that the sword flew out of the bull into the arena and the bull ran off, while the fifteen thousand yelled their derision.

"If he'd done that right," said Cliffe, "the sword would have disappeared and the bull dropped down dead."

"You seem to know a lot about it," observed Lucy, sarcastically, recovering herself.

"Yes. Out of the guide-book."

"Good heavens!" he exclaimed contemptuously, when the illustrious espada had missed again and yet again. And to himself, challengingly: "I'm not going to have any of her sauce."

At length the bull, bored and indifferent, did drop dead.

"Sixteen minutes," said Cliffe, looking at his watch. Teams of brightly-draped mules cantered into the arena and cantered out again, dragging over the stained sand what a quarter of an hour earlier had been a living bull and three living horses. A few people cheered. The band played.

"Some of the cloak play was goodish," Cliffe remarked, judicially. "The fellow in gold, the matador, he was the best with his cloak; but what a rotten swordsman!"

"Oh, indeed!" said Lucy, still being sarcastic concerning Cliffe's assumption of expertness in bull-fighting.

"Yes, 'oh, indeed!' " said Cliffe. And to himself: "I must teach her a lesson. But she's coming through rather well."

The whir of fans was heard again and the calling of hawkers. Part of the arena was now in shadow.

V

"*That* bull isn't five years old, I swear!" said Cliffe, when bull number two sprang into the arena, stopped, blinked and charged after a flaunted pink cloak.

"Oh! how do you know?"

"Well, I can tell."

"And what does it matter, anyway?"

"One of the rules is the bulls must be five years old. More difficult to deal with when they're mature. Anybody could play *that* bull."

"You, for instance?"

Cliffe was conscious of a rush of emotional resolve similar to that which had actuated his change of direction from Paris to Seville. He was subject to these singular and surprising waves. He made no retort to the irony of Lucy's tone, except to snatch her shawl (which lay folded on her knees) and scramble down the few steps. He vaulted easily over the first barrier and less easily over the second. He was in the ring!

"I *will* teach her a lesson!" said he to himself, and unfurled the shawl—his one defence against the bull. The bull was now mysteriously standing hesitant close beside him. The toreadors seemed a long distance off. He noticed that one of them was looking at him; the rest were giving all their eyes to the bull. The arena was limitless. No sign from the assembled populace; a million mute dolls!

"I'd better get away from the barrier," he thought, and ran. The bull saw something new, insolent and attractive, and rushed for him. Cliffe stopped and flung outwards the shawl. For the bull, who, like all bulls, was really an ass and not a bull—for the bull the shawl was the enemy, and he lowered his head and aimed furiously for Lucy's precious wrap. He flew past Cliffe in the manner of an express train, of an elephant, of a mastodon, so close that the youth might have smacked his huge shining flank. The youth felt the warmth of his breath and the wind of his passage, and felt also in an awful flash of understanding that he had never realized till then the capacity of a bull as a self-impelled projectile. The youth did not withdraw the shawl quickly enough. He heard a rending. The bull bore off a fringed fragment of the shawl on one horn. Laughter from the grim populace! The toreadors were now attending carefully to their own safety. Cliffe was exceedingly frightened. He was aware of the great heat of the sun on his head, for his Homburg hat had left him—he knew not when. Also he heard a loud knocking. At first he thought someone was hammering on the wooden barrier, and then he discovered that what he was listening to was his own heart.

"Why in the name of heaven didn't I go to Paris?" he reflected. And then: "Confound the girl! Well, she's got something to think about now! I wonder if she's fainted? I may never see her again. I am an idiot. There never was such an idiot as I am." And so on.

The return of the bull from several excursions cut short his meditations.

"No," he muttered in despair. "I couldn't possibly do it again." The mere thought of the bull, the whole vast bull, thundering past him with red eye, lowered horns and flying tail paralysed him. There were no gorgeous toreadors now, no populace; there was nothing but himself and the bull in the interminable and shelterless arena. However, he awoke from his paralysis in the nick of time, and by force of cruel necessity did do the shawl trick again—and the bull got no more of the shawl. From this moment he received full confidence from the skies, and took his turn with the other toreadors in playing the bewildered animal. The faces of the other toreadors grew quite familiar to him. They grunted to one another in Spanish, but appeared to ignore himself. And then as the bull terrifyingly overran Lucy's soiled and ripped shawl for perhaps the fifth time, Cliffe felt a touch, the slightest touch, on his leg. The bull's horn had frayed his trouser! Over-confidence, resulting in a quarter-of-an-inch grazing of death! Cliffe lost his head. Confidence, all of it, exuded from him like an escaping gas; and he ran for the barrier. The bull swerved round and was after him. The bull was the better sprinter. Cliffe knew that he was doomed. He knew that he ought to stop and turn and use the shawl, but he could not stop. Reason had fallen off her throne.

Then he saw in front of him one of the wooden hoardings placed at intervals round the ring, with width enough between them and the inner barrier for a man to pass, but not width enough for a bull; refuges for pressed toreadors. He slipped into the interstice and found salvation. Instantaneously confidence came back to him. The horns of the baffled bull were within a foot of him, and yet he was safe. Rage seized him, and angrily he flung the shawl at the bull's colossal head. The bull tossed his head and ran off with the shawl, half blinded by it. Roars of laughter from the populace. Cliffe was appeased.

He leaped lightly over the barrier into—no, not into safety, but into the receptive arms of two Spanish officials in funny hats. He was a captive. In doing what he had done Cliffe had transgressed the statutory law of Spain and subjected himself to grave penalties. His offence, indeed, was not uncommon. There was no going back to Lucy. He was separated from the entire world by the power of the law. What the Herculean Spaniards said to him he could not in the least comprehend. But in less than a quarter of an hour he comprehended that beyond the slightest doubt he was locked up, hatless, in a Spanish prison. The remainder of the bull-fight had no interest for him. He forgot the heat of the sun in the chill of the cell, where he had leisure to wonder what the other toreadors thought of him.

VI

It was not till after a highly unpleasant night in the indescribable cell that Cliffe Forrest resumed contact with the great world. The authorities had other occupations on Easter Sunday-night than to show mercy to malefactors. He might have been released earlier if the British Consul had not been out of town. Lucy, having learnt, as much by intuition as by anything else, the nature of Cliffe's fate, had hurried to her uncle and begun by confessing a clandestine visit to the bull-fight. Mr. Brest had the brilliant idea of searching for the Consul, but was not unduly disturbed by the Consul's absence from home. Indeed, Mr. Brest contemplated with amazing equanimity one night's incarceration for Cliffe Forrest. The criminal's release was preceded by a bed of justice, sinister interviews (by means of an imperfect interpreter) with the Alcalde and the chief of police of the city of Seville, and a cash payment of five hundred pesetas plus some important sundries. After which his crime was purged.

That afternoon, while Mr. Brest was allaying his fragile wife's alarms in the latter's bedroom, Lucy had a conversation with Cliffe in a secluded corner of one of the endless, winding, tiled corridors of the Hôtel de Madrid. The noise of a little fountain and the song of a canary in a cage accompanied their talk. Both of them had a comically guilty air.

"But you might have been killed!"

"I might, of course. But, you see, I've baited my old father's pedigree bulls with a horsecloth before now in a field three times the size of that blooming bull-ring."

"Oh! Then you were a bit of a toreador. You ought to have told me before you started. D'you know I nearly fainted!"

"Served you right if you had fainted!"

"Why, it wasn't my fault!"

"Of course it was your fault."

"But I never challenged you to go."

"Not in words! But you did! And you jolly well know it!"

"Indeed I didn't! I never dreamt of such a thing. And what's more, I'll never speak to you again. You simply aren't safe."

"Yes, you will. You must come with me to the shawl shop by the Alcazar and I'll buy you a new shawl. After that you needn't speak to me any more."

"You just won't buy me a new shawl, then. I've got one."

"Already! You don't lose time."

"I've got the old one and the bit that fell off the bull's horns, and I've started to mend it, and I shall never wear any other shawl, dirty as it is, as long as I live."

"Oh!" murmured Cliffe, transfixed by her words and her downward glance.

Lucy said:

"Naturally I'm bound to marry you now, seeing how seriously you take me. You aren't safe. However, I must risk it. I'm in for a lively time."

But she said all this to herself, with her gaze on the large black and white tiles.

MIDDLE-AGED

I

THE yacht *Aphra* was sailing down the Channel, and the company, which consisted of the owner (usually addressed as Jackie) and Mr. and Mrs. Proctor, were having tea on deck. The skipper was at the wheel, the engineer was in the engine-room, and the rest of the crew lounged about forward. The yacht *Aphra* was a ketch of one hundred and twenty-five tons, and whenever she put into a minor port she was referred to in the local Press as "the fine ketch," because no yacht of any size is allowed to put into a minor port without a complimentary adjective.

With just a breath of wind dead aft, the yacht *Aphra* was on an even keel; her sails were wide outspread; the engine was helping the sails. The sea was smooth—and empty, save for one or two tramp steamers in the offing. At a distance of four or five miles low, undulating hills, with an occasional cove, cliff, village, church-steeple, white tape of road, were all that could be descried of that enigmatic, weird, self-sufficient isle, England. The sun shone; half-concealed within its warm rays was the tang, the nip, which throughout the English summer wholesomely reminds humanity that winter is not far behind and winter not far ahead. In a word, the scene was one of ideal peace and felicity, and nobody could have guessed that a tremendous upset—moral, not physical—was about to happen.

The huge mainsail suddenly flapped with a report like thunder.

"This wind is getting tired of life," said the owner, who often spoke in metaphors and images, and he rose and went and sat on the poop on the opposite side of the wheel from the captain. He was a stoutish man of fifty or more; so was the captain; the chief difference between them seemed to be that the captain had brass buttons while the owner hadn't.

In a few minutes the owner returned to the slightly-swaying tea-table.

"Look here," said he. "I don't know so much about this sailing-all-night business to-night. Glass is rising. There'll soon be a dead calm. Of course, we shall carry the tide for another two hours, but after that, with the tide against us, we shall do no good with the engine alone, especially round the Nose. Moreover, the engineer can't be expected to work all the clock round. So I think we'll just drop an anchor in Polpooe, and leave early in the morning, say seven-thirty. We shan't be losing any time, and we shall have a quiet night." Which was not what he thought, but what the captain thought. He always came back full of marine knowledge and wisdom from chats with the captain.

"Polpooe!" cried Mrs. Proctor, with surprising vivacity. "Are we near Polpooe? Why didn't you tell us? That's where Elizabeth lives."

* * * *

The social atmosphere of the deck was changed in an instant; waves of excitement radiated from Mrs. Proctor and disturbed the serenity of her husband and the owner. She was a little woman, slim, lively, dynamic. Her complexion might be in ruins, but not her eyes and her emotions. Though the twenty-fifth anniversary of her wedding was nigh, though she had two daughters and two sons, all of whom were adult or adolescent, and all of whom could and did attempt to give her lessons in everything, from lipsticks to politics, she still violently counted with men, and on them, and could be as wilful, capricious, naughty, and charming as a girl.

Mr. Proctor lazily agreed that Polpooe *was* where Elizabeth lived. Mr. Proctor was rather a big man, who knew all about women through the study of his wife—his wife being all women rolled into one—and was cheerfully, if sardonically, resigned to the facts of Nature.

"I must call on her to-night," announced Mrs. Proctor.

"But look here, Tikky, why?" Mr. Proctor protested. (Her name was Marcella, and nobody, not even Mr. Proctor, knew why he called her "Tikky." By the way, her children called her Tikky, too.)

"You can't go calling on people like that!"

"Elizabeth isn't 'people.'"

"But it's only by chance we're going into Polpooe. Supposing the wind had held—"

"What's the good of supposing?" Mrs. Proctor demanded. "Men are so queer. We are going into Polpooe, and I couldn't possibly go there without calling to see Elizabeth. She'd never forgive me."

"She wouldn't know anything about it."

"But I should know, silly!"

"Good heavens!" ejaculated Mr. Proctor, and, turning to the owner: "Look here, Jackie, if I were you I should refuse to have a boat lowered."

"Jackie wouldn't be so disgusting, would you, Jackie?" Mrs. Proctor took the owner's hand and smiled at him, the smile of the unscrupulous enchantress. "Elizabeth's one of my best friends. She was a bridesmaid at my wedding. I haven't seen her for twenty-five years, but we write to each other every year and tell each other *everything*. Now don't be horrid, Jackie. And *you*'ll have to come with me, Arthur."

Arthur Proctor groaned.

Off and on Mrs. Proctor talked about Elizabeth until the yacht *Aphra* dropped an anchor in Polpooe harbour.

"Oh, what a lovely little place!" cried Mrs. Proctor, and kept on crying, "Oh, what a lovely little place!" And it was, indeed, a pleasing small port, with hills on either side, and the houses of a tiny town climbing up them.

"Oh! And there's Elizabeth's house!" cried Mrs. Proctor, pointing to a greenclad residence with a steeply-sloping garden that ended in a long, curved, irregular flight of stone steps leading down to the sea's level.

"How do you know it's Elizabeth's house?" asked Mr. Proctor, stroking his sparsely-covered cranium.

"From the photographs, of course, stupid! Jackie, don't bother to have the launch lowered. I know it's an awful lot of trouble. We'll go in the dinghy."

Soon after the sails had been stowed two tired mariners lowered the dinghy, and Mr. and Mrs. Proctor, somewhat titivated for the occasion, stepped into it and were rowed ashore, and presently were seen from the yacht breasting the slope towards Elizabeth's house. Mrs. Proctor continued to laud Elizabeth, and to express her absolute certainty that Elizabeth would be just the same as she had ever been. Nevertheless, as she and Arthur entered the porch of Elizabeth's abode Mrs. Proctor was seized with a great fear and terrible apprehension.

"It's a ticklish affair," thought she, "seeing someone you haven't seen for five-and-twenty years. I feel frightfully awkward. I shan't know what to say to her. Supposing she's— Arthur, you're so good at small-talk. Now mind you keep the conversation going."

The little thing's heart fluttered most disturbingly. It told her that this was the most dangerous enterprise that she had ever undertaken in all her life. She wished to Heaven she had never left the yacht *Aphra*. If the well-beloved Elizabeth proved a disappointment—provided a tragic disillusion!

Ages seemed to pass. Mrs. Proctor, restless, looked round at the coarsely-carved wood of the porch, at the cheap imitation stained glass in the door. Suburban! No, provincial! She felt the nocturnal deadness of the little town. She was ashamed that her husband should see the environment in which lived the adorable Elizabeth, whom she was always vaunting to him. She was about to say to him, "Nobody in. No use waiting any longer," when the door slowly opened, and as she saw it opening Mrs. Proctor had a sense of disappointment. She would have preferred that nobody should be in. Strangeness of human nature!

A middle-aged, rather unkempt, and lanky man stood in the doorway. He had a moustache, a beard, neither of which would Mrs. Proctor have tolerated in a husband. A bony and apprehensive face! Dishevelled grey hair! A brown suit that in the friction and strain of life had lost both shape and pattern! One pocket bulged with a garden-trowel; the other bulged with articles unseen—no doubt pipes and pouches and matches and things. The man must have long since ceased to care what he looked like.

"Oh! Good evening," Mrs. Proctor began, impulsively, desperately.

"Good evening," said the man, coldly, and added: "We don't let rooms."

"Oh, it's not that!" protested Mrs. Proctor. "I—we—just called to see Mrs. Draver. I—"

"Mrs. Draver is not in this evening," said the man, still coldly; but he did suggest: "Can I do anything?"

"Are you Mr. Draver?" Mrs. Proctor asked, with a distressing attempt at a seductive smile, and death in her heart. Surely impossible that this man was the husband of the beloved Elizabeth!

"Yes," said he.

Mrs. Proctor glanced at Mr. Proctor for help, because Mr. Proctor always charmed everybody.

"Our name is Proctor," said Mr. Proctor, with the whole of his charm. "We're yachting down the coast, and as we've put in here for the night my wife thought—"

"Proctor? Proctor?" murmured Mr. Draver, blankly.

"Yes," exploded Mrs. Proctor, impatiently. "I'm Marcella—Tikky."

"Ah, yes!" Mr. Draver seemed to be drawing up something long-forgotten from the deepest depths of memory. "Ah, yes!" And then again: "Yes, yes!" And then an original idea visited him. "Do come in," he said, as if saying: "We're in a great difficulty. Somebody must act, and I suppose I'd better act."

He went even further and shook hands.

"Come through into the garden, will you? It's beautiful evening. I was just pottering about and watering. You fond of gardening? Elizabeth's gone to the pictures with the mayor." (A sort of naïve satisfaction in the word "mayor"!) "She hasn't been out at night for months. I never go out at night myself. Doesn't suit me. Lovely view here, isn't it?"

It was a lovely view, and Mr. and Mrs. Proctor said so with perhaps exaggerated enthusiasm.

"Elizabeth will be sorry to miss you," said Mr. Draver. "But I'll tell her you've called."

"How kind you are!" thought Mrs. Proctor, in fury.

No suggestion that they should wait until Elizabeth returned from the pictures! No suggestion that they should call on the morrow!

"I expect you'll be leaving again early to-morrow," said Mr. Draver.

"I'm afraid we shall," said Mr. Proctor. "You see, we mustn't miss the west-going tide. The skipper says we ought to weigh anchor not later than eight o'clock."

"Elizabeth *never* gets up early," said Mr. Draver, with much sincerity and conviction. "Servant doesn't get up till eight o'clock. They won't, you know, in these days. It's *her* night out, too."

"Great Scott!" ejaculated Mr. Proctor, simply, as they descended the slope again towards the quay. "Great Scott!"

Mrs. Proctor ejaculated nothing at all. She was thinking: "So that's my Elizabeth's life!" And the thought filled all her mind, and devastated it, and was unutterable.

"The whole thing is perfectly plain to me," said the owner, when the trio were sitting in the green-tinted saloon and he had heard the story—or rather had heard two different stories, one sardonic from Arthur Proctor, and one resentful and half-tragic from Tikky.

"What's perfectly plain to you?" Mrs. Proctor demanded, quite ready for a shindy with her host and determined to tolerate playful nonsense from nobody.

"I will interpret this dark matter, lady. And you shall see a great light," Jackie smiled, teasingly.

Mrs. Proctor raised a warning finger. "I don't mind what you do as long as you don't try to be funny. I can't stand funniness to-night."

"My dear Tikky," said the owner, "let me say that I never thought more highly of your phantom friend Elizabeth than I do at this moment. She is evidently a wise woman. She thinks as I do, that to search out a friend whom one hasn't seen for a quarter of a century is an act of madness. Why were you kept so long at the front-door? Obviously because Elizabeth at a bedroom window happened to see you coming up the street. She—"

"Ridiculous!" observed Tikky. "She wouldn't have recognized me after all that time."

"Not recognized you, my dear Tikky? I've known you for more than a quarter of a century, and I assure you that you haven't changed in the least."

Mrs. Proctor told him not to be absurd, but in spite of herself she could not help believing him.

He went on: "To resume. Your Elizabeth saw you from her bedroom window, where she was probably turning down the bed—or beds—the servant being out, and conscientiously imitating the ways of servants by taking a spell off to watch the interesting street. 'That's Tikky!' said she to herself, horror-struck, and ran down into the garden to her husband to tell him to lie to you. She had grasped in an instant that it would be fatal for you and her to meet again. She taught her somewhat stupid husband exactly what to say to you, and in what tone, and then she fled upstairs again, and no doubt leaned over the banisters to peep at you going through the house. And now she's making her husband repeat to her everything that you said in the garden and congratulating herself on having preserved her dearest illusion—namely, yourself. For twenty-five years you've been growing more and more perfect in her eyes, just as she's been growing more and more perfect in yours. And she was bent on keeping you perfect. Yes, a wise woman, your Elizabeth! I should have liked to make her acquaintance. Of course her illusions about you may have been a bit damaged by what bit she saw of you and heard of you, but speaking broadly—"

The oration was cut short by Mrs. Proctor snatching a handful of cigarettes from the box and wildly flinging them at her host's features.

"Never mind, Tikky!" Arthur Proctor soothed his wife, benevolently.

The owner laughed. Husband and wife retired to their cabin. But in the wakeful middle of the night Tikky reflected: "Did she keep out of my way on purpose? *Did* she keep out of my way on purpose?"

III

The next morning was marvellous. Tikky, lying in her bunk, watched a spot of earliest sunlight wander up and down the wall of the cabin as the yacht *Aphra* swayed very gently in the water. There, in the opposite bunk, lay the immense, mountainous form of Arthur, sleeping as usual just like a child. Nothing less than the wrecking of the ship would wake Arthur. He slept peacefully even through the deck-scrubbing, which to those below presented the characteristics of something apocalyptic and final in the earth's history. Well, Tikky had to get up. Why? Foolish creature, she wanted to gaze across the sunlit water at Elizabeth's house. She arose. She contented herself with a cold bath (for the routine of the yacht *Aphra* must not be disarranged), and she dressed summarily, in an athletic or sporting fashion, and hid her hair in a sort of mob-cap contrived out of one of Arthur's coloured silk handkerchiefs. Then she went and sat in the deckhouse, and she gazed across the sunlit water at Elizabeth's house, with its hanging garden and its long flight of stone steps descending to the sea's edge, and it was just as beautiful as she had imagined. The whole port had the air of being enchanted.

Then, glancing below, she saw Bill, the senior steward, punctual to the minute, on his way to her cabin with two large cups of tea and a plate of bread-and-butter.

"Here, Bill," said she. "I'll have mine here. Wake Mr. Proctor and give him his, will you?" And she took her cup and two pieces of bread-and-butter.

But instead of drinking and eating she gazed and dreamed. Twenty-five years married, with offspring who taught their mamma how to suck eggs! Not a bit. She was a young girl—and Elizabeth was a young girl.

Half-way between the shore and the yacht a row-boat was approaching, with a rough-clad fisherman in it, and a woman.

"Am I going to faint?" thought Tikky, and it seemed to her that life was leaving her as she suspected, guessed, divined that the woman was Elizabeth. (Elizabeth, who *never* got up early!) Never was a young virginal girl more excited, more ecstatic, more purely thrilled than the mother of four adults in that dizzy moment. Her faith in her own sex and in humanity returned like a great tide and swamped every other conviction. She sprang up, ran on to the deck, and stood over the bulwarks. The boat was a thousand years in reaching the yacht *Aphra's* side!

"Elizabeth!"

"Tikky!"

The names were whispered as though the women had a secret to share. The deck was deserted, the crew being now at breakfast. No gangway had been let down, because the yacht *Aphra* was a self-contained unit that morning and nobody had to go ashore. But Elizabeth seized hold of the mizzen shrouds and hauled herself over the rail with the agility of a child. (It was wonderful!) The fisherman murmured that he had to pay a call at a neighbouring schooner and would come back for the lady in half an hour.

"Come, come!" whispered Tikky, in agitation, and, having cruelly hugged her, led Elizabeth through the deck-house down the staircase. There was an unoccupied cabin, and into this Tikky pushed her friend. It was the sole place in the yacht *Aphra* where the cronies would be safe from intrusion.

"Darling, you haven't changed a bit!"

"Nor you!"

They spoke quite sincerely. Each of these fond middle-aged creatures saw in the other a mere girl.

"Wait!" said Tikky, and skipped out of the cabin and fetched first her tea and bread-and-butter from the deck-house and, second, Arthur's tea and bread-and-butter (the giant still slept), and she shut the door of the cabin. And Tikky sat on the bunk and Elizabeth sat on a chair, and they drank and ate and looked at one another and gradually perceived the mature women in the girls.

"You silly!" said Elizabeth, in just her old, remembered, somewhat caustic tone. "You're crying into your tea!"

"I know I am, and I don't care!" Tikky replied, gruffly, with just her old, remembered, tone of sturdy defiance.

IV

"I suppose you wonder what on earth I do with myself all the year round in this little pudding-basin of a place," said Elizabeth, breaking the first little silence that had occurred in their talk. This was after they had been "at it" for some time.

"No, I don't," said Tikky, admiring Elizabeth's graphic phrase, "pudding-basin of a place"—so characteristic of her, as Tikky now recalled. "I'm jolly sure you find plenty of interesting things to do."

"That, infant, is a whopper! You know I don't," said Elizabeth, calmly, and looked Tikky full in the eyes.

Elizabeth had a shrewd, tolerant, somehow negligent face. She was a large woman, not stout, but spaciously built. Her hair was still as black as coal. Although the hour was early, she had several fine rings on her fingers, and she was excellently dressed, and with much care.

"Is it a whopper?"

"It is a whopper. Ever since you called last night to see me you've been adding up the situation, and you've been asking yourself what in the name of Heaven I do with myself here. Me, the high-spirited young thing that used to go to two parties a night and make havoc among a whole sex. Do you think I don't know what my reputation was?"

"Well, what in the name of Heaven *do* you do with yourself, then? Your Joey is engineering in Durham. Your Anna is learning frock-making in Kensington. You were never one for reforming the poor against their will. You've nobody—"

"Except my husband," Elizabeth interrupted, quickly and positively.

"That was what I was going to say," Tikky agreed, almost guiltily, fearing lest the perspicacious Elizabeth was already reading her secret thoughts about Mr. Draver, whom Tikky certainly regarded as the dullest, flattest, stupidest, untidiest, most commonplace of created males. Here indeed was the disconcerting problem for Tikky: how could Elizabeth stand her husband?

"Now, I'll tell you what I do. If it's fine I sit in the garden and admire the view up the coast. And if it's wet I sit inside at the window and admire the view up the coast. You won't deny it's a marvellous view. Also, if I feel particularly energetic, I watch my husband gardening. As for going out of a night, never in the world! Last night at the pictures was an astounding exception—one of those things you simply can't explain. I tell you it was so unusual that it was an event in my life."

"Your husband's a great gardener, isn't he?"

"Not at all, my dear. He's a gardener. He doesn't garden all the time. He reads the *Daily Telegraph* through every day, and that takes him from two to three hours."

"Well, you are a slothful pair."

"I shouldn't call Leonard slothful," said Elizabeth. "He's twelve years older than me. He worked a lot too hard until he retired from engineering. And his health isn't too good. If he's idle, he's earned it; but he isn't."

"I'm sure he's earned it," said Tikky, eagerly and kindly, for she had noticed a touch of genuine seriousness in Elizabeth's humorous voice.

"Tikky," Elizabeth began in a new tone, leaning forward on the chair, which was too small for her. "I am about to confide to you the secret of my life. I've never written it to you because it isn't the sort of thing that sensible people write about. My husband is jealous. My Leonard is a jealous husband, fiercely and untiringly jealous."

"Oh!"

"I have to put up with any old stick of a servant because my Leonard hates me to be human with servants. We might have kept Joey at home, or near home, only Leonard really preferred him to go, because Joey and I were always so thick together. Same with Anna. I really only went to the pictures last night in order to defy Leonard—you see, I have to keep him within bounds. He's always been jealous of you—yes, though we only write to each other about once a year! He's always finding excuses to move your photograph off the bedroom mantelpiece. And I bet anything he was pretty rudish to you last night when you called. You see, he can't help it."

"I wouldn't say he was rude, my child," said Tikky, without conviction.

"I didn't say rude, I said rudish," Elizabeth laughed. "I had to take him firmly in hand last night. Yes, I got angry because he hadn't made you stay till I came home, or come and hiked me out of the cinema. I frightened him." Elizabeth looked grave. "We had a great scene of reconciliation after he'd apologized. But I made him get up at six-thirty this morning and go out on his bicycle and find me a boat. I say, of course I wouldn't talk in this style to another soul! You know that, don't you?"

"Naturally I know it, you silly fool!" Tikky retorted, blandly. "But, I say—"

"What?"

"Seeing as we're talking like this, isn't it rather trying for you, all this—er—jealousy?"

"Trying!" exclaimed Elizabeth. "You bet it's trying. But it's lovely, my child. I'm that man's passion. I'm his atmosphere. I'm his climate. I'm his life. I'm all his life. I'm the last thing he thinks about before he goes to sleep and the first thing he thinks about when he wakes up. He's in a perfect fever this very moment because I insisted on coming off to you alone. I dress for him. I wear jewels for him—jewels that he pays for. And it's been so for twenty-four years. And I'm in my fiftieth year. Can you beat it, my infant? Isn't it enough? What does it matter to me in what sort of a pudding-basin place I live? I've succeeded."

Tikky dangled her leg against the side of the bunk. Her face had the look of one to whom revelation has been vouchsafed and the dark meaning of existence rendered clear.

V

Suddenly Mrs. Proctor slipped off the bunk and seemed to be listening—or at any rate to be fixing one or other of her five senses on some mysterious phenomenon. She swayed slightly. The teaspoon in the cup and saucer which she had placed on the little tip-up table by the bunk shifted its position with a slight metallic click. She dashed out of the cabin. The second steward was rubbing the walls of the corridor.

"What are we doing?" she demanded, anxiously.

"We're at sea, madam."

"But I never heard the anchor-chain."

"No, madam. While you were ashore last night, as there was a mooring-buoy not being used, the captain thought it would save time this morning if we got the anchor then and just moored to the buoy. So we only had to cast off this morning."

Mrs. Proctor did not entirely understand these technical statements, but she thought she did, and was more than ever convinced that seamanship was an odd business.

"But the engine isn't going!"

"No, madam."

"And I didn't hear the sails go up."

"No, madam. You see, there's a very nice fair breeze, and so the captain only hoisted the staysail, so as not to disturb anybody below."

"But—"

Mrs. Proctor did not proceed further with the steward. She perceived in a flash how an awful thing had come about. Neither the captain nor the crew had seen Elizabeth arrive on board. They were all at breakfast in the forecastle. Elizabeth had embarked silently, used no gangway, and her own boat had vanished for the time being. Breakfast finished, the captain had given his orders, beautifully ignorant of the presence of a stranger on board, and the yacht *Aphra* had stolen away and stolen Mrs. Draver from her spouse.

Mrs. Draver appeared with a puzzled face at the door of the cabin.

"My dear, something simply frightful has happened. The captain didn't know you were on board and we're at sea."

"Well, the captain will have to put back, then," said Mrs. Draver, calmly.

"Put back?" Mrs. Proctor repeated the phrase. A hundred-and-twenty-five-ton yacht did not put back. You didn't ask a train to put back because somebody had boarded it by mistake, and you could not ask the yacht *Aphra* to put back. If you did, Jackie would think that the end of civilization had come.

Mrs. Proctor ran into her own cabin, Arthur was still sleeping heavily.

"Arthur! Arthur!" No response. Men were astounding.

She then knocked at the door of the owner's cabin. Equally no response. These males had slept brutishly through wondrous incidents and could not be roused. Mrs. Proctor flew up on deck, followed by Mrs. Draver. Yes, the fine ketch *Aphra* was at sea right enough. The staysail was well filled. The captain, unaware of calamity, was at the wheel. Various members of the crew were quietly cleaning brass. The kitchen chimney was blowing off pleasant smoke. The ship pitched very, very gently in the smooth, glittering sea. The ship had something inexorable about her movement. Cry "Stop"? You could not cry "Stop." Mrs. Proctor, nonplussed, looked behind. The little pudding-basin of Polpooe was getting smaller every moment. It was fading. It was like a historical event, receding irrevocably into the past, and never to be recalled. To see Polpooe from the moving ship was like reading about Polpooe.

Then was heard the distant sound of a siren, several times sharply repeated. The captain gazed aft. All the sailors on deck ceased work and gazed aft.

"What's the fellow making a noise about?" asked the captain.

"Hadn't you better stop, skipper?" Mrs. Proctor weakly suggested, utterly unlike herself.

"Stop'm? We can't stop. She's got the tide under her. Besides—"

At this point the captain caught sight of an unknown woman, Mrs. Draver, and was transfixed with astonishment. The look on his face was so comical that Mrs. Proctor laughed the laugh of incipient hysteria. Both stewards came on deck. The cook's white-capped head appeared at the forecastle hatch.

"That's that old coal-barge a-coming," said the captain. "If she wants us she'll soon overhaul us. She's got a motor in her enough to shake her to bits. I seed her last year."

The pursuing vessel showed a foaming prow, and was visibly growing larger and larger.

"*Leonard is in that barge!*" exclaimed Mrs. Draver, solemnly.

"Lower yer staysail!" shouted the captain.

"Lower yer staysail," repeated two deck-hands, according to ritual, and the staysail came down with a rattle.

"Hoist yer staysail!" the captain cried a few minutes later. "He looks as if he was coming alongside, and I must have steering way on her."

"Hoist yer staysail," repeated the deck-hands.

The staysail rose again. The coal-barge bore down with the ruthlessness and the inevitability of pursuing justice. Soon could be heard the murmur of the divided white water at her prow.

"Leonard's always watching in the garden with his glasses," said Mrs. Draver, clasping Mrs. Proctor's hand. "He saw me come on board and the boat go away, and then he saw the yacht move off and he got excited. Hence the coal-barge. He'd have chartered a steamer if he couldn't have got anything less."

"But surely—" Mrs. Proctor began.

"Yes, of course, infant," Mrs. Draver cut her short. "But, you see, Leonard doesn't think. He feels."

The coal-barge, slackening speed, drew alongside. There was a shock and a great pother. The captain of the yacht *Aphra* bawled something in the confusion to the grimy steerer of the coal-barge, and the steerer of the coal-barge bawled back to the captain of the yacht *Aphra*.

"Hi! Look out!" the captain almost screamed.

But Mrs. Draver had leaped from the yacht's rail into the vile depths of the barge; and a hatless old man had caught her by the waist and was holding her, and also kissing her.

"Well," muttered the captain. "That was a fine set-out, that was!"

The coal-barge sheered off, and in half a minute was making for Polpooe. Mrs. Proctor felt lonely, for Mrs. Draver seemed to have quite forgotten her.

"Alb," said the captain, gloomily, to the mate. "Have a look there—see how much he's done to our paint. And swab down again here. He's left half his coal-dust behind him."

Lastly, at a distance of a quarter of a mile, Mrs. Draver turned and waved from the barge. And Mrs. Proctor waved in reply. She was smiling, and she was crying, too—not from grief at parting with her beloved friend, but from another emotion. Might it be envy, or something nobler?

VI

It rained softly in the afternoon. Arthur Proctor took the opportunity to have more repose in his cabin. Mrs. Proctor sat in the saloon with Jackie, listening to the gentle patter of the rain on the deck above. The two men had not heard the whole truth about Elizabeth's adventure of the morning; they had heard only part of it—the mere physical events of it. Tikky had not even begun to relate the rest, because she felt the hopelessness of trying to convey its significance to those comfortable, lazy, teasing, sardonic males. They laughed good-naturedly and quizzically at what they did hear. How could they possibly understand?—the one a nice, heavy husband, sunk in ease and satisfaction, the other the lowest of created beings, a bachelor profoundly decent and indifferent to women.

Jackie and Tikky were discussing housekeeping, upon which Jackie justifiably regarded himself as an authority. They sat close together; she was holding his hand—in a friendly, affectionate way, for she liked Jackie while despising him. Arthur, having wakened, and feeling the need of tea for his refreshment, strolled into the saloon.

"Hullo!" he murmured. "Here you are!" Tikky did not move—even her hand. Presently she went into their cabin. Arthur followed her and carefully shut the door. She looked at him and waited.

"I say, Tikky," said he, "I think I shall have to speak to Jackie."

"Oh, what about?" cried Tikky, as it were hopefully.

"His confounded Ceylon tea. He really ought to give us China."

She stamped her foot impatiently, quite recovering her regular form of a very capricious, unpredictable young woman.

"Puh!" she exploded. "Is that all?"

A little later she said: "Arthur, were you ever jealous?"

"About you?"

"Yes."

"Certainly not. Why should I be?" he asked, with perfect tranquillity. "Why do you ask?"

"I won't tell you—you wouldn't even know what I meant."

"Oh, all right!"

"It isn't all right," Tikky asserted, contradictory. And she thought of Elizabeth, eternally watched and longed for, and she sighed.

THE UMBRELLA

I

ALTHOUGH the village of Slipcup was larger and more opulent and more beautiful than he had gathered from his sister's rare letters, although it had a quite imposing bank and a cinema (open one night a week—*this* night), although its railway-station was a junction, with three platforms and four tracks, Mr. Arthur Malpatent felt as he passed up the steep main road as if he was passing out of the world, his world, into something unknown, strange, queerly romantic.

He was a man of fifty or so, grey, thin, lively, with a thin, mobile, and highly-expressive face, elastic lips, vague eyes. He talked confidentially to himself and smiled to himself, now and then flourishing his umbrella. Anybody with any knowledge of the physiognomy of professions would have seen at once that he was an actor—who dreamed when he was not acting. He was neatly dressed in a lounge-suit to match his ample hair, and wore buttoned boots, a grey wide-awake hat, and a club-necktie carelessly knotted.

It was a beautiful warm evening, and at half-past nine night had not yet fallen. Mr. Malpatent had inquired the way to "The Weald," his sister's house. He had to continue up the main road and then take the second on the left. He did so. If the main road was steep, the by-road was steeper, with a bad surface for frail buttoned boots. He saw two low bungalows (semi-detached), neither of which was The Weald; and then he saw a house, and an inscription on its open garden-gate named it The Weald. It was the last house, the highest house, and it stood in its own garden on the moor. (The moor, however, was pleasingly covered with shrubs and small trees.) Mr. Malpatent mounted the steep slope of the small front-garden and rang his sister's bell. He then turned round to view the scene from the doorstep, and saw a marvellous panorama of the distant estuary.

"Charming! Charming!" he ejaculated. "But in winter it must be deuced bleak up here."

So this was the abode, and this the situation, which Muriel had chosen for herself! Here she lived with one servant. Her letters had announced that her neighbours were without exception very odd people, but Mr. Malpatent thought that few of them could be odder than his queer, beloved Muriel. The door did not open. No sound within the house. Mr. Malpatent rang again He rang thrice. Still no answer.

"Yes," he reflected, impartially. "It might have been better to warn her. Still, what does it matter, after all? Man's life's a vapour. One is here to-day and gone to-morrow."

An immense semi-clouded moon was approaching him over the summit of the hill. Indeed, all was romantic. Accidentally he pressed with his back against the door and it opened.

"Tut-tut!"

He saw the dim hall of Muriel's house.

"Anybody about?" he cried. No response. "Have I the right to enter my sister's house merely because it is my sister's?" he asked, and answered the question by entering, and clinched it by shutting the door. "Why not?" said he. "We have always been on the very best of terms. But how astonishingly careless timid women are!" He cried once more, "Anybody about?" His voice resounded in a sinister manner. No response. "Well!" he said, and walked first into the drawing-room on the left, and second into the dining-room on the right.

Nice rooms; full—too full—of old furniture, engravings, knick-knacks; some of which he recognized with a gentle thrill. Yes, Muriel evidently knew how to make herself comfortable. He came back into the hall. The stairs invited him.

"Well!" And he went up the stairs into the even more unknown. "Perhaps the poor dear is in bed and asleep," he said.

Four doors on the landing at the top of the stairs, all shut, all as it were hiding secrets! He knocked at one of the doors and opened it and peeped in. A bedroom, empty. This happened twice. The two rooms were swathed in dust-sheets.

"She can put me up handsomely," said Mr. Malpatent.

The third door was locked. Mr. Malpatent's skin crept.

The fourth door proved to be the door of the largest and richest bedroom—crammed with a miscellany of furniture. Empty, but the state of the dressing-table indicated use!

"I am alone in this house," said Mr. Malpatent, impressed, and he invaded the room boldly.

From one of the windows he could see the large back-garden. It was much better tended than the small front-garden, whose drive, indeed, showed a deplorable array of weeds. But the back-garden was as deserted as the front-garden and as the house. Turning again into the room, he noticed, to his astonishment, a telephone by the bedside.

"Telephones out on the moor!" he murmured. "The world does revolve after all. But what does Muriel want with a telephone?"

Of course, he did not know that his sister had inherited the instrument from a previous tenant, and that she had kept it on account of its convenience for giving orders to the chief village tradesmen.

"Well," said he, brightly, to the room. "If my darling sister thinks I am going to wait here all night for her, the chit is mistaken."

He had not yet been in the house for more than a quarter of an hour; but he was an impatient man, if genial and kindly. He dropped his umbrella on the floor by the bed and picked up the telephone-receiver.

"Please give me the station," he said, sitting carelessly on the bed.

The Exchange asked him whether he wanted the police-station or the railway-station.

"The railway-station."

"What railway-station?" the Exchange demanded.

"Slipcup, naturally."

It did not occur to him that the Exchange was situated in a big seaside town five miles off and had at least a dozen railway-stations on its list of subscribers.

When he got to Slipcup Junction he blandly inquired:

"Have you any trains to-night?"

"Where for, sir?"

"Oh, anywhere. Doesn't matter."

He was like that. He learnt that in twenty-five minutes there was a train whose chief destination was Bristol.

"Oh, Bristol!" said he. "Very well, then, I'll go to Bristol. I've never been there, but I think Bristol will do quite nicely, thank you. I left my luggage with the head porter in the porter's room." (Slipcup, though a junction, was rural and informal and had no left-luggage office.) "Will you please ask him to get it out on to the platform ready for me?"

"What name, sir?"

"Malpatent. Professor Malpatent. It's all labelled."

The student of the physiognomy of professions would have been wrong in putting him down as an actor. He merely resembled an actor. He was professor of mathematics in the University of Leeds. There is, however, a marked similarity between the appearance of actors and the appearance of professors who have abandoned themselves utterly and passionately to mathematics.

In five minutes he had departed from his sister's house. He might have encountered Muriel in the road, in which case he would have returned with her, and probably sent down to the station for his luggage. But as he did not happen to meet her, he allowed her to fade out of his mind. He was extremely casual. Finding himself on the coast not many miles from Slipcup, he had had, suddenly and unexpectedly, the idea of paying a visit to his sister. A charming and brotherly idea! She was not at home. He dropped the idea, forgot it completely; and it was as though it had never been! He was like that.

Not till well on the way to Bristol did he observe that he had left his umbrella behind at The Weald. Regrettable, perhaps; but what did it matter? He could do without an umbrella. He had the temperament which makes for happiness.

II

The next morning, which was a marvellously beautiful morning, a slim and somewhat elegant lady, dressed entirely in white and dangling a pair of white gloves, might have been seen issuing from the front-door of The Weald. This was Miss Malpatent. Even in Bond Street, or on a Sunday afternoon in Hyde Park, she would have passed as being quite presentable. As a fact, she made a point of being presentable—even to powder and rouge (though these aids rather clouded her reputation in Slipcup). But she did so in order to disprove the detestable masculine theory that women only dress "for" men.

A quarter of a century earlier Miss Malpatent had been jilted by a rake with whom she had most foolishly permitted herself to fall passionately in love. From that moment all men, except possibly her brother—whom she rarely saw—were alike to Miss Malpatent. At first she hated them; then she loftily pitied them; but she never distinguished between them. She was delighted when a strange man glanced at her with admiration. All admiration is good, and doubtless Miss Malpatent liked to be admired, but what she liked far more was the opportunity to return the admiring glance with a glance of cold contempt.

She was fifty, and despite grey hair did not nearly look it, because she had retained her figure, and because the charm of her pretty face depended not on complexion but on the excellent shape of its bones and the sparkling beauty of the eyes. She had a secret dread—common to all slim women—the dread of getting too thin; and she was always trying to achieve plumpness and never succeeding. She envied her servant Annie, who was a big, bouncing wench of forty or so. Annie looked older than her mistress, but she possessed what was for Miss Malpatent the incomparable charm of magnitude. There is a moral lesson to be drawn here.

Annie was cleaning the drawing-room window as Miss Malpatent issued forth on to the weed-encumbered gravel.

"I shan't be long, Annie," said Miss Malpatent, with the sweetest, most sisterly smile, as of a pearl of mistresses to a pearl of servants. "I'm only going down to see about the weed-killer."

Annie nodded. An ideal relationship, you would have said, between those two women who lived their solitary lives in appreciative amity together at The Weald.

Miss Malpatent stopped outside the first of the two semi-detached bungalows. A Mrs. Pastow lived in the first one and a Mr. Pastow lived in the second one. They were man and wife, and they were friends, yet they lived in separate houses! Slipcup, however, as Miss Malpatent always maintained, was inhabited by odd people. Mrs. Pastow, gloved and aproned, was polishing the brass of the front-door. She was a downright lady, who had no shame. Her husband kept a servant, but she didn't—and didn't want one—and her bungalow was assuredly the cleaner and neater of the twain.

"Can I come in?" asked Miss Malpatent, deliciously, if abruptly.

* * * *

Now Mrs. Pastow in her downright way objected to morning callers. She held that friendship and nearness and the general simplicity of village life could in no wise justify informality of intercourse, and especially the informality of morning calls save for very pressing reasons. She knew that Miss Malpatent shared this view with her. Hence she divined at once that Miss Malpatent had something urgent on her mind.

"Come right in, Muriel," she said, heartily, and removed her thick gloves.

Her robust common sense, her time, and her knowledge of human nature were always at the disposal of her friends when her friends needed them, though she was apt to be curt with those who made merely frivolous demands on her sound qualities and her leisure.

"Here, sit here," she said, picking up a book that lay on an easy-chair. "I'm half-way through the second volume of 'Orley Farm.' I couldn't help reading a bit this morning in the middle of my work. I shall beat you if you don't buck up."

Both of them were fervent admirers and students of Anthony Trollope. Indeed, they read little else, and were rather scornful of the Brontë and Jane Austen sects in the district.

"Now I can see you're a bit upset."

Thus did Mrs. Pastow enjoin Muriel Malpatent to begin the recital of her woe. Twelve years younger than the spinster, she nevertheless treated her as a niece. Both women sat.

"Am I upset?" Muriel's tone was a little weak, uncertain. She knew that it was useless to try any pretences with Mrs. Pastow. "Well, it's about Annie."

"O-oh! The model maid! She's not taken to drink, has she? I always said she would, remember. Here! I shall take my apron off too." Mrs. Pastow took her apron off and put it under her chair.

"Oh, no! It's worse than that."

"Worse than drink? No, it isn't. Because there's nothing worse, my dear."

Muriel Malpatent shook her head and smiled sadly.

"That girl," said she, "was determined to get me out of the house last night. It was cinema night, you know. She went last week and saw something called 'Daughters of the Storm,' and liked it. And it was such a success last week they brought it again yesterday, and the girl would have me go to it. Never was anything so beautiful, and so on and so on! She knows quite well I don't care for films. However, she was so insistent that I said I'd go. I didn't want to hurt her feelings. Anyhow, she got me out of the house. But I didn't go to the films after all. It was such a lovely evening I walked over the hill instead, right down into Mersington. When I came home her ladyship was in bed—at least, she was in her room and no light burning. But do you know what I found in *my* bedroom?"

"No. What?"

"I found a man's umbrella! Yes, my dear! A man's umbrella in my bedroom!" Miss Malpatent's voice shook as she announced the outrage. "And what's more, it was lying by the side of my bed. She must have had a man in the house. Of course, I saw at once then why she'd been so anxious to get me out of the house. She'd arranged a rendezvous."

"But are you sure?"

"Well, the umbrella couldn't have walked upstairs by itself, could it?"

"But why in your bedroom?"

"My *dear*! The telephone, of course. He'd wanted to use the telephone. I do wish I'd had that telephone moved long ago, as I said I would. It's frightfully inconvenient. And I'll tell you something else. The umbrella is a very good umbrella. Which seems to me to prove either that Annie's carrying on with some rake above her own class, or, if he's of her own class, he's a thief and stole the umbrella. . . . Well, what do you make of it?"

"I don't know what to make of it. Have you tackled her about it?"

"Indeed, I haven't tackled her about it! It was for her to speak. I simply put the umbrella on a chair and left it there. I needn't tell you I had very little sleep. A man been in my bedroom and using my telephone and probably sitting on my bed! When she came in with the tea this morning, naturally she saw the umbrella. You should have seen the start she gave—though she tried to cover it as well as she could. She blushed. And I felt so queer and nervous, I'm afraid I blushed too. Still, I said nothing. I was most sweet to her, as I always am. I gave her every chance to make some explanation. But did she? Not a word! She knows she's in a hole and there's no escape—all through her gentleman forgetting his umbrella—and yet she doesn't say anything! Talk about an ostrich. She didn't even ask me how I liked the film. Yesterday afternoon she was all film, film. This morning not a syllable about the film! Can you conceive it, my dear? Here that woman has always pretended she's got no use for men—silly thing she is! One would have thought she had a positive sex-complex against men! And I believe she had, too! But not now! Now she's carrying on. I've treated her more like a friend than a servant—"

"That's always a mistake."

"I know! I know!" cried Miss Malpatent, admitting guilt. "But I have. And this is how she rewards me! But I've noticed several little things lately. In her work. Forgetful. A bit capricious. Careless. I understand now! Instead of getting on with her work she was thinking about the owner of the umbrella. Of course, she'll have to go. I couldn't possibly keep her. She was *perfect*, that woman was! So devoted, so thoughtful. *And* punctual."

"There's no such thing as a perfect servant, and I've always said so," put in Mrs. Pastow. "Where's the umbrella now?"

"It's where I put it—on the chair. But she's done the room. Oh, yes, if you please, she's done the room and left the umbrella where it was. Can you imagine it? The brazenness! I don't know what to do, I really don't."

"I know what I should do," said Mrs. Pastow, with characteristic robust decisiveness.

"What?"

"I should tackle her about it. I should have it out with her, and at once."

"Never!" Miss Malpatent protested. "It's her place to speak. She knows all about the umbrella and she owes me an explanation."

"Well, she does. I admit that. But supposing she doesn't give you the explanation? Supposing she lets it drag on? You know what servants are."

"I was wondering whether—"

"What?"

"Whether Amelia mightn't know something."

The ancient Amelia was Mr. Pastow's servant, in the adjoining bungalow.

"Oh, I never talk to Amelia more than's necessary," said Mrs. Pastow, curtly.

"But she talks to Mr. Pastow, doesn't she? I know he's often made me laugh repeating the things she says to him."

"Well, Charlie's coming in for lunch to-day. When he gets so sick of Amelia's cooking he can't stand it any longer, then he asks me to ask him to lunch. I'll see whether he's heard anything, if you like. Not that I'd trust anything Amelia says!"

"No, of course not."

"It's very trying for you, my dear," said Mrs. Pastow, kindly, as Miss Malpatent rose to leave. "But I'm sure I'm right. You ought to tackle her straight."

Miss Malpatent sadly shook her head. You would have thought that she was broken by misfortune. Nevertheless, she held herself proudly enough as she passed down the road towards the village. And when she returned to The Weald her charming manner to Annie was absolutely faultless—so faultless that umbrellas might never have been invented. But Annie, for her part, was startlingly and disconcertingly glum—to the point of rudeness. It was a hard world for mistresses.

III

Mr. Pastow came to his wife's lunch in a particularly jolly mood. He was a stoutish man of forty-two, with a reddish, rural face; brown beard and moustache; fairly robust voice; country clothes. He was not always jolly; on the contrary, like many fat men, he was addicted to moods of grave depression, when his conscience or something of the sort got hold of him and worried him. It was in such moods that his wife preferred him; when he was jolly she was apt to be a bit sardonic, and he never knew why; she never told him, being well aware that it advantages a woman to practise mystery with a man. There were only two things in him to which she objected: his beard and his irresponsibility. As to his beard, he clung to it because it saved the terrible daily task of shaving. He had held the Chair of Psychology in University College; but when he inherited some solid money he gave up the Chair, saying that he could conceive no reason why he should work when he need not. He still published pamphlets and small books on his own subject; his wife smiled indulgently at them and asserted that the worst novel of Anthony Trollope's was a better text-book of psychology than any that any lecturer on psychology ever issued.

The twin bungalow arrangement was one of the fruits of his irresponsibility. Looking for houses, they had seen the twin bungalows.

"Let's each have our own home," he had suggested, humorously.

His wife had laughed disdainfully.

"But why not?" he had demanded, defending the sudden, capricious, unconsidered notion.

Whereupon his wife quickly agreed, just to try him. He was entirely ready to enter on the wild experiment. She wondered how far he would let it continue. He had now been letting it continue for four years. To her surprise it suited her at least as well as it suited him. It seemed to combine most of the blessings of marriage with very few of the drawbacks.

They lunched in the kitchen, for reasons of cookery, Mrs. Pastow being cook as well as wife on these occasions.

"You'll never believe it, Sally," he began, as he put the first mouthful of welsh rarebit into his eager mouth, "but Muriel's losing her sex-complex."

"What on earth do you mean, boy?"

"She's getting herself tangled up with some man."

Mrs. Pastow did not believe it, but she was startled, and, as always when startled, she grew cautious.

"Oh!" said she, dryly.

"Yes," said he. "I've had such a morning as I think I've never had. Muriel's Annie was down confabulating with old Amelia at eight o'clock or soon after, and, of course, I had it all—no, not all, but a lot of it—with my bacon at nine. I should say this must have been the greatest morning, the most dramatic, in the whole history of Slipcup."

"Oh!"

"Yes. It seems that our dear Miss Malpatent pretended to go to the cinema last night; only she didn't go. We know she didn't go—when I say 'we' I mean, as usual, Annie and Amelia—we know she didn't go because the girl that takes the money is a friend of ours, and she swore last night that Miss Malpatent had not been in. Now, the question is: Where was Muriel last evening? Well, we can answer the question. Annie was out; it wasn't her night out, but she went out, as there was nothing to do at home—she went down to the village; that was how she learnt from the cinema girl that Miss Malpatent hadn't been where she set out for. When she came home—it was rather late—she saw Miss Malpatent coming down the hill, from the moor. 'Oh!' says Annie to herself, 'this is rather odd.' And she hid in the hedge until Miss Malpatent had got into the house, because she wasn't sure if Miss Malpatent would quite care for her taking a night off without leave. Then she crept in afterwards—quietly. But Miss Malpatent must have known she'd been out all the evening, and counted on it, because this morning, when Annie took up the tea, she found absolutely convincing, undeniable evidence that there'd been a person of the male sex in Miss Malpatent's bedroom last night. When she saw the evidence she didn't say a word, and Miss Malpatent didn't say a word, but Miss Malpatent blushed, I can tell you, blushed like anything. The theory is that Miss Malpatent, guessing that Annie would go out, surreptitiously introduced a man into the house and then got him away and accompanied him over the moor—probably to Mersington."

"Oh!"

"Yes."

"And what was the absolutely convincing, undeniable evidence?"

"The fellow forgot his umbrella—left it in the bedroom! The pair had no doubt been up there to use the telephone. Hence I say that Miss Malpatent is losing her sex-complex. I say further that she is somewhat ashamed of losing it. Otherwise, why should she make a secret of her man, why should she pretend to go to the cinema and not go? Why should she blush when Annie catches sight of the male umbrella?"

* * * *

Silence fell between husband and wife. Mrs. Pastow snatched, rather than removed, the empty plates from the table, and threw, rather than placed, the clean plates on the table for the ham and salad.

"My dear," said Mr. Pastow, "you are strangely moved."

Mrs. Pastow burst out laughing.

"My poor boy," said she, "I wonder how you can interest yourself in such ridiculous tittle-tattle. That's all." And she laughed again.

"It's nothing to laugh at, believe me!" the husband reproved her. "From all I can gather the excellent Annie regards herself as positively insulted and outraged by what has occurred. After all, she and Muriel have been most beautifully at one in their attitude towards the sex which—which is not theirs. And now the male umbrella! Personally I am delighted at the news. It would be idyllic to see Muriel philandering—perhaps marrying. I should attend her wedding with the utmost satisfaction. I should esteem Muriel's marriage as the greatest lark that ever was or could be." He smiled thoughtfully. "Ah!" he said, reflectively. "For fun, for real fun, give me village life every time. For pure diversion, no town is in it with a village."

"If you want fruit," said Mrs. Pastow, "it's there on the dresser."

"Are you leaving me, my dear?"

"I am. I'm going out—now, this instant."

"But you haven't eaten your delicious ham and salad."

"No, and I shan't; at any rate, not at *this* meal."

IV

"My dear!" exclaimed Mrs. Pastow, when she reached The Weald and found Miss Malpatent walking to and fro somewhat agitatedly in the front-garden. Tears, she noticed, stood in Miss Malpatent's eyes. She had hurried up the hill in order to tell Miss Malpatent without the loss of one moment that some mistake, some misunderstanding, some misapprehension, had occurred on somebody's part, and that assuredly Annie was not guilty of the umbrella. If this mistress and this servant both lacked the ordinary sense to talk plainly to one another, and so clear up a silly and dangerous situation, then Mrs. Pastow was determined to talk plainly to each of them for their joint good and their earthly salvation.

"What is it now?" Miss Malpatent demanded curtly, almost rudely, in a broken voice, stifling a hysterical sob.

"I've found out one thing," answered Mrs. Pastow, in a tone intended to tranquillize the disturbed. "Annie knows no more of the umbrella than you do yourself. She was just as astonished as you were to see it in your bedroom."

Whereupon Miss Malpatent's glance blazed down destructively upon the robust Mrs. Pastow.

"My good woman," said she, with extraordinary bitterness and resentment and rudeness. "My good woman, I've no doubt you mean well, but please don't annoy me any more than you can help by such a silly tale. *Of course* Annie knows more about the umbrella than I do. I asked you before and I ask you again: Could the umbrella have walked upstairs—or couldn't it? You don't accuse me of putting it where I found it, I hope?"

"No. Certainly not."

"Well, then?"

Mrs. Pastow was wise enough to know when she was beaten, and so she strategically withdrew with the minimum of loss. She perceived that reason had vacated the throne of Muriel's intelligence. And, therefore, she decided on the spot that she would, and indeed must, postpone any further remarks until reason had returned to its seat. She laughed sadly at human nature as she went back to the bungalow, and the first thing she did on arriving was to snub Mr. Pastow.

Later in the afternoon Miss Malpatent, having eaten nothing at lunch, and having recovered some of her self-control, rang for tea, which was brought into the drawing-room by stout Annie in a defiant style.

"Wait one moment, Annie." Miss Malpatent stopped her at the door as she was going out. "This milk has turned." Miss Malpatent's voice was a sugary masterpiece of dissimulation.

"And what if it is turned?" Annie retorted. "Can I help the weather? There's no pleasing you, miss, and that's all there is to it. Look at the lunch I cooked for you, and you snorting at every dish. I've got my feelings same as other people. And now it's the milk, *if* you please."

Inflammable matter had at last caught fire and exploded. It was bound to be.

"I will not permit you or anybody to talk to me in that way," said Miss Malpatent.

"You mean you'd like me to leave?"

"You must do as you choose, Annie." Pathetic attempt of Miss Malpatent to be indifferent!

"So I will leave!" said Annie with excessive heat. "So I will leave! This is no house for me nowadays, this house isn't. I'll leave now, and you can keep my wages in loo of notice."

She slammed the door and went upstairs. A moment later Miss Malpatent also went upstairs and came down again bearing the umbrella. In twenty minutes Annie, in all her best clothes, hot, flustered, and very warlike, came down in turn. The drawing-room door was open.

"I'm off, miss," she nearly shouted from the hall. "I'll send up a man with a barrow for my box."

"Annie," said Miss Malpatent, approaching her, "you'll take away this umbrella," and she held forth the umbrella. Both women gazed in horror at the incriminating object, origin of an immense disaster.

"I'll take no umbrella, let alone that one."

"*You will take away this umbrella,*" Miss Malpatent repeated, with icy and devastating authority.

It was a duel. By sheer force of will Miss Malpatent won. Annie took away the umbrella.

Alone in the house the victor tragically wept.

* * * *

Now, as she was descending the hill into Slipcup Annie met a gentleman ascending. He had grey hair and was harmoniously clad in grey. His manner of walking was flamboyant. And he was singing to himself. He looked at Annie and then at the umbrella, and then he stopped, and under some strange influence Annie also stopped.

"What are you doing with that umbrella, madam?" the gentleman inquired, looking Annie straight in the face and frightening her.

"Nothing, sir," she faltered.

"I say, what are you doing with that umbrella?"

"Miss Malpatent told me to take it away, sir."

"Well, you'll just take it back, then! Quick march! That umbrella's mine. I left it behind me last night, by inadvertence. I am Professor Malpatent. Are you the perfect 'Annie' that I've heard about from my sister?"

Annie was somehow glad of the excuse to return to The Weald. But she let the Professor precede her.

V

"I do think, Arthur, you might have left a note to say you'd called," said Miss Malpatent to her brother.

The reconciliation between the mistress and the servant was one of those intimate and elemental affairs in which the barriers of class break down utterly.

"We mistrusted one another," murmured Miss Malpatent to Annie. "Never let us do it again. It's too serious."

"Yes, miss."

Mrs. Pastow benevolently smiled. The village laughed. Mr. Pastow roared.

HOUSE TO LET

I

WHEN the great Sid Smith came down from his dressing-room into the wings of the stage of the Victoria Empire (usually pronounced by its patrons as though it was written "Victoria Rempire"), Miss Nella Nora, his "lead," and the two young men who completed the cast of Sid's sketch, "House to Let," were already waiting. The stage-manager, absorbed in the sole idea of flying time, was also waiting, with his eye on the clock. The orchestra was getting towards the end of the "Selection" which divided the performance into two halves. Sid's sketch always came next after the "Selection," because the "Selection" gave the stage hands fair opportunity to "set" the stage for the sketch; the Victoria Empire, though a large and prosperous music-hall, engaging some first-rate talent, did not possess one of those whirring, revolving stages which enable a scene to be set at the back while another one is being used at the front.

Sid Smith casually glanced at his wig in the long mirror hung for the use of artistes by the side of the assistant stage-manager's little lair, and he happened to see, in addition to his wig, Miss Nella Nora making an impudent face at the nape of his neck, and then giving a pert smile to the two young men as if saying to them:

"Look what *I* think of the old codger!"

Now to understand the full enormity of Nella's gesture it is necessary to grasp the high importance of Sid Smith in the ranks of his profession. For fifteen years at least Sid had toured the provinces as a music-hall comedian, had had a certain success, and had rarely been out of an engagement; but he had never reached the top-line of a bill. Then one night in an emergency he had been whisked off to the Alhambra from the Holloway Palace (which theatre, though only a few miles distant from the Alhambra, is morally as far away from it as John o' Groat's); his appearance on the classic stage of Leicester Square had been heralded by the words "Deputy Turn" in the illuminated number-frame; a quarter of an hour later, by exactly the same kind of performance as he had been doing for over a decade in provincial towns, he had torrentially brought the house down, and was deranging the whole remainder of the programme by his extra encores. On the following day the "Stone Palaces Circuit" had agreed to cancel his contract and give him a new and immensely superior contract and in a fortnight he was a top-line star.

Such are the hazards of life. Sid Smith was surely a common enough name; yet now it was differentiated from all the other million Smiths; and nobody asked "Who is Sid Smith?" because everybody knew. At the Victoria Empire Sid was receiving three hundred and fifty pounds a week for his sketch, which cost him much less than fifty pounds a week in salaries. His name and no other name burned on the façade of the theatre. When patrons booked seats many of them would ask: "What time does Sid Smith come on?" Sid Smith filled the house; he did not fill merely the "second house" of a night; he filled the "first house," which began at six-fifteen. Even Sir Joshua, the managing director of the V. E. and of various other music-halls, treated Sid as an equal, and ordinary persons were proud to be seen in his society. Lastly, when his programme number shone in the number-frame, it was always greeted with applause—the audience apparently not being able to wait for the sight of the actual man on the stage to express its gratification.

Considering that Nella Nora's salary was ten pounds a week, that Sid could have got fifty other girls to play her part at the same salary, that she was a mere chit without experience and without marked talent, that Sid had the right to sack her at any time on a fortnight's notice, and that in a word she was nobody at all—considering these matters, the enormity of her ribald gesture could not easily have been exaggerated. Sid Smith believed she fancied herself because she happened to be the granddaughter of the Great Macdoodle, a super-star comedian of the music-halls in the 'eighties and 'nineties, long since retired but not wholly forgotten; he held the reason to be an inadequate one.

II

In the very famous sketch "House to Let," Sid Smith played the part of caretaker. The scene was the reception hall of a large tenantless house, with doors here and there all round, and a grand staircase leading to the upper storeys. (The staircase, of course, curved away out of sight of the audience, and the persons who climbed it, when they also were out of sight of the audience, found themselves at the edge of nothing except a step-ladder.) The plot of the sketch was concerned with a young house-agent's clerk; and with a rich young couple on the eve of a clandestine marriage who dallied with the idea of taking the house and who, incidentally, used the house as a place of meeting. There was also a telephone. Why the landlord should have been fool enough to keep a working telephone in an empty house was not explained; and anyhow it was not a real telephone; it was only a stage telephone; put there so that Sid could be side-splitting into it. Sid's telephonic conversations with the police, the fire brigade, the house-agent's office, the doctor, the post-office, and the dairy shop made a large part of the success of the piece. Then there was the caretaker's maiden aunt, for whom he had a nephew's passion; a strange creature who did not appear at all, but from whom he received letters of advice and to whom he wrote letters describing the fearsome things that happened to him in the course of his calling as a caretaker.

And in fact the things that did happen to him were of the most astonishing kind, and the deeds which he performed in order to cope with the dilemmas into which he fell were even more astonishing. He—that is, the caretaker—was a muddle-headed, untidy, dirty, rather besotted old man, very slow of speech, very slow in the uptake, very ready to take tips—nay, bribes, and quite capable for his own private purposes of repelling all desirable prospective tenants. (Why, he argued with himself, should he help to let the house when the letting of it would deprive him of a job upon which he entirely depended for a livelihood?) On the other hand, he could be fatherly in an agreeable, benevolent way, and would continually offer sound worldly advice to all the young characters in the piece. Further, although muddle-headed, he had moments of startling insight and rapidity of thought and action; you thought you were deceiving his simplicity for your own ends, but you were not; indeed, in one of his moments of vision and decision he succeeded in locking up the three other characters in three different rooms—a singular proceeding on the part of a humble, stupid caretaker. His snatches of letters to his well-loved, unseen aunt, and the snatches of letters received from her, convulsed the audience from gallery down to fauteuils. And his every remark was so contrived by the author, and so uttered by the strange, rich, juicy genius of Sid Smith, as to draw laughter, and cataracts of laughter. If any of his lines failed to cause considerable amusement, those lines were cut and better lines substituted.

Thus, despite his wicked, unscrupulous, dishonest, idiotic disposition, the caretaker was as deeply adored by the audience as the maiden aunt was deeply adored by the caretaker. And twice every night Sid Smith was called before the curtain again and again to bow to ovations which he had thoroughly deserved.

It should be mentioned that none of the other characters had lines to raise laughter. If in practice it was found that they had, the lines were cut and dull lines substituted, or the players were instructed to say them in a different and duller manner. And why not? The show was Sid Smith's show; Sid Smith had all the talent; and the audience came and paid to see Sid Smith—not a trio of mediocre nonentities. Sid would have preferred—

and justifiably—to do a sketch in which figured one character only—himself; but such a sketch was not to be had. He was therefore bound to employ other artistes: they were his necessary evil.

III

As soon as he opened the front-door of the empty house for Nella Nora, the great Sid Smith perceived that she meant mischief. She followed him down the stage, but not far enough. "Come below me," he muttered to her in the midst of their first bit of dialogue. By which he meant: "Get nearer to the footlights than I am and turn towards me."

The audience of the Victoria Empire heard not the muttered order, nor did they reck of the complicated technique which goes to the making of a star's success. It did not occur to them that the first rule in a music-hall star turn is that the star should always keep his expressive face in full view of his admirers; nor did they ask themselves how he could possibly accomplish this if he had to talk to a partner who kept *her* face in full view of his admirers. (Not *her* admirers—she had none!) In these painful circumstances the star is obliged either to talk at the audience, ignoring his partner, or to turn away from the audience so as to confront his partner. Nella Nora simply did not obey the muttered order. There she stuck, displaying her dark, chubby, pretty, simpering, extremely youthful features to the audience; and Sid Smith, being an artist, felt himself compelled to deprive the audience of his own features. Sid was furious. But he dared not show his fury; he dared not even let his fury possess him, lest it might spoil his acting. He was helpless; he was at the mercy of the chit. He could do nothing whatever—short of walking right off the stage in dudgeon, or telling the assistant stage-manager to ring down the curtain. At rehearsals, and before and after shows, he was the boss and could enforce obedience; but with the curtain up he was an actor with no more power than the meanest of his troupe. Thus as the sketch proceeded he had to continue being benevolent to the chit; he had to hide all his anguish.

However, when the telephone bell rang he fairly let himself loose on the telephone, with a movement and a tone which brought a roar of joy from the house but no joy to his heart. The roar did not blind him to the fact that his performance was suffering. He thought that Nella Nora must have gone mad. Why else should she risk her livelihood by this inexcusable vagary?

Nella Nora next broke the second rule in a music-hall star turn. She was deliberately "slow on her cues," by which is meant that she deliberately delayed her replies to the caretaker's remarks, holding up the action of the piece and generally impairing effects. Her tendency had always been in this direction.

Sid Smith began to forget his own lines, and once the minx audibly prompted him!

He still controlled himself, for his own sake, but with a most exhausting nervous effort, and he felt like a camel who sees the last straw being brought along. But at the end of the short scene, as he locked her in the little room on the O.P. side, he locked her in savagely, and in addition gave her *sotto voce*, with masterly brevity, a goodish piece of his mind. The mischief was that she actually won applause on her exit, which was an outrage upon professional etiquette. She had not been engaged to win applause; she had been engaged to help the star to win applause.

The next scene, with the two young men, went better for Sid Smith. The two young men at any rate would never dare to play tricks on him; they probably had young wives to support, or chocolates and flowers to pay for; also they had sense, and a sense of decency too. The surcease was short. On her second entrance Nella Nora made clear her intention to break the third rule in a music-hall star turn. She simply would not stand stock-still and utterly expressionless while Sid Smith talked. Obviously every underling who attempts to act while the star talks distracts the attention of the audience from the star. Nella Nora improvised "business" of her own during Sid's wonderful back-chat—or perhaps she did not improvise it, perhaps she had carefully thought it all out beforehand! She actually got laughs; the audience actually laughed at her when it ought to have been laughing at Sid Smith! Sid swallowed the medicine as best he could, and he swallowed it nobly, because he was a man of vast experience; but if somebody had called out "Fire!" and so brought the safety curtain down and the show to an end he would have been rather pleased; and it is doubtful whether he would have been very annoyed to see Nella Nora a bit singed by the flames.

Well, he would dismiss her that very night! He would give her a fortnight's salary on the spot and send her packing. No, he could not quite do that, because he had no other pretty young woman trained and rehearsed to take her place.

Why was she trying to ruin him and to ruin herself? What was her grievance against him? He admitted that he had been rather severe with her on the previous night, had employed in his observations to her a vocabulary perhaps too free and varied. But if chits were to begin to resent plain speaking and expressive English from stars of the largest magnitude there was an end to discipline on the music-hall stage—indeed, there was an end to the British Empire and to the world itself!

When the curtain fell Sid fancied that the applause was less voluminous and frenetic than usual; but quite possibly the diminution existed only in Sid's deranged fancy. His worst trial came then; for it was etiquette that he should hand his leading lady before the curtain. A desolating ordeal! Involuntarily he crushed her frail little hand in his, crushed it with ferocity. She did not blench nor flinch. She just smiled and bowed—to the audience and to him—with an amazing impish sweetness.

"Now!" he said to himself, rolling up the shirtsleeves of his soul for a fighting display, as he followed her off the stage amid the hands who were "striking the set" and amid the acrobats who were waiting in the wings for their turn.

"Not very good to-night, Mr. Smith," said the assistant stage-manager to him.

"What the Hades do you mean?" Sid demanded, ferociously.

"Thirty-one minutes," said the assistant stage-manager, who judged every turn by its length.

The official allotted time for "House to Let" was twenty-nine minutes. Two minutes lost, and the A.S.M. knew well that he would never get them back!

"Here, you! Miss Springfield!" said Sid Smith (Springfield was Nella Nora's name in the archives of the Registrar of Births). She turned and faced him, still smiling, but rubbing her crushed hand.

"Getting your lines out of you's like drawing teeth out of a cow, that's what it's like!" said Sid, glaring at her. "And I told you the same last night."

"Yes, you did," answered Nella, with an astounding pertness. "And if you tell it me again to-morrow night I'm finished with you, Mr. Smith, *and* at once, and so I don't mind telling you."

She ran away, and he could say no more.

She had finished with *him*. *She* was threatening to get rid of *him*. Ah! She had youth, her prettiness, her charm; and she was trading on them. That was it! Sid Smith was very unhappy, chiefly because he did not know what to do. Fortunately the acrobats were Italian and did not understand English.

IV

About a week after the events above described Sid Smith stood one afternoon in fashionable Lowndes Street, staring at a large house which bore a notice-board to the effect that it was to let, and in Sid Smith's pocket was an order to view the house, which had five storeys and was very fine to the sight. Also in Sid's pocket was a new contract with Sir Joshua for four years at the rate of four hundred pounds a week—instead of three hundred and fifty.

Sid's income was still rising, and, of course, his prestige was rising too. He was rich, and he was steadily getting richer. His wife, a stout lady of bourgeois tastes, had had the idea of moving from Clapham to the West-end; the idea pleased Sid. He had looked about, and the particulars of the house in Lowndes Street had taken his fancy. Nay, more, they had intoxicated him; so much so that he had more than once mentioned the enterprise, and at least once shown the particulars of the house, to admiring acquaintances and fellow-performers within the Victoria Empire and elsewhere; and on the previous evening he had told Sir Joshua himself and one of the young men in his sketch that the following afternoon was to be consecrated to an inspection of the property, which was variously set forth in the particulars as a "noble mansion," a "town house," and "a gentleman's residence."

* * * *

And now at last, having crossed the street, he was on the threshold. Being an artist by temperament, his imagination moved very quickly and grandiosely, and already the house was his and a powerful and luxurious motor-car stood throbbing at the kerb and he was coming down the front steps with his dresser behind him and a respectful chauffeur holding open the door of the car, and a few watchers saying to themselves, "Here's the great Sid Smith going out to do his night's work." The front steps were of marble, broad and massive. He looked up and saw storey lifting above storey into the skies. He contrasted this magnificent abode with his mother's grubby little house in Slip Street, Salford, where he was born, and, justifiably proud, he decided that the world was good and life worth living, and that virtue and industry and genius were much less than their own reward.

Withal he felt a little nervous, for he knew that a viscount lived next door. He thought it was queer that he, the great Sid Smith, the idol of populations, should feel nervous, but feel nervous he did.

Then he perceived, on a card hung crookedly in the dirty but immense dining-room window, the words "Caretaker Within." He smiled, with pleasant anticipation. He had been interpreting the *rôle* of a caretaker of a large house for many months; but he had never to his knowledge actually seen a caretaker; he knew absolutely nothing about caretakers, never before having inspected a house important enough to need the services of a caretaker. He had created his character of a caretaker entirely out of his own head, basing it upon his notions of what a caretaker ought to be like; and nobody had ever questioned the substantial truth of his ideal portrait. It would certainly be very interesting, amusing, and just possibly helpful to see what a real caretaker was in fact like. He rang the bell; after a considerable interval he rang again; the majestic front-door opened to his summons.

"Are you the caretaker?" asked Sid.

"Yes."

It was an old man with whitish hair, a very wrinkled face, and small watery eyes; thin grey hands; somewhat baggy and shabby and indistinct as to clothes; a blue kerchief round his neck and a red one sticking out of his pocket. He spoke without the formula of respect usually offered to prospective tenants of important town mansions, but there was benevolence in his full tone; also he spoke contemplatively, as though answering not Sid Smith but informing the whole universe.

"Got your order to view?" he added. He took the card from Sid and, without glancing at it, transferred it to his own pocket. "We have to be very particular," said he.

Being rather pleased with the old fellow, Sid Smith nodded amiably, if nonchalantly, sure of his power to impress and reassure real caretakers as he had a glimpse of himself in a large mirror on the wall of the vast entrance-hall. What signs of prosperity in that slightly portly figure! The pearl tie-pin alone. The vastness of the parqueted hall, however, was as much as he could stand up against; it was far larger than any room in his house at Clapham! The mouldings on the panels of the various visible doors were gilded. The staircase was terrific!

"You know what happened to the man who was too particular?" observed Sid Smith, quizzically.

"I know what happened to the man as wasn't," the caretaker replied. "Three doors away. Burglars came with a lorry and took off all the marble mantelpieces in the place! And the individual as came first to look round was wearing a pin on his chest with a pearl as big as a gooseberry. That's how they does it. But not me, they couldn't do it on! Not me!"

Sid Smith felt a little uncomfortable, and the emptiness of the town residence gave him an uneasy sensation.

"Now this is the dining-room." Opening the door to the right, the caretaker began to reel off the beauties of the house in the style of a museum guide. Then he suddenly stopped, while yet enumerating the advantages of the dining-room, and he looked Sid Smith up and down.

"Excuse me, but aren't you the great Sid Smith?"

"I am," Sid admitted, not deprecating the word "great."

"I thought you was. I thought you was. It struck me all of a heap." From his pocket he pulled the order to view, already a seriously damaged piece of cardboard, and examined it. "Yes, that's right. You're Sid Smith, right enough. I thought you was. I said to myself as I was speaking, I said: 'Either that's Sid Smith or it's the devil.'"

"Might be both," said Sid, brightly.

"Excuse me, sir, but I should like to shake your hand. No offence."

A weak grasp; and as the caretaker waggled Sid's hand he looked up naïvely into Sid's face. Sid was highly pleased by this encounter with one of his million admirers; it seemed to certify his position in the world, and he was glad that by so simple an act he could give such keen pleasure to a common mortal.

"Well, that's done," muttered the caretaker, casually, and dropped Sid's hand as though he was letting something fall on the floor.

Sid began to think that he might have something to learn about real caretakers; they appeared to be more subtle and more mysterious than he had supposed.

* * * *

But it was on the first floor, in the huge imposing double drawing-room, that the caretaker revealed himself fully as a true character. Sid Smith had never seen such a spacious apartment in a private house. He tried to imagine himself giving a Sunday-night party in it; and he could not, or hardly. He feared that he would feel a self-conscious fool in it, and he was quite sure that his stolid wife would.

"Aye!" said the real caretaker. "Well may yer look scared!"

"Scared! What do you mean, my good man?"

"Scared!" the caretaker repeated, grimly now. "Of course I know as you music-hall swells make pots o' money. But what I say is—what d'ye do with it? Do you save it? No! I've had my eye on you swells for many a year, and when yer retire from the grease-paint and footlights, how many of ye is there as don't have to have a benefit to keep 'em out of the workhouse? Only one as I can remember, and I've had my eye on yer. Only one. What does a man like you want with a house like this? This house takes some keeping up, this house does. Lease seven, fourteen, or twenty-one years, and in three years *you* might be flat on yer beam-ends. Supposing yer had a stroke!"

The great Sid Smith might have been flabbergasted had he been less great than he in fact was. He remained calm and massive.

"My friend," said he, pushing his hat to the back of his head, "do you make any charge for these sermons?"

"A silver collection at the door," the real caretaker replied.

("Not a bad line, that!" Mr. Sid Smith reflected, wondering how he could best bring it into his sketch. "Not at all a bad line.")

"And should *you* know how to slang a butler?" the real caretaker continued. "Why, a gent of your sort wouldn't dare to wipe his nose in front of a butler. You take my advice, Mr. Smith, and don't take this here house, nor no house round about here. Bloomsbury's more in your line. But Lowndes Street—I don't think!"

"You come out of an asylum, my man?" asked Sid Smith, assuming that he had to do with a lunatic.

"Not lately," said the caretaker. "But *you* ought to be in one if you're set on this house. If you're only wasting my time, that's all right. I've got lots of time. I've got all the time there is in the world. Like to see the second floor?"

Sid Smith did not lack courage nor physical strength, and he was twenty years younger than the caretaker; so he bravely asserted that he would see the second floor. He saw the second, third, and fourth floors, and then saw them all again in the reverse order. Back in the echoing hall once more, the caretaker, who had been silent down eighty-nine stairs, remarked:

"Of course, yer'd have to put house telephones in on every floor. Never keep modern skivvies with all them floors unless ye have telephones to save 'em a-running up and a-running down. See what I mean?"

"Yes, I see," Sid agreed, blandly. "What I don't see is how you keep your job as a caretaker."

"Oh, well," said the caretaker, "don't you go and let worrying about that spoil yer show to-night, Mr. Smith."

"And the basement?" Sid suggested.

"Eh, I'm not forgetting the basement. You come down along o' me and mind the steps. They're dark, and they're hard on yer spine if yer slip."

The basement seemed endless to Sid Smith, and full of marvels. The wine-cellar! The strong-room for plate! The butler's pantry! The butler's bedroom!

"And there's something here," said the caretaker, "as yer wouldn't find in another house in Lowndes Street, and that's a servants' bathroom. When yer ring for yer butler and he doesn't come, ye'll know he's having his bath with verbena bath-salts."

The servants' bathroom was a daylightless cubicle beyond the scullery. The geyser was in the scullery, and in the dividing wall was a little hole with a shutter like a theatre gallery ticket-office, through which the occupant of the bathroom, by means of his bare arm, could manipulate the geyser in the scullery: an ingenious arrangement.

"A bit dark here," said Sid Smith in the bathroom.

"Yes, and it'll get darker soon," said the caretaker, slamming the door and locking it from the outside.

"Here!" cried Sid Smith, who was a prisoner.

"Here and there!" retorted the caretaker, and his face showed itself to Sid on the scullery side of the little aperture. "So you're the man as libels and slanders us caretakers!" He grinned fiercely at Sid. "I've seen yer sketch all right. I know all about it. We pinch things, we caretakers, do us? We bully young women, do us? We blackmail people, do us? We lock people up in rooms, do us, and take money to let 'em out again, do us? All that's in your sketch. Here, caretaking's my trade, and as honest as any and more honest than most; and yer make yer blooming living by holding us up to shame and scorn twice every night. What d'yer think ye are? A man? Yes, and speaking of locking people up in rooms, well, us *do* lock people up in rooms—bathrooms as it happens. And so now ye know it!"

The real caretaker walked deliberately away, and Sid could hear his heavy, slow footsteps resounding through the kitchen and the passages.

"Here!" cried Sid again.

No answer. Not a sound!

An impossible situation! The victim of it was obliged to admit that in his sketch he had drawn a much truer character of a caretaker than he suspected. In fact, the reality surpassed his wildest notions of it.

He struck a match and peered at his watch. In half an hour he would be due at the Victoria Empire. At this point he lost his head and began to thump and kick. But in and out of his resentful fury ran the tiny thought that there might be some justice in the caretaker's complaint. He *had* traduced the great race of caretakers! And herein was the explanation of the queer, dangerous old man's supposed madness.

V

However, therein was not the explanation of the queer, dangerous old man's supposed madness. For after what seemed to be an interminable interval, during which Sid had burnt his last match in consulting his watch, and was obliged to hold it at arm's length through the aperture to take advantage of the scullery light, the caretaker returned, and, having snatched the watch and chain out of Sid's startled hand, uttered these memorable words:

"And there's one more thing, mister. You've insulted my granddaughter."

"Insulted your granddaughter! I've never set eyes on her."

"Yes, you have. A nice remark to pass to a respectable young woman— telling her that getting her lines out of her's like drawing teeth out of a cow! And on top o' that yer give her notice!"

Sid Smith caught his breath as a blinding illumination came upon him.

"Are—are—are you the great Macdoodle?"

For answer the caretaker (who was not a real caretaker after all) pulled off a wig.

"Here. Take your watch, Mr. Smith," said he, in a new, dignified voice, ceasing to act.

"This is a have!" exclaimed Sid.

"You may call it that."

"I shall put the law on you—shutting me up like this!"

"If I were you, I shouldn't, Mr. Smith. Because if you do it will all come out what I did it for, and everybody'll know that you bully young women, and what sort of language you use to them. You wouldn't care for that. And here is my granddaughter come to see why you're staying here so late. It seems you told pretty well everybody where you were going to-day!"

Nella Nora had followed her ancestor into the scullery. She positively exuded pertness.

"Do let him out, grandad!" she laughed. "He'll be late."

"Well, I will, to please you, my dear, and so that the public shan't be disappointed. It's the public I always think of first. But he must apologize. See how nice and kind and forgiving she is!" he added to Sid Smith. "And you'll withdraw the notice you gave her, won't you? I'm sure you will."

Behind Nella there appeared a very fat, slatternly woman, the real caretaker this time. The old comedian gave her a ten-shilling note. And Sid Smith having been set free, gave her another ten-shilling note. And then Sid Smith burst into laughter, long and free.

"May I ask what you are laughing at, Mr. Smith?"

"Myself," replied Sid Smith, when he had recovered his composure. "And may I add one thing? You *are* the great Macdoodle—you've proved it."

They shook hands. Sid took Nella Nora swiftly off in a taxi to the Victoria Empire.

CLARIBEL

I

CLARIBEL FROSSACK, after attending a rather late tea-party at the flat of her only friend in Paris, an American widow named Sonnenschein, was returning home on foot along the Boulevard du Montparnasse on an evening in October. A tall, well-made, nice-looking blonde girl, tremendously English, with big bones and a good stride to her gait, she officially gave her age as thirty, and her face was a fair confirmation of the statement. The expression on her features was sometimes bright and sometimes overcast, according to her varying attitude towards the phenomena which she encountered; but a sanguine cheerfulness predominated. Her hat and coat were splashed with vivid crimson—the innocent, unconscious signal of the maiden to whomever it might concern.

Rain began to fall, and, in falling, to shape her destiny. She was rather beautifully dressed, with all the skill and sense which she had industriously acquired in six months of Paris. Some years earlier she would have enjoyed and scorned the rain, but she had replaced the physical ideals of her athletic, sporting youth by quite other ideals; she took scrupulous care of her clothes, and even of her complexion, with an anxiety which would have earned merely the contempt of her old self. The sky had given everybody in Paris good notice of a change, but Claribel had ignored it, from a certain vagueness of mind; and she had no umbrella. There was no taxi in sight. Trams and motor-buses there were; Claribel, however, had not the courage and decision to try to halt them in their implacable progress, nor did she know where they were going. Moreover, they were all suddenly full.

Putting her trust in the reputation of the Parisian climate, she hoped that the rain would soon cease, unaware that in Paris the rain is capable of raining for three days and three nights without a moment's mercy. And she was optimistic about a taxi, unaware that a sharp shower will miraculously empty every street in Paris of plying taxis. Opposite the Montparnasse station an empty taxi passed her. She timidly hailed it. The driver, with an odious grin, sneered at her simplicity and held his rapid course.

The rain was now pouring down. A serious crisis was at hand in the history of Claribel's attire and complexion. The famous and vast Café de

Versailles was in front of her, with its covered *terrasse* full of occupied chairs and tables, and its white-flowing waiters. She hesitated. She certainly could not sit out on the *terrasse*; such a proceeding was in her opinion utterly impossible for an unaccompanied girl. But might she not go inside? She had never been in a *café* alone. There is probably not a more decorous public resort on earth than the old-established Café de Versailles. Yet Claribel feared lest terrible things might happen to her if she entered it. She was a solitary creature, wistful, undecided—she felt as though all Paris was leagued against her friendless, unsupported self. Then, between the rain on one side and the glances of the quizzing people of the *terrasse* on the other, she nerved herself to a frightful, perilous resolve, and strode with beating heart and the most absurd bounce into the crowded interior. Inside she took a long breath.

The first thing she clearly saw was a young man standing up and smiling and bowing to her—with much deference. She blushed a little, just as though she had been caught in a questionable act.

"Just my luck!" she thought, scared. Like everybody else, when anything untoward happened to her, she imagined that her luck was as a rule worse than other people's. However, he was a very nice young man, whose ingenuous face and dark, lustrous, wistful eyes she well remembered.

"I came to one of your At Homes," he explained himself. "A friend of mine brought me—François Polin. We'd been shopping together. My name's Arroll."

One of her At Homes! Well, she had had two, and the guests had been almost exclusively her various professors, who taught her French, Italian, music, painting. François Polin was her piano-instructor. She was ashamed of her two miserable fiascos of At Homes.

"Yes," said she. "James Arroll, and he introduced you as 'Jimmie.'"

"It's awfully nice of you to remember me," said Jimmie, obviously pleased that this tall, opulent powerful, rather imposing lady did remember his timid little self.

The *café* was very full. Claribel looked about vaguely for a free table, and saw none.

"Will you sit here—if you don't mind sharing a table?"

"If you're sure *you* don't mind."

"I should simply love it," said Jimmie, eagerly.

She sat down by him, feeling adventurous, imperilled, and exalted in spirit. She suddenly loved life; her face shone. Then of course she had to account for her entrance into the *café*. Naturally a fib came first into her mind. She had to meet a friend—a girl, oh, a girl! The friend wouldn't arrive, and the explanation of her absence would be the downpour. Somewhat clumsy. The truth was simpler, and she told the truth, brushing drops of rain off her shoulders as it were in corroboration of her story.

"I came," said Jimmie, "because it was too dark even to draw—bad gas, you know. I usually draw a bit when my painting's done. But I get lonely, and then I have to go out. Paris is fearfully lonely."

"Oh, it *is*!" she agreed with strong sympathetic emotion. She had always assumed that men were never lonely. They were free, with a free code, and they picked up acquaintances easily; they understood and trusted one another; they were all freemasons together. She thought of her desolating loneliness in Paris and liked Jimmie tremendously for being lonely. His admission gave her ease.

* * * *

A waiter stood in front of her.

"May I—?" Jimmie began.

She cut him short by ordering tea. Jimmie was having a bock. All around people were drinking coloured and exciting liquids out of various shapes of glasses. She would have loved to drink something dangerous out of a glass, but her upbringing compelled her to keep within a traditional respectability; besides, she would not have known what to order.

She was now sufficiently composed to examine the *café*. She adored its foreignness, its stuffy smell, the click of billiard balls far, far up the great room, the flowing gestures of the waiter as he deposed the shiny tea-things on the marble, the murmur of strange tongues, the perpendicular rain through the glass walls, the constant swishing of the revolving doors, the ring of checks on the cashier's counter, the occasional sharp cry of some impatient little bearded customer, the newspapers furled on sticks, the dominoes, the chess, the writing of letters on vile blotting-pads. Enchantment!

"Quite a number of Germans here now," observed Jimmie.

"Yes," she said, cautiously hostile.

"I think it's rather a good thing," Jimmie continued. "Of course, it's unpleasant in a way, and you wonder how they have the nerve; but it gets people used to what they've got to get used to sooner or later. They can't go on hating and sulking for ever. Of course I don't know, but that's how it seems to me." He gave a little nervous laugh.

This piece of political wisdom greatly astonished Claribel, for two reasons. First, because it had issued from the almost babyish mouth of one whom she had supposed to be interested solely in the arts—and here he was taking notice of the great world and thinking for himself internationally; he had ideas! And secondly, his ideas were so at variance with those with which she was familiar. Germans had not many years since killed her only brother, and killed her brother-in-law—both professional soldiers. The people whom she knew in England never discussed Germans, save in regard to their brilliant military qualities. Germans had to exist, but they must be ignored as human beings; they were outside the pale. Certainly it was like their unspeakable nerve to force themselves on Paris; but they were Germans, and there was nothing to be said—though much to be suffered in silence. And Jimmie was accepting them with calm, unprejudiced, far-seeing satisfaction. It was a feat on his part.

"Oh, I quite agree," she said, warmly.

The curious thing was that she did agree. And she was aware in herself of an accession of wisdom and broadmindedness.

Further, she admired the baby James. He was assuredly not of her class, which had owned land and hunted and shot and stuck animals and men for centuries; he did not wear a club-necktie, though he wore a necktie which reminded her of the sacred scarf of the Eton Wanderers; he had obviously never been to a public school. But his manners were nevertheless perfect; and he was not dull, as she and hers were; and his mind was free and easy and alert and not afraid of new notions; and his accent was faultless. She admitted that his clothes might have shocked her males; his hair, too, not to mention his dark, lustrous eyes.

"It was so beautiful it made me cry," he was saying, the conversation having shifted from politics to river landscapes.

Not a man of hers but would have killed himself rather than confess to such a weakness! Then there was an interruption. Customers were looking with hope into the street. A few departed; a few more departed. The rain had ceased. Claribel must go. She would have liked to stay; she hated to go. But she must go. She simply could not be free. She had sheltered from the rain; the rain was over; there was no reason for staying. True, neither was there any reason for going, for she had no appointment and naught to do. Still, she must go. She paid—no silly attempt on Jimmie's part to settle for her tea—and she went. Jimmie also paid and went; and he put her into a taxi. No suggestion about meeting again. He said not a word. And she could not.

* * * *

Fate, however, had Claribel's affairs in hand. Its method of action was violent but effective. Another taxi, turning the corner, as Paris taxis will, on the wrong side of the road out of the Rue de Rennes, caught the bonnet of Claribel's taxi before the latter had moved a dozen yards, and, in addition to putting it out of action, gave Claribel a shaking in body and mind. A small crowd, a policeman, an altercation between two vituperative chauffeurs, a trunk in the roadway, note-taking by the policeman! The rain then sharply resumed its baptismal work and did something to tranquillize the fever of men.

"Excuse me. Hadn't you better come back inside again?"

It was Jimmie, who had apparently witnessed the accident from afar and returned.

"Oh, no. I'm perfectly all right," said Claribel, in a voice rendered loud by excitement.

"You look rather pale. I think—"

"Very well, I will," she agreed. She did feel a little unsteady. The policeman detained her a moment; Jimmie talked to him; and then they re-entered the *café*.

"I'm awfully sorry," said Jimmie.

They sat down.

"I think you'd better have some brandy," said Jimmie.

She yielded to his caprice. She did not need the brandy, but she found pleasure in obeying his suggestion. As soon as he had ordered the cognac she suspected that perhaps she did need it, and after drinking it she had an idea that she might have fainted without it. They discussed the accident, and the naughtiness of French taxi-drivers, at great length.

The *café* was now becoming a restaurant. Waiters covered table after marble table with white linen, and the white linen with cruets and cutlery. Odours multiplied; warmth increased; the place grew even cosier, homelier, more congenial; it proved itself the resort of a race that understood the art of living.

"I think I shall stick here for dinner," said Claribel, with a sudden audacity that rather frightened her.

"I wish *I* could," said Jimmie. "But it's too dear for me. I eat at a pension-restaurant. If I wasn't so frightfully poor I should have ventured to ask you to dine with me." He spoke quite simply, neither ashamed nor defiant, and he gave her the sweetest smile.

"But you can't leave me," said she, with a flash of the imperiousness of the governing class. "You must dine with *me*, of course."

"Well," said he, "I won't be silly about it. It's awfully nice of you to ask me."

His tone was faultless. Claribel thought he was out of sight the most sensible young man she had ever met. She imagined how any young man of her own set in England would have bridled and jibbed and blushed and protested under such an invitation—and ended by accepting it!

They dined—slowly, savouringly, and towards the close of the meal lusciously. Years seemed to have passed since Claribel first entered the adorable Café de Versailles. And it had been raining for years. Existence was transformed for Claribel. The pall of loneliness had been lifted from her. She formed part of humanity; she had a contact. Not ordinarily a facile talker, especially with mere acquaintances, she was now talking with marked ease. Jimmie talked without any effort. He was a natural talker, and he talked naturally. He seemed to say whatever came into his mind, but his mind was an interesting mind and a nice mind—no necessity to filter or censor its contents before letting them forth!

At intervals, in pauses of argument, Jimmie would point out celebrities or notorieties among the customers. Possibly not notables of the world, but notables of the Montparnasse quarter, which honestly considered itself the centre of the world.

The ornate clock over the cashier's counter behaved in an extraordinary manner; its fingers raced round the dial. Claribel tried to will them into deliberateness, but they would not be restrained. They showed twenty-five minutes to twelve when the other clock, in Claribel's head, said that the hour could not be later than twenty-five minutes to ten. An evening unlike any other evening that ever was in Paris or in paradise!

Just as Claribel was beginning to make a successful fight against the mysterious magnetic force which held her to her chair and absolutely prevented her from rising to depart—the bill had long ago, through Jimmie's agency, been paid and the change handed over and the tip given—Psichari came up, on his way out of the *café*. Psichari was one of the celebrities already indicated to Claribel by Jimmie. Claribel had felt an artistic thrill at being even in the same *café* with Psichari. You could tell how great a painter Psichari was in Paris by the fact that Jimmie blushed when he most surprisingly stopped at the table, and rose with much deferential ceremony to greet him.

"Present me," murmured the handsome, bearded hero of the studios in an undertone. And he was duly presented to Claribel. Thereupon he sat down at the table, and talked in French.

"You will pardon me, mademoiselle, but I have not been able to prevent myself from regarding you all the evening. You are so exquisitely an English type. It is so romantic to me. No women exist save the English. There are none save the English."

Still, in a more general vein, he talked admirably—better than Jimmie. Claribel, however, was now restless—pleased, but confused and apprehensive. She said that she must leave. And she did leave, escorted to the pavement by the two men. The rain continued with infinite strong perseverance to descend in generous cascades. Claribel got into a taxi, and, while Jimmie was giving the address to the driver, Psichari also got into the taxi. He was not intoxicated—or at least he was not suffering from anything more deleterious than the romantical quality of Claribel's blonde English appearance; but he was uplifted. He stated in an uplifted voice that it would not be safe for Miss Frossack to travel home unaccompanied. Claribel glanced with a certain appeal at Jimmie. Jimmie seized the great painter first by one arm and then by two, and pulled him out of the cab. The two men, Psichari taller than Jimmie and ten years older, faced each other on the pavement.

"*Fiche-nous la paiz!*" Jimmie exhorted the celebrity.

And as Psichari would not listen to the exhortation to leave them in peace, Jimmie hit him on the chest, and the idol of Montparnasse subsided on to the pavement. Jimmie nipped into the taxi, which drove off.

Little was said, but the cave-woman in Claribel could not sleep that night because she had been fought for by two artists on the Parisian pavement; and the English girl in Claribel could not sleep because the delicious Jimmie had asked her to sit for him and she had consented to do so.

The next really thrilling thing that happened to her was the arrival, one evening, of an express letter, which ran: "May I call to-night about nine? I want very much to see you about a matter which is important to me.—Your devoted Jimmie."

Claribel blushed and shook. She blushed and shook all by herself in her own drawing-room.

II

On the morning of the day on which Claribel received the express note from Jimmie in the late afternoon, she had been sitting for him in his studio in the Rue Léopold Robert, a street south of Montparnasse and plenteously inhabited by Anglo-Saxon youths of both sexes of a status similar to that of James Arroll. It was the final sitting for the portrait, and nearly three months had passed since the great scenes inside and outside the Café de Versailles. Claribel had just gone, and Jimmie was still watching her as she primly and brightly descended the four double flights of stairs that separated his lair from the solid earth, when he heard footsteps above him. A figure was coming down from the heights of the fifth storey—a young man dressed in golden brown, very baggy corduroys, heavy boots, a black wide-awake hat with a circumference of about one yard, and a muffler that seemed like a slice off a blanket. The ferocity of the black moustache argued, perhaps falsely, that the hip-pocket held a revolver to match it. Of course, an English painter; French and other painters no longer wore the classic uniform of art.

"Josh!" called Jimmie, shivering in the icy January draughts of the staircase. "Come in and have a look at this blessed thing I've just finished."

"Thy wildest caprice is an order. Let her loose," replied Josh, entering with a swagger the large, naked, and dirty studio of his friend. He examined Claribel's portrait with a lofty and judicial air for an extraordinarily long time. Then, in silence, he went and poked the stove, and then he examined the portrait again.

"Look here, brother," said he, at last. "What in the name of the late esteemed Lord Leighton have you been trying to get at?"

"Don't you like it?"

"Rotten!" said the critic. "Rotten! It's all over the place. It isn't like anything on earth."

"I feared it," murmured Jimmie, with submission.

"You don't mean to tell me you have the nerve to like it yourself?"

"Frankly, I don't. But she does."

"Oh, she does, does she? Well, that settles it. They never like anything but the completely putrid."

"But really she isn't quite the—"

"Silence, sir!" the bandit stopped him. "If you're thinking of informing me that she's subtly different from all other girls, think better of it and don't. Because I doubt if our friendship would stand it. No girl is different from all other girls. And when she says she likes this portrait, she simply and unaffectedly means that she likes *you*. Have I lived, or was I born this morning?"

"That's where you're wrong, Josh. She may be a bad critic, but there's no nonsense about her of that sort. She's even cold. You can talk to her just as if she was a man."

"And you do?"

"I do."

"Laddie, you must introduce me to her. It will be the day of my life. I bid you good morning."

"I say," said Jimmie, timidly, to Josh in the doorway. "You might let me doss in your studio to-morrow night."

"Not on your life!" said Josh. "I have other arrangements in view. Why?"

"The landlord was here at eight-fifteen to-day. I owe him two quarters and I can't pay. He's given me till to-morrow."

"The dirty dog!" exclaimed Josh, with feeling, the basis of his philosophy of existence being the axiom that all persons not painters ought to be willing and proud to be owed money by all painters.

"I haven't had my supplies from London, and I shan't have just yet, and it's six months since I sold a thing," Jimmie explained, gloomily.

"Serious, eh?"

"Yes."

"Then sell a thing at once. Sell her this portrait. From the look of her raiment, wealth is not what she's short of."

"Oh, she's rich all right," said Jimmie, "but I couldn't possibly ask her to buy this."

"Why not?"

"Because it's not good enough."

"What an ass of a reason! Unload the bad, my excellent fool. Unload, I say. If *I* do anything decent I always want to keep it. Besides, there are 'passages,' as we critics say, in this that aren't positively criminal. I don't mind stating that the hair is the best bit of pure painting you ever did. But the rest—oh, Mohammed and Buddha!"

Jimmie shook his head.

"No. I won't do it."

"Then touch her for a thousand francs. Tell her she's helping the sacred cause. She'd love to lend it to you."

Jimmie coloured slightly.

"I was wondering whether I might ask her. But she's so jolly decent I don't really care to take advantage—" He gave a nervous laugh.

"Well I beg leave to say no more. She has the stuff. You want it. Which is the same as saying she has your future and you want it. Ask her to lend you a thousand francs, and report to me to-night or to-morrow morning, if you please. And have a care!"

Josh stalkingly departed.

After some hours of mental travail, Jimmie brought himself to the point of telephoning to Claribel about money, from a *café*. She was not at home. Then he dispatched the express note, to which he received an answer at seven o'clock: "Delighted to see you. Nine o'clock.—C. F."

III

Claribel put the little blue note from Jimmie away, with several other specimens of his handwriting, at the back of a drawer in her dressing-table. Then she pulled it out and read it again and replaced it in the drawer. And all this in the middle of her dressing! And, further, she was dressing after dinner, not before it. She was dressing all over afresh, in the light of her beautiful bedroom lamps and of the note, which had arrived after her first evening dressing.

She was far gone in love with Jimmie. Jimmie was unlike any other man she had ever known, and especially unlike the men of her own tribe. She admired these men, in a fashion, but how dull and narrow and rigid and incurious they were in their subconscious self-satisfaction and their dependable honesty! Jimmie had dependable honesty, too, but what a different, what a superior and finer mind! Of course, he was five years younger than herself, but did that matter? Besides, she had frankly told him her age—after he had guessed twenty-seven; and he did not seem to mind in the least. She knew him now, at the end of twenty-five or thirty sittings; she knew him through and through; and he was sound through and through. And she had decided that he was, or would be, a great painter—no doubt the greatest painter of the age. He had taught her an immense amount about life and art and Paris and the European outlook and such things. Indeed he was a Titan. Yet not on these counts did she adore him. She adored him because he had fought for her on the pavement in front of the Café de Versailles, and because he had such dark, lustrous wistful eyes, and such an appealing voice and such gentle gestures, and because he was a baby. Strange that he could be at once a Titan and a baby. But so it was. He had no more notion of looking after himself than a baby.

And if he had taught her, she had taught him. She had softened some crudities and she had shown him what a woman thinks, and how and why. And he had learnt eagerly and thankfully.

* * * *

Her maid (French) now came in.

"Monsieur Arroll."

"A little moment," said Claribel. "Arrange me this tulle, Louise."

She was agitated—and for an excellent reason. She was convinced in her heart that Jimmie had come to ask her to marry him, and she very well knew that she would not refuse him. She had noticed the frequent tendernesses in his voice, the admiration in his eyes, the shy hesitations in his adoring demeanour. At least once, she judged, he had been on the very edge of a proposal in his studio, but timidity had held him back. She could not be mistaken. In half an hour, in an hour, she would be an engaged girl, with vistas of thrilling happiness stretching before her.

Fortunately she was under no obligation to consult anybody. She had no ties; she had full control of her own plenteous money. Imagine having to obtain consent to marry a painter from one of those queer, good, misguided persons who had given her the ridiculous name of Claribel—after some ridiculous poem of Tennyson's! Awful!

She passed shaking into the drawing-room, Louise following her as far as the bedroom door with pats and smoothings of her skirt. She stood hesitant, frightened and blissful in the doorway, showing herself for admiration, at her very best; not offering herself, but expecting to be demanded. She smiled exquisitely, and her lower lip trembled. Nothing of the outdoor athletic girl in her now! She was the indoor, the boudoir girl, richly attired—moulded and prepared for love. She made a splendid vision in the luxurious, luminous drawing-room.

And there stood Jimmie, somewhat threadbare in his neat lounge-suit. Might he not be disconcerted, impeded, by her luxury, by the economic difference between them? Not he! He had a mind above such accidents of fortune. He had genius, outweighing any quantity of money; and moreover, like all artists, he had a taste for luxury—could not resist it.

They sat down. She noticed that he was just as nervous as she was, and this lessened her own nervousness and gave her confidence.

"I'm so glad you've come," she said, brightly "because I wanted to ask you something."

"Yes?"

"I want you to let me buy that portrait. I should have mentioned it this morning, but I felt a bit awkward about it."

"I'm glad you didn't," said Jimmie. "And I'm sorry you mentioned it now. Because I don't want to part with it."

"Why not?" She asked the question, but she knew the answer. He wished not to part with it because he felt the absolute necessity of having her reminding portrait in his studio. Still she repeated, "Why not?"

"It's not good enough," said Jimmie. "I don't like it well enough to let it go."

"But, Jimmie, I've set my heart on having it. I think it's simply beautiful."

Jimmie shook his head. "No, I must be firm about that." His voice sounded hard to her. He added: "May I tell you right out what I've come for? I want—"

The fatal words were on the very edge of his lips when he stopped and jumped up. Claribel was crying; she was sobbing. His attitude concerning the portrait, acting on her extremely excited nerves, had overset her. She was perhaps quite as startled by the tears as himself. But there they were! And Jimmie was gravely disturbed. He was absurdly disturbed. For it is a remarkable fact that, though a woman's tears mean vastly less than a man's, her—shall we call it?—effervescing point being much lower than a man's, a young man will treat those tears just as seriously as if he had shed them himself.

Jimmie thought it was his duty somehow to stanch them; but he could not devise any method of doing so. And he was aware of remorse. Also he saw the utter impossibility of asking her for a loan. Indeed, the situation was excessively delicate and demanded for its handling all the experienced, wise, diplomatic ingenuity of a man of the world. And Jimmie knew too well that he was by no means a man of the world.

He merely hovered around the fount of tears in a state of rather silly indecision, suffering acutely from the shock which always accompanies an increase of knowledge of the baffling psychology of women. At the same time his emotions were not wholly unpleasant. He actually enjoyed the spectacle of her woe. The tears softened her. They gave her a touch of "nonsense" which hitherto, according to Jimmie's observation, she had lacked. They indicated to him that never in the future could he talk to her as to another man. Formerly he liked her because she could be treated as a male comrade. Now he liked her rather more because she had suddenly ceased to be a male comrade. Her tears melted her, and they melted him too.

As for Claribel, what she chiefly felt was resentment and disillusion. And she also enjoyed her tears. Then she remembered her Spartan youth, and with a heroical effort resumed command of herself. And then she opened her bag and began to rebuild her damaged complexion. Never in the old days would she have put powder to her face in the presence of a man. But things were changed. Neither of them spoke a word. It was most ridiculous. Jimmie sat down again.

At length he said:

"I'm awfully sorry. You shall have the portrait."

She looked at the radiator, there being no fire.

"But, of course," he added, "I shall give it to you. I really couldn't take anything for it."

Whereat she sobbed once more.

"Can't you see I can't accept presents from you?" she mumbled, inarticulately.

"I beg pardon," said he, comprehending nothing.

She made a new attempt.

"I say it's fearfully nice of you, but I can't accept presents from you."

"Then I'll sell it to you at any price you like," he yielded, beaten.

But she continued to weep and to mumble.

"I know what a genius you are, and I wanted to be able to say I'd bought a picture from you when you were unknown." And more loudly and distinctly: "However, it doesn't matter!"

Jimmie stood up again. He wanted to cry himself for she had become to him the most touching and heavenly sight ever seen in the world. She had become exquisite, fragile, defenceless, and desirable. Simultaneously it occurred to him that in certain circumstances there is only one right method of stanching a woman's tears. He used that method.

* * * *

The mayor of the sixth arrondissement, with the French flag tied round his rich waist, united them in marriage. Claribel never knew that, had she begun to weep five seconds later than she did, the direction of her whole life would have been changed, for her sentiments would never have survived the blow of being asked for money when she was expecting to be asked for love. And Jimmie's heart would stop beating at the mere awful recollection of the moment when her tears in the nick of time saved him from stepping over a precipice into—into what?

TIME TO THINK

I

A LARGE car stopped outside one of the narrow entrances (Nos. 172-216) to a very large block of very small flats near Chelsea Bridge. The chauffeur got swiftly out and opened the door of the car, and at precisely the same moment an extremely beautiful girl, dressed richly in white satin, with tulle and certain blossoms which indicate the imminence of a certain ceremony, tripped down the narrow, steep, curving stone steps from an upper storey of the block and, bending her head, stepped into the car and laughed lightly; and the chauffeur shut the door on her laugh, and the car shot away towards the West-end, where it belonged.

A triumph of accurate organization, for a girl in Enid Ledburn's situation, to vanish from a building occupied by several hundreds of persons passionately curious concerning the private affairs of their neighbours, without arousing the least interest! Such a triumph could only have been accomplished by individuals who knew how to keep themselves to themselves and who were thoroughly accustomed to the idea and the discipline of time.

"Alf, you're wonderful!" said the girl.

There was a man in the car, a man of about thirty-eight years, fifteen years older than the girl. Enid was referring to Alf's clothes, which were undeniably wonderful, from the Malmaison in the buttonhole and the white slip in the waistcoat to the white spats over the patent-leather boots and the podgy white gloves at the end of the long arms. Alfred Ledburn indeed was more than wonderful; he was rather too wonderful. Alfred looked just like a shop-walker at Prim's Stores, arrayed even more superbly than usual for a special occasion. And this was not surprising, for Alfred was in fact a shop-walker at Prim's renowned stores, arrayed for a special occasion.

"Did Val want to pay for them?" the girl asked.

"He did, but of course I wouldn't have it."

"I told him you never would," said the girl in a firm tone.

"To tell you the truth, girlie, the under-manager of the men's department's a friend of mine, and he fixed me at a special discount, and it's all as good as there is. And what's more, he thinks he can take the suit back if it's pressed properly. You look a bit of all right."

"Oh, I'm all right!" the girl agreed, with confident conviction.

And she in fact was, being a saleswoman at Karkeek's, one of the most fashionable firms for women's attire in Regent Street, an establishment not one-twentieth of the size of Prim's, but twenty times smarter and more exclusive.

"Of course Val will have the bills for this lot," said the girl smiling contentedly.

"Naturally." A pause. Alfred looked at his watch. "We're in good time—and not too early."

They were. And this was not surprising either, for both brother and sister had had to "clock in" of a morning and "clock out" of an evening for years.

"This his best car or his second best?" Alfred asked.

"Well, which do you think it is?"

"If it's his second best the best must be some car."

"It's neither. It's mine. It's one of his presents. He only told me last night at the Savoy."

Mr. Alfred Ledburn merely raised his eyebrows and whistled.

At two-thirty precisely by the clock in the tower of the church of St. Agnes, Mr. Alfred Ledburn handed his sister out of the car, and arm-in-arm they passed over red cloth, under a striped awning, between two thick walls of people addicted to the spectacle of the greatest of all human institutions, into the fashionable fane. Enid's extraordinary exquisite dark beauty—what large glittering eyes, what black eyelashes and eyebrows, what curves of the lip!—caused necks to crane, and mouths to open and even to ejaculate words of amazement. But both Alfred and Enid were thoroughly used to the public gaze; Alfred addressed thousands of strangers, and Enid some scores or hundreds, every week. Their deportment on the red cloth was perfect in ease and correctness. The Press photographers, victims of routine, saved their plates for the ceremonial exit of bride and bridegroom, and foolishly ignored the brother and sister.

II

Almost at the same moment as Enid's wedding car was leaving the neighbourhood of Chelsea Bridge another car was leaving a house in Hyde Park Gardens. It held two men, Mr. Valentine Porter, of the same age as Alfred Ledburn, and his brother Rudolph, a little the senior of Enid Ledburn.

"I hope she won't keep us waiting. They generally do," said young Rudolph, full of the worries of a best man.

"She will not," replied his elder. "She won't keep us waiting at all. On the other hand, she won't make us look awkward by getting there first."

"Why, she's unique, then!"

"Well, she is. And if you'd left New York last month as you said you would you'd have had more opportunities of judging her. Have you got the ring in your pocket?"

"What a question! Many men have been killed at dawn for a less insult than that."

"Sorry!"

"If you want to know, I've got two rings, one in each pocket. Do you suppose I've never been a best man before?"

"You'll like Enid," said the bridegroom.

"I *do* like her, you idiot."

"You'll like her more and more. She'll appeal to you. She's so practical. She thinks of everything. She's never at a loss."

"You call her practical. I should call her lovely."

"She's the most beautiful girl in London."

"Well, there are lots of girls in London, but I shouldn't be surprised if she is."

"She *is*. Everybody says so. But if she hadn't had character, do you suppose I should have looked twice at her?"

"Yes, I do suppose you'd have looked twice at her."

"I shouldn't have married her, anyway."

"You said you met her first in the shop?"

"Yes. I happened to go in there with Rebecca. What a bit of luck! You know, sonnie, those shop people know a thing or two about things. It's a terrific education being in a shop. And if it's a good shop like Karkeek's, they learn style. Enid would be equal to anything."

"She'll have her work cut out, being the mistress of your modest establishment."

"In a month she'll be doing it as well as the mater ever did. She'll go slow at first. She'll watch and she'll keep her mouth shut until she's got the hang of it. And then she'll act. You'll see. I haven't the slightest fear. It isn't as if I didn't know what marriage is and what women are. Some women can't rise. Some women are born to rise. She's one of the born. And I thank heaven she's not passionate."

"Isn't she? I should have thought she was."

"Well, you're wrong. She isn't temperamental, and I'm glad."

At two-twenty-eight precisely the car stopped gracefully before the porch of the church of St. Agnes. The brothers descended on to the red cloth. The head verger was excessively deferential. In thirty years of professional marrying he had never known such glorious and expensive floral decorations as Mr. Valentine Porter had caused to be provided; and his expectations about tips were enormous.

"I 'ear there's to be no bridesmaids," said a disappointed voice in the crowd.

"She wouldn't have bridesmaids at any price," Val murmured to Rudolph. "She was right."

The brothers walked nervously up the centre aisle of the church, crowded with well-dressed and other persons who had been drawn partly by friendship for the contracting parties, partly by the rumours of a highly romantic marriage, and partly by the rumours of the bride's astonishing beauty. The brothers came to a halt near the altar, within whose railings stood one young clergyman. Then the organ began to breathe o'er Eden, and, looking round, the brothers saw the dazzling advent of the self-possessed bride and her majestic brother.

III

In the back or more recondite parts of the church—and chiefly in the vestry—there was a certain excitement, for the Reverend Johns Marjoribank Banks, rector of the parish of St. Agnes, and chief officiator at the wedding of Valentine George Joachim Porter, member of the Stock Exchange, and Enid Ledburn, spinster, had not appeared. Only his surplice was present. Odd and nondescript people get into vestries on the days of fashionable weddings—friends of the clergy, of the organist, of the choirmaster, and privileged friends of the parties, in addition to minor functionaries of the church itself. All these persons were now becoming feverish, with a tendency to lose their heads. The vestry telephone was working. The vestry clock ticked disturbingly onwards into the future. The sole soothing influence was that of the distant organ. Excuse, however, might well be made for everybody concerned, for assuredly the failure of the rector to arrive punctually for a ceremony so important was utterly unprecedented.

At length—twenty-three minutes to three—the Reverend George Fitch entered the vestry, having quitted his post behind the altar railings; and his departure from the sight of the contracting parties and the crowded congregation produced a commotion in the church even surpassing the commotion in the vestry. A hum of talk arose, and the contracting parties actually spoke to each other—before the commencement of the ceremony—a thing hitherto unknown in the history of marriage-celebration in the Church of England.

"The rector isn't here," explained a sidesman to Mr. Fitch.

"Not here! Impossible!" Mr. Fitch was a tall and vigorous curate, neither dark nor fair, with hazel eyes and a sincere, persuasive manner.

"And we can't get an answer on the telephone, either."

"I'll run round to the rectory myself and see if the rector is unwell or anything," said Mr. Fitch. "I can be back in six minutes, and if necessary I can perform the ceremony myself. It will not be quite the same thing, but it will be just as binding."

He threw off his surplice, seized his broad-brim and almost ran out.

Relief! The rectory was but two minutes distant in Upper Pulteney Street. Then gradually, as the vestry clock ticked on, tension again; tension turning to horror. The verger himself invaded the vestry, gave terrible accounts of the state of affairs in the church, and demanded advice as to the management of hysterical crowds. Someone followed the curate to the rectory, and returned with the news that neither the rector nor the curate was to be found. Somebody else telephoned to the rector's churchwarden, who arrived at eight minutes to three, and, confronted by a unique situation, proved singularly unhelpful. Urgent messages of distress were dispatched for other parsons, as for doctors in a dreadful extremity, but, like doctors, the other parsons were out. By this time the best man had visited the vestry thrice and the bridegroom once.

And then a frightful thing occurred. The great clock of St. Agnes struck three. Now it is well known, and everybody knew, that for some reason, completely baffling to the reason of mankind, no marriage can be celebrated in England after the hour of three o'clock in the afternoon. In the coarse phrase of the verger, the milk was spilt.

News of the calamity spread with fantastic speed. Even the journalists present got hold of it, and scurried away to the offices of their newspapers. The state of the congregation was really alarming—made up as it was of fever, sympathy, resentment, a horrid, inexplicable human joy in the misfortunes of others, and pride at having assisted at a very remarkable event. People spoke of the ruined reception at Claridge's, the unusable seats booked in honeymoon trains, the unluckiness of the mishap, the decadence of the Church of England, and the awful predicament of the poor bride. But the bride was the most composed person in the multitude. For composure she beat the bridegroom easily.

She remarked, calmly:—

"Never mind. It means only a delay of twenty-four hours. Less. Because we can be married at nine o'clock to-morrow."

"But I doubt if I can get off to-morrow," said her brother, for whose convenience the ceremony had been fixed as late as two-thirty that day.

IV

The Reverend Johns Marjoribank Banks lived in a house which was like all the other houses in his street: a costly house, with window-boxes of flowers, a sun-cloth over the front-door, a basement, a butler, several other servants, innumerable stairs, no lift, no central heating, two bathrooms, and a wine-cellar. Mr. Banks enjoyed a stipend of over two thousand a year for spiritually guiding the expensive souls of his wealthy parishioners, and his wife, Lady Sylvia, had considerable money of her own. So that they were able by strict economy to make both ends meet in a showy, earthy world.

Mr. Valentine Porter, severe, was talking to the butler in the narrow hall.

"The fact is, sir, that as soon as Mr. Banks had left for the church, knowing that I should not be wanted for at least half an hour, I stepped out to see some of the wedding myself, having noticed a portrait of your bride-to-be in the paper this morning. You can see the front of the church from the windows here, and I have no doubt that the maids were leaning out of the top-floor window. Perhaps that explains why the telephone was not answered."

"The rector left in the ordinary way for the church?"

"Not quite the ordinary way, sir. He left earlier than I expected. Consequently I was not in the hall to give him his hat."

"But when Mr. Fitch came to fetch him, who opened the door for Mr. Fitch?"

"Mr. Fitch has a latchkey, sir."

"Then no one saw him?"

"I think not, sir. But I've told the police all this, sir."

"Quite. But now you're telling me."

"Yes, sir."

"And you've not seen or heard anything of either the rector or the curate since?"

"No, sir."

"Where is Lady Sylvia?"

"Her ladyship has been away for some days, sir, on a little motor tour."

At this moment a taxi stopped in front of the house, and the butler, neglecting Mr. Valentine Porter, rushed to open the door.

"What's happened, Roberts?" said the rector sharply, stepping in and snatching up a telegram that lay on the hall table.

He was a ruddy, grey-haired, slim man of fifty, with a countenance habituated to authoritative cheerfulness.

"Er—this is Mr. Valentine Porter, sir," replied the butler, cautiously.

"Ah!" the rector greeted Val. "The bridegroom. Yes. I hope everything passed off smoothly. I hope that my curate Fitch officiated to your satisfaction, Mr. Porter."

The rector then heard the truth in the clear, masterful, not quite inoffensive tones of Mr. Porter.

"Great heavens!" exclaimed the rector, calm but shocked. "How dreadful! How dreadful! Really, Mr. Porter, I cannot sufficiently—I cannot sufficiently— Be good enough to step this way." And he led Mr. Porter to the back room on the ground floor. The marrier and the unmarried began to talk coldly, politely, with much admirable restraint. The clock on the mantelpiece struck five.

"Do you mean to say that you haven't seen the newspaper posters?"

"I have not," said the rector.

" 'Strange disappearance of a London rector and his curate.' 'Hitch at a fashionable wedding.' And so on!"

"No."

"Nor seen the police either?"

"I saw the police at Leytonstone."

"At Leytonstone? Why Leytonstone?" Mr. Porter sprang deplorably from his chair.

"Let me explain," said the rector, with tranquillity well maintained. "I was in this room at a quarter-past two this afternoon when the telephone rang. You see the telephone." The rector pointed. "The call was from the police-station at Leytonstone. They said that my wife, Lady Sylvia, had had a very serious accident with her motor in the Lea Bridge Road, and that I had better come at once. My curate, Fitch, was waiting for me in the hall. I told him what had happened, and gave him instructions to perform the ceremony in my absence. We went out together, he put me into a taxi, and I went off instantly to Leytonstone. At the police-station there they denied all knowledge of any accident and assured me that they had not telephoned to me. I thought I must have heard the name wrongly on the telephone. They made various inquiries by telephone, with no result. And after a fruitless search in the Lea Bridge Road I came back home."

"A hoax, then?"

"Certainly. Here is a telegram replying to one I sent to my wife from Leytonstone. She is safe at Winchester."

"But Mr. Fitch told them nothing of this at the church," said Mr. Porter, quite ignoring the glad tidings about Lady Sylvia's safety. "When you didn't arrive he said he would fetch you himself, and since then he's missing."

"It is all most disconcerting. No doubt Fitch lost his head through nervousness at the prospect of having to conduct the ceremony."

"Where does Mr. Fitch live?"

"He has a bedroom here. You see, the Church of England provides very inadequately for her curates, very inadequately, I regret to say, and as a convenience to both of us, and to save him expense, I give him a bedroom upstairs."

"He may be there now!"

Mr. Banks rang the bell. But Mr. Fitch was not in his bedroom, nor anywhere in the rectory.

Both the rector and the still prospective bridegroom were philosophers and had a proper sense of the true relative proportions of things. They therefore arranged the most important matter first: a marriage at ten o'clock the next morning. The rector masterfully charged the bridegroom with all his excuses, sympathies, and condolences to the bride-elect. And at last the police themselves discovered Mr. Banks.

That evening Valentine took Enid to the dinner-dance at the Berkeley Restaurant. And he was very gentle and apologetic. They were not recognized.

"My dearest," he said to her, gently, apologetically, but passionately, "you don't suspect that anybody had any reason for trying to prevent our marriage to-day? Anybody who—er—"

"Not so far as I'm aware, darling," Enid answered placidly. "But of course you can never be sure. More people know me than I know. And I'm so beautiful. Well, I am, aren't I?"

Val thoughtfully agreed, drove her to her flat, where naturally she insisted on spending the night; then he proceeded for the third time that day to Scotland Yard.

V

The frustrated bridegroom had scarcely had time to drive away before Enid heard a knock at her little front-door on the fourth storey of the block. She thought that Val had returned for a last kiss or something less valuable; but the tall form of Mr. George Fitch (curate, though not now in clerical attire) stood in the doorway. There was a silence.

"May I come in?"

Another silence.

"I suppose so."

Mr. Fitch went in. Enid opened another door, and murmured:

"I've got another visitor, Lizzie."

"Oh!" came the low, startled cry of a girl who had been about to enter the tiny sitting-room in a state of undress. Then more composedly: "All right!"

Lizzie was the friend and colleague with whom Enid had been sharing the flat. The frustrated bride shut the door again.

"Sit down, please."

Mr. Fitch sat down, and dropped his hat, which Enid picked up. Mr. Fitch, though he entirely lacked the traditional curate's accent, had a considerable flow of words, and he was soon in full spate.

"Yes," he said, after a few preliminaries. "At first it was deliberate on my part. I did arrange for Mr. Banks to be called away urgently to Leytonstone—on false pretences. Then I repented. In fact, I was in a desperate state of funk because of what I'd done, and I determined that after all I must perform the ceremony myself. But when I saw you and *that man*—"

"What man?"

"Mr. Porter."

"If you meant Mr. Porter, why not have said Mr. Porter?"

"Sorry. When I saw you and Mr. Porter standing together at the altar-rails, I knew that I could never bring myself to marry you to him. Never! I simply couldn't do it And so I ran away. I've been in the parks most of the afternoon and evening, wondering what I ought to do. I decided that I ought to come to you. So I hung about here until Mr. Porter had brought you home and gone again."

"I was sure all the time that you were at the bottom of it all. I must say you make it all sound very ordinary. I expect you think you've done nothing to be ashamed of?"

* * * *

Sarcasm was in her tone, and a troubled fire in her eyes. This was not the placid, lovely girl that Val Porter knew, but a passionate, feverish, lovely creature apparently capable of fearful deeds. She looked magnificent in the plain and simple dinner-frock which had been in her valise for use that evening in a hotel. Her main trunks were awaiting further events at Victoria.

"No. Nothing."

"And why did you do it?"

"I did it because I wanted to give you time to think."

"Think what?"

"Think about what you're letting yourself in for. You don't love Mr. Porter. He loves *you*, in his way, tremendously, no doubt. But you don't love him."

"How do you know that?"

"From the way you stood and looked at him now and then in church. He's dazzled you with jewels and presents and things, and flattery and adoration. He's swept you clean off your feet. And you're marrying him for money. You have beauty and you're selling it to him—no doubt at a very high price. It's a commercial transaction, that's what it is, I wanted you to realize this."

"Very kind, I'm sure," said Enid, with voice shaking. "And why are *you* so interested in my private affairs?"

"Well, I knew your father and mother. I've known you ever since you went to school, and you're perfectly aware that I've always been very interested in your private affairs. Otherwise, how did you guess just now that I was 'at the bottom of it all'?"

"I must say I think you're very impertinent, Mr. Fitch. And, what's more, you're quite wrong about Val. I do love Val—very much, and that's the only reason why I'm marrying him."

"That," said Mr. Fitch, "is a lie. I know it's a lie, and you know it's a lie. You do not love Mr Porter. A girl like you couldn't."

Tears—whether of rage or of fear—glittered in Enid's great eyes. Her mouth worked, but nothing articulate issued from her lips.

Mr. Fitch continued:

"You'll soon be unhappy. In the end you'll be very unhappy. You're going exactly the way to ruin your life, all because you can't resist the temptation of luxury and the lure of being idolized by a handsome man."

"And so you think it would be better for me to keep on at Karkeek's and work ten and sometimes twelve hours a day in the season, and be always soothing and flattering and kotowing to women better off than I am and not half so good-looking, in a stuffy shop and trying-on rooms, and all for a miserable salary, and walk with girls in parks on Sundays, and get old and dried up instead of being the mistress of a beautiful house and wearing lovely frocks and jewellery and driving about in a motor, and going to restaurants and theatres and balls and being adored by a man who thinks all the time of nothing but me. That's what you think, is it?" demanded Enid, taking no notice whatever of the curate's assertion that she was a liar.

"Yes, I do," Mr. Fitch replied, boldly. "I mean I think anything would be better than marrying a man you don't really care for and couldn't care for. But I see no reason why not marrying him should mean that you'd be compelled to do all the unpleasant things you've just mentioned. For instance, walking about in parks on Sundays with only girls. You might walk about in parks with me, for instance."

"Why," she ironically protested, "Sunday's your busy day."

"It won't be in future," he said. "I shall have to leave the church. Mr. Banks will dismiss me, of course, and I shan't get another curacy. And I'm rather glad about that because I ought never to have gone into the church. The church isn't my line."

"And what is your line, may I inquire?"

"You're my line," said the curate. "And you're a million times too glorious for a curate's wife."

"What?" Enid cried. "*Me*—your line!"

"Yes," Mr. Fitch courageously insisted. "You—my line! If curates got salaries of ten thousand a year and drove about their business in cars, I should have married you some years ago. So far as I'm concerned, what's put you off is not *me*, but my being a curate with an income of fourpence halfpenny per annum. Indeed you rather like me, and if your head had given your heart only half a chance you'd have liked me very much. Even now you think I'm good-looking and have charm. I don't say that I'm good-looking and have charm; all I say is that you think I have."

Miss Ledburn flamed and stood up. And in her speechless wrath she was a marvellous sight—a sight however, which Mr. Val Porter, accustomed to placidity, would scarcely have recognized. She still could not speak, and so she gave a loud, passionate scream, which must have been heard in the flat below, the flat above, and at least four other adjacent flats. On the part of a woman whose success in life had depended so much upon self-control and perfect tact, it was a surprising exhibition. Mr. Fitch was at a loss; for he had unloosed mysterious forces which he could not direct.

* * * *

The next moment the door of the bedroom flew open, and there appeared Enid's friend Lizzie, well and resplendently covered in a negligeé which formed part of Enid's trousseau and had been intended for the delectation of Mr. Val Porter. Lizzie's hair was not "down" because it was shingled—proof of the practical value of shingling in the supreme crises of existence. Lizzie was a fair and plain undistinguished girl—her interests and those of Enid did not clash—and her arrival set off to still greater advantage the distinction and the dark beauty of her companion.

Enid glanced at Lizzie and then sank back into her chair and sobbed.

Lizzie did not quite know what to do or say.

"Good evening," said Mr. Fitch. "My name is Fitch, and I'm an old friend of Miss Ledburn's."

Lizzie stooped and put an arm round Enid's lovely neck, and Enid continued to shake herself with sobs.

"What is it, darling? What is it?" murmured Lizzie.

"He's—he's—" More sobs.

"I think you'd better go," said Lizzie wisely to Mr. Fitch. "I don't know what you've been doing to Miss Ledburn, but you'd best hook it, and quick."

"I shall not hook it," replied Mr. Fitch, "until I have finished my chat with Miss Ledburn."

" 'Chat!' " repeated Lizzie, scornfully. "If you call this sort of thing 'chatting'— Will you go, or not?"

"Not!"

"Then you're no gentleman," said Lizzie with conviction and brutality. "Any gentleman who won't leave a lady's flat when he's asked to is a cad, and that's all there is to it."

Enid sat up straight, suddenly ceasing to sob.

"He isn't a cad," she assented vehemently, freeing herself from Lizzie's arm.

Lizzie also straightened herself. She looked around, and a new, comprehending expression came into her eyes.

"My mistake!" she snapped, sniffing. "Seems to me I'm one too many here."

And she marched back into the bedroom and banged the door. An intense silence followed.

The two enemies, the injurer and the injured, were again alone together in the small, mean, neat, feminine room. Both were breathing hard. Enid wiped her wondrous eyes.

"What else do you want to say?" she grievously inquired.

"Nothing, really," Mr. Fitch confessed. "I've told you all I had to tell you. I may perhaps add that I've done you no harm. I've not compromised you, or interfered with your new plans. You can be married to your Mr. Porter to-morrow morning just the same. And I hope you'll be happy. I mean it, honestly. But I had to give you time to think. I had to warn you. I'll go."

"Well," said Enid, calm now, "you *had* better get away. You'll have the police after you."

"Why shall I have the police after me? I've done nothing that's against the law, and I can look any policeman in the face. Good-bye. And I'm sorry." He did not hold out his hand.

"What are you thinking of doing for a living?"

"What's that got to do with you, please?"

"Nothing. Only you seem to have ruined yourself by this day's work."

Mr. Fitch laughed easily.

"Not a bit of it!" said he. "I can make a living somehow. There's more than one string to my bow. And I don't mind saying that if I'd been given the chance I could make a living for you too."

"I don't want anyone to make a living for me," said Enid with independence. "I can make my own, always have done. And if I tried I dare say I could make your living too. That would put the boot on the other leg, wouldn't it?"

"Enid!"

"I'm afraid of you."

"Why?"

"A man who'd do what you've done to-day would stick at nothing."

"Enid!"

Mr. Fitch began to stroll towards her round the table which separated them.

* * * *

The verger of St. Agnes lost his tips. The floral decoration of the church was wasted. The Rev. Johns Marjoribank Banks had to seek another curate. Karkeek's welcomed back its unique Miss Ledburn. Mr. Valentine Porter was badly, even scurvily, treated. He had committed no crime, except that of being wealthy, generous, and furiously in love. And yet he was humiliated and robbed of an unparalleled treasure, and nobody felt very sorry for him. The world is unfair. However, he got all the presents back—including the car.

ONE OF THEIR QUARRELS

I

THE yacht *Alice II*, a ketch of one hundred and eight tons, with auxiliary engine and a crew of nine, was just leaving the small haven of the Rotterdam Yacht Club, whose hospitality she and her owner, James Thorpe, had been enjoying for two days. The haven was studded with many mooring posts, to each of which a yacht was tied up; so that there was little room to spare for the manœuvring of a biggish, beamy, and sluggish craft like *Alice II*—easily the most important vessel in the cove.

Now Rotterdam is one of the greatest river ports of the whole world, and it is certainly the most feverish and busy of all European ports whatever. At the open mouth of the haven the mighty tide of the Maas streamed past at a speed of four or five knots, and the rushing water thereof was covered with tugs, motor-barges, sailing-barges, passenger steamers, sailing-ships, terrific ferries, and Atlantic liners—not to mention dredgers and such monstrosities as floating cranes. But chiefly tugs, of which scores and scores rushed to and fro, navigated by their skippers with more than the nonchalance of taxi-drivers navigating taxis along the Strand.

The wind was fresh; flags and burgees stood out pretty straight. The much-disturbed water was lolloping and splashing against the banks of the haven; a few rats as big as rabbits were to be seen foraging on the deep sides of the banks; sirens and whistles were sounding menaces everywhere; steam-cranes were creaking as they raised huge burdens of barrels, cheeses, and grain out of the holds of ships or off wharves, and flung them down again like toys. And railway bridges and road bridges were swinging high gigantic arms on steel joists to let trains and lorries and people go across or to let ships go through.

In brief, the scene was bewildering to an extreme degree, and Captain Abbott, who possessed the two finest qualities of a skipper—to wit, a strong sense of danger and a gloomy outlook upon the future—was glad that he had a Dutch pilot on board. Captain Abbott and the pilot between them were moving the *Alice II* out of the haven stern foremost. The dinghy, with a crew of two, was afloat carrying ropes to mooring posts and generally executing shouted orders from the poop—orders of which details need not be given here, as this story is in essence domestic and of a purely family nature.

The family, now leaning critically against the rail on the port quarter and watching the operations, consisted of efficient James Thorpe, his efficient wife Alice, and their daughter, who was usually addressed as Alice II. The yacht had been called *Alice II* because the name of Jim's previous yacht, a mere fifty-tonner with a crew of only four, was *Alice*. The increase in the size of Jim's yacht was a measure of the increase in his prosperity since the earlier days of *Alice*. Real yachtsmen are always selling the smaller for the larger if they are getting on in the world, or selling the larger for the smaller if they are not. The Thorpe family were beyond doubt real yachtsmen. They lived for yachting, and occasional sea-sickness never daunted them. As for Alice II, aged four, she had had a narrow escape of being actually born on *Alice*. (*Alice II* was acquired after the birth of Alice II. It may sound complicated, but is not.)

Right at the mouth of the yacht-haven was a station for tugs, and just as *Alice II* was feeling her way out backwards, a tug swayed casually to a berth, and her nose stopped about a yard from *Alice II's* stern. The skipper, not used to such circus performances, was alarmed, but neither the Dutch pilot nor the Dutch captain of the tug showed any sign of fever, though the two men in the dinghy certainly did. And the family, while outwardly tranquil, were aware of qualms.

"Come along, darling," said Mrs. Thorpe. "Time for your afternoon snoozelet."

"Is it, daddy?"

Jim Thorpe, tall, with a tendency to bulk, glanced at his little, slim girl of a wife (aged thirty-three, but not looking it) with a secret appeal.

"It is," said Alice Thorpe, staring down her mass of a husband. So that was that. Mother and daughter disappeared below.

When Alice returned to the deck there was a considerable noise of voices both on the yacht and in the dinghy, and the engine-room bell was ringing a new order about every thirty seconds.

"Look out for that dinghy," cried Alice, leaning over. Jim Thorpe was making the same cry, but only in his mind. He was not like Alice, of whom it might be said that, as a rule, whatever came into her mind went out through her lips.

"Shut up," Jim remonstrated, "Don't confuse them. They know exactly what they're doing."

"Do they? Well, they'll have the dinghy nipped between the yacht and that post in half a minute."

"Not they!"

But in about exactly half a minute the dinghy did get nipped, just as the tiresome Alice had predicted, and the general outcry was multiplied.

"Good gracious!" Alice exclaimed, with all her efficiency. "I never saw such clumsiness. And why is Pete in the dinghy at all?"

The post was immovable, and the hundred tons of the yacht uncontrollably and ruthlessly moved towards the post; and then there was a startling sound of crushed wood.

"A dinghy smashed!" said the skipper under his breath, gloomily justified of his pessimism.

Then one side of the dinghy rose up on the post and the dinghy suddenly filled with water; and the two men sprang out of her, clutched madly at the mizzen shrouds, and somehow got aboard the yacht. Jim had seen panic and the fear of death upon their bronzed faces. The yacht forged safely ahead, dragging after her the nearly submerged dinghy, in which oars and other gear were floating. A rope attached to the mooring post was tightening as the yacht moved.

"Ye'll have to cut that rope, Alf!" the skipper shouted to the mate. "Get your knife ready and cut it!" he repeated, savagely.

The rope was cut, and the tail of it left hanging round the post, a memorial to all Rotterdam of the inefficiency of British seamanship. The yacht was now safely away in the stream.

But there had been an accident, and the drowned dinghy dragging astern was the awful desolating proof of it. Alice had never before seen a marine mess, and she was outraged by this one. When the dinghy had been salved, and hauled up on its davits and emptied of a ton or so of water, it looked better, for not much damage had been done, the wretched boat having slipped under the yacht's quarter instead of being squeezed to matchwood. But red-headed Pete was now lying on deck, feeling his ankle and having his ankle felt. The man could not stand.

"Carry him down into the port-cabin. He'll be more comfortable there," Jim Thorpe ordered, curtly.

"But Alice is asleep there. It's her cabin," said Mrs. Jim, tensely.

"Take Alice out, then, and put her in your cabin—or mine," said Jim, still more curtly. "There's no room for a crippled man in the forecastle. He must be made comfortable, and he can't be comfortable in that box-room of a forecastle with eight other men and a kitchen in it."

II

"Jim," said Alice, quietly, when she had finished, with considerable efficiency, putting a cold compress, surrounded with flannel, upon the severely sprained ankle of Pete, "I want just two words with you."

They were in the narrow corridor, at the door of the port-cabin, which Alice had closed, and she led the way into Jim's own cabin, which was on the starboard side; and, having got him within, she closed the door of that cabin also. The yacht was breasting the densely-populated stream of the Maas, and on deck the excitement of the accident had died down. But below, between the pair in Jim's cabin, the shut-in atmosphere vibrated to unseen forces more dangerous than electricity. The big man and the small woman, who till that moment had talked together (in the presence of others) with an admirable sweet reasonableness, were now formidably glaring. Their bodies almost touched, for the cabin was not quite as large as a drawing-room on a liner, and Jim's high head was bent a little to avoid a beam in the ceiling of his private apartment.

"Well, child?" growled Jim.

"You made me look very silly just now in front of the captain and the mate and all of them, insisting on Pete being put in Alice's cabin when you knew I strongly objected to it."

"Not a bit," Jim replied. "I was perfectly polite. So were you, as far as that goes. Also, I carried the kid out myself, and she's asleep now all right. Where's the harm done?"

"The harm is this. This yacht is our summer home. Am I the mistress of the house, or am I not? I never interfere on deck—"

"Oh, yes, you do, my girl."

"I do *not*—and I don't expect you to interfere in the cabins."

"Oh, don't you?"

"No. I certainly do not. Imagine that great hulking fellow in little Alice's cabin! It's simply disgusting. If a dustman slipped on the front steps at home and hurt himself, would you bring him into the flat and put him into Alice's bed *there*?"

"No, I shouldn't."

"Why not?"

"Because the kid's bed there is only a cot, and Pete wouldn't hold in it."

Mrs. Jim stamped her foot, but she could not stamp hard because she was wearing indiarubber soles.

"Moreover," Jim continued, "the two cases are not quite on all fours. This is a—"

"They are exactly the same," Mrs. Jim insisted. "And there's another thing. It was all Pete's fault. I asked you before: Why was he in the dinghy at all? He isn't in the dinghy's crew. He's steward, and of course he only gets into a muddle in the dinghy."

"Pardon me. Pete's as handy a man as anybody aboard the vessel. He was in the dinghy because he likes to vary his work sometimes—surely that's natural! This isn't the Royal Navy."

"Then he must take the consequences, like anybody else. You always favour him. And if there's any difficulty between him and me you always take his side. I shan't forget the trouble I had in the old yacht."

The first honeymoon quarrel between the married pair had indeed happened in *Alice*, and apropos of precisely red-headed Pete.

"Anyhow, Pete was quite innocent then."

"I absolutely insist on him being taken to the forecastle, where he ought to be. You understand—absolutely."

"That's your ultimatum, is it?" said Jim, darkly. He was reflecting that if he allowed himself to be defeated in this battle he would lose all moral authority for ever. "Well, my heated darling, I'll just tell you two things. First, you're a horrid little piece, and a snob, and entirely without the milk of human kindness. Why on earth *shouldn't* the poor fellow be treated decently, as a fellow-creature, for once? Second, that he is not going to be moved back to the forecastle—not if I know it! Is that clear?"

It is astonishing with what perilous foolishness married people can behave to one another when prestige seems to be at stake; but somehow they will do it.

"Very well," said Mrs. Jim, raising her chin.

At that moment a hopping noise was heard in the corridor. Jim opened the door to see what was happening. It was happening that Pete, feeling ill at ease in the solitary splendour of the port-cabin, had arisen from his bunk and was hopping through the saloon towards the forecastle, his natural home. Mrs. Jim watched his retreating figure, and saw his great dirty hands imperilling the beautiful upholstery of the saloon as he balanced his way on one leg over the floor of the heaving vessel.

"Of course, his bandage will all come loose," she observed, dryly. "A lot of use it was me taking so much trouble over him!"

III

The episode would have ended at this point if the married belligerents had had as much common sense as the rest of mankind. Pete's independent and instinctive action had given Alice a clear, notable triumph in the affray, and yet a triumph which could not humiliate Jim. But with all their efficiency and all their mutual affection and other fine qualities, the married belligerents suffered from a lack of common sense. In the supply of that precious commodity they were our inferiors. And therefore the episode did not by any means end with the vanishing of red-headed Pete into the forecastle and the evacuation of Alice II's cabin. The personal dignity of the parties had been engaged, and the question of personal dignity had been the source of nearly all their marital differences. Each wanted to laugh lightly and make peace, but personal dignity prevented either of them from laughing.

"As usual, you've been very inconsiderate to me," said Mrs. Jim. "And, of course, I shall expect you to apologize."

To which Jim replied:

"Expect—by all means. Keep on expecting with all your might, my child." His tone was cold and cutting as a razor.

"And seeing how carefully I've looked after the ankle of that man," said Mrs. Jim, following her own thought and ignoring Jim's, "I don't quite see the point of your saying that I've no kindness in me. However—"

And yet that night at dinner, which in the regretted absence of Pete was served by the second steward, the atmosphere was as smooth as the canals and rivers upon which *Alice II* was so beautifully sailing in a fair wind. The most penetrating of stewards could not have detected a false note, much less a rift within the lute. And little Alice, upon whom both parents were lavishing all sweetness, was present at the soup stage of the meal as a special treat. Mrs. Jim had suggested this departure from the routine of discipline, and Jim had agreed to it with positive ardour. The fact was, of course, that the belligerents desired to be alone as little as possible.

"About where shall we be to-morrow afternoon, Jim?" Mrs. Jim inquired, graciously.

"I should think not so awfully far from Flushing, my pet," Jim graciously replied, stroking his offspring's golden hair.

"Then I think I *shall* take the steamer to Folkestone," said Mrs. Jim. "With all those urgent things to see to at the flat. . . . And Alice had better go with me, hadn't she?"

For a moment Jim, with all his acuteness, was at a loss to understand what Mrs. Jim was at, for there had been no previous suggestion whatever that Mrs. Jim should return to the flat, or that there was anything urgently needing her attention at the flat. Then he comprehended. He had not apologized to her, and never would apologize (deeming himself, of course, to have been entirely in the right in this dispute); she had therefore determined to show her displeasure, and prove her unconquerable mind, by leaving him alone in the yacht and taking Alice II with her. But she wanted to achieve her purpose smoothly, and without giving any hint to the child or to the little world of the yacht that a serious state of war existed. Hence she was displaying her remarkable skill in the art of acting. But Jim also could act, and Jim's mind also was unconquerable.

He said, charmingly:

"I think you're quite right, my dear, though I shall be very sorry to lose my two darlings. Of course, if you'd like me to come with you—"

"Oh, no! You must finish the cruise, dear."

"Very well, then. We'll keep going all night. You can take the train at Vlake and you'll be in plenty of time to catch the steamer at Flushing."

* * * *

And so it came to pass. Early the next morning he helped her to pack, and Alice II felt obliged also to help her mamma to pack; he gave her money; he saw them both off at Vlake station; and very trim, neat, charming, and efficient mother and daughter looked as they leaned their heads out of the carriage window and waved good-bye to daddy. It was a lovely morning. But for some twenty hours husband and wife had not exchanged one word save in the presence of others.

"Women are staggering," Jim reflected, naïvely. "Absolutely staggering." Just as if he hadn't been married for six years or so. He did, however, show some gleam of an appreciation of the fact that men also are staggering, when he asked himself: "I wonder why I didn't apologize to her? It would have cost me nothing." Then he resumed his masculine bias by adding: "No! Not on your life! It would have cost me my position in the home."

IV

Alice and Alice II sat together side by side in a red-velvet-covered compartment of the train to Flushing. It was a boat-train, sure enough, but a boat-train that stopped at every station. So that as she gazed casually at cows, dykes, steeples, barges apparently sailing through fields, maids and matrons in high-waisted "native" costume with gold-ornamented headpieces, station-gardens, and windmills, and explained the various phenomena of the journey to Alice II, Alice had plenty of opportunity to reflect upon the quarrel. Like all their quarrels, it had arisen out of almost nothing, and a word, even a tone, might have stifled it at birth. The important thing, however, was not the originating cause, but the nature of the issue engaged. And the issue in this particular quarrel was about the same as in all their previous quarrels—namely, the rights and dignity of man and the rights and dignity of woman.

"Jim is an idiot," thought Alice; and then: "I am an idiot too!"

But idiots are apt to have a powerful sense of dignity, the same as the wise. Alice could not imagine how the quarrel would end, but of course it would end; and the end would be delicious, as the ends of all their quarrels always were. In the meantime Alice felt a fine artistic interest in the quarrel, and contemplated calmly its growth, and conceived different dodges for concluding it with advantage to herself—an advantage which, having won it, she would cheerfully throw away as soon as the affair was over. She contemplated also, with satisfaction, the vision of Jim alone in the yacht. Put on what proud, careless air he might, he would certainly be rather miserable that evening!

She liked the thought of his misery; and she assured herself that *she* would not be miserable—and the assurance was not the least in the world convincing. Certainly she had Alice II, whereas Jim had nobody except his silly old captain and his sillier old red-headed Pete.

Alice II had begun by being prim, more prim than her mother. But soon Alice II grew tired of dangling her legs a dozen inches off the floor, and she slipped down and carried out a complete inspection of the compartment, and fell violently once when the train stopped with a jerk. Being very like her parents, she did not cry over her fall; she had a full share of pride. Then she climbed on to her mother's lap, and hugged her mother with much love.

"You're very demonstrative this morning, my pet," observed Alice.

Strange that Alice II knew precisely the meaning of that long word which she had never heard before.

"Mummy, won't daddy be awful sad all by himself?"

"Mummy, when's daddy coming home?"

"Mummy, why didn't daddy kiss you at the station?"

"Well, he was very busy with the luggage," Alice answered the last question uneasily. Nothing could be hidden from the child. The child knew as well as anybody that trouble was in the air. Nevertheless the demeanour of both the child's parents in her presence had been unexceptionable in its show of friendliness and affection. Alice ought to have made Jim kiss her. She hated nothing more than to give away the fact of a family quarrel to the innocent child. They, idiots both of them, were gods to the child. In another minute Alice II was fast asleep, and Alice could feel through her thin frock the warm, regular breathing of infancy. And she squeezed the child and woke her.

* * * *

The train had seemingly no intention of ever arriving at Flushing; but it did arrive. And there was a Flemish horse on the platform dragging bits of luggage about at the end of a long chain: a spectacle which made Alice II shriek with glee. Alice arranged matters efficiently with a porter and walked off the platform and turned to the left in obedience to printed instructions for boarding the steamer. And then she heard a call in Dutch-English:

"This way for passports, please."

At first she had an idea that the Dutch authorities were going to present her with a passport for the purpose of returning to England, and she tripped forward until she came to a wide gap with the view of a steamboat in the middle distance. Just at this gap was a table, with a bald-headed official seated thereat. He at once perceived that Alice was English, and he addressed her in her own language:

"Your passport, please, madam."

"But—but I haven't got a passport," Alice replied. A dreadful truth vaguely took shape in her mind.

"But it is forbidden to go on board the steamer without a passport."

Now she saw the dreadful truth very clearly. With Jim she had gone to various foreign countries in the yacht, which, belonging to an officially recognized yacht club, flew the blue ensign of the Royal Naval Reserve. On arriving in a foreign port Customs officers had come aboard for a formal inspection, but no officer had ever asked for passports. She and Jim had just walked ashore, and no questions put and no demand made. Similarly for re-embarkation. And similarly on the return to Britain. Yachting people were exempt from all passport complications. But on the present occasion Alice was no longer a yachting person. She was a mere common traveller. She explained matters to the urbane official, whose urbanity, however, proved to be of no help to her.

"But what am I to do?" she asked plaintively. In her war-days that celebrated efficiency of hers was habituated to dealing successfully with every crisis that arose, but now her efficiency failed her.

"Ah!" exclaimed the official suddenly. "Here is a gentleman from the office of the British Consul here. Good afternoon, sir," he greeted a young man who had put down a passport on the table. "You are going to England, sir?"

"On leave," said the young Englishman, who, indeed, was dressed in holiday style and had a bright face to match.

But immediately the Dutch official began to state the case of Alice, and Alice joined in with explanatory remarks, the young man's face hardened into the face which he wore in the Consular office. He was well used to petitioners who had foolishly omitted formalities, and, moreover, on the very threshold of his holiday, he objected to being worried with professional affairs. He was most definitely off duty. He said, finally:

"If you go to Rotterdam, or to the British Legation at The Hague, and fill up the proper forms and furnish references, you will be able to obtain a temporary passport, but you wouldn't get it under four or five days at the earliest. . . . Where is this yacht of yours, madam?"

"Near Vlake."

"Anybody on board who could help you?"

"My husband, the owner."

"Well, then, madam, I think your best course would be to go back at once to your husband." And, his own passport having been inspected, he raised his hat and vanished away in the direction of the steamer

Alice very unjustly considered him to be a rather unpleasant young man. "Return to your husband!" "Return to your husband!" The young man had not the slightest notion of the horror implied in his words. Go back—ignominiously! Go back—defeated! She cursed men in her heart, and particularly the ex-Kaiser Wilhelm, author of wars and therefore of passports.

"Darling," she said, sweetly, bending down to Alice II, "we must go back to daddy." And the thoughtless child clapped her hands.

"There's a train—" the helpful official was beginning.

"Can you tell me where I can hire a car?" she asked, and to herself: "Anyhow, it shall cost him as much as possible."

But supposing the yacht had already left her moorings!

V

That same afternoon, which happened to be full of sunshine, Jim Thorpe, the august owner of the one-hundred-and-eight-ton auxiliary ketch *Alice II*, sat on his deck with a book in front of him. But he was not reading and could not read. For he was in a state of nervous apprehension surpassing anything in his experience since the other war—the Great War. The same thought ran round and round in his mind: "What a Hades of a row when we do meet!" Then he heard the noise of an automobile approaching on the long, tree-shaded, straight road that skirted the canal. He jumped up, and in the distance saw in the car two figures that looked like his womenkind, together with certain luggage, the aspect of which seemed familiar.

"By Jove!" he exclaimed to the captain, who came aft to meet him. "They've come back. I wonder what's happened?" He acted as well as he could, but not too well.

"I thought it was them, sir," said the captain, anxiously, and glad of an occasion for anxiety.

The car stopped on the quay alongside the yacht.

"Hello! Hello!" cried Jim, despite his notorious manliness almost shaking with fright. "What's this, my children?"

"Missed the steamer," called Alice, nicely, and with a calm smile.

The chauffeur lifted down the baby whom Jim and the captain passed across the abyss that separated the quay wall from the yacht's side. Alice stopped the chauffeur from unloading the luggage.

"We were just waiting for the lock to open to put to sea. How lucky you had the idea of hiring a car!" The first statement was misleading, for Jim had no intention of putting to sea.

"Jim!" said Alice, persuasively, "just come here for a moment, will you?"

He obeyed, saying to himself: "She's playing with me like a cat with a mouse. What an idiot I was to let her go off like that!"

The assembling crew, aroused from torpor by the unexpected *contretemps*, saw the car turn and drive off with Mr. and Mrs. James Thorpe, while Alice II ran forward to her friend, red-headed Pete, who was stretched on deck near the forecastle-hatch.

"Jim," began Alice, in the speeding car—the chauffeur could not possibly hear for the loud rustling of the trees—"I wanted to have a bit of a chat with you, and I thought this was the best way. There's no more privacy on a hundred-ton ship than there used to be on a fifty-tonner. I was wrong to run off like that, and when *I'm* wrong I prefer to say so frankly. I don't agree at all with the attitude you took about that cabin, but I can see now you were acting for the best, and you honestly thought you were right, and so, of course, you couldn't conscientiously apologize."

"Oh, my child!" said Jim. "Please! Please! I dare say I was wrong, though I didn't think so, as you say." His heart was magically lightened. For once he had been lucky. She hadn't been near the steamer. She hadn't found out about the passport snag. She had just taken fright at the enormity of her rash foolishness in leaving him in a tantrum, and had turned tail. And she had had such fear of missing the yacht that she had hired a car. She had simply flown back to him.

"*But*," she continued, and Jim's heart was heavy once more—heavier than ever, "why did you let me and Alice II go away when you knew perfectly well that we couldn't get on to the steamer without a passport?"

"I—I—" the coward stammered.

"Did you know or didn't you know? Do be straight and tell me the truth."

"Yes, I knew."

"I suppose you thought it would be a lesson to me?"

"Well, I did," said Jim, shortly, intimidated by the formidableness of her tone, and wishing to Heaven he had never had the notion of teaching her a lesson.

"Well, it *will* be a lesson to me. But not the lesson you think. I'll never trust you again. You aren't a man, and you aren't a husband. You're a horrible brute. That was what I wanted to say to you, and I'll never forgive you."

She touched the chauffeur in the middle of the back, and motioned to him to return to the yacht.

"Of course," she proceeded, "I'm in your power. You know it, and I admit it fully. I couldn't get away from you, no matter how much money and pluck I had. I'm fast, simply because I haven't a passport. I shall have to fall in with your wishes, and there's nothing more to be said. So I won't say another word. But I must say this—" She went on talking until the car was once again alongside the yacht.

"The whole thing is perfectly silly. It's infantile," Jim muttered.

"You may think so, but I don't," said Alice.

They stepped on to the yacht. The crew got the luggage aboard.

"You'd better pay him, dearest," said Alice, silkily, for the benefit of the crew.

"Pilot!" Jim shouted. "Find out how much that fellow wants, will you? And you pay him, skipper."

"Lock's opening, sir," said the skipper.

"All right. Get her through."

Jim planted himself on the deck, feet wide apart and hands deep in his pockets, a statue of ferocious gloom. Up forward baby Alice II was pretending to bandage Pete's ankle. And she was absurdly like her mother at the task, though she had never seen her mother bandaging Pete's ankle. The resemblance was wonderful, incredible, very touching. Even while they were casting-off the crew gave sidelong glances at the sight and smiled; and as for the engineer, he could scarcely bring himself to descend into the engine-room, so spellbound was he by the group of red-headed Pete and Alice II.

Alice herself smiled.

Only Jim would not smile. He went below and dropped disgustedly on his bunk and glowered at the ceiling, cursing himself and cursing Alice, and resolving to sell the rotten yacht. Then Alice invaded his cabin.

"Oh, lor'!" thought Jim. "More to come!"

"You great silly!" murmured Alice bending over him and kissing him. "You great silly!" And she kissed him again. "Now kiss me. A good one."

He kissed her. All was light. In an instant of time all was happiness. But in the secrecy of his soul Jim stoutly maintained that you never knew where you were with women. When they seemed to be most serious they really weren't serious at all. And if she hadn't happened to be touched and flattered by the sight of Alice II imitating her Red Cross work upon Pete—

"WHAT I HAVE SAID
I HAVE SAID"

I

RALPH and Maidie, his wife, were walking up Grosvenor Place on a fine warm morning. He was forty and she was getting on that way. She had a snub nose, freckles, and red hair. On the other hand she was slim and pretty, and she did not look her age. He had married her, long after his very sensational rise in the world, from his own original class.

Just as he had once been a working engineer, so had she been a Board-school mistress, in the Five Towns. She had left a Board-school to enter and rule his town house, his country house, his yacht, and to make the acquaintance of his swell friends and keep even with them, and with forty or fifty servants, and to keep her end up in general—and especially with him. In the main she had succeeded, by learning some things and flatly refusing to learn other things. They had had many and magnificent quarrels and one baby.

The baby was her strong point, for he adored the infant with all the undisciplined fury of his nature. But she had other strong points. In addition to loving her in his neolithic manner, he respected her because she belonged to the select band of persons who had absolutely no fear of him.

They were going that morning to a wholesale house behind Holborn to buy the finest perambulator in the world for the baby. They were walking because she desired to walk through the streets by his side. They had walked from Belgrave Square as far as Grosvenor Place when he was overtaken by an attack of his notorious restlessness.

"Here, lass," said he, snapping at her. "I've had enough of this. I take my exercise with tennis. Let's have a taxi. We should be all day getting to Holborn at this rate."

"No!"

"*Yes!*"

"See here!" said she. "We'll go on the top of a bus."

Now he had not been on a bus nor in a bus for many years. The notion of a bus made a romantic appeal to him. There was something most amusing and strange about the notion of *him* travelling by bus.

"*No!*" he repeated.

She laughed happily, knowing that he meant yes.

"Yes," she said. "It's number 99. It passes here and goes right past the place. It'll be here in a minute."

They waited. 25's, 25*a*'s, 25*b*'s, 125's, 44's, 16's went by, having duly stopped in front of them. But not a 99. It happened that Maidie was just as impatient as Ralph himself, though differently.

"Oh, come on," she said at length. "We'll take a 25 and change at the top of Bond Street."

He loved to see her impatient—if she grew impatient first. The spectacle of her girlish impatience would put him into a mood of superior and benevolent serenity. He would treat her as a placid, experienced, kindly old gentleman might treat a charming, capricious child.

"Now don't be impatient, my dear," said he. "We have all the morning before us. You decided we should go by a 99, and we'll go by a 99 and no other. It's bound to be along soon now. And I'm not going to stir from this pavement till it does come along."

"Let's walk on a bit, then."

"No. I'm going by a 99, and I shan't stir from here till it comes," he repeated. "Not on your life."

"I know they don't run often," she said.

"You ought to have told me that before," he said.

Five minutes elapsed. At last Ralph, whose serenity was beginning to wear thin, beckoned to a policeman.

"How often do the 99 buses go past here?" Ralph inquired.

The policeman answered:

"Oh, they took that service off yesterday, sir."

"The deuce they did!" murmured Ralph in a queer tone.

At that moment a 25 bus came up.

"Come *on*!" said Maidie; she was very quick in resolve.

She had one foot on the step when he pulled her by the arm.

"Here," he said; "I said I wouldn't leave this pavement except by a 99. Not on your life, my girl."

"Pah!" she burst out, in blazing disdain. "You can't come that sort of thing over me, my lad. Are you coming or aren't you?"

As he made no reply, she shook off his arm and boarded the bus, which instantly departed.

II

"Officer," said Ralph, approaching the policeman again, "I wonder whether you could do something for me? I'm Lord Furber."

And he was Lord Furber—Lord Furber of Bursley: the first person who had ever given to the mother of the Five Towns the distinction of serving for a territorial title. Public munificence connected with a Midland University, and his extreme distinction in the engineering world, accounted satisfactorily for the title. And, unlike many peers of the lower middle-class, he had used his peerage where a peerage ought to be used—namely, in the House of Lords. He spoke frequently, and trenchantly, in the House of Lords, exasperating the aristocrats therein by telling them what he deemed to be the truth about themselves, and then soothing them by telling them what he knew to be the truth about the labouring class. His speeches were well reported, especially in his own newspaper, *The Echo*; so that of late he had become a celebrated figure in two worlds, if not in three. He was known of the populace. Newspapers no longer said: "Lord Furber, the great engineer." They said: "Lord Furber."

The policeman did not blench before the dazzling name. He was wearing the blue-and-white armlet of duty, and all the majesty of Great Britain was behind him. He just benevolently nodded.

"Are there any habitual loafers around here that I could send on an errand?"

The policeman looked about, and Ralph looked about. Not a loafer! Everybody seemed to be either busy with his own urgent affairs or well-dressed. The policeman said he knew of none.

"I suppose you couldn't go yourself—and risk it? Worth your while."

The policeman gave a grandiose grin at the extraordinary folly of such a suggestion.

"I tell you what I *could* do, my lord," said he. "I could do it for you when I come off duty—twelve o'clock."

"Thank you. I'm very grateful for your offer," answered Ralph, turning away and instantly and entirely forgetting the policeman.

He had a sensation of discomfort. He was being baulked, he who was never baulked, he with whom to want was to have in all material things. He was marooned in the middle of Grosvenor Place, on a triangular area of pavement, which an invisible barrier prevented him from leaving, and he wanted immediate contact with his establishment of servants, secretaries, and other persons whose function in Nature's plan was to do his bidding. Once contact was effected, the rest would be easy to his masterful volition, limitless resources, and organizing ingenuity.

He saw a man standing by a horse near the pavement. The horse was attired in a costly black mackintosh upon which were printed in white the words "Our Dumb Friends' League." The business of the horse, which was fed, lodged, and clothed by an association of kind hearts who had somehow never heard of the existence of the motor-van and the motor-lorry, was to help, free of charge, overtaxed horses up the hill from Victoria to Hyde Park Corner. The horse had that minute arrived from Victoria with another horse and a coal-cart in tow, and was very proud because this was his first job in three days.

"See here," said Ralph to the horse's attendant. "I'm Lord Furber." The attendant touched his hat. "I live at Essington House in Belgrave Square— you know, the big house on the corner. Can you run down there—it isn't a couple of minutes—and ask for my secretary, Miss Hummel, and ask her to come up here to me now, as quick as she can? It'll be worth ten shillings to you."

"Will you hold my horse?" the man asked.

"Sure!" cried Ralph, rather gleeful at the picturesque prospect of Lord Furber holding a horse in Grosvenor Place.

He seized the rein, and the man set forth. But the horse, inexcusably forgetting that he was a dumb friend, gave a loud neigh and set off after the man. Lord Furber was dragged into the roadway and became, with the horse, the centre of a protesting mix-up of motor-cars, taxis, and vans.

"Hih!" shouted Ralph to the man, who returned. "Take your damned nag! He's too thoroughbred for me."

The policeman had to straighten out the disorder.

It was at this juncture that Ralph found the idea which he ought to have found at the start. He stopped an empty taxi.

"See here, driver. I'm Lord Furber. I live—," etc., ending with: "Bring her back here. It'll be worth a pound to you."

The driver, whose taxi was gay with curtains and flowers, and who was accustomed to the unfathomable caprices of the rich, merely touched his smart hat and sped away throwing over his Melton Mowbray shoulder: "Back in five minutes, guv'nor."

He was back in four minutes.

"The young lady wasn't in, my lord. They've telephoned for her to your City office."

"She'll know where to come to?"

"Yes, my lord."

"You're a smart fellow," said Ralph, paying a pound. "D'you want a job?"

"No, my lord. Thank you, my lord. I own this here bus. She's my wife. And she'd miss me."

It seemed to Ralph as if, after a long period of sheltered existence, he was out again unprotected in the bleak winds of the wide world. He had three things rarely found in combination: great brains, character, and great wealth. He was also a realist about human nature, and he was well aware that such a combination is and must always be surrounded by flattery. He thought that in his estimates of himself in his relations with mankind he had made all due allowance for flattery. Now he discovered that he had not.

The young policeman had maintained all his nerve and independence; the horse-keeper had shown no great disappointment whatever at the loss of ten shillings, and the taxi-driver had humorously turned down the mighty peer.

Worst of all, Ralph had believed in the dependableness of Miss Hummel as deeply as he believed in anything. Miss Hummel ought not to have budged from Essington House; but, counting on a free morning, and drawn away by the attraction of love, she had failed in the supreme duty of not budging.

Yes, his tremendous confidence in himself as a manipulator of men was slightly impaired. He was in the most difficult moral quandary that he had ever been in. He could not decently escape from it without help. But could he rely on his power over anybody?

III

Still, after all he was well served. In less than a quarter of an hour a taxi stopped at the pavement, and two people emerged from it—Miss Hummel and St. John. St. John, a fashionably and ceremonially dressed man of forty, with an immaculate silk hat over greying hair, and manner to match, was Ralph's principal secretary. (There were other secretaries, but they had no share in the events under narration.)

"Here, what's this?" Ralph inquired brusquely. "I didn't ask for two of you."

"Sorry, sir," said St. John. "The message was that you wanted your secretary, and as we didn't know which, both Miss Hummel and I came."

"The message was for Miss Hummel," said Ralph. "But she wasn't at home."

"Sorry, sir," St. John repeated, showing absolutely no trace of the thought ever present in his mind that, whereas he was a Balliol man, his employer's father had been a working potter.

"No, keep the taxi," said Ralph to St. John, who was feeling in his pocket. "Miss Hummel, stroll down there and take the number of that policeman."

Miss Hummel strolled. Ralph did not want the policeman's number; he only wanted to speak to St. John alone. He continued:

"St. John, it would be a great convenience to me, and perhaps to you too, if you'd get that affair over and propose to the young woman and marry her. I'll give you a flatful of furniture for a wedding present. She's spoiling."

St. John smiled and blushed.

"Very good of you, sir. I know you wish us well."

"Think about it. I don't want you now. Thanks for coming."

St. John got back into the taxi and departed, having dutifully displayed no anxiety as to the reasons of the great man for sending for a secretary to meet him in the middle of Grosvenor Place—and waiting for the secretary. Him—waiting!

Nor was Miss Hummel any less discreet. She gave the policeman's number, and also wrote it down on her tablets, and then waited with dignity for ukases.

Her father and grandfather had been Colonial judges. Ralph liked to be served by members of the ruling classes. She was thirty, plain, a fatalist, and had no notion of making the best of herself by means of clothes.

Ralph was one of those men who can confess themselves only to women. He would confess himself shamelessly to Miss Hummel on nearly every subject except his wife. Miss Hummel liked it, had lived for it until the excellences of Mr. St. John had begun to affect her.

Ralph had meant to tell her of his fearful quandary. But confronted by her calm, expectant face and her shabby gloves, he suddenly knew that he could not. Miss Hummel had many most admirable qualities, but not that of greatness of soul. The scale of her soul was restricted, and Ralph felt that the first necessity for him was to be understood, and that only a great soul would be capable of understanding his unique predicament, and the nature of those invisible barriers which prevented him from leaving the pavement in the middle of Grosvenor Place until a 99 bus came up to remove him. His intention had been to discuss ways and means with the usually resourceful Miss Hummel, but he couldn't begin, in practice, without disclosing the awful secret of the quandary; and so he did not begin.

His brain, impeded therefore in one direction, jumped off in another, and, working furiously, soon informed him that the sole way out of the quandary was to invoke the highest possible human aid.

He was an extremely influential man, and enjoyed the friendship or the acquaintance of nearly all the other extremely influential men in London. And he used them and expected them to use him. Thus, if he needed at a day's notice a suite on a crowded liner, he would start at the top and ring up the chairman of the line and say: "See here, Alfred, I want a—" And he would assuredly get it. This system has its advantages, but few can make it work. Ralph now determined on a course of amazing audacity—even for him. He would send for the sublime overlord of all the passenger traffic in the streets of London, a personage so lofty, so recondite, so hidden in mysterious clouds of authority that not one bus-driver in five hundred had ever even set eyes on him, a personage who controlled and co-ordinated tubes and buses and even taxi-owning companies, and whose name caused dozens of company directors to tremble.

Ralph stopped a taxi.

"Miss Hummel," said he, speaking with slow solemnity and emphasizing his words with smacks of the right hand on the palm of the left. "You will go to Sir John Hipwood—you know, the general offices—and you will insist on seeing him at once, no matter what he is doing. You understand—no matter what he is doing."

"Yes, sir."

"You will ask him to come to me at once, *at once*, here, *here*. Tell him I want to see him on a matter of the very greatest urgency, and that I rely on him. Got it?"

"Yes, sir."

Miss Hummel sprang into the taxi.

"Hi!" Ralph halted the moving cab, and added, through the open window. "And I rely on *you*."

"Yes, sir."

After he had been striding up and down the pavement for what seemed to be about thirteen hours, and was, in fact, about half an hour, someone touched him lightly on the shoulder. It was Lady Furber, cheerful, agreeable, infinitesimally pert and ironic.

"Here, Rafie," she smiled. "You'll probably be here for quite a long time, unless I'm mistaken in you. I know you'll be hungry soon, so I've brought you some sandwiches from a Lyons'. I've chosen the perambulator."

Before he knew it he was holding a white packet. Lady Furber passed prudently on.

"Great heavens and Scott!" hissed Lord Furber, and pitched the packet fiercely over some green hoardings into a temporary enclosure that encumbered the middle of this particular isle of refuge in the middle of Grosvenor Place.

IV

A car drove up, and out stepped Sir John Hipwood. An older man than Ralph, his hair and moustache were white, though perhaps prematurely.

Without doubt he was under sixty. His expression showed benevolence and a thoughtful habit of mind. His eyes were soft and liquid (so different from the blazing, challenging orbs of Ralph), set in a broad, cautious face that all the time contradicted them.

"Jack!" said Ralph, in his deep voice. "This is very decent of you, awfully decent. I knew I could count on you. I'm grateful."

"Not at all," said Sir John, deprecatingly.

"Yes, I am. I'm sure it must have been d—d inconvenient for you to come like this." And Ralph, while in secret dwelling proudly on the fact that he, once a working engineer, had now influence enough to drag such a Titan as Jack Hipwood out of all his engagements without any explanation whatever, was indeed quite emotionally grateful to Jack.

"Not a bit!" Jack assured him warmly. "Not a bit inconvenient. I'm only too glad to be of use." Then his tone became much graver and more compassionate, as to one who was in the very last ditch. "But what's the matter? And why are you waiting here in the street? Come along with me to the Yacht Club. We can talk in the card-room at this time." He looked at his watch.

"Jack, listen to me. Bear with me. You're one of the few men who'll understand. And I'll tell you why I can't go to the Yacht Club—why I can't even get into your car and talk there."

When he chose, Ralph could be a very dramatic and persuasive talker, and Jack, already affected by the exordium, patted him sympathetically on the shoulder. Nevertheless, Ralph felt fully the immensity of the task before him. He saw clearly that if he did not succeed in it, and succeed completely, he would make himself completely ridiculous. He therefore mustered all his powers for the narration of the quandary.

"That's how I'm fixed, Jack, my lad," he ended. "And that's why I can't leave here except in a 99 bus. What I have said I have said, and I'm bound by it."

Sir John Hipwood's reaction was rather spectacular. He turned away, roaring with laughter—so much so that his pink skin deepened to purple and people stopped to look at him. He walked a dozen paces and then back, and faced Lord Furber, still laughing; then he wiped the tears from his eyes.

"And what is my *rôle* supposed to be in this affair?" he demanded, somewhat curtly, the laughter having finished as suddenly as it had begun.

"I want you to give orders for a 99 bus to be put on. But, of course, it's got to be a real 99, with the proper label on it—a public bus—none of your 'Private' labels, hire department. It's got to ply for hire, and follow the right 99 route, with a proper conductor and all. I must play the game properly. No hanky-panky with myself. I'll pay all expenses."

"No!" said Jack, with increased curtness.

"No? But believe me, Jack, it's a very serious thing for me. It's everything to me. My self-respect is at stake. I said it, and I said it to my wife, and I've got to stick to it. You're my friend, and you can save me. What's the good of knowing great men if you can't make use of them in a crisis?"

"Crisis be hanged!" cried Sir John Hipwood, who was gradually losing his benevolence and showing that he was just as accustomed as Ralph to being top dog. "Crisis be hanged!" He moderated his tone. "Now look here, Ralph. You say I'm your friend. I am. Take the advice of a friend. You walk right off this pavement and go home—it isn't five minutes off. Go to your wife and say to her just these words: 'Maidie, I'm a fool.' Tell her I told you to. She won't crow over you. She's fine, Maidie is, and there isn't a mean streak in her."

Lord Furber replied quietly and collectedly—his demeanour was a masterpiece of self-control:

"You mean all that?"

"I mean it. Not only will I not send a bus for you, but I'll give positive orders that a bus must not be sent."

"Well, then, you're a dirty dog, Hipwood!" Ralph retorted, calmly and bitterly savage.

Sir John bit his lip and responded:

"The matter with you is that you're an overbearing idiot, Furber. You think you own the earth, but you've got to learn that you don't. You've made a fool of yourself, and you think because you're the mighty Furber you can evade the consequences. It just happens this time that you can't. You're beaten—and a good thing too, for this once. You talk about your self-respect, but self-conceit is what's the matter with you. 'What you have said you have said!' Bosh! I say Bosh! And here you have the infernal impudence to take me away from my business on this fool's errand. D'you know that I broke up a directors' meeting to come to you, and put off a lunch, too, because I thought you were in trouble—real trouble? I never dreamed I was being summoned by a swollen-headed lunatic." At this point Sir John relented. "Forgive me, old thing," said he coaxingly. "Mustn't lose our sense of humour. Come along with me now and I'll stand you a lunch."

Ralph's answer was to walk away, with a lowering face. The next moment Sir John Hipwood drove off in his car.

Ralph had not moved a dozen paces when he saw the patiently waiting Miss Hummel. He laughed shortly.

"Miss Hummel," he addressed her in calm tones, as though nothing had happened. "You did very well, very well indeed. Now go back to the city and get Mr. St. John. Tell him he is to go down with you to the 'General' depot at Battersea. I know there's about sixty old motor-buses for sale there. Tell him to buy one and pay cash and see it's in going order. Make them lend you a conductor and a driver—they always have emergency reserves—and borrow two '99' number boards, and come right back here with it. Don't spare money. If bribes are needed, give them. Doesn't matter how much. Got it? Got it all?"

"Yes, sir," said the imperturbable.

<h1 style="text-align:center">V</h1>

The Right Honourable the Lord Furber suddenly felt very hungry—even to the point of physical weakness. He felt also that he had supported long enough the rigours of Grosvenor Place and needed a little privacy. Such were his reasons for nosing round the green-painted enclosure, rather in the manner of a dog excited by hopes. He then heard a strange tapping within the enclosure. His next act was to knock on the door of the enclosure, which bore an authority from the London County Council to exist up to a certain date; the date was already passed, but the enclosure continued to exist.

A grey-bearded man, clothed in white from head to foot and holding a chisel, appeared at the door.

"My man—" Lord Furber began, benevolently.

"Something wrong there," the grey-beard interrupted him. "So far as I know I'm not your man."

"I beg your pardon," Lord Furber apologized. "I thought you were a workman."

"So I am," said the grey-beard, "and I hope you are, too."

"Certainly," agreed his lordship quickly. "I'm sorry to trouble you, but I'm afraid I threw a packet of sandwiches into your wigwam a short while ago."

"Why are you afraid?" the grey-beard inquired. "Either you did or you didn't—you must know. If you mean that you are afraid *because* you threw the packet on my head, that's all right. You ought to be, now that I see you. When the packet fell I thought it came from Providence—or from the devil. Probably the latter. I thought it had been sent to tempt me from my hygienic brown bread."

"May I have it?"

"No, you mayn't," said the grey-beard. "I regret to say that the temptation was too strong for me, and I ate your sandwiches—all of them, and am now suffering from the inevitable indigestion. I don't blame you. I only blame myself. But you can have the brown bread. Here it is."

Lord Furber, after some hesitation, took the brown bread.

"Of course, I couldn't eat it inside here?"

"You're wrong again. Of course you could eat it inside. Come in."

Lord Furber gave thanks and entered the enclosure, and was relieved to see that he was still on pavement. A large group of statuary occupied the middle of the enclosure.

"Very fine," observed Lord Furber, amiably.

"Only posterity can decide that," said the grey-beard. "Now make yourself at home while you eat. I don't know who you are, and I don't care."

"I'm Lord Furber."

"Who's he? Never heard of him."

"Don't you read the papers?"

"Of course I don't. I haven't looked at a paper since the day after I was elected to the Royal Academy."

"Oh! Perhaps I ought to say—"

"No, you oughtn't," said the grey-beard, firmly. He began to knock chips off the statuary. "I'm just putting the finishing touches to this shameless young woman, and I desire you to follow the example of Renan's barber. When the barber asked Renan how he would like his hair cut, Renan answered, 'In silence.' I want you to eat my brown bread in silence. I'm engaged and mustn't be disturbed."

Lord Furber, with a deplorable lack of self-control, pitched the whole of the brown bread full in the face of the shameless girl and left the enclosure. No sooner was he outside than he regretted the rash act. But he impartially saw that a man must abide by the consequences of the defects of his qualities.

His sole sustenance was now the self-induced joyous conviction that St. John and Miss Hummel might arrive at any minute with the bus, driver, and conductor.

About an hour later he noticed a group of idlers staring at him from the opposite side of the roadway, by the gates of Constitution Hill. He swung round. From the west also groups of idlers were staring at him. The groups waxed in size and came nearer to him. He thought hard, and would have retreated into the enclosure; but the door of the enclosure was forbidden to him by an invisible barrier. Then, gazing across to the corner by St. George's Hospital, he descried a newspaper poster: "Strange freak of a Millionaire Peer." And another: "Lord Furber's Dilemma." (The poster of his own newspaper, *The Echo*, said: "Bloodhound Hunt for Girl's Murderer.")

He blushed; he wished to sink down through the earth to the Antipodes; then he cursed, swore, shrugged his shoulders, and grew brazen again. He especially anathematized Jack, who must have been talking at a late lunch.

A young man approached. "I'm from *The Standard*."

"D'you know I own *The Echo*?"

"Yes, my lord."

"Dog doesn't eat dog," said Lord Furber oracularly.

"I only thought you might care to tell me—"

"DOG DOESN'T EAT DOG," thundered Lord Furber. "Get off!"

He was obeyed.

The multitudes of quidnuncs were still waxing. The policeman, a new one, had to begin to handle them—always with tact. Three photographers came, one after another, and snapped Lord Furber. But Lord Furber had tenacity, and held doggedly to the theory that everybody in the world was mad except himself.

Then Miss Hummel—alone. No St. John.

"We've bought the bus, my lord."

"And how soon will it be here?"

"It isn't coming, my lord. The police licence for it was withdrawn when it was put up for sale. We can't get a new one for four days, and no driver will take the bus without a licence."

After a terrible pause, during which Ralph's face underwent the most shocking contortions, Lord Furber said with an affrighting imitation of calm:

"You'd better get away if you value your life, Miss Hummel. Come back in an hour. I shall be here."

In less than a minute Lady Furber herself arrived. Ralph glared at her.

"Come to keep you company a bit, Ralph," she said. "Sandwiches all right?"

"Fine," said Ralph.

"Good. I must tell you about the pram."

She seemed to accept the situation as though it was perfectly ordinary. She did not argue, cajole, nor complain. She was richly experienced in Ralph.

VI

Ralph's face was enigmatic. He smiled to himself, and occasionally even snorted a kind of monosyllabic laugh. But his feelings were terrible; they included despair. He did not know what to do; he only knew that he could not and would not give in. He saw nothing for it but a lingering death on the pavement, and such was his silly, grandiose, tremendous character that he was not unprepared for this, because a surrender was inconceivable to him. He had never surrendered.

At the same time he clearly realized the vast extent of his folly. But he happened to be of those few who are ready to pay honestly for their follies. Meanwhile he walked to and fro the full length of the pavement, and at intervals right round the three sides of the pavement. And Maidie walked with him; and he said not a word to her. Still, he saw that she was a great wife. She withstood the ordeal of the ever-increasing crowds perfectly—better even than Ralph. They were now quite accustomed to being pointed at, and to hearing: "That's him," and "That's her." Or, "Is *that* him? Good heavens!"

Then there was a strange diversion. Three young men hurried past; one carried a saxophone, one a sort of flageolet, and one a kettledrum. Ralph for one appalling moment thought that some newspaper (not his own)—perhaps *The Evening Press*—had engaged them to serenade. The *Press* would be capable of anything. However, they passed on, winding through the throng, towards Victoria, and the diversion ended.

"Look!" said Maidie suddenly; they were now at the extreme south of the pavement and could see the string of buses climbing the hill.

Ralph looked, and beheld on the forehead of one bus the number 99! It was not a "General." It was what people very unjustly called a "pirate." Its colour was a brilliant green, and it belonged to the "Emerald" tribe of motor-buses. A heavenly and triumphant satisfaction permeated the whole soul of Lord Furber. He had held out, and he had won.

"You did this," he said to Maidie.

"Well, my lad," said she, "I thought of it."

"And why I didn't think of it myself absolutely beats me," said Lord Furber.

Lady Furber was very happy. She heard no praise with her ears, but in her heart she plainly heard the unspoken, enthusiastic laudations of his lordship. The 99 came nearer—the gallant lifeboat of his lordship's self-respect. But music was soaring from its roof. The trio of musicians had boarded it and were playing "I Want to be Happy" with an amazing stridency, and flowing from the trumpet end of the saxophone was a long streamer with the words "*Evening Press*."

The multitude of gapers gave an immense roar of delighted cheers. Those nearest the bus made way for Lord Furber to mount. But Lord Furber turned his back on the bus, and, accompanied by his wife, walked right off the pavement towards Belgrave Square. He was laughing.

"Dog does eat dog after all," said he.

"It *is* a shame!" said Lady Furber, with the full vivacity of her red hair. "But you've won, Rafie, really."

"*You* have, wench!" said he. And after a pause: "But I'll get even with the *Press*."

This was not the right spirit. If he had understood the only way to happiness he would have forgiven the *Press*.

DEATH, FIRE, AND LIFE

I

Mr. Curtenty lay in bed in the winter morning darkness, and reflected upon the horrible injustice of destiny. Mr. Curtenty was a most respectable gentleman—indeed, a connection of the celebrated Jos Curtenty of Long-shaw, and, be it admitted, a great deal more dignified than Jos ever was. He had never done anything wrong; his conscience was sinless. In sixty years his dignity and his respectability had not been ever compromised. He could, and he did, look everybody unyieldingly in the face. By nature and long practice he was intensely proud and independent. All the world addressed him as "Mr." Once he had lost a situation through his employer omitting the "Mr." Of course he had not openly resented the omission, for he was not a fool, but the omission had put him in a frame of mind favour-able to quarrelling, and a quarrel about some trifle had ensued. Neverthe-less he had soon obtained a new situation, which unhappily he had lost through the death of the new employer.

Since that disaster—now rather more than a year ago—he had been workless, and therefore wageless. Society seemed to blame him for being sixty years old. The fact that he had no particular trade also counted against him. He had always had posts such as watchman, doorkeeper, timekeeper, inspector—posts which meant doing nothing with dignity. Hence no doubt his feeling of superiority to people who actually did things.

Somehow he could scarce hide this feeling—even from his daughter's husband, who secretly resented it. Jim Crowther was a young miner living at Longshaw, and in the opinion of Mr. Curtenty, Jim's wife, Harriet, had married beneath her. Mr. Curtenty was mistaken in supposing that he had concealed this opinion from Jim and Harriet. Every week he disliked Jim and Harriet more and more, because they were contributing to his subsis-tence. They were not so crude in their methods of charity as to give him money direct. Certainly not. Such clumsiness would have made an ever-lasting breach between the two generations. Mr. Curtenty knew naught, officially, of any help. Only it invariably happened that when Curtenty had not a shilling, Mrs. Curtenty had ten shillings or so, which she produced as it were apologetically. Mr. Curtenty was diplomatic enough never to inquire whence she had obtained the money.

Thus the twelve lean months had run precariously and unsatisfactorily on.

But a crisis was now upon Mr. Curtenty. For his wife had told him that Harriet had told her that Jim had told Harriet that Mrs. Curtenty could go and live with the Crowthers at Longshaw if she liked, and Mr. Curtenty too. And little by little Mr. Curtenty was given to understand that either he must submit to this humiliation—or starve. Well, Mr. Curtenty had his pride, and he swore to himself that he would not submit to it. He simply could not imagine himself as a helpless pauper dependent in the home of his son-in-law. He conveyed his decision to Mrs. Curtenty, and the next thing he heard was that if he wouldn't go she would! Ah! He saw well enough that the notion was to force him into submission! As if anybody could force him into submission!

Two days previously, it being then a Wednesday, Mr. Curtenty had been informed that Mrs. Curtenty would migrate to Longshaw at the end of the week, Saturday. It was now Friday. The supreme catastrophe was indeed shaping. All his life Mr. Curtenty had worried about the future, and his relatives and acquaintances had laughed at him for worrying. But was he not justified by the event? Had he ever been wrong? They twitted him about being miserly. He was not miserly. He had always been careful, and was he not now justified of his carefulness also? Financially, there was the matter of the Post Office Savings Bank account. They did not positively accuse him of keeping a private hoard in the Post Office Savings Bank; but they hinted at it, and no amount of denials by him would stop their hints.

His ear caught a *puffpuff-puffpuff,* the same being the first irregular coughings of the engine of Clayhanger's Steam-Printing Works, which extended from Duck Bank down the opposite side of the lane. These coughings were Mr. Curtenty's morning clock—he had no other, nor watch either. Soon followed the sound of sirens from different parts of the town of Bursley. The hour was seven. Mr. Curtenty slid out of bed from his wife's side, and began with deliberation to dress. He did everything with deliberation. He even looked for work—when he looked for it—with deliberation. (But he had an idea that work ought to look for him.) His nature demanded that he should always have plenty of time in front of him. Time was the basis of dignity; hurry was the enemy of dignity. The first part of his dressing he did in the dark. Then he lit a candle, behind the bed's head, and with a morsel of blacking and an old stumpy brush he softly cleaned his boots—or such poor fragments of them as were left to clean.

A miserable small room, but the totality of Mr. Curtenty's home! Once he had rented a whole house, and could walk from one room to another and go upstairs and downstairs and still be at home. . . . A few pitiable bits of furniture, including the little oil-stove on which his wife cooked their so-called meals! Once she had held sway over a whole kitchen-range!

In a dignified way he was sorry for his young and ingenuous, quietly grumbling wife. Not really young, for she was the mother of a mother! But he, at thirty, had married her at nineteen, and to him she had always remained curiously young. There she lay, on the verge of fifty, and looking to the impartial observer more than her age—she had had a wearing life—but to him, in her tranquil, pathetic sleep, she seemed rather like a girl, foolish, feckless, helpless. Yes, he was sorry for her. . . . So she intended on the morrow to migrate to her daughter's at Longshaw whether he went or not! Unless he yielded she meant to leave him—leave him to his own devices. It had come to that.

On the old tin tray was just enough bread, and dripping, and bits of cured fish to last them till the next morning. Thenceforward, the fiat had been issued from Longshaw, there were to be no more supplies. And then what? He knew that his wife was wondering, and Harriet was wondering, and Jim was wondering what the obstinate, secretive old man would do—what would happen. He alone knew what would happen.

* * * *

When he had laced his boots under the candle, and combed his hair, he extinguished the candle and finished his toilet in the dark. But the dark was now twilight; the earth was revolving as usual, and in its revolution baring Bursley to the dawn. Mr. Curtenty buttoned his greenish jacket, tied an antique woollen muffler round his collarless neck, put on his cap, and went forth into Woodisun Lane.

He knew he would be too early. He always was too early. He paced smartly but with dignity about Duck Square. A huge tram, packed with people who had work and were going off to it, rumbled past the Wesleyan chapel down Duck Bank towards Hanbridge. Mr. Curtenty stamped his feet into the pavement and rubbed his hands, for January mornings are always dank and chill in the Five Towns. Yet while doing this he pretended with dignity not to feel the cold. At last he descried the postman, and returned to the front-door of the cottage in which he occupied one room; and he received the postman majestically on the doorstep.

"Good morning," said the genial postman.

"Good morning to you," said Mr. Curtenty grandly, and took from the postman a small yellow official envelope.

In the privacy of the cottage stairs he opened the envelope. Its contents were quite in order: an authority to withdraw the sum of two shillings from the Savings Bank department of the Post Office. Then Mr. Curtenty drew from his breast-pocket a yellowish bank-book, which showed that twenty pounds stood to his credit, and he carefully put the withdrawal form within the book and replaced the book in his pocket.

Surely you are not surprised! A prudent man must have something up his sleeve for the last emergencies. Mr. Curtenty had maintained that twenty pounds in reserve throughout a year of privation and humiliation. He had lied about it for a year and more than a year. No matter how terrible a plight you may be in, it is always possible to conceive yourself in a still worse plight. That twenty pounds was Mr. Curtenty's bulwark against the imaginable worse—the fear of which had plagued him for forty years. It was the last defence and resource of his independence.

"Where ye been?" asked his waking wife, as he re-entered their home.

"Getting a breath of air," said Mr. Curtenty.

II

In the evening, about half-past seven, Mrs. Curtenty was lying in bed (for warmth) and Mr. Curtenty was sitting on one of the two chairs, all in the dark, when Mr. Curtenty, after a little shuffling of his legs and scrunching of the chair legs on the bare boards, suddenly rose and felt his way to the door, where his cap and muffler hung on a hook. The pair had had two lean meals and one snack; all the fish was eaten, but not quite all the bread; some tea remained for breakfast. Mr. Curtenty had been abroad once, in the afternoon, and during that period he had cashed the warrant for two shillings. Whether or not his wife had gone out in the same interval he did not know. They had scarcely spoken to each other, not from unfriendliness, but from habit. Not a word had been said about the morrow, or Mr. Curtenty's intentions regarding the morrow. Mrs. Curtenty had not dared to challenge him on the great matter. Indeed, he could not safely be challenged.

Mrs. Curtenty thought to herself now, as she sometimes remarked to her daughter:

"Things'll work themselves out if you leave 'em alone."

This was her philosophy in face of Mr. Curtenty's terrible estranging dignity and independence. All she said was, as Mr. Curtenty fumbled on the cheek of the door:

"Where ye going?"

And all he replied was:

"A breath of air."

He left without looking at the companion of his life. Even if he had looked at her he could not have seen her in the darkness. Still, he might have lit the last inch of candle for a few seconds and looked at her, for the moment was one of farewell after a companionship of thirty years. But his sentimental emotions had been numbed, frozen by misfortune, by spiritual pride, by privation, by secretiveness, by hidden anger against fate, and by self-righteousness. So he just went. He knew that his young wife would fall asleep and stay asleep.

It was a raw night in Woodisun Lane, and a muddy.

He had not meant to visit the Free Reference Library in the Wedgwood Institution, but as a measure of precaution he decided to do so. He was at home in that warm refuge of the unemployed, the Wedgwood Institution. The horrid, stuffy, damp smell of the Reference Library delighted his nose. After the usual formalities he obtained Quain's Dictionary of Medicine, and, taking the thick volume to a desk, he turned over its pages with the deliberate majesty of a vicar searching in the Bible for the lesson appointed to be read.

His brain was absolutely clear. He was not out of his mind, nor out of any part of his mind. In no circumstances would he migrate to his son-in-law's. His wife might go; she indeed would go; and she would be happy there, or at least contented. The twenty pounds (less two shillings) which he had guarded for an ultimate contingency would be useless to him, because too soon exhausted. He might of course fend for himself, all alone, for a time on the twenty pounds; but if he did so his family would know for sure that he had had a secret hoard after all, and he could not bear that revelation; it would too seriously humiliate him. Moreover, when the twenty pounds was gone—what then? Merely the same crucial, unanswerable problem as now! No! He had had enough, and there could be but one answer to the question, To be or not to be?

Quain was perfectly explicit: "The soluble cyanides, more especially the cyanide of potassium, largely used by photographers and by electroplaters, are common articles of commerce, and produce the same deadly results as the acid itself. The fatal dose of prussic acid is the equivalent of less than one grain of the anhydrous acid."

Nothing could be simpler to the understanding. He had read it before, but he wished to refresh his memory and so avoid the possibility of blunder. He refrained from proceeding to read about the effect of the poison; he had read that also before; it was rather disturbing, sensational.

He closed the stately tome and grandly handed it back across the counter to the pert young thing in a jersey who had dominion there. None could have guessed, as he calmly descended the broad steps of the Institution, that he was solemnly marked out and divided that night from every other soul in the town.

* * * *

He made his way to Critchlow's in St. Luke's Square. Critchlow was the oldest chemist in Bursley. He knew Critchlow slightly—a sardonic and antique being who would as lief as not sell poison to a customer who he guessed meant to drink it. Not that there was any trouble about buying poisons in those distant days at the end of the nineteenth century. You could pick a phial of tablets out of a mahogany case and pay for it and walk off with, for instance, as much sulphonal as would finish a whole family—and no questions asked and no eyebrow lifted. And if perchance Critchlow should ask a question about "Scheele's Acid," the trade name of the anhydrous prussic, Mr. Curtenty (who had never heard of sulphonal) could easily refer to electro-plating; for he had once had a temporary job on a small electro-plating works in Knype; hence his knowledge of the matter.

Critchlow's, however, was closed. Monstrous that the shop should be closed on that night of all nights! Holl's clock across the Square showed six minutes to eight, and Critchlow's had no right to be closed until eight. But Critchlow's was closed. The old fellow was allowing himself to become a bit capricious in his latter years.

Mr. Curtenty had purposely driven the transaction as late as convenient, for he desired a deserted, nocturnal town for his mortal work; but he now saw the possibility of having cut the thing too fine. Still, there was Salter's, in the Market Place—all on the way to the empty playground, beyond the Town Hall, which he had selected for his end. He walked to the top of the Square, and turned to the right where the Market Place was. He had an idea that Salter's kept open till nine o'clock. Salter's was open, and he entered the shop, which happened to be empty behind the counter as well as in front of it.

Salter's was the new chemistry in Bursley. Salter, a daring and optimistic fellow from Birmingham, had taken over the ramshackle old shop from the dying hand of the historic chemist who, for more than fifty years, had sold drugs and given advice to the old-fashioned *élite* of the ramshackle old town. Salter had provided a new ideal for the ramshackle old town. The interior of the shop had been expensively refurnished from floor to high ceiling. It shone; it glittered; it was orderly; it was the cleanest thing in Bursley; it had an antiseptic, tonic odour; its clock was accurate; it offered chairs, mirrors, and a weighing machine for the use of customers. It displayed more toothbrushes than a quarter of a century earlier had been employed in the whole of Bursley. Mr. Curtenty was not impressed. He had the native's distaste for and suspicion of all that was "showy" and that was not ramshackle.

A fine young gentleman, Mr. Salter himself (no apron), appeared from the dark backward of the establishment, glided along the length of the counter, and became a note of interrogation to Mr. Curtenty, whose tongue—very surprisingly—clave to his palate and whose throat grew parched.

"I want some Scheele's Acid."

Mr. Salter stared at Mr. Curtenty, and Mr. Curtenty, invigorated and challenged by the stare, returned it.

"Photographic work?"

Mr. Curtenty nodded. "Aye!"

"How much?"

"Dun' know. Smallish bottle."

"Half a pint?"

"Aye! That'll do."

"I'll get you to sign the poison book."

"Aye!"

Mr. Salter moved about behind the counter, and in a startlingly brief space of time was slapping a salmon-tinted poison label on a corked bottle. (Never within Mr. Curtenty's experience had seconds passed so quickly.) The next instant he had screwed the bottle into a bit of wrapping-paper, and he was in the act of handing it to Mr. Curtenty when a great lady entered the shop and Mr. Salter turned to her with eager and yet dignified deference, excusing himself negligently to Mr. Curtenty.

But Mr. Curtenty held the bottle. He held it victoriously; and it was no longer a bottle in a bit of paper—it was a sacred phial, magic, omnipotent, more powerful than man and than God. It held the key to the riddle of the future, and the short answer to the arguments of the past. It gave Mr. Curtenty a sense of absolutism, of independence, of dignity, of conquest over earth, such as he had never had. It rendered Mr. Curtenty heroic, magnificent. Already he was leaving earth. He had no interest in earth; he was sick of it, disgusted with it. He yearned bitterly to be quit of it. He had little or no fear, for fear presumes imagination, and he had little or no imagination. He forgot the teachings of religion and the wrath of God, or, if he remembered them, remembered them only to despise them. He was the supreme egotist. He thought of nobody but himself. He was absorbed in himself. Some faint vision of an inquest flickered transiently through his brain. He sniggered at it and it vanished. He was triumphant. He was a hero, a conqueror, a poet. He was God.

"One-and-twopence, please," murmured Mr. Salter, between two respectful sentences addressed to the lady.

"*One-and-twopence!*" cried Mr. Curtenty, dropping the florin which he was holding suspended in mid-pocket. "*One-and-twopence!* Why! It hadn't ought to be more than tenpence-halfpenny!"

"I'm afraid it's one-and-two," said Mr. Salter, calmly.

"Not *me*!" Mr. Curtenty growled with finality, and, dropping the bottle on to the round indiarubber mat intended to receive coins, he walked with fury and grandeur out of the shop, not caring for forty Salters nor forty great ladies.

He muttered things to himself. Did Salter suppose that *he* was going to help to pay for all the fal-lals and gimcrackery of his new shop? Not him! They called him a miser and a skinflint. They might. But fair was fair, and impudence was impudence. Impudence, that was what it was! Impudence. Let Mr. Salter charge his one-and-twopences to them as had quarterly bills and wouldn't pay cash. But not to *him*! He knew to a certainty that Fresson the "cash chemist" in Hanbridge, the great price-cutter, would sell him half a pint of Scheele's Acid for tenpence, if not ninepence-halfpenny. And to Fresson's he would go. Fresson's did not close until ten o'clock. Fresson was the friend of the poor, and a hard-working man who toiled early and late. . . . Impudence! Impudence! . . .

People passing in the Market Place heard and saw Mr. Curtenty muttering and chuntering to himself. He noticed with resentment that he was observed, and walked off in the direction of Hanbridge. His resolution to carry out his plan was as firm as ever—for nothing could shake it—but he was equally determined not to be done in the eye.

III

Woodisun Lane is one of the ways from Bursley to Hanbridge. Indeed, from Bursley Market Place it is the shortest and the oldest way, but by far the worst way, by reason of its gradients and its foul surface. However, Mr. Curtenty took it, in order, by a glance at the window of his home, to see whether Mrs. Curtenty was wastefully burning the last inch of the candle. She was not; the window gave no sign of light. Strange to say, Mrs. Curtenty's thriftiness disappointed him, because he wanted another grievance, he wanted dozens of grievances, to gather into his breast as St. Sebastian gathered arrows.

He had to be content with the one great grievance against Mr. Salter— Mr. Salter, who by his rapacity was forcing a determined and desperate man to walk unnecessarily over to Hanbridge on a dank night. Soon, by dint of reflection and savage concentration, the grievance swelled till it filled his whole mind and heart and soul.

Nearly at the top of the hill, at Bleakridge, Woodisun Lane debouches into the main thoroughfare, Trafalgar Road. Somewhat farther on is the football ground, where Bursley had never yet defeated Knype, and then there is a corner upon which had stood for centuries a small earthenware manufactory—one small manufactory succeeding another there from Plantagenet times onwards. Young Eddie Colclough had recently razed a small manufactory to the ground and was just finishing the erection of a new one of an experimental type wherein various modern dodges of economic organization were to be tested.

As he passed the building Mr. Curtenty's watchman's nose sniffed the air, in the manner of a tiger sniffing distant blood. Mr. Curtenty became a nose and nothing but a nose; and his grievance and his purpose were equally forgotten. It might be said that Mr. Curtenty had no trade, but that he had a profession was richly demonstrated in that sniffing moment. He sniffed the night-watchman's arch-foe—smoke, indicating fire.

He looked at the façade, whose upper windows were still unglazed, and could see no curling wisp of smoke. But he had faith in his nose. Though the gates of the large central archway had not yet been put in place, the archway was stoutly boarded, and Mr. Curtenty could not get through it. He ran along and climbed a rough fence at the side of the manufactory, and so reached the back, which was less securely protected than the front from marauders. The next instant he was in the strewn quadrangle, or "yard" as it is called. And his nose was justified, for he saw smoke meandering furtively, ominously, from a first-floor window. And his eyes detected a faint glow within.

Mr. Curtenty was gloriously alive. The price of Scheele's Acid was nothing to him. He was professionally inspired. He was happy in the midst of calamity and conflagration. He knew the first thing to do and the second thing to do, and did not hesitate a moment. In a quarter of a minute he was in Trafalgar Road again. A policeman, a policeman to take charge! But there was no policeman. In the Five Towns, so different from other localities, when you are engaged in the practice of virtue and philanthropy there never is a policeman within a mile; it is only when you happen to be delinquent that policemen spring magically out of the earth. There was nobody except three giggling and shrieking girls, arms mutually entwined round necks, swinging along the oozy pavement. Mr. Curtenty ignored them. But at the corner of the tiny Square, in front of Bleakridge's yellow church, burned a red lamp. Dr. Ackerington's, of course! Mr. Curtenty, forgetting dignity, and yet somehow preserving it, ran to the house and violently rang the bell. He rang it three times with increasing violence.

The door opened.

" 'Ere! You're in a 'urry," said a stern, fat, middle-aged maid in cap and apron, as soon as she had satisfied herself that Mr. Curtenty did not belong to the ruling class.

" 'Ave ye got th' telephone here?" Mr. Curtenty demanded stiffly.

"And if we have! You can't use it."

"Who wants to use it? You tell your master or missus as Colclough's new pot-bank's afire, and they mun telephone for th' fire brigade." And as the wench, startled and impressed and stricken, did not immediately move, he added: "And look slippy!" Then he ran off.

* * * *

Within the quadrangle of the works once more, he descried in the darkness what looked like a mound of sand. He put his hand into it. It was a mound of sand. Seizing one of several buckets which the builder's men had left, he filled it with sand and searched for and found stairs and gingerly mounted them in the black darkness, and guided by his triumphant nose he passed through a corridor and into a large suffocating room, which room was illuminated by the fire.

Planks of wood were just beginning to crackle. With the sand he smothered their ardour. But there was not enough sand. He descended again, with empty bucket, bungled the stairs, fell, hurt his ankle, swore, limped, got more sand, ascended. After three such ascents he had extinguished the fire and was in darkness. But he had seen enough to decide the origin of the fire. The usual thing! Workmen's negligence. They had been bivouacking in the room, they had made a fire in the grateless hearth—one of your sprawling fires—and they had not put it out on leaving. A few embers had reached a plank leaning at a broad angle against the mantelpiece, had patiently attacked the root of the plank—a slow business, but in the end successful; the plank, deprived of its base, had fallen sideways on to a heap of other planks. And so on. Had not the entire place sweated with damp it might have been a heap of ruins at the moment when Mr. Salter's rapacity had driven Mr. Curtenty in the direction of Hanbridge.

Mr. Curtenty, his occupation gone, limped through other corridors and rooms until he saw the light of Trafalgar Road street-lamps through an unglazed window. He looked out, himself unseen. A crowd, small but increasing, was gazing stolidly up at the façade of the works. It could perceive nothing of interest; it had no impulse to do anything; it merely gazed, in the faint hope of witnessing some terrific catastrophe. No policeman! No fire-engine! A tram-car roared by, unheeding. Mr. Curtenty continued to look out, proud, patient, invisible, scornful of the crowd. He was triumphant— nearly as triumphant as he had been fifty minutes earlier when he held the sacred phial in his hand. What a world! What destiny!

The expectant crowd in the mire was in due course rewarded by the exciting arrival, from Hanbridge way, of a motor-car full of people—Eddie Colclough, a young newly-married wife, and friends. Dr. Ackerington being out, Mrs. Ackerington had telephoned not only to the fire brigade, but to Eddie, who lived at Cauldon, between Hanbridge and Oldcastle. Mr. and

Mrs. Eddie were entertaining at dinner two gentlemen and a lady, and, all being young and adventurous, they had instantly decided to leave dinner and come in a body to the scene of the announced conflagration.

Mr. Curtenty, seeing them and guessing that Mr. Colclough must be among them, went downstairs with pain in his ankle. Eddie, followed by Mrs. Eddie and the others, was in the quadrangle almost before him.

"Where's the fire?" Mr. Colclough demanded fiercely, in bewilderment; he was intensely relieved to see no evidence of a fire, but also—rather illogically—annoyed to see no evidence of a fire.

"It ain't anywhere. I've put it out," answered Mr. Curtenty, coldly, challengingly.

"And who the devil are you, anyway?" cried Mr. Colclough, who was of an aggressive and hasty disposition.

"Mr. Curtenty's my name," said Mr. Curtenty, "and if you'll come upstairs I'll shownd ye a thing or two." His tone gave pause to Mr. Colclough, and at the same time allayed Mr. Colclough's rising suspicion of some hanky-panky in the rumour of the fire.

"Strike a match," ordered Mr. Colclough at the dark stairs, feeling vainly in his pockets.

"I dunna' smoke," said Mr. Curtenty, grimly.

However, one of the other gentlemen had one of the new-fangled electric torches. The six of them stood in the scene of the conflagration and heard Mr. Curtenty's description of the great episode: how he was passing, how his nose gave the alarm, how he sent for the fire brigade, how he used the sand, how he sprained his ankle, and how all's well that ends well; the whole recital being supported by charred timber and the heavy odour of wood-smoke.

The ray of the electric torch lighted Mr. Curtenty's smoke-grimed face. The rest of them—the fashionable aristocracy, including two young and beautiful women—were in shadow. Mr. Curtenty's tale was faultless; it extorted admiration, a little unwilling perhaps at first from Eddie Colclough, but spontaneous enough from the others, and especially from the women.

"Well, here's something for you," said Mr. Colclough, and handed Mr. Curtenty a sovereign.

"Thank ye."

"You must be used to fires," said Mrs. Colclough, smiling warmly.

Mr. Curtenty majestically offered some of his personal history.

"And who are you working for now?" asked Mr. Colclough.

"I'm playing [out of work]," said Mr. Curtenty.

Mr. Colclough paused.

"What did you say your name was?"

"Mr. Curtenty."

"Well, look here, Curtenty," said Mr. Colclough, and paused again, as though hesitating in his mind.

Mr. Curtenty did not repine at the rough careless omission of the "Mr."; experience had been teaching him.

"Look here, Curtenty. There's no watchman here yet. D'you want a job?"

Mr. Curtenty was engaged on the spot.

Suddenly he hurried from the room. The others followed him. The electric torch lighted him from behind. His ears had been copying the excellent example of his nose. He reached one of the front unglazed windows and put his head through a square. A fire-engine had arrived with an enormous fluster and bluster and glint of brass helmets. A fine effort on the part of the Bursley Fire Brigade—forty minutes!

Mr. Curtenty bawled angrily, disdainfully, to the brigade:—

"It's out! Get away wi' yer sprinklin' mashane! It's out! I'm a-telling on ye!"

Then he turned and faced the torch.

"You perfect *duck*!" exclaimed young Mrs. Colclough, and carried away by gratitude for a great deed, and by her youthful sentimentalism and the general influence of a honeymoon and the comicality of Mr. Curtenty's dirty tweed cap—in all her beauty and all her finery she put her ringed hands on the shoulders of the old man and kissed his sooty plain face.

IV

In Duck Square (which is really only a bit of Duck Bank and not a square at all) there is an establishment (not to be confused with the Boro' Dining Rooms two doors off) which stays open till a late hour nightly, brilliantly lit amid the surrounding gloom, and which exudes from its interior an odour so appetizing and powerful that it has been known to interfere with the Wednesday evening prayer meeting in the Wesleyan chapel a hundred yards away on the opposite side of Trafalgar Road.

Mr. Curtenty entered this establishment and, pulling a florin from his pocket, bought two plenteous portions of the finest fried fish. He then bought a candle, though candles were not in her line of business, from the white-clad proprietress, who gave him a few matches into the bargain. Then he went across to the fast-closing Dragon Hotel and in the nick of time bought a bottle of beer. Having unlocked the door of the cottage in Woodisun Lane with his own key, he took off his boots at the bottom of the stairs, struck a light, and proceeded upwards, heavily encumbered, into his one-roomed home.

Young Mrs. Curtenty was fast asleep; the blaze of the candle did not awaken her. He examined her face with a new interest. His heart was loudly beating (but that, of course, was the effect of the stairs—what else could it be?). He was vaguely aware too, of a non-fleshly throbbing, a quaking, a half-pleasant, half-frightening general disturbance in his mind or his soul or somewhere. He could not quite surely identify the phenomenon. It might have been some imperfect realization of the dread fact that but for the accident of a fire he would at that moment have been elsewhere, or nowhere at all and nothing at all. On the other hand, it might be due to alarm at his own wild and reckless expenditure in the fried-fish shop and the Dragon Hotel.

It was the heavenly odour of the fried fish that first caused his wife to dream a delicious dream and then woke her. As her senses gradually brought her back into the sphere of reality, she opened her ingenuous eyes and saw Mr. Curtenty bending over her, candle in hand. The memory of Mrs. Colclough's kiss was now the chief thing in Mr. Curtenty's mind. It somehow thrilled him, and it somehow took thirty years off Mrs. Curtenty's age.

"Rally thysen up, wench," said Mr. Curtenty in a tone so startlingly new and attractive to Mrs. Curtenty that she could not move.

He wanted to bend down and embrace her, but was prevented by an unconquerable complex that held him fast and told him not to be ridiculous.

"Rally thysen up," he repeated, "and put th' blanket round thy shoulders."

"Jimmy," said she, hopefully, "then us'll go to Harriet's at Longshaw to-morrow?"

"Not me!"

"I shall," said she, sadly. "They'll make me. Aye, lad, I'm going, I am!" She sighed.

"Thee isna'," he almost shouted. "I've gotten a job. Rally up and set this 'ere fish on a platter."

She raised herself on her elbows and kissed him; she had no forbidding complex. The kiss was what he wanted. This kiss was the second in one hour, and the second in perhaps six months or more. And the lips were as cool and fresh as Mrs. Colclough's. And the kiss had a quality mysteriously surpassing that of Mrs. Colclough's.

Mr. Curtenty felt himself obliged for form's sake to show impatience at the salute.

" 'Ere," he grunted. "Thou'rt shaking candle-grease all o'er th' bed."

Nevertheless, he himself adjusted the blanket round his wife's exposed arms and neck.

THE EPIDEMIC

I

QUITE a little crowd of men and women, chiefly young, were assembled in the drawing-room of Mrs. Miss's boarding-house, "Fairbourne," at Exquay, when the stopping of a taxi outside put them into a state of excitement.

Exquay, that city of pleasure and health, set on seven wooded hills overlooking a lovely bay, is one of the five English seaside towns proudly known as the Queen of Watering Places. Once it was select and exclusive. Once it was "residential," its residences being villas each in a garden with butler and dinner-gong all complete; and its casual visitors crowded themselves into four old-fashioned hotels (six bathrooms between them), and into a few prim and expensive boarding-houses where the difference between class and class was deeply understood. Once nearly all its seekers after health and pleasure were retired military and naval officers and Anglo-Indians and their perfect ladies. Once it had no pier, no orchestra, no taxis. The coming of the motor-coach changed everything. The town ceased to be select. The number of boarding-houses enormously increased. The villas declined. The superior shops declined. Cheap shops and *cafés* multiplied. Tramcars multiplied. And innumerable dust-raising motor-coaches brought people from everywhere and took them everywhere—usually for about ten shillings.

These people knew and cared nothing for the fighting services and the Indian civil service. They mistrusted, feared, and ignorantly admired sartorial smartness, a correct London accent, and polished manners. They had their own code of manners, hearty, rough, and no-nonsense. The old residents cast ashes upon the old residents' heads and wept for the glory of the vanished past. The superior shopkeepers said that the end of the world was come, and sometimes went into bankruptcy. Wags began to call Exquay "Birmingham-on-Sea."

"Yes, it's him. Yes, it's the Magician. Look at his red moustache," said eager voices as a man descended from the taxi.

"I'll go and open the door," said Mr. Abel Hipgood.

In that astounding suggestion, which astounded nobody in the drawing-room, was shown the whole difference between the Present and the Past of

Exquay. Imagine a guest at a boarding-house going to open the front-door to a caller! You cannot imagine it—if you happen to be a retired colonel.

But these comfortable, unconventional Midlanders were indeed strange. It was ten o'clock—were they in evening-dress? Not one of them. They dined in the middle of the day, took a plentiful tea at six, and ate a bit of bread and cheese before going to bed. Their blouses were blousy, their suits were apt to have two different patterns of check, their boots were strong and large, their ankles massive, their accents ditto. Sad sights and sounds for a colonel's lady! But they quite rightly thought very well of themselves, and were quite rightly convinced that they constituted the backbone of the country.

* * * *

Mr. Abel Hipgood in particular thought well of himself. He was a man of thirty-three, small and neat, with a notable scarf-pin. He was obviously a Leader, and he led "Fairbourne." A plumber, he had succeeded to the moribund business of a deceased uncle in Wolverhampton and in a short time had restored it to prosperity. He accounted this a considerable feat, and seriously doubted whether any other person on earth could have accomplished it.

"Where's Miss Tansley?" he inquired on his way out of the drawing-room. (Miss Tansley was the young woman who knew the red-headed Magician and had arranged the séance.)

"She's not come in," said someone.

"Oh, never mind! We'll dispense with introductions," said Mr. Hipgood, composedly, and proceeded to open the front-door.

"Good evening—er—Mr. Magician," he welcomed the gentleman with the red moustache. "Do come in. We're all waiting for you." He held out his hand, which Mr. Magician, after glancing at it, accepted and duly shook.

"*All* waiting for me, are you?" said Mr. Magician with an urbane, reserved smile. "Isn't that rather a lot?"

Mr. Hipgood perceived from his accent that Mr. Magician was a "real" gentleman. And he was glad, and at once began to imitate the style and accent of the real gentleman.

"I hope you won't *mind* all of us," said he, grandly. "We rather understood from Miss Tansley—Your crystal's come. The boy brought it. We've been looking at it."

"Oh, my crystal's come, has it? That's all to the good. Shouldn't have been much use without it, should I?"

The Magician laughed soberly, and, Mr. Hipgood having courteously taken his hat, passed through the smiling and inquisitive throng, which had followed their Leader to the hall, into the drawing-room.

And there was the crystal, in its opened case, on a table in the midst of the room!

"Would you prefer the curtains drawn?" Mr. Hipgood inquired.

"I should—certainly."

The electricity was turned on and the curtains drawn.

"And now for our promised Peep into the Future," said Mr. Hipgood.

It was curious that though, when Miss Tansley had first proposed the visit of the crystal-gazer, everybody had laughed at the notion of there being anything whatever in crystal-gazing, now that the crystal-gazer had arrived and given a glance at the crystal, everybody began to believe in crystal-gazing, and to quake at the possibility of terrible prophecies.

"All sit, please," said Mr. Magician.

All sat except Mr. Hipgood.

"You too."

Mr. Hipgood sat—next to Miss Bertie Thaxted. (Bertie, in her case, was the diminutive of Alberta.) He had meant to remain standing—sign of his leadership!—but by a curious affable gesture signified to Miss Thaxted that he had only been waiting an opportunity to secure a seat near herself. It would never have done for Miss Thaxted to think that the Magician had any moral dominion over him, Abel Hipgood.

* * * *

Miss Thaxted, in Abel's eyes, was by far the most important lady in the room. She was not staying at "Fairbourne," but had come in for the séance with sundry others from other boarding-houses at the suggestion of the missing Miss Tansley. Abel had made her acquaintance, through Miss Tansley, on a warm evening in the neighbourhood of the bandstand, and had instantly been struck by her handsomeness, her dignity, her finished manners, her smart clothes, and her slim ankles. So much so that he assumed a certain doggishness and remembered that he, a very eligible bachelor, had come to Exquay partly with the object of "looking out."

But he was ever suspicious of finished manners, finery, and especially of slim ankles. He rightly thought that they connoted expensive tastes and an imperfect appreciation of the true value of money. One day, however, Miss Thaxted, in a casual conversation concerning a proposed motor-coach expedition into the moors, had unconsciously shown to him that she had minutely studied the prices of such tours, and objected to either herself or anybody else paying seven-and-six a head when the same end could be obtained at six-and-six a head by a slightly different route. "What I say is," she had said, "a shilling is always a shilling," and had uttered this indubitable truth in a serious and quite unashamed tone, as one confessing a faith. Henceforward Mr. Hipgood had been perfectly reassured about her, and all her acquaintances, and he knew that matters were slowly and correctly pursuing their normal course. Miss Thaxted was secretary and book-keeper to a fashionable dentist in Leeds—source of her finished manners.

* * * *

Mr. Magician was gazing sternly into the crystal. Hearts throbbed with expectation. Mr. Hipgood hoped that Miss Thaxted would be the first to be called upon; he hoped further that everyone, except perhaps himself, would be asked to leave the room while the future was being revealed to Miss Thaxted. Indeed, with others, he was surprised that Mr. Magician had so far said not a word as to the arrangements which he usually made for securing privacy to individual clients.

"No!" said Mr. Magician, fiercely and startlingly looking up. "No! I should prefer to do nothing to-night. You must be good enough to let me exercise my discretion and—be dumb." He glanced around almost menacingly, his prominent moustache sticking out on either side of his firm lips.

"Oh! But—" cried Mr. Hipgood. "We've heard so much about you. Surely you can—"

The hearts of several persons present were now in their mouths; they feared that Mr. Hipgood, too audacious, was inviting trouble. Clearly the Magician had seen trouble for some of them in the crystal, and if the future held unpleasantness they preferred to be spared foreknowledge of it. They were human, even if despicable, in their cowardice. They prayed in their secret bosoms that Mr. Magician would maintain his attitude—and they were disappointed.

"Very well, then! Very well!" said the crystal-gazer, quite blithely. "If you must have it! Five persons staying as visitors in this house to-night are about to be struck down by an extremely contagious disease—extremely contagious." And he gazed around for the second time, as it were, cruelly triumphant. Then he shut up with a snap the box containing his crystal.

At the same moment, such is the power of suggestion, nearly everybody in the room felt a conviction that throughout the day he or she had been suffering from grave and mysterious symptoms of oncoming illness. All looked at all with a wild, questioning surmise.

"But may I inquire—?" the undaunted Mr. Hipgood began.

"I can say no more. That is all I have seen in the crystal, or can see."

In twenty seconds Mr. Magician had left the house.

"He hasn't asked for his fee!" exclaimed Mr. Hipgood, who had collected the amount of the fee and had it in his pocket.

"And what about his crystal?" Bertie Thaxted demanded.

The scene is now the surgery of that very popular Exquay general practitioner, Dr. Cedric Ryper, M.R.C.P., M.R.C.S., ten minutes later. Dr. Ryper was sterilizing some surgical instruments and restoring them to their cases, when in walked quite unceremoniously a gentleman with a red moustache.

"Hullo, Rooding," said Dr. Ryper, turning his head. "You've been quick enough, I will say! Do you deal with your own patients as rapidly?"

"*You've* got some deuced funny patients, my lad," said Dr. Rooding. "Believe me, I've had an adventure—yes, an adventure. Mind you, I'm not complaining. I accept what comes. I offered to take that call for you, seeing how absurdly worried you were about that abscess case that blew in on you. And, by the way, I tell you again that you're over-working. However, that's your affair. Further, I'm thoroughly enjoying my holiday here in your house, though I must confess that Exquay is not in the least what it was when I left it nineteen years ago, and I keenly regret the change. But—"

"Is this an oration you're making, Jack?" Dr. Ryper interrupted.

"But," the red moustache proceeded implacably, "I do think it's a bit odd that when I arrive at the house I'm sent to I should be greeted as 'Mr. Magician' by a crowd of people evidently of the sort that have made Exquay what it is to-day—and then introduced to a crystal and expected to gaze into it! No time allowed for explanations. A complacent ass with a startling tie-pin insisted on my getting to work at once with the blooming crystal."

While Dr. Ryper, entirely puzzled by this affair, laughed with much freedom, Dr. Rooding filled in the details of his entrance and continued—

"I know how it happened, because I heard the words 'red moustache' through the open window. They were expecting somebody else with a red moustache, some rascal of a necromancer, and they mistook me for him. My moustache has always been my undoing, and I'd shave it off to-morrow morning if I wasn't too proud."

"But what did you *do*?"

"What did I do? I saw at once that several of 'em were sickening for mumps—couldn't miss seeing it—and so I prophesied that five of 'em would be struck down by a highly contagious disease—I thought I should be on the safe side in saying five—and then I just left."

"But, my dear charlatan, didn't you see Mrs. Miss?"

"Who's Mrs. Miss?"

"The keeper of the establishment, an old lady who wears an embroidered silk apron."

"No. I didn't see any old lady."

"But it was she who sent for me. I told you so."

"Did you indeed! Well, anyhow, I didn't see her. If you think she's in danger you'd better run along yourself—and explain."

"Nobody could explain what you've done," Dr. Ryper laughed, again in a rather unprofessional manner. "Here. Let's have a whisky-and-soda apiece."

"I never in my life saw such a collection of oddities," remarked Dr. Rooding, reflectively, over his whisky-and-soda.

"My dear Jack," Dr. Ryper reproved him, "there are no 'oddities' among the visitors to Exquay. They are all very respectable and very decent people who pay their way, and they've made the town more truly prosperous than it ever was before. And don't you forget it. I'd like to know where I should be without them." He rang the bell.

"Clara," he said to the maid, " 'phone for a taxi for me."

"Mistress has just come back with the car, sir."

"Oh, all right. I'll take it, then." And to his guest: "I've had several mumps these last few days. We may be in for an epidemic. But fancy adults helping themselves to it."

"Those adults at 'Fairbourne' would catch anything," said the red moustache. "I hope I've left them with the impression that it's smallpox they're in for."

III

In spite of the fact that his scarf-pin had not met with the approval of Dr. Rooding, Mr. Abel Hipgood was a thoroughly good fellow and full to the brim with sagacity. Of course he laughed at the prophecy of the Magician. He walked Miss Thaxted home to her lodging and laughed at the Magician's prophecy all the way—nor was the way the shortest way.

He thus derided the Magician, partly by reason of sagacity and partly in order to reassure Miss Bertie. For Miss Bertie was obviously somewhat upset. It goes without saying that she pretended not to be upset, and that she bravely joined in Mr. Hipgood's mirth. Still, she was upset. Mr. Hipgood casually pointed out that Miss Bertie could not possibly be affected by the prophecy, which was expressly confined to people staying at "Fairbourne" that night, whereas Miss Thaxted was not staying at "Fairbourne" either that night or any other night. To which Miss Bertie replied that the whole thing was in her eyes ridiculous, and she hoped that Mr. Hipgood did not for one moment imagine that she was taking it seriously. To which Mr. Hipgood replied that naturally he did not and that all he had said was purely jocular. Nevertheless Mr. Hipgood knew that Miss Bertie was indeed taking it seriously, and she knew that he knew.

You might suppose that this absurd irrational weakness of Miss Bertie's would lower her in his esteem. Not a bit! Quite the reverse! He liked her all the better for it. It demonstrated her true womanliness. It enabled him to give her some of his moral strength. It intensified his tender feelings towards her. She was a wonderful girl, at once stylish, lovely, prudent, sagacious, but she simply had to have some frailty—otherwise would she not have been unlovable?—and this particular frailty was delicious in the sight of Mr. Hipgood.

So that his attitude to her during the longish walk was adorable and did credit to both of them. And at her door they clinched a proposal for making an excursion together on the morrow—an excursion which should start early and end late. And Mr. Hipgood set off alone for "Fairbourne" in a most romantic mood.

But no sooner had he bidden Miss Bertie a soft good night than a change came upon him. He himself began to take the Magician's prophecy seriously. Preposterous, of course, such a prophecy, and yet—! *What* contagious disease? *Five* persons, the magician had said. Odd, that! Because, the holiday season being scarcely opened, there were only six persons in all staying as visitors at "Fairbourne," including the absent Miss Tansley. Miss Tansley would surely return to sleep, which left a margin of one. Mr. Hipgood comforted himself that he would be the margin. It was not that he feared contagious diseases in the abstract. No! What he feared was that the onslaught of contagious disease might prevent him from accomplishing the excursion with Miss Bertie. (Rapidly was his common sense ebbing out of him.)

And astonishing, disconcerting developments awaited his arrival at "Fairbourne." The door was opened not by one of the two maids, but by the aged landlady, Mrs. Miss, herself. Mrs. Miss's glance reproachfully informed him that the hour was very late for a respectable house. But this was nothing.

"Miss Tansley returned?" he airily inquired.

"Miss Tansley has telephoned that she has to stay the night with friends at Plymouth."

Mr. Hipgood gave no sign, but he was thunderstruck. The margin of safety had vanished away. Five persons staying that night as visitors in the house were to be stricken down, and there would be only five visitors— including himself! Therefore he was doomed. Grotesque notion! But he could not shake it off.

And this too was nothing.

"I'm sorry to say," Mrs. Miss went on, "I've had to have the doctor in. I thought one of my maids was sickening for mumps, so I sent for the doctor. They've both got it. And what's more, Mr. and Mrs. Benbow and Miss

Tweedie and Mr. Belfield have all got it. They're all in bed now, of course, and being poulticed."

"Mumps, eh? Glad it's no worse," Mr. Hipgood murmured, feebly, staggered by the marvellous and terrible fulfilment of the Magician's prophecy.

"No worse?" repeated Mrs. Miss, hurt, and fidgeting with her apron. "It could hardly be worse for me, Mr. Hipgood. And I must ask you to kindly overlook any little shortcomings there may be in the service to-morrow morning."

Mr. Hipgood gave a very polite and sympathetic reply. He was about to mention the Magician, but fortunately refrained. Had he done so he would have added to the mental disturbance of the old lady, who knew nothing whatever of the Magician's visit. Nobody had had the courage to refer to it in her presence.

Mr. Hipgood retired to bed.

IV

But not to sleep. What was mumps? He had of course often heard of mumps, but he had never seen it. He had thought in his ignorance that it was a mere ailment of infancy. And here it was attacking grown-ups. It might be very grave in grown-ups! He lay in the dark for about a hundred hours, and then, full of a desperate resolve, arose, turned on the light, and with proper precautions crept down the stairs in his pyjamas, making, despite the precautions, creaking noises that sounded like explosions in the night. And so to the dining-room, which smelt of stale food.

On some shelves in a corner of the dining-room he had noticed an old edition of the Encyclopædia Britannica—a relic of Mrs. Miss's more opulent married days. He found the right volume, after opening two wrong ones, and, his chill feet on the bare linoleum scanned the article entitled "Mumps."

"Parotitis." A serious word! "A contagious disease, characterized by inflammatory swelling of the parotid and other salivary glands, frequently occurring as an epidemic." Good heavens! Where *were* the parotid, etc., glands? ". . . . Soon the nature of the ailment is announced by the occurrence of swelling and stiffening in the region of the parotid gland in front of the ear." He felt in front of his ears. "The swelling speedily increases in size and spreads downwards. . . . under the jaw. . . . The effect is to produce disfigurement, which becomes still greater should the inflammation spread, as often happens, to the glands at the other side of the neck and face." Disfigurement! "Pain. . . . Febrile symptoms. . . . Suppuration. . . . Interference with mastication and swallowing. . . . Four or five days. . . ."

He heard a noise across the hall in the drawing-room. Mrs. Miss was afoot and after him! He felt like a criminal. He shut the horrid volume and padded upstairs again as rapidly as he could.

Back in his bedroom, he examined himself in the glass. Swelling? Yes! No! Yes! Had he not had febrile symptoms during the day? Yes! No! Yes! He made the motion of swallowing. Did it cause him pain? Certainly! He was without doubt ill, and with disfiguring mumps. To-morrow instead of an excursion—poultices! He thought he had better keep warm, and so slipped into bed and put his head under the clothes.

What made him arise again within two minutes? A strange noise? A premonition? A mysterious warning? He could not say; but being very matter-of-fact he put it down to a strange noise. This time, before going downstairs, he donned his dressing-gown; on the other hand he did not turn on the staircase lights. From the darkness of the hall and the back-hall he saw a thin slit of light in the doorway of the small room (behind the drawing-room) which was Mrs. Miss's private apartment, the chamber where she kept her books of account, held delicate interviews with boarders or servants, and, presumably, stored her money. And he heard unusual half-muffled sounds in this room.

He very quietly pushed open the door, which had been ajar, and peeped, and saw a man busy with the bottom drawer of Mrs. Miss's old-fashioned bureau-desk, in the corner by the window. The man was taking out of the drawer a cash-box. Mr. Hipgood had never seen a burglar; nor could he be sure that burglars as a class had any distinguishing appearance peculiar to themselves. But he at once leapt to the justifiable conclusion that the fellow, whose clothes might have been those of a clerk in, say, a wholesale fruiterer's establishment, was indeed a burglar. He could be no other.

* * * *

The situation had no terrors whatever for Mr. Hipgood, who forgot even his parotid gland. In such a pass Mr. Hipgood was at his very best. He was incapable of physical fear. He had powerful muscles. And in moments of crisis he would keep all his wits, and his brain worked admirably. The joy of life burned bright in Mr. Hipgood. What did he do? Spring? Shout? Throw a chair with unerring aim? Not at all. He first quietly withdrew the cord of his dressing-gown from its loops and hung it round his neck. Then like a panther he crept forward to his prey, and, as the prey turned in alarm, he dashed at him and clasped him by the neck with both hands. The burglar gave an awful yell of pain.

"Loose my neck, guv'nor, and I'll stand quiet," the burglar breathed in a stifled voice, his arms limp.

But Mr. Hipgood only gripped him the tighter; whereupon the burglar collapsed, a mere carcass, on the floor. Mr. Hipgood then let go of the neck and tied the man's hands behind his back with the cord of the dressing-gown. Mr. Hipgood knew how to make knots; in his apprenticed youth he had often had to tie two short ladders together to form a long one, and no operation calls for more secure knots. The burglar was helpless. (If Dr. Rooding with the red moustache could have seen Mr. Hipgood in this moment he might have altered his disdainful opinion of northern visitors to Exquay.)

"My neck's that tender!" moaned desperately the defeated burglar. "Give me a drink, for Gawd's sake, or I shall faint right off."

Now in the upper part of Mrs. Miss's bureau—the burglar had let down the flap—stood shyly in one of the compartments a small bottle of brandy. Doubtless Mrs. Miss kept it there for great emergencies. Mr. Hipgood, impressed by the burglar's pallor, and not at all anxious for the burglar to die on his hands, uncorked the bottle and unceremoniously put it to the lips of the plunderer. The plunderer swallowed some brandy—but with obvious pain and difficulty!

The glorious truth suddenly and blindly illuminated Mr. Hipgood's mind.

"You've got mumps!" he cried, with joy overflowing.

"Copped 'em from my young woman," the burglar agreed, weakly.

Mr. Hipgood ceased in an instant to feel any of the symptoms of mumps. He had no longer the slightest sense of discomfort in the indicated regions of the face and neck. He was, in two words, perfectly well. The menace was lifted. He could now interpret the oracle, who, like the oracle of old, must be interpreted strictly. *"Five persons staying as visitors in this house to-night."* Those were the exact words; Mr. Hipgood was in no danger of forgetting them. Four persons staying in the house as visitors were already "down" with the inconvenient disease. The fifth was clearly the burglar. Two questions arose as to the burglar. First, could he be described as a visitor? To which the answer was that he could not possibly be described otherwise than as a visitor. An unwelcome visitor. That was it. Everybody would naturally describe him as an unwelcome visitor. Unwelcome—but a visitor! Second, was he "staying" in the house? Well, the point was easily settled. He was in the house, and Mr. Hipgood himself personally undertook to see that the fellow stayed in the house until morning.

Thus were the five victims accounted for—and Mr. Hipgood not among them! Mr. Hipgood could not by any chance be a victim, because that would have raised the number to six, and the oracle had distinctly said five.

The oracle now enjoyed a terrific prestige in the esteem of Mr. Hipgood. He had proved to be so miraculously, so dazzlingly, so incomprehensibly right that he could not conceivably be wrong in any detail. The oracle of the red moustache had in fact destroyed all Mr. Hipgood's scepticism concerning the mystical powers of seers and discoverers of the future. Henceforth he was a believer, and prepared to fight and defeat sceptics out of his own vouched-for personal experience. New horizons opened out for Mr. Hipgood.

"You seem quite pleased I've had a burglary, Mr. Hipgood," said Mrs. Miss when, a little later, she was fetched down to view the captive. "But I can assure you it's all very upsetting for an old woman like me. And no servants and all! And no sleep either!" Mrs. Miss whimpered.

"I can assure you I'm not!" answered Mr. Hipgood, clasping his dressing-gown more closely around him. "I'm only pleased I managed to catch him for you before he could get away or even do any damage."

"I thank you kindly," said Mrs. Miss, tardily giving justice to her star boarder.

But Mrs. Miss's first remark was true enough. Mr. Hipgood *was* delighted that she had had a burglar, and he could not conceal his delight— would be at no pains to conceal it.

Two policemen, summoned by telephone, arrived at seven o'clock, by which time Mr. Hipgood had had a little sleep.

"There's a police-court this morning, as it happens," said one of the policemen to him. "Of course you'll attend as a witness, sir."

"I shall do no such thing!" exclaimed Mr. Hipgood, offended.

"But you must, sir."

"I shall attend no police-court this morning. I've got an extremely important appointment elsewhere. The prisoner must be remanded."

And Mr. Hipgood conscious of magnificent health and vigour in spite of a somewhat disturbed and broken night, went upstairs to make himself beautiful and impressive in the eyes of Miss Bertie Thaxted. He ate heartily such apology for a breakfast as the martyrized Mrs. Miss could put before him, and he went off to the boarding-house which was honoured by the bright presence of his angel. There was some delay in answering the door, but Mr. Hipgood did not notice it, for he was dreaming of the *tête-è-tête* excursion.

"Are you Mr. Hipgood?" the maid inquired.

"I am."

"Miss Thaxted's very sorry, sir, but she's got mumps and won't be able to see anyone for four or five days."

A VERY ROMANTIC AFFAIR

I

IT was the Saturday before the August Bank Holiday, and Beach Street, the principal shopping thoroughfare of the great and justly popular resort of Rustingor, was overrun with crowds, throngs, and multitudes of visitors.

Rustingor, whose prosperity was founded upon a broad, smooth sandy beach two miles long, had come into prominence in the fifties of the nineteenth century, and with all its popularity it had maintained its mid-Victorian architectural character. A dingy, stuccoed town, where everything was cheap, it appealed to parents with more children than money. Admittedly it had defects; but its answer to all accusations was that its unsurpassable beach was a paradise for the little ones and tiny tots. Ninety-nine per cent. of its clients travelled to it third-class, and stayed in boarding-houses or took rooms where they boarded for themselves. Hotels were few, and restaurants almost non-existent.

The shops in Beach Street lacked grandeur and display, but they were full of customers: women who knew the difference between fivepence and sixpence a pound, who wore imitation silk stockings and imitation leather shoes and imitation jewellery—save the wedding-ring, which was invariably of genuine gold.

The side-walks of Beach Street were embarrassed with many perambulators and their pushers and their escorts, and also with young men and young girls, effectively if cheaply dressed, who were obviously determined in due course to have weddings and perambulators of their own. Nothing smart; nothing fashionable—to the aristocratic or the plutocratic; but to the average Rustingor visitor, who knew no better, all was smart and fashionable.

The roadway of Beach Street was embarrassed in its turn with a welter of huge char-à-bancs, small motor-cars, side-car combinations, motorcycles and a few plain foot-driven bicycles; for the progress of civilisation had been such that even at Rustingor the majority of pleasure-seekers were quite used to moving to and fro by means of petrol. At the point where a high road crossed Beach Street, white lines to direct drivers had been painted on the tarred macadam according to the London method; and the entire movement of wheels was under the control of a policeman who wore white sleevelets according to the London method. This policeman's job was very difficult and very responsible—and he knew it—for a full half of the drivers were acutely inexperienced and, without being in the least aware of it, were indeed little better than potential killers and maimers and breakers of limbs; sometimes they would manage to assassinate even themselves.

The august and omnipotent policeman, by means of his white-ended right arm, was holding up all the wheeled traffic in Beach Street in order to allow cross traffic to pass. A youngish man, rather fat—indeed fat, stood on one side of Beach Street and he desired to get over to the other side, but the vehicles awaiting the fall of the arm of the law were packed so close together that he hesitated to insinuate himself into the press. At last, however, he found a space of eighteen inches between two motor-cars, and stepped into it—only to be prevented from further progress by a van whose driver was creeping up every foot he could steal.

There stood the fat young man, eyed with undisguised interest by all the young women in all the stationary cars. For the young man, though fat, was obviously differentiated from the ruck of these seaside males by his distinguished attire and his distinguished bearing. The humble persons who gazed upon him wondered what *he* could be doing in a place like Rustingor. But the young man showed no self-consciousness. All the young women who saw him compared him with their own young men—to the serious disadvantage of the latter; they felt themselves capable of any sacrifice if only they could lean, rightfully, on the arm of just such a young man (despite his girth), and talk to him in low tones on the pier by moonlight.

The policeman's arm fell. The young man, seeking in vain an opportunity to dash, did not stir. He was safe from the car behind him, which dare not run into him, and he was of course safe from the vehicle in front of him. But—in motor-traffic there is and can be no "of course." The car in front of him backed instead of going forward. It was a small car and a cheap car; even the smallest and cheapest car, however, when colliding with the human body, is very ruthless and unyielding. The girl-driver gave one "Oh!" of surprise, and instantly corrected her mistake; but the elegant fat young man by that time was lying in the road, and in a moment crowds of people were all around him, and other people were standing up in cars to see him, and the entire traffic was once more immobilized.

The girl-driver of the deadly car blushed red, knowing that her sex was against her. If a man had depressed the wrong foot-pedal and put the car into reverse-gear, nobody would have thought twice about him. Accidents will happen. But because the offending driver was a woman, and not a beautiful woman nor a smart woman, every man in the vicinity was saying either aloud or to himself: "Ah! These women-chauffeurs! Why are they allowed?" Etc.

The policeman pushed through the crowd like a steam-roller, and became something between a deity and a prosecuting counsel. All the surrounding persons who had been in a hurry were no longer in a hurry, and all felt that a bit of luck had fallen their way.

The young man, white as the woman was scarlet, had fainted for a moment, but he very quickly recovered. Clearly one of his legs was broken. A doctor magically appeared, as doctors will. The doctor said to the young man, after examining him:

"Would you prefer to go to the town hospital or to a nursing-home? Rather a good nursing-home."

The young man weakly nodded in favour of the nursing-home.

"I must trouble you for your name and address, sir," said the policeman, note-book in hand, after the young man had been lifted into the offending car, whose occupants, except the wicked driver, had been turned out of it.

Part of the wicked driver's punishment was that she should be compelled by the policeman to drive her victim to the nursing-home.

The victim made no reply to the policeman's respectful request. The policeman, still more respectfully, repeated his request.

"Arthur Beachcroft," answered the young man. "90, Piccadilly, London."

Then he shut his eyes and sighed. The doctor sitting next to him, signalled to the policeman that his patient must be spared further inquiry for the present. The car moved forward—very gingerly. All other cars made room for it. The crowd dissipated itself, and hundreds of individuals went about proudly describing the unique accident which they had witnessed with their own eyes.

II

"It's you who are the queer man to be giving a false name to the police yesterday afternoon, Mr. Purfill."

These opening words from the young and lively dark-eyed nurse as she came on duty at eight o'clock in the morning, gravely disturbed the owner of the broken leg. He had passed such a night as one is liable to pass in a well-run nursing-home. The limb had been admirably set, and the nurse had done her work admirably, and, in a light-hearted way, sympathetically; and the nurse had finally gone off duty, and then the patient had become aware that a bell was installed on the landing outside his door (as a bell always is installed in a well-run nursing-home), and that this bell functioned irregularly and often. It seemed to be connected with thousands of bedrooms, all of whose occupants wanted something urgently. The patient began to be hungry, and there was nothing to eat, and the blind rattled, and when he switched on the electric lamp its crude ray dazed his eyes. In the end he had the audacity to ring the bell himself, and it emphatically did ring. In twenty minutes he had made the bell ring emphatically three times. At the end of thirty minutes the night-nurse entered and inquired with sympathetic and yet warning blandness:

"Did you ring?"

When the patient confessed hunger, the air of the night-nurse indicated an exquisite and sympathetic divine discontent. She regretted that the kitchen was closed. However, she accorded biscuits, and to stop the blind from rattling she shut the window: it was ingenious of her, but drastic. Also she gave the patient aspirin, and reassured him that he could not fail to sleep. He did sleep—between five and five-thirty; the night-nurse wakened him by coming in to see how he was getting on: most kind of her. She generously brought him a cup of tea, which at an earlier period of its existence had probably been hot, but was now merely strong. When he answered her question about sleep, she said first that people always slept more than they thought they did, and second that people could scarcely expect to sleep the first night in a strange bed, especially with a leg in splints, upon which remark she went off to administer similar comfort to other patients.

So that by seven o'clock the patient was living for one event only—the arrival of his bright, vivacious, Irish nurse. These two had grown very friendly indeed during the previous afternoon and evening. The hour between seven and eight comprised some six hundred and sixty minutes. And then in burst his old and valued friend the Irish girl with her:

"It's you who are the queer man to be giving a false name to the police, Mr. Purfill."

Somehow she knew his real name! Perhaps the night-nurse had known it too, and the knowledge would explain the extraordinary fortitude with which the latter had borne his infelicities. No wonder that the patient was gravely disturbed. His fractured leg became an affair of secondary importance. He felt like a criminal detected.

"Didn't I give the right name?" he asked, with feeble cunning. "It must have been because I was dazed, then. What name did I give?"

"It's yourself that ought to know," the smiling girl replied. "Talking so free. The policeman wrote 'Beachcroft' in his big black beast of a book and the matron saw it."

Mr. Purfill tried to laugh, not with complete success.

"Well," said he. "That must have been because I was in Beach Street."

"It's in Beach Street you were. But what power put it into your mouth to say your address was Piccadilly, London, seeing that you were staying at No. 19, Channel View, here, and it's the landlady called here all in her finery because you didn't go home to the fine tea she'd cooked for you, fish and all, and she'd heard of a fine fat young man knocked down to the earth by a woman and him brought in here with a leg dangling?"

"I do live in Piccadilly," Mr. Purfill insisted.

"You say it, and you wouldn't tell a poor girl a lie, for I judge you're quality by the smallness of your feet. But it's the policeman himself's been here this morning, as I'm telling you, but the matron pushed him out again, and the way she did it, saying you were asleep yet, and the giant said he should come again. And now it's this thermometer in my hand for your sweet mouth. Ah! Would you suck the very mercury out of it?"

While sucking the mercury out of the thermometer, Mr. Purfill was debarred from speaking, but not from seeing. He gazed foolishly at the nurse. What he liked in her, more than her undeniable fresh comeliness, was her Irish speech—both phrase and accent. There is no ground to suppose that the Irish are less cruel, more conscientious, more benevolent, more unselfish than Anglo-Saxons, but their speech always predisposes Anglo-Saxons in their favour, and undoubtedly Mr. Purfill had taken quite a fancy to the girl of whose very name he was ignorant. He did not say to himself that the picturesqueness of her tongue was a reason for counting on her and trusting her: but that was what it amounted to in his mind.

"I can't see any policeman to-day," he said fretfully, as soon as she had withdrawn the thermometer.

"And you shan't," she exclaimed, examining the instrument. "It's myself that will stop him. Your temperature is the temperature of a calm and holy saint—98.7—but I'll write it down on the chart 102, and it's the doctor will shut the door on any policeman, and him with his squeaking boots and his roaring great voice." She laughed lightly, and wrote on the chart and showed it to the patient.

As for Mr. Purfill, he was thunderstruck by her irresponsible audacity. To tamper with the record of a sick man's temperature! She frightened him. With nurses so fantastic and conscienceless, no patient could feel safe anywhere. And every patient was helpless. He spoke not a word. His breakfast arrived on a green lacquer tray, and on the tray a bit of paper with the name in pencil, 'Mr. Purfill.' It was a breakfast for a weak girl after an operation. Mr. Purfill ate it in a moment, and in another moment was hungry again. But he dared not ask for more. A maid came in to clean the room; she kept covertly and fearfully glancing at him, as a murderer, for he had given a false name to a policeman. The matron herself came in, evidently out of curiosity to see a murderer caught and rendered innocuous by the deserved accident of a broken leg. The doctor came in. The nurse respectfully offered to him the chart, and made surreptitiously a face at Mr. Purfill, who trembled.

Surely the doctor could not fail to see through the trick of the false temperature chart. But the doctor did not blench.

"Yes, I expected it," said the doctor.

Another knock at the door, which the nurse cautiously opened a few inches.

"Mr. Purfill can see nobody to-day," said the doctor.

"It was Miss Brewer," said the nurse. "To inquire after your health. And she's brought these flowers." In her hand was a miserable bunch of cheap flowers.

"Who's Miss Brewer?" Mr. Purfill questioned, at a loss.

"Sure, and isn't it the untidy creature who broke your honour's leg with the tail end of her Tin Lizzie? And did you ever see the match of it?" She held up the flowers to derision. "And it's to soften your heart not to fetch the law on her for her sinful clumsiness that's she's brought them—ferns and all."

Once more Mr. Purfill tried to smile and fell short of success.

It was in the afternoon, while Mr. Purfill was looking at a photograph taken from a pocket-book which lay on his bed-table, that Nurse (with a capital letter in his mind now because they had been steadily growing more and more intimate) hurried in with the news that she had beaten off an inquisitive journalist—a poor local young man of the *West Sussex Weekly Courier and General Advertiser*.

" 'Take yourself from this, young fellow,' said I," she said. " 'Or the holy saints themselves will not protect you from me.' He was up on the stairs. You didn't hear his impudence, and the door not latched?"

Mr. Purfill shook his head, putting away the photograph as nonchalantly and innocently as he could. Then Mr. Purfill suddenly resolved on a certain course of conduct. He would confess the truth to Nurse. To do so would give him satisfaction and would not disturb her, because she took everything for granted, even a broken leg; moreover she showed intense interest at the slightest symptom of the emergence of a bit of personal gossip.

"It was the thought of journalists that made me give a false name to the policeman," he began.

"Then it wasn't dazed he was!"

Mr. Purfill proceeded:

"I'll tell you what nobody else knows, except the landlady at Channel View. I came to Rustingor to get my weight down. I weighed nineteen pounds more than I ought. And I came here to hide myself while I took it off. I didn't want all my friends in London teasing me about my diet. Because you know I haven't to eat bread or pudding or cakes or butter or milk or ham or bacon or potatoes or sugar, and I mustn't drink alcohol at any time or drink anything at all with meals. Stiff, eh? Especially when you're asked out to dinner, eh? But I'm told if I stick to it I shall lose a stone in a month."

"You'll be losing a stone in a month if you stop here and eat every scrap they give you," Nurse put in, casually realistic.

"I'm really doing it," Mr. Purfill finished, "because my doctor says that fat men are liable to die early. And I don't feel like dying early."

"Nor look it, either. A man with a fine paunch on him it's yourself ought to be proud of." She pointed to the hillock in the middle of the plateau of bedclothes. "Well, it's a strange and wild story I'm hearing."

"But don't you believe me, Nurse? I assure you it's quite true."

"Oh! Is it myself that would be disbelieving you? I can see truth in your eyes. But the matron and those other wiry pagans downstairs and upstairs! Not they! Because they've made you a mysterious conspirer and criminal in their hearts, and they wouldn't be letting you go and fade off into a mere fat young man. No! And it's the truth I'm saying to you—every syllable. But a grand romantic story it is you've told me."

"Why romantic?" Mr. Purfill demanded. "Nothing very romantic about avoirdupois!"

"What!" cried Nurse. "And will you tell me next there isn't a woman at the bottom of it, and she likes a man slim, and you carrying her photograph about with you and all?"

Mr. Purfill blushed in spite of every effort to remain pale. The directness of the perceptions of Irish nurses was simply terrifying. Also he was becoming rather too intimate with this particular one.

III

There came a morning when one of the most romantic and thrilling episodes that ever did happen in a nursing-home happened in the nursing-home at Rustingor. Mr. Purfill would have felt the romance of it in any case, without the help of Nurse, but her chance use of the adjective "romantic" had caused him very clearly to realize, with his brain as distinguished from his heart, that the whole affair did indeed possess the true romantic quality.

Weeks had elapsed. Perhaps in ordinary circumstances Mr. Purfill would have already left the home; but his landlady in Channel View (to whom he was steadily paying rent) had expressed a certain unwillingness to take care of a cripple, though she had been quite ready to cook meals for a man who proposed to maintain life without bread, puddings, cake, butter, milk, ham, bacon, potatoes or sugar, and without drinking at meals. Hence he was staying on at the home. He had long ago learnt that Nurse's

Christian name was Eileen, and she that his was Oswald; but he had not allowed the intimacy to grow, nor had he ever admitted that his yearnings for slimness had any bearing on his relations with any lady.

On the morning of the episode a heavy arm-chair had been delivered at his room in the home. It resembled the ugly arm-chair of commerce, except that it had a platform for the feet, and that parallel with the right arm, and outside it, ran a steel bar along which a pendant brass weight could be moved to and fro. Nurse Eileen had remarked on the costly look of the chair, and it was a fact that Mr. Purfill had not spared expense; but then there was no need for him to economise on his romances; for not only had he that curse of the unambitious, a substantial private income, but he had also a sound practice at the Chancery Bar.

The last words uttered by Eileen as she quitted him that romantic morning to attend to another patient were:

"God have mercy on your soul if you go trying to sit in that chair this day."

He replied that he would not dream of trying to sit in the chair, either on that day or on any other day, in her absence. He was alone, free, unobserved; he knew that Eileen would not return for at least half an hour. So he took out the photograph, which Eileen had never seen close, and gazed at it according to his daily custom.

A woman! Odd thing for a firm-lipped, sharp-chinned Chancery lawyer to spend many minutes per day over a woman's photograph! But such things are not quite unknown at the Bar. Christian name, Caroline (a wondrous name, he thought). Surname, Otway (famous in English literature, he thought). Age, in the immediate neighbourhood of thirty. Dark. Soft eyes. Long eyelashes. An enigmatic smile. A wedding-ring on her fine, delicate finger.

Yes, she was a widow, and not a bit a rich widow; rather the contrary. She had a son, Alec, aged eight, who was one of Oswald Purfill's best pals and showed a semi-religious devotion to him, and was a peculiarly bright boy with a nice, tolerant protective attitude towards his beautiful mother.

It was on an occasion when Alec had been inquiring about George IV and Mr. Purfill had been explaining what a great dashing fellow George IV was, that Caroline Otway had remarked:

"Yes, but he was fat."

This simple five-word remark, spoken in what had seemed to Mr. Purfill a disturbingly significant tone, had led the lawyer the same evening to contemplate his own figure, and to decide to alter it as quickly as possible, lest it might undo him with Caroline. Then had followed the quest of professional advice, and the decision to vanish, to diet himself strictly, and to practise various exercises ingeniously calculated to modify those portions of his body whose appearance had moved Caroline to put such a disquieting emphasis on the monosyllable "fat." Then Rustingor—and the accident.

Oswald continued to gaze at the photograph of the woman who had affected him a thousand times more than any other woman had affected him in all the thirty-five years of his self-centred existence, and then his eye roved and the vision of the chair caught it and held it. Oswald became a bird and the chair became a snake; the snake fascinated the bird. With the most singular precautions Oswald slid very slowly out of his bed, placing one foot, and only one foot, on the floor, and when a board creaked he stopped, petrified, as though fearful of being trapped by unseen detectives in the perpetration of some awful crime.

Then he moved on again, advancing, without a noisy hop, by manœuvring of heel and toes of one foot, till, while still holding to the bedstead, he was within a score of inches of the chair. The other foot had not touched the floor.

At this point he happened to see himself in the mirror of the white-enamelled wardrobe. He looked earnestly and anxiously at his figure as revealed by a pyjama suit and could perceive in it no change or modification whatever. He had been dieting, he had been hungering, he had been thirsting; he had even been able, while lying on his back in bed, and without disturbing the repaired leg, to accomplish several of the—shall we say?—equatorial exercises. . . . And yet no visible modification of the too full contours! Nothing to suggest that the hated word "fat" was no longer fairly applicable to him!

He felt distressed. Still, he was bravely determined to know the worst, and he reached the chair and fell down on it, with one leg sticking out like a warning to the unrighteous. For a few moments he dared not manipulate the sliding weight on the steel arm; he dared not glance at the steel arm. But Oswald had British grit in him; he had proved it in the war. And now he proved it again. He looked squarely at the notched steel bar; he pushed the pendant weight about until the bar balanced itself motionless and precisely horizontal. Then he faced the figures. . . .

No! His eyes must be cheating him; they had misread the figures. His heart was thumping. Good news is apt to be shattering, until it is realized. Oswald at last realized his luck. Since the last weighing, at a Turkish bath, he had diminished by eight and a half pounds. At the Turkish bath he had worn a towel; the pyjamas must weigh quite as much as the towel—probably a few ounces more. He had lost appreciably more than half a stone. Triumph! Ecstasy! Romance itself! A tremendous scene in the solitude of the sick-chamber! What a world was this world! Why hanker after Paradise when it was all around you? He saw (by faith) Caroline Otway smiling approval upon him.

And this was by no means all. There were a few bath chairs in Rustingor, which followed on the footsteps of Brighton at a distance of twenty-five miles. Oswald Purfill was being drawn in one of these vehicles by an aged fellow-creature the same afternoon when he met a little boy running hard in the opposite direction. The little boy halted violently at sight of the bath chair and shouted out to its propeller:

"Hi! Please stop, you!"

The little boy was Alec Otway, all in blue linen. He had recognized his admired friend, and the two shook hands.

"Where were you running to so fast?" asked Oswald, with a good imitation of casualness.

"I'm running after Miss Phipps," said Alec. "She left me on the sands. At least I mean I left her. Mamma's brought me down here because I need a sun-cure. It's called helio-therapy." He remembered all the funny words uttered in his hearing. "We're staying at the Grand Hotel. We've got two rooms, and I sleep in Miss Phipps' room, but I'm going to sleep in mamma's room to-night because Miss Phipps is restless and mamma isn't, and I'm a bad sleeper for one so young. And I shall bathe to-morrow and ride on a donkey this afternoon. But I must catch up Miss Phipps or she'll be sulky and won't give me enough jam for my tea, and perhaps she'll stop the donkey too. Why are you in that bath chair, Mr. Purfill? Is it your broken leg?"

"Broken leg, brother? What broken leg?"

"You broke your leg. I know you did, because I saw it in the paper, and I showed it to mamma, and it was just like a lady-driver to go and break your leg. You know I always study the press, don't you? And mamma's been wondering why you didn't tell your friends—us, for instance. She says you're fearfully secretive. Are you? Shall you come to our hotel? Mamma's lying down. She says this is the finest beach on the South coast." Alec ceased, from breathlessness. Then he concluded: "You said once you'd teach me to fly a kite *properly*, if ever we were at the seaside together. Well, we are, and it's the finest beach on the South coast. *I* don't think it is, but it must be. I saw it on a poster at a railway station. I say— how thin you look!"

The next moment Alec, apprehensive concerning jam and donkey, and perhaps also uncomfortably full of a really great item of news, fled away in pursuit of his nursery governess. But at intervals he turned his head and smiled and waved a hand to his friend, who was craning his neck to watch the boy. The final words of the boy's speech still sang sweetly in his ears.

IV

It was a new Oswald Purfill that went up to his room that day in the rumbling lift (wide enough to hold a stretcher) at the nursing-home. An Oswald drenched in romance. An Oswald, too, full of a notion at once enchanting and malicious and somewhat conceited. He had never before heard that his friend Alec suffered from any malady or constitutional defect. The boy was understood to be the incarnation of perfect health. Why then the need of a sun-cure? And why Rustingor for the sun-cure? Could it be—? No, absurd! Could it possibly be—? No, preposterous! But still, however absurd, however preposterous, could it conceivably be that the boy's mother had manufactured an excuse for coming to Rustingor in order to make fresh contact with Mr. Purfill? Well, it could not. And yet—! She was annoyed with him. She had even remarked to her son that he was secretive. Ah! If she knew the romantic truth she might laugh—ironically—at the foolish sentimentality of men. He would not like that.

Why had the improvident girl gone and put up at the Grand Hotel? She could not afford the Grand, which was one of those aloof and costly hotels which are generally to be found on the outskirts of popular resorts—scorning the popular resorts and arrogantly disowning connection with them. She had little sense of the value of money. What she stood in want of was a wise, protecting person to look after her, and incidentally to shower money upon her and rid her of financial care. It was monstrous that such a delicate heavenly creature should be compelled by fate to keep accounts. . . .

So the accident had reached the London papers, and in its correct form as regards the true name of the principal actor. And the boy himself had found it. Charming and gifted boy, naturally, being the son of so charming and gifted a mother!

It was a pity the boy had been in too much of a hurry to remember to ask for Oswald's address. Oswald knew Caroline's address, but Caroline did not know Oswald's. So that she could not call to see how he was getting on. Pooh! As if she *would* have called, in any case! When would he see her again? He desired to see her immediately, despite her annoyance, and yet he desired not to see her immediately. He would prefer that she should not set eyes on him until his obesity cure was completed. Eight and a half pounds! It was naught. (Still—"How thin you look.") He must and he would part with at least a couple of stone. He would send her some flowers. But he could not send flowers unless he bought them himself at a flower-shop, and he could not go down to a flower-shop before next day. Never could he entrust the transaction to Nurse Eileen! She would grin at the mere mention of the sex of the recipient. She would tease him, charge him with deceiving her for weeks. His dignity could not have borne it.

The fact was, he was weary of Nurse Eileen. She was admirable and she was cheerful; but how monotonous! Being with her was like paddling along a shallow pretty river that ran perfectly straight and unvaried for endless miles. She had no depth, no variety. He had finished with Eileen, who would doubtless behave to her next male patient exactly as she had behaved to himself.

The next day he left the Nursing Home, and the weighing machine also left the home. The landlady at Channel View had to receive him and make the best of the cripple. Not that he was a cripple for long. Within a few hours he started to walk a few steps on both legs: which placated the landlady. Nevertheless, the landlady thought him a queer fellow, and perhaps not right in the head. He was always weighing himself on his weighing machine; and when not weighing himself he was weighing his clothes and making calculations on bits of paper. His chief quality, in the estimation of the landlady, was that he ate scarcely anything, while paying a fixed inclusive price for board. He had begun by being very cheerful: but after three days he became melancholy and irritable. He was always driving out, in a horse-carriage, and each time he had to be helped in and out of the carriage. Why he had abandoned the bath chair she could not imagine. And indeed how could the old woman be expected to guess that there was a lady in the case, and that it would not do for him to meet the lady while being humiliatingly drawn to and fro in a bath chair?

For three days Oswald promenaded the edge of the sandy paradise of children; he also drove past the garden of the Grand Hotel at very frequent intervals—but never a glimpse of Caroline or Alec! Had they left Rustingor? Blank despair!

Then he saw her in the distance, hand in hand with the boy. A marvellous sunshade over her divine hat and head. The boy descried him first and scampered forward, all heels and arms, leaving his mother. Oswald stopped the carriage. The mother followed sedately.

Romance! Oswald was thrilled, but he was frightened. Romance! He was hungry and thirsty for her sake. He had had his leg broken, for her sake; because he had gone to Rustingor in order to render himself pleasing in her sight, and if he had not gone to Rustingor, he would not have had his leg broken. And he could not tell her!

She blushed as, leaning out romantically over the side of the victoria, he took her hand. The boy did nearly all the talking; his tongue would not cease—fortunately.

"It was most kind of you to send those flowers," said Caroline gravely. "I should have written to thank you, but there was no address."

"But I told the people at the shop to pin my card on the packet!" said Oswald, relieved at the explanation of what had seemed to him to be a bodeful remissness.

"There was no card." She smiled.

"Then how did you know who they were from?"

"Alec was sure they must be from you."

Alec! Not Caroline!

He gave his address—she did not ask for it. Soon afterwards she departed, and the boy with her. It was all very chilling. Had she noticed that he was thinner? No! The carriage rug had hidden his shape. Really, she had not said a great deal about his leg—fractured for her sake. He was disheartened, and the spectacle of the paradise of children, with its glorious smooth sand, joyous infants, castles, pier, kites, flags, minstrels, punch-and-judy, clowns, bathing-machines, sand-yachts, and distant dappled sea and coloured boats thereon and coloured bathers therein, the whole warmed and vitalized by the tremendous downpour of the sun—this superb spectacle made no appeal whatever to Mr. Oswald Purfill.

V

The next morning all was changed for Mr. Purfill by the arrival of a letter from the Grand Hotel addressed in a handwriting with which he was not entirely unfamiliar.

"Dear Mr. Purfill, I wonder whether you could bear to dine here on Friday at 8. Yours sincerely, Caroline Otway."

No more than that. It might have been considered curt by the fussy. It was certainly quite unlike her usual invitations.

Oswald got out of bed and weighed himself. Two and a half pounds more gone! And it suddenly struck him, as he gazed anxiously at the mirror, that his cheeks were noticeably thinner. The old cherubic look was going—or gone.

"Of course," thought Oswald, as if he had made a sudden and startling discovery. "She's a woman. They're always changeable. I used to imagine that she was an exception, but she isn't. Yesterday she was stiff because she wanted to make out that she had a grievance against me so that I shouldn't suspect that she really only came to Rustingor to see me. Then after I left her she was afraid she'd been *too* stiff. Three days to Friday. Why didn't she ask me for to-night? What about the next three days? Well, now she wants to demonstrate that she isn't in the least hurry to see me."

His mind returned to the singular brevity, even brusqueness of the invitation.

"Dash the girl!" he exclaimed aloud, and sat down at once in the parlour adjoining the bedroom and wrote:

"Dear Mrs. Otway. So many thanks for Friday at 8. I could. Yours sincerely, O. Purfill."

"That'll teach her," he said to himself.

With all this he was insensately uplifted and happy. It is a fact that he sang aloud, and ate less and less, and did more and more physical exercises, and made a rule against weighing himself more than twice a day.

In the three days he had no sight of either Alec or Alec's mother. His state of happiness fell somewhat. Still, there were two advantages: his leg was getting stronger and his weight was diminishing.

On the evening of the third day, which came at last, though Oswald had feared that it would never come, he arrayed himself with special care and walked out to his carriage unaided. He was early, despite a determination not to be early, and therefore he instructed the coachman to go slowly. The coachman went very slowly. It was just his luck, he thought, that he should encounter Nurse Eileen, who was taking a night off. Eileen negligently signalled to the coachman to stop. She noticed Oswald's attire, smiled peculiarly, and said:

"So it's yourself that's going to meet her this evening in the half-light."

Unparalleled effrontery! But nurses always knew you too well. They mowed down your dignified reserves as with a scythe. This was the last time he ever saw Nurse Eileen. In three months he could scarcely recall what she looked like.

Caroline Otway stood in the foyer of the hotel when Oswald entered. She was looking at a poster. Others were there but they were candles to a dazzling headlight. Tall! Slim! Dark smooth hair, large and rather melancholy, dreaming eyes, and a wonderful olive complexion! Some powder, but no rouge. A dark, discreet frock. Long fingers! And the poise of her body! Thrilling! And she knew it. They shook hands without a word. She blushed.

"And Alec?" Oswald questioned, after a few ceremonious politenesses.

"Oh, Alec's in bed. He doesn't stay up to dinner. We shall be alone. Do you mind?"

She had secured a table in a corner.

"No soup," said Oswald to the waiter.

Caroline offered no comment.

"Now as regards drink?" the hostess asked.

"Thanks. I don't drink anything at meals," said Oswald, and continued upon the subject, which she had introduced, of nursing-homes.

"No thanks," said Oswald, when the waiter presented an omelette. (Naturally at the seaside fish was unobtainable.) "Flour in it," he added, to Caroline, who said nothing.

"No potatoes, thanks," said Oswald to the waiter, at the meat course. "No, no sauce."

"No thanks," said Oswald, when the waiter presented trifle, at the sweet course.

"No sugar. No milk," said Oswald, faced with a coffee cup.

"I'm afraid you've had a very poor dinner," said the hostess.

"On the contrary I've had an excellent dinner."

"Have you lost your old appetite or only mislaid it for to-night?" she quizzed.

"I've thrown it away. I'm dieting. I'm getting my weight down. Nearly a stone already. Don't you notice my face?"

"I thought it looked pinched. Worry, I thought."

"Not at all. Hard work and iron resolve."

The music began, and they went to sit in the lounge.

"But why all this dieting?" Caroline demanded suddenly.

"Because George the Fourth was so *fat*," said Oswald.

"I don't quite follow," she murmured.

"Yes you do," Oswald firmly contradicted.

She would not meet his glance.

"Surely," she murmured. "One can state a fact about a historical character, without being misunderstood!"

"No, one can't," said Oswald.

She looked up timidly at him, and her olive-tinted face with its wistful eyes melted into a smile.

"It's all very romantic, I think," she murmured.

"That's just what it *is*!" said Oswald. "And I'm glad you think so."

And he was overcome with the romance of it, and she too. Oswald was overwhelmed with the romance of his own resolve to continue in the most ascetic well-doing until—well, you know how flat the front of a house can be. And Caroline was overwhelmed by the romance of the thought of what Oswald had done and was doing to satisfy her caprices. Romance was so strong upon them that they could hardly talk sense any more.

"A stepfather," said Alec to Miss Phipps a day or two later, "is the man who is your mother's husband when he isn't your father." As usual, Alec had got it right.